I0524232

KENT WYATT

Ears to Hear
A Special Heroes Book

by

Kent Wyatt

https://pixabay.com/

Winged Publications
Surprise, AZ 85374
All rights reserved.
ISBN: 978-1-947523-96-8

Inspirational thriller
Religious fiction

ISBN: 978-1-0881-6278-1

Dedication

To those special heroes who live in the world of autistic uniqueness, a world of extreme perceptions and experiences. Thank you for sharing with us your extraordinary view of the landscape of this life.

To the Children of Israel. You have, longer than any other race, endured bigotry and attack for nothing more than the genetic makeup of the blood in your veins. May the Lord protect you and bring you into the true promised land of a life lived in the knowledge of the Messiah who has come.

To Patrick. Thank you for the opportunity to walk beside you for a while, learning your perspective and gaining understanding through your experiences. (For those who would like to read Patrick's fascinating story, you will find it on my website: https://www.kentwyatt.org/stories-from-the-red-and-blue-world/the-santa-claus-man/)

To all those who suffer violence in the womb, and to the young women with child who find themselves at the mercy of those who pressure them to make a deadly choice. May the Lord quicken us all to support both in their most vulnerable time. We pray for a new day when no longer will we sacrifice the helpless, the innocent, and the voiceless on the altar of our fears, our philosophy, or our greed.

A big thank you to Betty Hutton Poublan for your translation of the French in this book. Having the

"Française" reviewed by someone who is living in the land and speaking the language daily made things much more authentic.

Special Heroes

This story includes a character with special needs, particularly Autism Spectrum Syndrome. I have tried to render the conditions accurately based on my research. However, only someone walking in that skin can truly know the challenges and the triumphs they experience. Any errors in portrayal of these fascinating people is due to my limited viewpoint, and I ask forgiveness. While each syndrome has its own unique traits, people with special needs are as varied as the individuals that they are. We know from Psalm 139:13-14 that God guides the forming of every person. He makes no mistakes. Any fault is in our limited, flawed perspective and our arrogance to believe that any of us are anything more than vessels of clay waiting for the Master to fill us.

This story is part of our Special Heroes series, which we hope to be a tribute to the many people with special needs Rebekah and I have had the privilege to know. We appreciate your contribution to our world. How much we would miss without you.

You can learn more about Autism at the following links:

https://www.autism.org/

For further resources and information about the lives of people with special needs and their caregivers go to:

https://www.ellenstumbo.com/

https://embracingimperfect.com/

https://embracingimperfect.com/autism/raising-autistic-kids/

Chapter 1

**For there is nothing hid, which shall not be
manifested; neither was anything kept secret, but that it
should come abroad. If any man have ears to hear, let
him hear.
Mark 4:22-23 (KJV)**

Amelia noticed Gabriel had stopped chewing and was listening. The strange world her younger brother lived in was such a part of her that she noticed his subtle expressions. After a moment, he relaxed.

Amelia tipped her head back and stretched. The quiet and cool of the dark park was a welcome relief after a sweltering day of interaction with customers. The other vendors had packed up and left long ago. The extra money she made by catching the latecomers would help since the home was increasing Gabriel's rates again.

The last of the kids from the apartments across the street had been called in from the playground. Now Gabriel could wander around the equipment without the pressure of all the people. Most of the farmers market regulars knew Gabriel, but

Amelia didn't want anyone worrying why a 22-year-old man was fascinated with the mechanics of the swings and the knots on the climbing web. Amelia was two when Gabriel was born and had spent her lifetime watching her brother be misunderstood.

Gabriel got up from the gazebo's table and took his plate toward the trash can. Amelia finished the last bite of the crackers and jam. No use wasting the samples her customers didn't take. *Mamma would have liked the new recipe.* She picked up her own plate and headed after her brother. The frogs from the creek chirped in varied tones and rhythms, making the quiet seem even richer.

She almost ran into Gabriel. He had stopped, empty paper plate suspended over the large trash can, ear in the direction of the trees behind them. He looked intent, wary.

Amelia searched the dark silhouettes of the trees that hid the creek at the edge of the park. "What is it, honey? What do you hear?"

"Car." Gabriel spoke in his perfectly pronounced voice. He used only the words he needed unless stress or excitement put him into a loop of repetition. No one was more conscious of the airspace necessary for sound.

Her brother closed his eyes, and the flavor of the evening changed for Amelia. Gabriel heard cars all the time, mixed and mingled, encroaching on his ears that perceived all the things she heard and a thousand more. He wouldn't mention it unless it concerned him. Gabriel had a sense of right and wrong as acute as his hearing. "What about the car?"

"Car in trees. Not allowed in trees. Sign says no motorized vehicles."

The sign he spoke of was far across the park to the east where the woods began. With her eyes, Amelia followed the wide walking trail that came from that area and skirted the grass and playground before it turned into the trees and disappeared into the leafy darkness.

Probably kids messing around. She wrinkled her brow. It

was time they went home.

Gabriel spoke again. "Man chasing man."

She looked at her brother. He still held the plate over the trash container, eyes shut, ear toward the woods. *Chasing?* She grabbed his plate and dropped it into the trash can with her own. Their ancient Ford Econoline van was across the playground and past the market area, at the far end of the parking lot. She had coveted the shade when she had arrived early that morning, but now she wished her van wasn't so close to the dark trees. Taking hold of her brother's shoulders, she tried to steer him in that direction. Gabriel put his arms up and moaned his disapproval. He slapped her hands away, still listening.

Then she heard it too, a car engine. Down the dark trail, a light glowed behind the trees.

She turned Gabriel to face her, but he still had his eyes shut. Her brother had every square foot of the park in his memory. He didn't need eyes to see it. She watched as his closed eyelids twitched. He was absorbing the current conditions, filling in the rest of the picture. The sounds, like strokes on a canvas, painted a mental image in Gabriel's extraordinary brain. With his ears, he might be placing a bird hopping on a branch, a rodent scurrying across the ground or…

A man burst from the trees to the left of where the trail went into the woods, exactly where Gabriel had his ear pointing. He was large, wearing tan cargo pants and a tight, dark polo shirt that accentuated his upper body. Even his protruding stomach looked tight and powerful.

Amelia's jaw quivered.

The big man in the cargo pants scanned the area. He assessed Amelia and Gabriel then continued visually searching the park as he spoke. "Excuse me. A man…a friend of ours…is playing a little joke on us. But we need to get going. We don't want to leave him behind. Did you guys see anyone come out of these trees?" In the lights illuminating the gazebo, the man scrutinized her.

Amelia shook her head and gave a weak smile.

Cargo Pants half raised his head in acknowledgment of her answer. Even in his shadowed expression, she detected suspicion.

The glow became headlights, and a large car lurched out of the woods, branches scraping the sides as it moved onto the grassy green of the park grounds. Two men bailed out of the back of the vehicle. The headlights obscured them. Circles of light panned the trees on either side of the vehicle. Amelia blocked the car lights with her hand and focused on one of the men. He had one arm extended and pointed something at the trees, moving it in unison with the flashlight.

"Hey!" Cargo Pants snapped at the men and jerked his head toward Amelia and Gabriel.

The man she watched brought his arm down and hid whatever he had been pointing behind his leg. The stream of light still played around on the foliage.

Cargo Pants raised his voice toward them. "I told these nice folks about how our friend is always messing around and ran off on us."

The men moved their separate ways. Their lights illuminated portions of the brush as they went.

Amelia whispered so only Gabriel could hear. "Parles très doucement en Français." If they spoke quietly in their mother's native tongue, the men shouldn't be able to understand. *I doubt these guys speak French.* It was the only other language in which she felt confident enough not to make a mistake under stress. She couldn't compete with Gabriel's skill.

Cargo Pants moved to the car and leaned in the window as the headlights went out.

All Amelia could hear was the car's engine. "Tell me what they're saying." The French she spoke to Gabriel calmed her thinking. *I better not try to call the police until we can get to the van.*

Cargo Pants' whispered words came from Gabriel's mouth, also in French. "I lost him in the woods."

A different French voice spoke beside her as someone in the car responded. "Do you think he got out of the park?"

Amelia shivered. It was always spooky hearing someone else's voice coming from her brother's mouth. She moved Gabriel toward the van. Distracted with his alternating dialogue, he offered no resistance.

"No. He wasn't that far ahead. He's still gotta be in those trees somewhere. We need some night vision."

"They're using it all up in Missouri, so we gotta figure out somethin' else. Okay, here it is. I'll get Roberts to set up as sniper where the park ends. He can test out that new silencer. Our man seemed to be heading that direction, so we'll keep pushing him that way. I got guys across the creek to make sure he doesn't come out over there. When he gets to the end of the park, he's gotta cross the street to get to cover again. There's enough open ground and lights down there that once he leaves these trees Roberts will tag him. Eriksen and Moss are going to the other side of town and make up something big to keep the locals busy. If we can do things quiet over here, even if someone calls the cops they won't be coming for a while. When Roberts drops him, we can go get him. We'll make like we're helping some drunk that fell. If you see a cat or possum in the trees, pop him. We'll need something to throw down to account for the blood." Gabriel's voice went silent.

Amelia wanted to run. *Not too fast. Don't let them suspect you know anything.* Her legs were shaking. She heard the frogs, but the peace had gone out of their song.

The voice resumed. "Where's your little girlfriend going?"

"Looks like she's heading to that van. Must be her wheels."

"She's hot, but that's a pretty poor ride. Doubt if anyone important will miss 'em."

Amelia drew in a breath at the words coming from

Gabriel's mouth.

Cargo Pants spoke in a snide tone. "That kid must be someone she takes care of. He acts like somethin's wrong with him."

The other voice ignored the comment. "She looks scared. Might be the type that will think too much about this." More silence, then the man in the car continued. "Better not let 'em go. Leave 'em in the trees over by the van. When we get done with our friend, we'll come back and put 'em in the van and make the whole thing disappear."

Another pause.

"You paying me enough for that kind of work?" Cargo Pants' voice was hard.

Gabriel's French took on a menacing tone. "Don't even take it there, Chandler. You'll get paid what you're worth if you do it right. I hope what we're doing means more than the money to you. Tonight, you better just worry about the fact that you're the one she got a good look at. She could make you a liability around here. Better go catch her before she makes it to her van."

Amelia grabbed Gabriel's hand and ran. He straggled. She pulled him as hard as she dared. Rushing him could lead to a meltdown. Then he would stop altogether and stand with his hands over his ears.

"Excuse me, Miss. I needed to ask you one more thing. Can you wait up a minute?" Cargo Pants' voice was just loud enough for her to hear.

Next to her, Gabriel mimicked the words in quiet French.

Amelia considered her vehicle, still some distance away. She'd never get to the van, start it and drive away before Cargo Pants caught them. All she had done was taken them further into the dark. Her fear made it hard to think. She didn't dare stop running. She turned and pulled Gabriel toward the woods to her right. Whoever they were after had lost himself in there, perhaps she could too. The dark foliage loomed before her. *This is crazy.* It was exactly where he wanted her, and she would never lose anyone with Gabriel in tow. She skirted along the trees and headed for her van again. She reached toward her pocket for her phone but stopped. *What if he sees me pull out a phone? He would know I was going to call the police. He'd have to stop me.* She imagined the man behind her with a gun, taking aim. She pushed Gabriel in front of her. *Please, Lord. Please help us.*

Feet pounded behind her.

She was out of places to run. What could she do? If she yelled for help, he would have no choice but to shoot.

He wants to keep it quiet.

She spun to face their pursuer. Cargo Pants sprinted toward her, still far enough away for it to work.

Amelia thrust out her hand. "If you come any closer, I'll scream."

The man skidded to a stop and glanced around him, examining the apartments across the park. He put his hands up as well. "Whoa. I didn't mean to scare you. I told you, we're just trying to find our friend." The man started to reach behind him. "I got his picture in my back pocket. I'm just going to bring it over, so you can look at it in case you've seen him."

"Stop!" she yelled over the French translation that Gabriel launched into. "I'll scream. I know you want things quiet. I'll keep quiet if you just let us go." Amelia poured out words while Gabriel did the same.

Cargo Pants gawked at Gabriel like he was a bad odor.

"My brother has autism. He doesn't know what's going on. He can't tell anyone. Please just let us go and we'll never say anything. You can trust me. I won't put him in danger."

"…Au cas où vous l'avez vu." Gabriel finished up beside her in the man's own voice.

Cargo Pants glanced back and forth between them. "What did he say?"

"Qu'est-ce qu'il a dit?" Gabriel repeated.

Amelia couldn't think between both versions. "Stop,

Gabriel."

The car had moved off in the other direction, leaving the big man to do the job.

The man eased closer, closing in on Amelia.

"I'll scream," she said again as she backed up, one hand toward the man and the other keeping Gabriel behind her. She was so scared. Could she even scream if she tried? *Don't give him a reason to kill you. Keep talking. Think of something else.*

There was a determination in the big man's eyes. Cargo Pants stepped closer. "Okay, you win. Let's just get you in your van and you can get out of here." The man's eyes were scanning the surroundings again.

He's looking for witnesses. He's going to do it. "Even if you have to kill me, just let my brother go. He will never be able to give you away. He's not a threat to you."

"You got this all figured out, don't you?" The man's narrowed eyes scrutinized her. "Okay, I'll let your brother go, but you have to be quiet." He was reaching behind him again. He inched further back into the dark, closer to the woods. "Leave your brother there, and come over into the trees."

He wants me in the dark...where no one will see him do it.

A shuddering breath escaped her. Tears blurred her vision as she moved toward the man. *Please let it be quick, Lord.* She had talked to God about dying. Told him she was ready. Their life had been so hard since...*I'll be with Mama and Daddy again.* But it always came to the same thing. What would happen to Gabriel? *Please, don't let him hurt Gabe.* She looked down as she took hesitant steps. The tree branch shadows slithered across the dim grass like fingers reaching for her. Maybe this was God's plan. Maybe she and Gabriel would go together. But it didn't feel right. Was it just her fear? Something inside her told her not to give up. But what could she do? Maybe she could save Gabriel. Could she get him to run for help? She'd say it in French. *It will take a second for*

Cargo Pants to figure it out – give Gabe a head start.

Something moved in the trees. A dark shape was behind the man, beside the man, now on him. Something snaked across Cargo Pants' chest. The big man's face disappeared backward. There were legs and feet in the air for an instant. A shape like the blackness itself covered the big man in a flurry of dark movement, and she heard muffled attempts at breathing.

Amelia turned, snatched Gabe's hand and pulled him toward the van. He planted his feet and tugged to get free, staring at the activity in the shadows.

She drew closer, inches from his face and placed her hand on his cheek. "Please, Gabe. I'm scared. We have to go. Please help me."

Her brother lowered his head and let her hand turn his face in the direction of the van. His body followed, and he allowed himself to be led.

Cargo Pants' muffled struggles had ceased. Amelia ventured a glance over her shoulder, and another man stepped out of the trees searching the ground for something. Black tight clothes covered his lean muscular body. A strap ran across his chest, which rose and fell from exertion. Shoulder length black hair framed a face that was too shadowed to make out. *He must be the one they were searching for.*

The man stepped forward to snatch an article from the ground. The park lighting revealed his striking features.

Their eyes connected.

Perhaps it was a trick of the light and shadows, but he seemed to have a longing expression of sadness like the look one gives a loved one they might never see again. He pulled the item in his hand over his head. It was a ski mask that left only the area around his eyes exposed.

When he saw she was still looking at him, the man's mouth came open and his eyes narrowed. "You better get out of here," his voice was firm and concerned.

The large car turned around. Amelia drew a sharp breath.

They're coming back. She fished for her keys. She unlocked the passenger side, got Gabriel in, then ran to the driver's door. As she worked the key, she made eye contact with the man again. Amelia stood with her hand on the door handle. What would happen to him?

He puffed out a breath and shook his head. "Go!" The large car accelerated. Its front end bounced over a sidewalk that ran across the park. It sped toward them, headlights off.

Amelia regarded the man. She couldn't leave. They would kill him. She was about to warn him, tell him to get in, when he heaved out a breath and said, "Go, now." The man turned and bolted, sprinting into the open.

One of the searchers shouted.

The car's headlights came on, and it accelerated in the direction of the black-haired man.

He dashed back into the trees.

The big car's headlights turned to face the foliage and headed to where the man had disappeared.

Amelia jumped in and fired up the van. Not only her life but Gabriel's life was at stake. She shot out of the parking lot without turning on her lights. The big car's brake lights lit up. She waited for the vehicle to spin around and pursue her. The brake lights went off. The car ignored her and continued toward where the black-haired man had vanished into the trees.

Chapter 2

Joshua weaved into the undergrowth. The car was after him instead of the woman's van. Good. At least she was safe. *You better forget her and get moving if you want to say the same about yourself.*

Behind him, he heard someone crash into the brush. A flashlight caused splinters of shadow on shadow as it tried to penetrate the tangled greenery. The reflection on the thick trees would prevent its operator from spotting him. *Time for a little misdirection.*

Joshua grabbed at branches as he went, breaking them off loudly. With a leap, he latched onto the thick silhouette of a low hanging dead limb. It joined his descent with a resounding crack. He used it to beat a noisy path to the left of him. *Come on. Key in on the sound.* He was risking the man taking a shot. *Where's your buddy? I saw two of you get out of the car.* Another pursuer broke into the dense vegetation behind and to the right of him.

Okay, follow the sound. Joshua threw the branch like a spear, over the thick brush, so it clipped through the lower tree branches. He dived to the right and slithered quietly beneath the dark foliage as the thrown branch crashed and snapped its way to the ground.

In seconds, feet crunched past his position. The noise of the man to his right moved past as well but further away.

The first man stopped. "That you?"

The other halted as well. "Yeah. I heard him just ahead."

Joshua's lungs shuddered as he silently pulled in air despite his body's urge to gasp.

The second man crept forward. Then the other moved up until they converged about fifteen feet in front of Joshua.

The first one whispered. "He must have stopped."

Joshua could perceive discreet movements—probably hand signals. Tiny glints let him know they were searching with their flashlights. Then the men split up again and moved off into the trees. He would let them get a little further ahead before he moved.

In the distance, he heard sirens. Had someone called the police? Maybe the woman in the park. The thought brought her to mind. The courageous resolve on her beautiful tear-stained face as she walked toward certain death had moved him. He suspected the young man with her had autism. In the quiet, waiting for his next move, Joshua found himself wondering if Caleb would have looked like the young man if he had lived to that age. *No time for that. Mind in the present.*

More of the wailing warnings joined in as emergency vehicles came alive from various parts of the town. They sounded like they were moving away. That was good. They couldn't afford any local involvement. But something big must be happening in the quiet town.

It was time he got going. Joshua slunk from his hiding place and followed the men, timing his movements with their own to mask the sound. He smelled the dankness of the creek and stopped—one splash and they would be onto him. Through the brush, he could see the water, bordered by the dense scrub, winding like a black road in either direction. A flashlight flitted onto the stream further down, lighting the eyes of the aquatic dwellers. He couldn't afford to scare a frog into the stream, but he needed to be on the other side. Ibbie would be at the pickup point and he had to cross to get there.

From across the creek, another light hit the water in front of him. More searchers were on the other side of the stream. Joshua froze, allowing only a quick tuck of his chin to prevent any reflection from his exposed skin.

The bushes around him lit up. It was too late to go for the Uzi slung across his back, and a body count was certainly not the way the mission was supposed to go. He prayed his black clothing would blend with the dark brush. The beam moved on in a slow pan of the scrub. When the light moved away, he allowed himself to breathe but not move.

If they had seen him, they might be smart enough not to let on. He watched his body for a laser dot. There was a faint rustling across the water. Was someone sighting him with a night scope, slowly squeezing a trigger? *It's up to You, Lord.*

The light moved further away, and the rustling steadily progressed along the opposite bank. He let them get further down. They were a little behind the searchers on his side of the stream. That could work to his advantage. He crouched and felt the ground, finally finding a palm-sized stone.

Joshua noted where the light illuminated the water and trees. He eased to where he could throw without causing noise. Targeting the area of black water ahead of the light, Joshua launched the rock. It hit with a loud splash.

The light snapped to the ripples in the stream.

On the same side of the creek as Joshua, one of his two original pursuers started tearing through the brush moving toward the sound. "Something's in the water behind us." The other one joined him in a noisy advance toward the creek.

Joshua scooped up a handful of pebbles. As he made a quiet dart to the edge of the water, he peppered the bank on the other side of the creek, sending frogs diving for the safety of the stream at the same time he scared the ones on his side. The noise alerted the amphibian world to danger, leading to a cascade of splashing entries into the water all along both sides of the creek.

In the glow of their own lights, Joshua watched the men on the other bank. They whirled in different directions at the noise around them and then relaxed at the realization of what it was.

One of the men who was running toward the creek yelled. "Watch out on the other side. He might be crossing."

Realizing they were in the line of fire, the men on the opposite bank called back. "We're over here. It's just frogs."

Joshua slipped into the water and soundlessly waded across as the two groups confronted each other, both blinding the other with their flashlights. He picked his way carefully up the opposite bank. His pursuers conferred below him. He could easily take them out, but instead he sneaked by them just inside the edge of the trees, moving toward his rendezvous. Earlier, he had no other choice but to take out the big guy. He couldn't let him kill the woman. But now Joshua hoped to slip away silently with no more confrontations.

He was ahead of the searchers now, but they would be coming. He couldn't move too fast and give himself away, but he couldn't let them catch up to him either. He needed to keep to the cover of the trees in case someone was watching the open areas. The park ended at Stone Street. Ibbie would be waiting in a parking lot just up the hill from there.

Chapter 3

Amelia drove through three stop signs before she slowed. *Thank you, Lord.* She was shaking. She was grateful they were alive. It had seemed hopeless, but God had brought the black-haired man. *Please protect him.*

Amelia took a left at the next corner. She pulled out her cell phone and dialed while she drove with the other hand. The phone rang on the other end. At the next intersection, she turned right, wanting to make it more difficult for anyone who might still decide to follow her. More rings and someone finally answered.

"Parnel county 9-1-1, where is your emergency?" The female voice sounded stressed. In the background, Amelia heard a police radio and multiple people talking.

"A group of men are chasing a man in Center Town park," Amelia rattled off to the dispatcher. "I think they're trying to kill him. They said something about setting up a sniper."

"Did you say sniper?"

"Yes, they said they were going to shoot the man when he came out of the trees." Amelia heard her own words. *They're never going to believe this.*

The sounds on the other end stopped and she heard a faint hiss. *Did she hang up on me?* Then everything was back again. "Did you see any weapons?"

"I'm not sure. I think two men had guns, but I couldn't really see them because of the headlights."

"Were they chasing the man on foot or in a vehicle?" In the background, radios were squawking. Another dispatcher was talking to a caller. Phones rang.

"Both," Amelia struggled with how to relate the complex scenario in as few words as possible. "They came out of the trees in the park. A big man was chasing him on foot and there were at least three men in a car. But two of them got out and started looking on foot.

"Can you give me a description of the car?"

"It was a large car...I don't...I'm not very good with cars."

"Can you describe the men?"

The tone of the woman's voice urged her to hurry and it made her brain fumble. "There was a big man with tan cargo pants and a black shirt, but I think the man did something to him because he was going to hurt me." Amelia faltered. "Please just send someone to the park. They might have caught him already."

"Okay, ma'am, calm down. We've already dispatched a unit. Everyone in town is tied up, so I am having a state trooper respond. It may take him a while to get there. Do you know these men?"

"No."

The radio in the background crackled. The line went blank again then came back. "Who was going to hurt you?"

"The big man."

"But you don't know him?" Someone on the radio asked for a vehicle description.

"No." The hiss returned. *She must be muting my call to talk on the radio. What is going on?*

The woman was back again. "Where are these men right

now?"

The dispatcher's frustrated tone made it hard for Amelia to think. "I don't know. I left the park."

"How long ago was this?"

"Just a few minutes."

Another phone rang. The dispatcher huffed, "Are you someplace safe?"

"Yes, I'm in my van. Someone needs to go to the park right away. They're going to kill him. I think that's why all this is happening." Amelia struggled to keep the car straight while she wiped her eyes on her shoulder.

"Ma'am, stay where you're safe or drive to the police department. We'll have someone there as soon as we can. Hold on while I answer another call."

The phone went quiet. Amelia let out a breath. *What kind of distraction did they create?* She pulled to the curb. The street behind was empty. Looking in the direction of the park, Amelia sniffed. Using her fingers to clear her vision, she looked at Gabriel for a moment. She sighed then worked the hand crank for the window. "What do you hear?"

Gabriel closed his eyes and turned his head. His face scowled, and he rolled down his window as well. Amelia turned off the engine. The night insects made an unobtrusive thrum.

"Do you hear any sirens coming?"

Gabriel rocked back and forth and shook his head. "Sirens went other way. All stopped now."

He must have heard them earlier, going to whatever distraction the men had created. Amelia leaned back in her seat. She stared at the steering wheel. *They're not going to make it in time.* She canceled the call and started the engine again. "Gabe, I'm going to drive back toward the park. I want you to see if you can hear the man that was running from the other men, the one who stopped the big man from hurting me. Can you find him for me?"

Still rocking, Gabriel nodded his head.

They said where the park ends. That would be Steel Street. Amelia started back. When she came to the sign for Steel Street she turned. She stopped a block away from where the end of the park woods butted up against the street at the bottom of the hill. Turning off the engine, she focused on Gabriel.

Eyes still closed, he turned his head back and forth like he was adjusting a television antenna. "Bad men making noise. Hitting bushes."

For Amelia, the frogs were back. She heard nothing more. She didn't waste her time trying. *They're driving him out. The sniper must be nearby. If he runs across that road, they'll shoot him.* "Can you hear the other man, the one I told you to find?"

Gabriel's brow squeezed tight. His head moved up and down and turned in tiny increments. "Animal," he murmured. Another slight head adjustment. "Birds." His head raised, lifting his ear as if his focus was moving up the hill. He rotated his neck to bring his other ear into the search. His finger raised up and he pointed. Leaning over she sighted down his finger to an area halfway up the hill, beyond the trees and out in the open. There was nothing but the lawn of a dark office complex.

"He's crawling," Gabriel continued to point out the location.

The grassy expanse was empty. She followed the line of his finger more precisely. Along the border of the lawn, a row of squat bushes edged a retaining wall. Where Gabriel pointed, one bush was thicker than the others. As she stared, part of the bush flowed into the next bush, increasing its dark shape. *It's the man. It must be.* He was crawling up the hill, the bushes concealing him from the street. Concern seized her chest in a grip that robbed her of breath. They had him trapped, and he must be trying to escape. Perhaps he was wounded, dragging himself with the last of his strength.

"Gabe, look at me."

Gabriel made a half-turn of his head in her direction, facing the floor and raising his eyes to meet hers.

"We have to help him. I need you to crawl in the back and get ready to open the side door when I tell you."

Gabriel looked back at the floor but didn't move.

Amelia touched his cheek and he met her gaze again.

"Do you understand?"

He clenched his eyes closed and started rocking back and forth. "Bad men in trees will hurt you."

"No. Listen to me. The bad men will hurt the kind man who saved us. He needs our help."

"He's fast and strong. He will hurt them."

"Look at him. He's crawling. He needs our help. Now, please get in the back and get ready to open the door."

Gabriel took rapid breaths, then hauled himself into the back and pulled on his seatbelt. He sat by the back door with his eyes closed, rocking. Amelia started the engine and headed down the hill.

At the bottom, Gabriel banged on the door. "Bad men in trees. Bad men in trees. Bad men in trees."

Her headlights illuminated men thrashing the last of the brush where the woods ended at the road.

She jammed the accelerator to the floor and roared past. Shocked faces gawked at her. On the dark running trail behind the men, headlights came on. *The car from the park.* In the rearview mirror, Amelia watched the lights rocket down the trail and go around the metal pillars meant to keep vehicles from doing what it was doing.

"No motorized vehicles on trail. No motorized vehicles on trail." Gabriel's voice was a mixture of offense and consternation.

The car fishtailed as it moved from concrete to slick grass. The bushes where the man was hiding were ahead. The big car flew across the sidewalk and threw sparks as it dragged bottom on the curb. *Oh please, Lord. What have I done?*

"Open the door." She glanced in the mirror but couldn't

see Gabriel. A quick peek over her shoulder showed him curled up on the rear seat with his hands over his ears.

She skidded to a stop near where she had seen the man crawling.

Gabriel was not budging. Behind her, the car raced up the hill.

Amelia threw the van in park as she unbuckled her seatbelt and dived across the center console to open the passenger door.

There was a loud crack and the seat shuddered.

Amelia screamed. Rotating her head, she spotted a chunk torn out of the headrest where she had been sitting. In the windshield was a bullet sized hole with a spider web fracture circling it. Crack! Another hole appeared lower down. *The sniper.*

"Stay down," Amelia hoped Gabriel would remain huddled on the seat. She wanted to do the same, but she forced herself to open the door.

Muffled machine gun fire blazed in her face sounding like a giant hornet.

She opened her mouth to scream but all that came out was a little squeak.

The ski mask hooded man was crouched behind the bushes firing a small weapon at something down the street in front of the van.

Amelia tried to speak. "I'm here to help y—"

The man turned, and his gun blazed at something behind the van. *He must be firing at the sniper and the car.*

"I'm here to—" The force of an impact threw Amelia against the back of the seat at the same time she heard the crunch of metal. The passenger door slammed shut. Gabriel let out a grunt. It took a heartbeat or two, as she sprawled across the seats, to realize the big car had rear-ended them.

The door came open and the man dived in on top of her. His legs landed on the back of her head, crushing Amelia's face into the seat. His weight came down and pushed the wind out of her. She felt suffocated and struggled to get her hands under her. Amelia pushed up and got a breath as the man crawled across her toward the driver's seat. She responded with groans and grunts as his hands and knees pressed places that didn't want to be pressed. When he got to the other side, she was able to pull her jean-clad legs out of the way and give him the seat. Amelia slid to the floorboard and huddled there.

The man in black jammed the van into drive. There was a grating, grinding, metallic cacophony as something jerked loose from the rear. The heavy van took off like the damage was superficial. The man leaned low against the door, viewing the road from the corner of the windshield. Headlights sparkled on the broken glass. A vehicle must be heading right at them.

Another round found their windshield and tore up the seat beside where the man scrunched against the driver's door. The windshield bowed inward where the rounds had pierced it, but the shatter proofing kept it in one piece. The headlights lit up the cab of the van illuminating his eyes. The glow of the lights swept toward the driver's side before disappearing out the window. Amelia jerked at the sound of another crash but felt no impact.

The man swung the van to the right and threw open the door. Through the opening, Amelia saw what was left of a shiny dark blue car embedded in the side of an SUV that was parked next to the curb. Another dark figure was extracting itself from the car, struggling with a seatbelt and airbag. The man in black leaned out and fired his machine gun at something behind the van. The new figure lunged to the driver's door of the SUV and fired a volley point-blank into the window. All the gunfire sounded subdued to Amelia. Not like the loud guns she had heard in the past.

The person across the street headed for them, blazing a weapon toward the same area the man in black had been targeting. Amelia screamed as she huddled on her knees on the passenger floor. The man in black was back in the driver's seat, his weapon hanging from a sling around his neck. He brought his leg up and used his boot to kick the windshield onto the hood. In one move, he threw his legs across the console, landing them beside her, and swung into the seat above where Amelia cowered on the floor. The other figure threw a black bag that hit the driver's seat like it was heavy. The man in black jerked it over to the console and the figure leaped behind the steering wheel. It was a woman with dark hair.

The man leaned forward with a gloved hand and shoved the largest portion of the windshield off the hood. He tossed smaller chunks of glass from the dash out the window. Metallic thumps came from the back door of the van where rounds were striking it. The man was thrown back as the van took off. Some of the glass slid off the dash onto the floor and Amelia's shoulders. She cringed, but when the avalanche was over and she opened her eyes, the man's gloved hands were shielding her head.

Gabriel stopped the moaning yell he had been emitting and was saying, "Not safe to drive without windshield."

The man opened the bag and pulled out a metal object. He removed an identical item from the compact firearm that hung around his neck and replaced it with the other one. The man ejected the last few bullets from the magazine he took out of the gun, put them in his pocket and threw the empty clip in the bag.

"Watch out, I'm going to freshen up your Uzi," The man grabbed the matching weapon around the woman's neck.

The woman acknowledged what he did with a slight turn of her body to give him more access as her eyes scanned ahead and in the side mirrors.

The man ejected the magazine from the weapon and replaced it with another from the bag. He emptied the spent magazine, deposited the bullets in the same pocket, dropped the emptied clip in the bag and zipped it up. It had taken him less than a minute to reload both weapons.

Amelia jumped a little when she felt the man's hands brushing glass pieces from her shoulder. Before she could object, he wrapped his arms around her and lifted her back onto the seat beside him. With one arm around her waist, he reached the other across her body and grabbed the seatbelt.

It was just in time because they were at the top of the hill and turning right. As her body pushed into the man's hard torso, Amelia glanced at the scene behind them. Wind from the open front of the van whipped her hair across her face. Through the wisps, she saw the large car sitting in the middle of the road, steam rising from the crumpled front. Several men gathered around it to check on the driver. Another couple of men ran to where the blue car protruded from the side of the SUV.

Chapter 4

"Was your car clean?" The man spoke to the woman driving.

"Of course."

After the chaos below them disappeared behind buildings and trees, inertia again cast Amelia against the man's firm grip as the woman reduced speed. Glass pieces slid off the hood. The woman killed the van's lights and made a quick left turn without touching the brake. The man's arm tightened around Amelia and kept them from sliding sideways.

In the back, Amelia heard Gabriel. "Not supposed to drive without lights at night. Driving too fast. Not safe to drive without lights. Not safe to drive fast. Not safe to drive without windshield…"

"Gabe, are you all right?" Amelia felt the man's warming touch encircling her. After the trauma, the strong arms around her felt comforting, but she pushed to get loose. "Please let me go. I need to check on Gabe." The man released his embrace but kept ahold of one arm and helped her move to the back seat as the woman maneuvered the van like a racecar. When it was safe, he released her, and she fell into the seat beside Gabriel. Amelia grabbed the middle seatbelt and put it on. In front of her, the man did the same.

Beside Amelia, Gabriel rocked and repeated his safety mantra.

Amelia tried to calm him. "It's okay, Gabe. We have to drive fast right now to get away from the bad men."

The man addressed the woman. "That was a bit of a radical solution back there, wasn't it? I thought you liked that car."

"It handled nice. I'd rent it again."

"Not that one you won't."

"We couldn't leave them with a working vehicle. It was the quickest way for me to take out the sniper and his ride."

"And ours."

"You just don't want to admit that I saved your life again. You know you weren't going to make it past that sniper without him putting a round through that door…and you."

"I was counting on him missing."

"I was counting on not letting him get the shot."

"Thanks. How did that airbag taste?"

"I was too busy to notice." The woman touched a large red mark on her cheek and grimaced. "Thanks for reminding me. Now it's going to hurt." Her hand went back to the wheel as she made another brakeless left turn.

The woman turned on the van's headlights and slowed to the speed limit. Gabriel's chant narrowed to only the windshield reference.

"Okay," the woman said, "We've doubled back enough and put enough distance between us that it will be hard for their reinforcements to pick us up."

The man pulled off his hood.

The woman frowned at him. "I would be wearing mine if I would have had time to get it out of my bag. Why are you—
"

"She's already seen my face. She was in the park and one of my friends back there decided she needed to be eliminated.

I lost my hood convincing him otherwise."

The lines on the woman's forehead went deeper. "Did he see you up close?"

"He won't be talking anymore."

The woman acknowledged with a nod.

Amelia noticed the man was gazing at her. "Please let us go. You can drop us off anywhere. We don't care what is going on, and we won't tell anyone what happened. Please, my brother can't take this. He has autism."

The man's expression seemed regretful. "That wouldn't be safe. I'm sorry this had to happen to you. Why did you come back? What were you trying to do back there?"

"They were going to kill you. I was trying to help you."

"Help me?" The man gave a small laugh. "You nearly got us all killed."

"You were crawling, I thought you were hurt and those men from the park were going to catch you."

"I was crawling past the sniper. My partner was waiting for me in a parking lot at the top of the hill. In another ten minutes, I would have been in the car with her, and we would have been gone without a trace. Now I think we left a little more than a trace. And that's not good."

"I'm sorry. If you just let us go, we won't cause you any more problems."

"Like I said, that wouldn't be safe and I mean for you. I'm not sure if they got your plate or not, but they will know this van. Unfortunately, you're linked with us now, and they will go through you to find out who we are. We can leave, but they will find you and get whatever information they can. Then they'll kill you. We've got to get rid of this van, just in case."

"What do you mean, 'get rid of this—'"

Glancing at the man, the woman spoke over Amelia. "Wait a minute. What we've got to do is complete the job and get out of here." The woman returned her eyes to the street ahead to avoid the look the man gave her.

"It's not her fault. She was trying to help."

The woman kept her eyes forward. "Help like that we don't need. Just let them go like she wants, and everything will be even."

The man let his eyes turn toward Amelia without moving his head. Then they went back to the woman. "We'll drop you off near the motel, so you can get the other car loaded up. I'll go with these two and get rid of the van and get them someplace safe. Once everything's settled, I'll contact you on where to meet." The man spoke to Amelia. "Does your brother have any special needs?"

"He needs to be home in bed. He gets nervous and irritable if he misses his sleep." Amelia ran her sleeve across her eyes. "Please just let me go to the police department. That's what the 9-1-1 lady told me to do. I know they're busy, but I'll be safe there until someone can help me."

The man's frown and downcast eyes shared her distress. "I'm sorry. We can't go to the police. And in this case, there would be no guarantee you'd be safe there."

Beside her, Gabriel added a new statement to his chant, which had gotten a little monotonous since the woman had limited her traffic violations. "Not safe to drive without windshield. Need to be home in bed…"

The man ran his hand through his hair and smiled halfheartedly at Gabriel. "I wish you could be there." He glanced at Amelia. "Does your brother… I heard you call him Gabe. Is that his name?"

Amelia started to agree but hesitated.

The man must have seen the concern in her eyes. "You're right. Best not to share too much information that might make us vulnerable later." There was a slight change in the man's voice. It had the same qualities as the look he had first given her, a tone of sadness and regret.

The woman behind the wheel glanced at him.

Gabriel changed what he was saying. "Gabriel. Amelia's brother is Gabriel. Gabriel needs to be home in bed. Not safe to drive without windshield. Gabriel needs to be home in bed…"

The man chuckled at Amelia's frustrated exhale. "Okay. Can't un-hear that. So, Amelia, does Gabriel have any medications or other needs that might be life-threatening before morning?"

"Morning?" Amelia's voice rose. "Where will we sleep? I am supposed to work in the morning. We live in a group home, and I have to cook for them. They'll be calling the police if we don't come home." It was a lie. Amelia and Gabriel were the only ones at the home for the next three weeks while the staff was on vacation and the residents were away at a special camp, but she hoped she could scare the man into letting her go.

The woman shook her head. "I doubt if the authorities will be responding to missing person complaints anytime soon. I was monitoring emergency traffic, and it sounds like there's a large fire and a sniper shooting out car windows on the highway on the other side of town. Doubt if that's a coincidence."

Amelia bowed her head. "That's why I came back to help you. I called the police and they were too busy to come. They had to call someone from out of town."

The man smiled. "I can't believe you did that. You risked your life for me. How did you know where I was? I like to think I'm pretty good at this and so were the people pursuing me. I got away from them. How did you find me?"

Amelia started to turn toward Gabriel but caught herself. *What is it about this guy that makes me trust him? I don't know these people.* She didn't like to lie but she had worked hard to keep Gabriel's abilities secret. "Just got lucky and spotted you from the hill."

The man gazed at her a moment. He shook his head. "That's impressive."

The dark-haired woman's head bent toward them, but she said nothing.

Gabriel stopped his call for safer driving. He tipped his

head toward the man but kept his gaze on the floor. "Gabriel could hear Rams One crawling."

Amelia cringed inside.

The man looked shocked. "How does he know my radio designator?"

"Rams One moves quiet, but Gabriel heard him. Other people don't hear him, but Gabriel heard him."

The van jerked to the right throwing Amelia sideways in her seatbelt. It bounced as it left the roadway and swerved again. The tires gave a little chirp as they came to an abrupt stop in a dark parking lot. Amelia's body went forward. When she sat up, the woman was turned in the seat pointing her Uzi at them. "Search them."

The man's shocked expression was now directed at the woman. "What are you…"

"They know your handle. Think about it. The only place we use our designators is over the handsfree. They knew where you were. We coordinated your pick up over our handsfree units. It's the only way they could have known you were crawling up that hill. This whole thing went wrong tonight. It was like they knew we were coming. Then she shows up and we have to take her with us. It's too convenient. They had to have been monitoring us from the start. That's how they almost trapped you. Now they've sent her to find out everything else about us. Search them. She probably has some type of transmitter on her."

Gabriel repeated again. "Not safe to point guns at people, Not safe…"

"Okay. Please, don't shoot us." Amelia positioned herself in front of Gabriel, holding her hands out. "His autism gives him savant hearing. He would be able to hear you talking to each other from over a block away. You can search us, anything, just please don't point that gun at us."

The man reached over to the woman and slowly pushed the barrel of the gun so that it pointed at the seat to the left of Amelia. "We'll search them, so you won't be worried, but there are some other things to think about here. The handsfree is encrypted so unless they got the key, they would not be able to understand it. She might be telling the truth. People with autism have heightened sensitivity. Maybe he's an extreme case. We can test what she's telling us once we get stabilized. I don't believe in coincidence either. Maybe this is all part of a plan, but maybe it's not the other side's plan."

The woman inhaled. "I know how you think, but if the Almighty really wanted to help us, He could have kept her out of this and helped us make a clean exit."

"Maybe He has something bigger planned and this was just a way to connect us. I've seen Him work like that before. Let's be open to the idea at the same time we're being cautious."

Rams One, as Amelia now knew the man, searched Gabriel which was hard on both of them. Gabriel batted at his hands as he tried to be as understanding and as gentle as he could. The man made a point of showing the woman that Gabriel had no weapons or wires, but he did not seem to really suspect he would find any. Then the man had the woman search Amelia. She was very thorough.

Rams One asked Amelia, "Did you give the police my description?"

Amelia thought for a moment. "No, I gave them the description of the big man that you stopped from hurting me, but they were too busy for much more."

"Good. Let's get going," he said to the woman.

They drove to the back lot of a fitness gym and stopped near a hedge in the back corner. The woman looked at the man, "You get the car. I'm not sure I trust you with these two right now."

"What's that supposed to mean?"

"It means that I'm not buying her innocent act, and I think you might be."

Rams One regarded the woman. Leaving his Uzi behind, he took a handgun and holster from the bag. "You have seen that they're not armed or bugged, so I know I can trust you not to be jumpy. You're right, we need to establish their credibility. It's a fantastic enough explanation that it should be easy to verify."

The man holstered the gun and tucked it into his pants, pulling his shirt over it. "Turn your radio on and kill the engine." his face had a slight smile as he looked at the woman then at Amelia and Gabriel. "Let's try something."

The woman shut off the van as Rams One got out. The man stretched nonchalantly by the van as he looked around. He then ducked into a small opening in the hedge. Amelia decided that asking the woman where he was going was not a good idea.

The man was gone only a few moments when the woman unexpectedly started talking. "Go ahead, I copy you." She turned to Amelia. "My partner says to have your brother tell you what he is saying."

"Gabe," Amelia spoke to her brother, "can you do that?"

The woman's eyes widened as Gabriel opened his mouth, but Rams One's voice came out. "I thought this would be as good a time as any to test this so here goes. Mary had a little lamb, his fleece was black as soot, and everywhere that Mary went, his sooty foot he put. Well, how did he do?"

The woman turned her head like she was listening and for the first time, Amelia noticed the small earpiece she was wearing. A thin microphone ran along her cheek and she spoke into it. "He's repeating everything, including what you just said over the radio. But the craziest thing is that it sounds just like you."

Gabriel went on, "Okay, I'm going to talk without the radio again. Old Mother Hubbard, went to the cupboard, to get her poor daughter a dress. But when she got there, the cupboard was bare, and so was her daughter, I guess."

Amelia smiled.

The woman spoke into the microphone again. "Either this guy has the same stupid sense of humor that you have or he's hearing everything you're saying."

"So, I guess she wasn't lying," Gabriel mimicked. "He's better than a parabolic microphone because I'm almost to the motel. I've got to be over…"

Gabriel kept talking, but the woman was speaking into the microphone at the same time. "Hey, stop. I'm hearing you in stereo only what he is saying is coming out a little later and it's confusing. Just say it without the radio because there's no difference. You won't believe this."

"…from you now. This is something that we might be able to…" Gabriel stopped where the woman interrupted the man. He paused for a moment and then resumed in the voice of Rams One. "Let's try something different. Numi numi yaldati," Gabriel's copy of the man's voice sang in a soft tune. "Numi numi nim. Numi numi k'tanati, numi numi nim. Aba halach lavodoh halach halach aba yashuv im tzet halevana yavi lach matana. Numi numi yaldati…"

"Stop," the woman said. "You're putting me to sleep. I'd say he's singing in perfect Hebrew, but it's you, so how perfect could it be? He also sings just as bad as you do."

"Hey, my mama used to sing that song to my sister. Have some respect," Gabriel mimicked. "You're the only one that hears any of my New York accent, so I think it's just you. I heard him speaking French back in the park. I was wondering how he would do with languages. Ask Amelia if he can translate it."

"Don't worry," the woman said. "You just asked her yourself because he is still repeating everything you're saying."

"Gabe," Amelia said. "can you sing the song in English?"

Gabriel sang in the man's voice. "Sleep, sleep, my little girl. Sleep, sleep. Sleep, sleep, my little one. Sleep, sleep. Daddy's gone to work. He left, Daddy left. He'll be back when the moon comes out. He'll bring you a gift. Sleep, sleep, my little girl."

The woman dropped back in her seat. "Tell him to stop."

"Gabriel, stop repeating, please."

The woman spoke into the mic again. "He translated it pretty much word for word. Finish up over there and I'll meet you somewhere. And watch what you say. It's obvious we have no privacy anymore." She ran her hand through her hair and looked again at Gabriel. "I've never heard of this before. I'm surprised your brother isn't famous."

"He's not supposed to do it around other people because my parents were afraid someone might try to exploit his gift. For some reason, he seems to trust your partner. He has always been fascinated with law enforcement. He likes all the gadgets they have on their belts. I think he's connecting you with that."

"How many languages does he know?"

"I don't know," Amelia said. "I know there are languages that he hasn't heard but we've never run across a need to translate those. My mother was French so we both speak French. When we were little my mother would put us to bed each night with the Bible in different languages. I picked up some, but Gabe remembers almost everything he hears. Things don't always make sense in his mind, but he remembers the sounds and he can repeat them, connect word for word, language for language. Now it's a game we play. I speak and he translates, and we learn languages together. My mother spoke five languages when she grew up in France, so it was important to her. She died when I was 12. It's…something of her that we try to keep alive."

"I'm sorry." The woman's face softened a little. "I heard you say that you used this van for your work. What do you do?"

"I sell organic vegetables and homemade jam. That's why we were at the park. But I have to be back at the group home tonight because I cook and clean there for my room and board."

The woman sighed. "Listen, I'm sorry you're caught up in this, but you are and none of us can change that now. The people we are…the ones that tried to kill us tonight will try again if they can find us, and 'us' includes you now."

"Why can't we just tell the police?"

"I can't discuss that. You'll just have to understand it's not possible." The woman softened again. "If you're able to speak so many languages, why don't you get a job as a translator? It's got to pay better than what you're doing. You should be worth a lot to some organization because they would only have to hire one translator instead of a whole team."

"Gabe couldn't do that. He needs to be in the group home. They understand his needs and he's comfortable there."

"How about you?"

"I need to stay with him. All we have is each other."

The woman's features changed, and she appeared to be listening to something else. "Rams Two copies," she said to the mic. "Okay, we're ready to go." She was talking to Amelia again. "This van is too conspicuous so Rams One will go ahead of us and warn us if we're about to run into any unfriendlies. We'll stay back a block and a half, so we can turn off if he sees something coming our way."

They drove for about fifteen minutes, winding around the streets of Gosnell until they reached the outskirts of town. They stopped on the street a short distance from the customer parking lot of an out-of-the-way salvage business. There was a tall wooden fence next to them that concealed the storage yard for the salvaged vehicles.

Rams One got out and came back to the van. Climbing in the passenger seat he said, "This place looks perfect. I see one camera on the back of the building." Opening the large equipment bag again, he brought out several items. The woman turned off the van. Amelia watched as the man assembled them into what she realized was a rifle of some type. The last thing he added was a long thick tube to the end of the barrel. From what she had seen in movies, Amelia decided it must be a silencer. He then took a large riflescope out of a padded case and attached it to the top of the weapon. Moving in the seat, the man set up the rifle on the dash of the van.

"There are some advantages to not having a windshield," he said as he pushed the barrel of the rifle out over the hood of the vehicle.

He sighted for a few seconds and the rifle fired with a muffled pop. Amelia heard glass breaking and saw some pieces fly from an object located just under the roof of the building.

Gabriel came to life. "Ooohhh, ooohhh," he was rocking harder than he had been already. "Not good to break things. Property damage is illegal. Gonna be in trouble."

The man turned to Gabriel and smiled. He reached out and moved his hand in front of Gabriel's field of view but did not touch him. "We'll pay for it, Gabriel. When it's safe, we'll send them enough for the owner to buy a better camera. We will make it right. We just can't let ourselves be videoed. It will be all right."

Gabriel's rocking slowed. "Better camera," he repeated. "Buy a better camera…"

The woman got out of the van and began doing something with the lock on the gate to the entrance of the lot. The man quickly disassembled the rifle and put it back in the bag. He turned to Amelia. "What personal belongings do you have in the van?"

Amelia noticed the woman had the gate unlocked and was swinging it open.

Chapter 5

Amelia sat in the back seat of the car with the woman. The man was driving with Gabriel in the seat beside him. The woman had insisted on the arrangement.

The salvage lot was far behind them. Amelia had watched numbly as they took everything out of her van, put her personal items in their trunk, and discarded the rest. Rams One had used a cordless grinder on various parts of her van to eradicate any identifying marks. They had concealed the bullet holes with duct tape, wiped away any fingerprints, and left her precious vehicle sandwiched between two other wrecks in the furthest corner of the salvage lot.

Rams One gave her a sympathetic look in the rearview mirror. "I'm sorry about your van. If we just left it sitting on the street or tried putting it on private property, there is too great a risk someone would call about it too quickly for our purposes. Besides we had a little time to kill while we let things cool down in the city. It was a little hot to be out on the streets."

The words impacted Amelia as she repeated them. "A little time to kill?"

In the mirror, the man's face appeared troubled.

The woman handed her a paper. "Here, sign this. It's the title to your van. I got it out of your glove box."

Amelia looked at the signature line but didn't know what to do. Who were these people?

The woman breathed in and her voice took on an understanding tone. "When someone from the salvage lot finally finds the van, they will think one of the other employees put it there. The next employee will think the same thing. Who would put a working vehicle in their lot? It will take time for them to all get together and figure out that no one at the lot knows anything about the vehicle. They will have a hard time identifying the van because the VINs are scratched off. To look further they will have to pull it out from between the other vehicles. Chances are they will be busy and procrastinate. They will put off calling the police. When they finally call, the police will have no record of a stolen vehicle. There are many hidden VINs on vehicles so eventually, they will find one, and we don't want the van to be in your name when they do. Just sign this and our people will take care of the rest. If they track it back to you, simply tell them the truth—you sold it to a woman that you never met before. We will set up an exchange on an internet buy, sell, trade site, and you can show them that. Leave tonight's events out of it."

"How is that going to be possible?" Amelia sorted through everything in her mind. "I needed my van to do my business. The Ozark Festival is coming up in a few days at the same park where I was at today. It's the biggest event of the year in Gosnell. People come from all over the country, and I make a lot of sales that day."

They stopped at a red light. The man turned in his seat. His face seemed to agree with the pain she was feeling. He put his hand on hers, and his voice was gentle. "I'll make sure you get a better van. It was dangerous for you to keep that one. Let the salvage company have it. The van has value to them in the parts, so you have done them no disservice. They can apply for a salvage title and take possession of the van like they do with the abandoned vehicles that they tow. Hopefully, by then, this will long be over."

"That sounds crazy."

"That's the point. It's too crazy to believe. The police will dismiss it as bad record-keeping on the part of the salvage lot. They won't be able to locate the current owner and it will end there. But the main thing is, we will have our mission completed by the time they start looking into it."

Amelia stared at the hand that covered hers. "What is that mission?" Amelia let the frustration she was feeling at all the secrecy creep into her voice.

The man slowly pulled his hand away and turned back to the front. "At this time, there is no benefit in you knowing." The light changed. As Rams One went back to his driving, Amelia saw his fixed eyes and brow furrowed with regret, in the glow of the dash lights.

Gabriel had been silent in the seat beside him, but he spoke unexpectedly. "Operation Jericho. Rams One wants to complete Operation Jericho."

The woman slapped the pen she was holding for Amelia onto the paper and arched her neck in frustration. "Now where did he get that?"

The man sighed heavily. "I'm sure he heard our conversation on approach to the compound. They were in the park, that's just a couple of blocks away. We might as well face the fact that the whole audio of our operation is locked in Gabriel's memory. This is not a secret to him. And, if Amelia wants the information, I'm sure he will tell her. I don't see any reason for me not to share an idea that I want to run by you."

"We need to talk in private about this," the woman tapped on the signature line and thrust the pen back at Amelia.

Amelia took it and signed, not knowing what else to do.

Rams One spoke calmly to the woman. "And just how do you propose we do that? Unless we are going to drop them off somewhere and drive far enough away that he can't hear us?

We are going to have to trust them one way or another, either not to run or not to talk. I for one think we can trust them with both."

Rams Two sneered at him. "Text me."

The suggestion brought a response from Gabriel. "No texting and driving. It's not safe to text and drive."

With a chuckle, Rams One continued. "Thank you, Gabriel. You see he knows what you're not supposed to do. He's on the right side. If they were spying on us, the last thing they would be doing would be revealing what they know. Gabriel has no deceit in him, that's obvious. And I have seen Amelia's heart."

The man's expression seemed to display admiration through the mirror. "She was ready to die for her brother. She risked her life to help a stranger. We've trusted people before with a lot less evidence of their character. If we give them a limited knowledge of the stakes, I think they can help us. It might be the only way we're going to succeed now that our adversary knows we're here."

"I appreciate your trust..." Amelia's insides ached. She needed to get Gabriel and herself away from them as soon as she could. "...but please just let us go. We are not cut out to be soldiers or spies or whatever you are. We just want to go home. I know you keep telling me it's not safe, but none of this sounds safe. I'm sure you have an important job to do, but I just don't think we can be part of it. We won't mention any of this, and I will take responsibility for Gabriel and me. Just drop us off anywhere you want."

"Tonight, you'll stay with us at a safe house." The woman's face was resolute. "In the morning, we'll see."

The statement felt like a sentence being pronounced on Amelia. She needed to do something. "I at least need to let the group home know we're safe and that we won't be there tomorrow."

"When we get to the house, I'll set you up with a secure net, so you can call your group home."

The woman was calling her bluff, or maybe Amelia had just fooled them. Either way, she would have to tell them that no one would really be waiting at the home.

The woman held two black cloth objects she took from the bag. "I'll have to blindfold you."

Amelia's mouth quivered. Would the man let the woman kill them? She closed her eyes as Rams Two moved toward her.

Chapter 6

The route to the safe house was a series of twists and turns that Amelia never saw. The hoods the woman placed over their heads seemed to bother Gabriel less than she expected. But he was used to comprehending things with his ears instead of his eyes. When the hoods were removed, they were traveling down a dark gravel road. A moon had risen and illuminated the open meadow they traversed. She could see that the drive ended at a log ranch house with several outbuildings. The closer they got, the more the moonlight was washed out by the powerful lights that surrounded the well-lit property.

When they pulled up, a woman opened the front door as they crawled out of the car. She was beautiful in the extreme. God had given her a lot to work with, and she had taken it from there. From her shimmering blond waves surrounding makeup artistry to her form filled pantsuit, the package was near perfect. The only thing that was out of place was the assault rifle in her hands and the penetrating way she assessed the vehicle's occupants. She seemed to be satisfied with everything except Amelia and Gabriel.

Rams Two opened the trunk and handed things to Amelia and Rams One. "They're guests." She addressed the woman on the porch as if there was nothing striking about her. Introducing them, she gave the blonde woman their names but not the other way around. Then she added, "Class four protocol, with the exception of this guy." She made a hand gesture toward Gabriel. "Nothing sensitive is to be voiced as long as he is present anywhere on the grounds unless it is in the communication room. We hope the soundproofing in there will be enough."

The blonde woman sized them up.

Ram's Two faced the blonde again. "You'll have to experience it to believe it, but trust me anything you say from now on, Gabriel will hear it and remember it. He has an interesting talent." Rams Two presented the woman with a humorous eyebrow raise. "He probably already knows what you said when we drove up."

The woman inspected Gabriel. "I burped. Did he hear that?"

Everyone looked at Gabriel who faced the ground as he spoke. "She didn't burp. She said, 'What are those two dragging in now?'" the voice a perfect mimic of the woman.

The sudden upward movement of the woman's head was faint, but her countenance appeared frozen. "Is he from the agency?"

Rams Two shook her head. "Chance encounter as far as we can tell. Caught in the middle of the operation. They might have been ID'ed by the other side. They need a safe place until we figure out what to do." She motioned toward Rams One. "He has an idea."

The woman's beautiful face dismissed Rams Two's comment. "It's all so convenient." She stood in the entrance like she might not let anyone in.

Rams One carried Gabriel's items onto the porch. "God works like that sometimes."

Amelia recognized a genuineness in the man's statement.

Earlier, he said something similar. I think he's a believer. They weren't talking like they planned on killing them. At least not right now.

The blonde finally held open the door as the hosts and guests filed through. "Not in my experience, lover. I don't like coincidences I didn't create."

Just inside the door, the man turned to Amelia, shaking his head. "She calls all the guys that. It's just her way. It doesn't mean anything."

As Amelia moved past the blonde, the other woman was evaluating her again as she muttered, "But he doesn't correct me to all the girls."

The house had a hunting lodge look that concealed a sizeable interior. Both women disappeared through a doorway.

"Do we need to make that call to the home where you live?" Rams One seemed ready to accommodate.

The bluff was called. Amelia might as well get it over with. "I was hoping you would let me go. There's no one there this weekend."

"Oh." Rams One gave her a curious scrutiny. "You think quick on your feet. That was a good try." He moved on without further comment. "The kitchen is stocked if you want to fix something for you and Gabriel," Rams One smiled and nodded to the open door. "There's a bathroom and utility room off of it."

The word bathroom struck Amelia like a slap to the midsection and made her suddenly aware of a suppressed need she hadn't allowed herself to think about until now.

"There's also a bathroom off your bedroom. This way." He moved down a hall in the opposite direction.

Amelia beckoned Gabriel and they followed to a bedroom at the end of the hall. Rams One placed their bags on the full-size bed in the center and motioned to the sides of the room. "Bunk beds fold out of the walls. You might want to use one of them for Gabriel if sharing your room would make him feel more comfortable. I know it's going to be hard to break from his usual routine."

Amelia glanced at the man's pleasant face. He seemed to pick up on Gabriel's needs.

"There's a bedroom next door if that would be better."

"No, he'll be better with me." The thought brought back the impossibility of the situation. Gabriel's wide eyes were glaring at all the strangeness of the room. His mind was probably putting together that they were expecting him to sleep there.

Something else was more pressing, literally. Amelia gave a thankful glance toward the bathroom.

She steered Gabriel toward a wall and Rams One pulled down one of the hideaway beds. Amelia spent a moment to show Gabriel how to work everything as she always had to do in a place that was new to him. Pulling his electronic tablet from his bag, she pointed out an outlet to charge it. In a moment, she had his audiobook playing in one app, the Bible and classical music in another and then a loop of woodland and water sounds.

"There's no fan," she told him. "I'm sorry. Please try to sleep without it tonight." She looked at Gabriel hoping for once he would be tired enough not to mind a break in routine.

Her brother surveyed the floor of the strange room as he rocked. Amelia followed as Gabriel's gaze moved to the bathroom.

Hurriedly she pulled items from Gabriel's bag and put them on the spacious headboard attached to the bunk. "Here's your headphones for when you're ready for bed. Don't leave the room. I'm going to…wash up, and then I'll come back and help you."

Gabriel reached out and touched the bare bed.

Rams One moved to a cabinet next to the bunk. "There's some bedding in here. He'll want something without a lot of colors, I imagine."

"That's right." Amelia turned her impressed expression

away from the man and placed a bag of trail mix in Gabriel's hand.

Rams One returned with white sheets and a plain brown blanket. Amelia took them and leaned over to place them on the bed. She was keenly aware of the part of her body that her bending put pressure on. "There." She stood up quickly. "I'll put these on…in a minute."

Gabriel looked at the blanket. "Gabriel doesn't have his pajamas. Gabriel needs his pajamas to sleep. Need to go to Gabriel's room. Gabriel's pajamas are in Gabriel's room. This is not Gabriel's room."

"I'm sorry, honey. Try to listen to your sounds. I need…to clean up, but I'll come back and check on you in a little bit."

Ram's One stood looking at her. "I can see you really love your brother. It's okay. We're not going to hurt him or you. We're just being cautious. It's something we have to do."

I think he really means it. Amelia clung to the words in hope.

The man had more to say. "I saw how you were willing to sacrifice yourself for him in the park today."

"I was so scared. I was about to wet…about to cry." *Where did that come from?* As if she didn't know.

The man lingered. "You *were* crying. But they were strong tears."

It was the first good look that Amelia had gotten of him in full light. His black hair laid wild around his face and accented his dark eyes. He had a sturdy chin that was covered in black stubble. His nose ran long from his thick eyebrows to his lips. She knew he must be Israeli because of all she had heard that day. But his face was the type that could be any number of different nationalities.

Amelia felt safe with the man, like he would protect them. She didn't want him to leave. Why did the pain in her bladder have to be increasing every moment?

Ram's One kept talking, "I know you must think we're Philistines."

For the first time she noticed the New York accent he had spoken of. It was so slight that most people wouldn't catch it. The work he was doing must demand that he bury it so that he could blend into different societies.

"If I can convince my supervisors to allow me to share our mission with you, I think you'll understand the importance of it." She thought he was going to turn to leave but he kept talking. "I don't want to promise that I will be able to tell you much. I have influence, but we're in a delicate situation."

"I'm sure you'll do your best," was all she could think to say. Amelia's leg had been slowly creeping across the other one. She uncrossed it, so she could move him toward the door.

"I hope you'll be able to sleep after all that's gone on today."

"I'm sure I will, right after I…freshen up." She bit her lower lip as she gave a longing glance over her shoulder to the beckoning doorway where she could see just a bit of white porcelain peeking out. She feigned smoothing her jeans and squeezed her thigh to stop the tiny bouncing of her leg.

"Now that I think of it, I'm pretty tired myself." The man smiled. It was perfect, a beautiful smile, a captivating smile and she had to get it out of her room, now!

Amelia slapped her legs and quickly took his arm and led him to the door and out into the hall. He smiled again as he looked at her arm wrapped around his. The man continued the expression. He looked up into her eyes as she backed up and closed the door in his face. She did not even care if he heard the bathroom door slam a second later.

Joshua clenched his jaw as he walked down the hall. This wasn't going to be easy. Should he even be considering the idea in his head.

The night's events tormented his mind. They had taken her van, held her against her will, and had to kill people right in front of her. *That's not going to go away.*

Even if she was strong, she had to be scared to death. It was going to take more than a little small talk to convince her she could trust him. The poor girl probably thought she had to talk to stay alive, to protect her brother.

What if it was Caleb? Would he want him to be a part of this? Joshua couldn't answer the question. The thought of his brother brought an ache to his insides. After Caleb was gone, his mother had kept him busy, so he didn't dwell on it. Now he did the same thing to himself. Always another mission.

Something about Amelia was like salve on that wound. Her care for her brother linked her, in his emotions, with all the good memories. Her self-sacrifice, her courage, her return to help a stranger at the risk of her life, all elevated his opinion of her.

He raised his eyes and followed the sturdy beams in the ceiling. He needed to concentrate on the mission and let God take everything where it was supposed to go. *Be anxious for nothing.* Sometimes it didn't seem possible. *I guess that's the point.* The impossible was where God liked to step in.

He still believed in what they were doing. The world was complicated, and there weren't always straightforward ways of taking on evil. They were in the U.S. with too few resources and no legal backing. Now the people they were up against knew someone was onto them, so they had lost the element of surprise. Gabriel might be the asset they needed, but could he handle the stress of such an operation, and what was Amelia going to think of him when he presented the idea to her?

The mattress jolted under Amelia's head. There was a

loud bang. Her brother was crying out. "Not Gabriel's bed. Not Gabriel's bed."

She jerked her head off the mattress and sat back from where she must have drifted off while kneeling beside him. She had been singing him their mother's French lullaby but had apparently fallen asleep for a few minutes.

In the dim light, her brother was huddled on his sheets, hands over his ears and he was kicking the wall. Stretching across the bed, she tried to wrap him in a hug.

He batted her hands away and screamed. "Gabriel needs to go home. He needs to go home to his bed. He needs to go home to his bed."

Amelia collapsed to a seated position on the floor beside the bed and buried her face in the mattress. She had done the best she could to repeat their bedtime routine, but it wasn't enough. Gabriel's autism demanded consistency. After she dozed off, Gabriel must have laid awake until he could stand it no longer. He was in meltdown stage. She was so tired, physically, emotionally. She was ready to have her own meltdown. *God, I need Your help.*

"Amelia, are you all right?" Ram's One called out from the other side of the bedroom door.

"Yes…"

Gabriel wailed. "Not Gabriel's bed, Not Gabriel's bed."

What was she saying? Nothing was all right. "No…It's Gabriel." She was sure the whole house had figured that much out already. She had to yell to be heard over her brother's broken record complaint.

The door opened and Rams One hurried in, swatting on the lights. He assessed the situation.

His arrival encouraged Amelia until he turned and fled the room almost colliding with Ram's Two and the blonde who stood in the doorway. Rams Two entered, gawking at Gabriel's tantrum, while the blonde gazed after Rams One with an amused countenance.

Even with his ears covered, Gabriel perceived the

unwelcome audience. He had reached his limit of stimuli and kicked the wall even harder and cried out breathlessly. "Home, home, Gabriel's home, home, home, home."

"Please, Gabe." Amelia touched his cheek, but he shook his head violently.

"Is there anything I can do?" Rams Two's face declared she had no hope that there was.

The blonde furrowed her brow at the situation. Her face changed to surprise as Rams One pushed past her.

The man held a long, thick, black vest with a large, white lettered "AGENT" emblazoned on both sides. He pulled loose Velcro straps, opening the side of the stiff panels. Shoving one half of the vest against Gabriel's back, Rams One scooped up the young man, ignoring the flailing arms connecting hard against his head. He timed his movements with the young man's windmilling limbs and brought the other half of the vest around the front of Gabriel and pressed it against his chest. The resistance continued as the man cinched the Velcro, making the vest snug.

Rams One pulled the boy in, wrapped his arms around him and pushed his head against Gabriel's so he couldn't move enough to strike out. The man rocked Gabriel and began a monotonous humming.

Amelia didn't know how he knew about "deep pressure therapy" or where he learned to use his work gear as a weighted sensory vest, and she didn't care. She plopped herself beside them and joined in the hug. She also didn't care if the other women could tell that it was as much for the marvelous man that understood her brother as it was for Gabriel.

Amelia resumed singing in French. Rams One went silent and they rocked together until Gabriel's tirade subsided. They continued as his breathing went from wheezing through his teeth to a slow normal rhythm.

Rams One straightened.

Amelia reluctantly let go and noticed that both women sat

on her bed, across the room, watching them. Rams Two erased the sweet look she had and sat up. The blonde continued her inspection, but her bemused smile softened her face.

Laying Gabriel on his bed, Rams One stood.

Gabriel opened his eyes and looked at the floor with his face turned toward the man. "Gabriel go home now?"

The man's wrinkled forehead showed his dilemma. "You can borrow my vest while you're here. I know it helps. We'll get you home as soon as we can. Just remember this is also Gabriel's bed now. As long as you're here, it's your bed. And I'll get you a fan today." He gave the young man a light swat on the thick ballistic panel covering his chest. "You look like an agent now. You better get some sleep. We might need you on our next mission."

Amelia found Gabriel's headphones in the covers and slipped them on his head. She leaned in and kissed his cheek.

His voice was quiet in her ear. "This is Gabriel's bed. Gabriel is agent now. Got to sleep for the next mission."

Amelia nodded and slid her hand across his cheek. Everyone was still watching as she got up.

Rams One took an uncomfortable breath. "Goodnight." He headed for the door.

Rams Two pulled the still smiling blonde to her feet and urged her out of the room. She clicked off the light and closed the door behind them.

In the silence that followed, Amelia listened to Gabriel's soft snoring. Even in the dark, she could see the bright white "Agent" covering Gabriel. Her fear had lessened. She was among humans, not uncaring killers. But why? *Why are we here?*

When she was satisfied Gabriel was sound asleep, she made her way back to her own bed. Looking up at the ceiling she repeated the question. *Why are we here, God?* Instead of an answer, He sent sleep.

Chapter 7

Amelia awoke in the morning to see Gabriel sitting on his bed, listening to his headphones. Sleep was always difficult for her brother, so she was grateful to see him looking rested. He would need time alone with his sounds to recover.

Thirty minutes later, Amelia emerged from her room showered and spruced, and, to her surprise, feeling refreshed. But that didn't take away the apprehension of what was going to happen. She found Rams One in her thoughts. He had become her only sense of security in the strange surroundings.

"Gabe, I'm going to go make us some breakfast." Her brother's head canted as he followed her to the door with his ears.

She meandered into the kitchen half hungry and half searching for that security.

The blonde woman stood at the counter, pouring a green smoothie from the blender. The woman's gaze snapped toward Amelia. She stabbed a straw into her glass, turned, leaning her backside against the counter, and took a long draw on the drink as she assessed Amelia.

"Good morning." Some of Amelia's encouragement left as she endured the inspection.

The woman lowered the drink. "You're looking better. Don't you wear makeup? Not that you need it, but I don't see that too often. Your hair has just the right shade of brown to go with your green eyes. You should accent them." She absently took a cookie from a package on the counter and bit into it.

"I've never been into makeup much. Only when I have a pimple or something." Amelia tried to appear pleasant. "You do yours very nicely."

The blonde swallowed the mouthful. "Tools of the trade. At night I clean my handgun and put on skin cream. In the morning I load it and put on makeup. Part of the job." She opened wide for another bite and stopped. The woman pulled the cookie away from her mouth as if noticing it for the first time. With a disgusted expression, she set it aside. "Just like watching what I eat." She gave a perplexed glance back at the cookie and shook her head.

"Sounds like an unusual job. You weren't with the others last night. Do you do the same thing as they do?"

"More or less. I just do my makeup better." The woman smirked.

Amelia returned the expression. *A sense of humor. Maybe she isn't so bad after all.*

"But our work is going to be a limited conversation, so we better pick a different topic."

"Can I ask where the others are?"

"They went to town for supplies and to pick up some things for you and your brother." The blonde looked at her watch. "I wanted to get my workout in before they got back, but I couldn't get my sorry rear out of the bed this morning." The woman raised her glass for a sip. The alteration of her face was immediate. Her stomach convulsed visibly. She slammed the glass down on the counter, and clamping her hand over her mouth, raced to the bathroom.

Amelia followed. The woman was on one knee, retching into the toilet.

Kneeling beside her, Amelia pulled a length of toilet paper off the roll and held it out to the woman. When the spasms subsided, she became aware of the offering and took it with a thankful nod. Even her cosmetics could not conceal the white in her face.

Amelia went to the kitchen and brought a chair outside the bathroom door. She assisted the woman into it with no resistance. She went back to the kitchen and poured a glass of water and took it to her patient. The woman took the drink but only examined it with wariness.

After a few minutes, the blonde's color returned. "Sorry, that took me by surprise. I drink those all the time. The first sip was fine, but then the smell got me."

Amelia put several things together in her mind. The woman appeared hungry, tired, and nauseated in unusual ways. Giving the blonde's shoulder a rub, she told her, "That's okay. Gabe and I volunteered at a Christian pregnancy center for a while. You should have seen all the strange things that set those girls off. It's not your fault."

"I'm not pregnant."

"Oh. I'm sorry. I—"

"I think I might have a touch of flu or something. I'll take care of it as soon as we wrap things up here."

A vehicle drove up outside. The woman turned toward the sound then looked back at Amelia. "I don't suppose I could ask you to keep this between us?"

"It's your business. I have no reason to spread it."

The blonde put her hand on Amelia's shoulder as she walked by. "I'm going to brush my teeth and then head to the gym."

The safe house command center occupied the basement of the building. Rams One ushered her and Gabriel into a room with a large table surrounded by chairs. Rams One invited Amelia and Gabriel to have a seat on one side of the table. The blonde and Rams Two sat on the other side and Rams One took the chair at the head.

He spoke first. "I need to beg an apology again. We had to conduct a background investigation on you with the information from your car title. I'm sorry to invade your privacy but it was necessary."

The dark-haired woman reached across the table and placed her hand in front of Amelia. "It sounds like you and your brother have been through a lot. I'm sorry." The woman's countenance conveyed approval. "But you have worked hard to overcome those obstacles."

The things they might know about her ran through Amelia's thoughts, but the woman interrupted them.

"We want to introduce ourselves, though we can't tell you more than our first names. I'm Ibbie." The woman put her hand on her chest. Using her open hand, she indicated the blonde. "This is Marsha." The hand moved toward the man. "And this is Joshua."

Joshua took over the conversation again. "Last night we received approval to officially make a request of you." He paused and smiled at Amelia. "Now, here is the difficult part. I cannot tell you who we work for. The only information I can give you is what we are trying to accomplish and the nature of the other side of the conflict we are in."

Amelia's face must have spoken for her.

"I know you might be thinking, 'Why would I want to be a part of any of this?' But please, before you decide, let me share something with you. What do you know about anti-Semitism?"

Amelia considered her response. "I read things about the threats to Israel from the Arab states around them. They talk about it at church. I always have to get Gabriel home, so I don't get to discuss it much. I am aware that for thousands of years the Jewish people have been the target of attacks all around the world. We pray for them."

Joshua nodded. "I am sure those prayers have helped bring us here. We are trying to stop one of the latest attempts to destroy the Jewish race."

"That's happening here in Gosnell?"

Ibbie nodded. "This is going to sound too bizarre to believe, but we have been tracking an organization that is operating under the guise of a DNA testing provider. We have intelligence that they are using their resources to identify people with a Hebrew background that are not openly Jewish. There is a phenomenon of many unlikely people finding that they are 'hidden Jews'—people that have a Hebrew heritage they never knew about. The company is owned by a group of Muslim doctors out of New York who have ties to terrorist groups. We believe they have come up with a new twist on genocide."

The word genocide made an impression on Amelia.

"The company provides testing for both ancestry and medical purposes. But we have intel that the data is being manipulated toward an anti-Semitic end. With every test, the lab searches for ancestry whether it is requested or not. When the testing identifies someone with latent Jewish ancestry, that fact is concealed, and the client becomes a target. The lab's ultimate goal is to eliminate Jewish DNA. So, in the case of medical testing, lab personnel discourage clients from trying to reproduce by lying to them about a variety of potential genetic defects. If it is a fetal test, the mother is deceived into believing she should seek an abortion because genetic abnormalities might make childbirth dangerous or cause the baby to be deformed. The lab is quick to provide a list of available abortion clinics, which are happy to work with the lab to perform discreet services."

It didn't seem possible to Amelia. "How can they get away with lying to people about their tests?"

Joshua was bobbing his head in understanding of the question. "DNA testing is so new, there is very little oversight. It has become a form of entertainment and it is growing so fast that no one wants to be on the wrong side of something so popular. Also, most politicians don't understand the science." Joshua shrugged. "The public isn't supporting regulation and lawmakers don't know how to write regulation, so who's going to stop them?"

Joshua's face said he regretted having to tell her more. "And that is only half of the picture. If they have no way to medically influence their target, they move to a more direct approach. They are not telling the customer about their Jewish heritage but are secretly providing the information to hate groups and sleeper terrorists, which they have been deploying to the United States for years. There have been random shootings and other acts of terror that might not be random at all. Depending on the individual's sphere of influence, they may be targeted directly for assassination which is concealed as a random or accidental death."

Ibbie seemed especially passionate when she said, "But there is a second prong to their direct attack. They are targeting the children of the tested families. We are not sure how many child disappearances can be attributed to them, but the number is significant."

Amelia felt heat rising to her face. It was unbelievable, but if there was any truth to it—

"They are operating on the belief," Joshua added, "that the impact of 'hidden Jews' in this country is a major contributor to the support Israel has received from the United States. It is the same old idea that Jews' genetic inferiority makes them an undesirable presence in the world. If they can eliminate the hidden Jewish strain, they believe they can turn the political tide in the United States, thus cutting off support for the Jewish community. Then anti-Semitics can eliminate the open Jews, and the enemies of the State of Israel will finally be able to destroy it and eradicate what they feel is the Jewish pollution from the gene pool."

Amelia shook her head. "Can't you simply expose them? Surely no one in their right mind would stand for this."

Again, Joshua nodded agreement. "We can if we have enough evidence, but I am sure you will admit that it sounds like one more conspiracy theory. The moment we make such an accusation, all the testing will turn legitimate. We have been told by our sources they have a system set up to make that happen at a moment's notice. Our operation the other night might have already set that in motion, but I doubt it. They don't know enough about us to cause them to shut down the whole operation, so if we let them get comfortable again, perhaps we can still stop them."

"The worst thing that could happen," Ibbie said, "is to make an accusation without proof. It could have the effect of bulletproofing the organization. No legal entity would listen a second time, too much bad PR and potential for a lawsuit."

"So now you're just waiting?"

Joshua gave a heavy sigh. "Waiting is dangerous because we have another problem. We are not the only ones that have this intel. Have you ever heard of a group called the Jewish Defense League?"

Amelia wrinkled her brow and then shook her head.

Joshua continued. "They are a radical band of loosely organized Jews that take the fight against anti-Semitism to a terroristic level. They were started in the 1960s and have been linked to many terrorist activities against individuals and groups they perceive as enemies of the Jewish people. Sometimes they might be right, but the methods they have decided to employ over the years have been a significant source of the negative publicity I mentioned. Some individuals that have been involved on the fringes of the JDL have now formed a new group called Fighters for Israel. They are a sophisticated and well-organized faction with ties to some wealthy and influential benefactors in the American Jewish community. Their tactics are far more advanced than their predecessors. They are more dangerous because they have the resources and the ability to carry out something big. We also understand that they have recruited some highly skilled ex-Israeli military personnel. Even former Kidon operatives."

Amelia blinked at the word. "What's Kidon?"

"Covert assassins." Marsha gave voice to the term, making it sound like a highly respected discipline.

Joshua wrinkled his brow. "We have to bring down this organization before the Fighters for Israel do it in the wrong way and cause a firestorm of political backlash."

"So what are you going to do?" Amelia felt like she shouldn't be hearing the information. The trio seemed sincere, but Ibbie was right. It sounded bizarre.

Ibbie reached across and took Amelia's hand. "We were hoping you and Gabe could help us."

"What could we do?"

Joshua supplied the answer. "We were hoping that if we got Gabe close enough, he would be able to hear some of the executives talking. We want to learn how things operate there, know who is really in charge, memorize their voices."

"Gabe's not a spy. I don't think he could take that kind of work, and I don't want him in any kind of danger. He wouldn't be able to take care of himself like you guys can."

"We don't want him in danger either," Ibbie said. "We'll keep him a safe distance from the action and make sure he's protected."

Joshua added, "Gabe's abilities make it possible for us to gain information without taking the type of risks we took the night we met. I cannot apologize enough for what you both went through. We certainly never intended for you to be in the middle of that."

"I know it wasn't your fault. I should have stayed out of things. I thought you were in trouble."

Joshua shook his head with a smile. "As I said, I think things happen for a reason. Now that you understand what is at stake, I want to admit that our organization has never had a very promising plan for how to accomplish the takedown of this group. Now with your help, I think we might."

Amelia frowned. Scenes rotated through her head. She remembered a documentary she had seen on the Holocaust. It was hard to imagine something so evil, but it had happened. Was it possible that an organization right there in Gosnell was targeting people simply because they had Jewish DNA? There was no mistaking the conversation between the men in the park. They were ready to kill her and Gabe and would have if it wasn't for Joshua. They had seemed that evil.

Joshua broke into her thoughts. "This is not your fight. If you don't want to be involved, we understand. But I don't think it's safe for you to go back to the group home. Even if the ones involved with this operation are arrested, you would still be a threat to them and the organization. I won't lie. I know personally that it is hard to run. I will do what I can to relocate you but I…we would not be there to protect you. I know it's not fair and I'm sorry."

Her entire life had changed…again. The weight of it seeped into her. It felt odd that it did not devastate her like it probably should. *Fair*. At least she had grown past thinking life was meant to be fair. Her parent's death had been life-altering, and now her life was altering again. Sitting in the company of people whose situation shifted with each mission, somehow, she didn't feel as alone as she had back then.

Was Joshua correct? Had God planned their meeting? Had He led Amelia to return to help Joshua, so she and Gabe would be here now? She had often wondered if God had a special purpose for Gabe's abilities. But what if something happened to him? How could she get him involved in something that might put him in danger? She didn't know the right answer. *God, if You want me to help these people, You're going to have to show me. I need a sign.*

If she had the power to help, how could she stand back and do nothing. She would never have imagined being faced with such a request, but here it was.

Amelia heard Gabe next to her. Turning, she listened.

In the middle of his gentle rocking, Gabriel spoke in a quiet voice. "Gabriel is an agent. Gabriel is ready for the mission. Gabriel could be a spy."

Gabriel never expressed that kind of enthusiasm. Could it be a dream come true for him? All the times he had fiddled with the spy kit she had talked her dad into buying for him when he was ten, were they preparing him for this? Had God put something in motion then? She had chosen the toy because it had the most gadgets to interest him. She wouldn't have believed Gabriel capable of understanding the concept of espionage. Her ideas of her brother were changing. *You must be up to something, God…enough to be giving out signs.* She looked back at the other three. "What's the plan?"

Chapter 8

The next day, Amelia was on a Gosnell street she rarely traveled. The building came in to view. It was a friendly, inviting design. A three-dimensional DNA helix wove its way up the side. Coming off the helix were large letters proclaiming the business name as "DNAble." Underneath, in letters that were smaller but still large enough to read from the road, was the slogan "Find the Hidden Chapters in the Book of Your Life." She recalled seeing the construction occurring on the other side of the creek and up the hill from the park where she sold her vegetables and jams. That had been over four years ago. Her life was so busy, working with Gabriel, cooking at the group home, tending their garden, making jam, selling at the markets. She had never taken the time to drive around to that section of town to investigate.

Using her latex-gloved hand to re-tuck stray strands of her long brown hair back into the short-haired wig, she repositioned the hard hat, trying to make it more comfortable. Then she put the work gloves back on.

Joshua caught her eye in the rearview mirror from where

he drove the bucket truck they were all riding in. "You know, if you keep doing that, you'll look more suspicious than if you have a few hairs sticking out." His voice was kind even in the warning.

"Don't make me any more nervous." she squirmed on the vinyl bench seat, trying any way to feel more natural in the unfamiliar clothes. "I've never done anything like this before."

"We shouldn't have any encounters. We'll let technology take the risks. I just want Gabriel to hear the original audio. Recordings might not pick up what he can hear. These getups are only in case someone sees you from a distance. You'll be fine." Joshua turned and gave Gabriel a wink. "You look like naturals."

Amelia noticed Gabriel almost had a smile on his face as he swayed and repeated, "Gabriel is a natural, Gabriel is a natural…"

She had to admit the gray work clothes and sunglasses looked good on her brother. Wearing Joshua's vest underneath gave him a beefy appearance. With his own hardhat on top, she barely recognized him. She had hardly recognized herself when she looked in the mirror at the safehouse, but she liked her look a whole lot less.

"The idea is to look manly," Ibbie had told her as she demonstrated how to position the girdle-type undergarment that was designed to cover her thin waist with padding in all the wrong places. But when Amelia emerged in her new outfit, Ibbie had frowned and Joshua smiled.

"We can't afford any curves," Ibbie had grumbled.

"What?" Amelia looked down, inspecting herself.

"Some things just weren't meant to be," Joshua snickered.

Ibbie gave him a look. "That's it, you're getting the potbelly model," she told Amelia as she spun her back toward the bedroom. "We'll make a man out of you yet."

Now, sitting in the bucket truck, she was cinched so tightly around her chest and had so much padding around her middle she could barely breathe. Her only consolation was when she looked over at Ibbie's naturally pretty face, she saw a hairy wild man with a hard hat atop a backward ballcap. *At least I didn't have to wear a beard like that.* The fake acne Ibbie had applied to Amelia's face was bad enough.

"You'll be the soft, teenage rookie, summer help," Ibbie had told her.

Amelia watched the DNAble building vanish behind the woods bordering the business's large grassy lot. The truck continued past the trees, and she saw the large office complex where Marsha would be waiting in the car, "just in case," as Ibbie had put it. She spotted the vehicle in an out of the way parking slot and saw Marsha's blond hair through the driver's window.

Ibbie lifted her smartphone and hit the speaker button. She looked toward the car as she spoke into it. "Hope we aren't disturbing your nap, princess."

"How could I sleep," Marsha sounded unaffected by Ibbie's remark, "knowing you two are in charge of this recon? I have to say, from here you all appear really natural. I think that's your look."

Ibbie tipped her hardhat as they passed the parking lot and encountered more trees. "Why thank you. I may never shave again."

"Your face or your legs?" was Marsha's parting shot as she slipped out of view.

Ibbie shut off the speakerphone and winked at Amelia. "Who shaves their legs?"

Amelia knew Marsha could still hear her. Ibbie had explained how the special cell phones always maintained an open channel. Amelia leaned toward the device. "The opinions expressed over this phone do not necessarily reflect the hygiene habits of all parties."

Ibbie leaned back in a silent chuckle.

Amelia regarded Joshua. The part that really wasn't fair was the fact that all Joshua had to do was wear a baggy uniform with the shirttail pulled out a little and a fake mustache that made him look Spanish. *Why didn't he have to have the potbelly model?* she mused as she watched him pull the truck onto an overgrown access road leading into the woods just past the office building.

Their vehicle was swallowed up by leafy foliage encroaching on the trail, giving them just enough room to navigate. Through the trees, Amelia caught enough of a glimpse of the office complex to realize the trail turned and went behind it, back toward the DNAble lot.

The rough access road ended at a power line running through the woods. Their cover was they were repairing there the line. Joshua had explained they needed a clandestine launch site with an unobstructed view of the back of the DNAble building.

They all donned the headphone style hearing protectors that Ibbie had handed out back at the base. Joshua and Ibbie were out in a moment, checking out the area, making sure there was plenty of blue sky above. Amelia urged Gabriel out of the truck, and they joined them. Ibbie climbed onto the back of the vehicle.

Gabriel began chanting the safety checklist he had memorized from the warning placard on the truck. His voice came clearly through her headset. Amelia remembered how Joshua had patiently walked around the entire vehicle in the driveway of the safe house while Gabriel called out the "safety circle check." "Check the vehicle exterior for broken, damaged, loose, or missing parts. Check tires for bulges, cuts, and pressure. Check for oil and hydraulic leaks…" He had gone on until the daily safety check was complete. Without irritation, Joshua congratulated Gabriel on being safety conscious.

Now Gabriel ran through the work-site checklist. "Do not park on uneven ground."

"Level ground verified," Joshua called out.

"Watch for drop-offs, holes, bumps, and debris."

"No such hazards present."

"Do not operate when wind gusts exceed 30 mph."

Joshua raised his finger to test the air. "Winds calm."

Ibbie chuckled and shook her head at the interaction while she was opening a large metal box strapped to the bed of the truck.

"Set emergency brake."

"Brake set."

"Position wheel chocks."

"Chocks in place."

And so, it continued until Gabriel stopped and stood rocking.

Joshua watched Gabriel. "Safety check complete?" He bobbed his head in satisfaction when Gabriel did not refute him.

Ibbie said, "Up I go." The boom arm lurched skyward as she used the controls mounted on the bucket.

Beside Amelia, Gabriel gave a running dissertation on the wonderful safety rating of the aerial lift device, providing all the safety guidelines were observed.

Joshua climbed in the passenger side of the truck and slid the seat all the way back.

Amelia and Gabriel stood outside watching.

Taking out a metal case, Joshua began assembling a high-tech console in front of himself.

Amelia heard beeps in her ear and knew he was remotely linking the wireless headsets with the communications part of the console.

"Rams One to Rams Two, radio check," Joshua's voice said in Amelia's earpiece.

"Rams Two check," Ibbie answered.

"Rams One to Rams Eleven, radio check."

Amelia kept her eye on Ibbie as she answered "Check...I mean, Rams Eleven check."

She could hear the smile in Joshua's voice as he said, "Rams One to Rams Twelve, how do you copy?"

Backward and forward Gabriel moved as he responded. "Rams Twelve copies loud and clear," in a perfect Sean Connery voice.

Amelia squeezed the smile from her lips. "I know you two think you're pretty funny for teaching him that."

Ibbie came over the radio. "Rams Two copies Rams Eleven's lack of a sense of humor."

Covering the microphone on her headset, Amelia leaned over and whispered in Gabriel's ear which prompted her brother to talk over the radio again in a perfect rendition of Joshua's voice sounding perturbed. "Rams One to Rams Two, you're out of line."

There was a pause and then Ibbie radioed, "What's got you so seri…?" She stopped, realization dawning.

Joshua came on again still laughing a little. "They got you, Rams Two."

"That was scary," Ibbie said, "I really thought that was…this is going to work isn't it?"

"Copy that, Ram's Two," Joshua said. "If we can find the right voice."

"I'm in position," Ibbie said.

Looking up, Amelia could see Ibbie, high above, crouched in the bucket. She had removed her hardhat and turned the camo cap forward to shield the sun from the strange boxy binoculars she held.

"Okay, I have eyes on the target, but I'm still concealed. The only complication I see is a camera mounted on a metal tower on the roof. It's not moving and seems to be aimed north toward the park. Okay, mark this."

Joshua scrutinized the console.

Amelia could just make out a screen that held the binocular view.

The view zoomed in close on the camera, and Joshua pressed buttons and worked the rollerball. "Camera angle added to the flight plan. Preparing for takeoff." The humor was gone from Joshua's voice.

He began flipping switches and screens came to life. "Video on." More switches and he verified indicators. "Computer flight assist enabled, binocular lasers on, obstacle avoidance functioning, searching for satellites." Joshua watched the display. "GPS satellites acquired." He took hold of the joystick controls. "Rotor test."

Amelia turned her attention to the box that Ibbie had opened.

"And we are live."

With barely a sound, an object lifted out of the box and hovered above the bed of the truck. Amelia appreciated what Joshua had explained about the drone. Built around the Israeli THOR military UAV design, the sophisticated surveillance craft had a special addition. It was nicknamed the "Owl" after the cutting-edge design of the 3D printed rotors that imitated the serrations on the wings of the silent bird of prey. The tiny fingerlike projections broke up turbulence that created noise. The rotor guards were also covered with sound-absorbing material. The drone was one quiet piece of hardware that could surreptitiously deploy multiple cameras and a powerful microphone as close to the target as possible.

Joshua fixed his eyes on the forward monitor and manipulated joysticks. The drone skirted around the cab of the truck and took off into the trees. Joshua pushed it toward the DNAble building, and the sensing devices and computer took the craft up, over, down, and around as it avoided leafy obstacles. It took time to get through the wooded boundary of the DNAble property. In the drone world, speed equaled noise, Joshua had explained. They didn't want anyone to hear them coming.

As the minutes passed, the monitors showed the aerial vehicle dancing just above the heavy undergrowth, dropping low into the brush to avoid the camera on DNAble's roof, and returning to the higher canopy once it approached the building. With a burst of speed, it shot across the opening between the tree cover and the roof so as not to linger in the open. The drone weaved around the various utilities on the DNAble roof until it finally came to a stop.

The screens showed the craft hovered approximately six inches above the surface. "I'm moving to the edge." Joshua maneuvered the drone rapidly across the roof as the laser sensors continued to avoid the obstacles. It stopped short of the edge of the building.

Ibbie came online. "You need to move south. That should be the CEO's office. Can't see past the window tinting, so we'll have to start listening and see what we find."

Joshua made the adjustment. "Okay, I'm putting the drone down to save the battery. That's the drawback of this equipment." Joshua sent the explanation over his shoulder for Amelia's benefit. "The increased payload shortens battery life. This might take a while to find what we need. I don't want to use up our ten-minute flight time hovering." Joshua eased the drone to a touchdown on the roof. "Deploying the surveillance cable. This microphone better be worth what we spent on it. It's supposed to be able to hear through that glass."

Amelia could see the microphone cable appear in the forward view and disappear over the side.

"Stop," Ibbie said. "You're right above the window. Any lower and someone might see it."

"I'm switching the audio to the headphones." Joshua pivoted in his seat. "Gabe, you ready?"

Gabriel stopped rocking and listened intently.

"Okay. Remember to use that dial on your headphones to adjust your volume since it will be louder for you. I'll start the sound low and gradually turn it up. You adjust so it doesn't hurt your ears."

Joshua turned back to the console, and the headphones filled with low sounds that got increasingly louder.

Gabriel rotated the knob the way he had been instructed back at the safe house.

The sounds became distinguishable. There were vehicles streets away, lawnmowers in multiple yards, distant highway traffic, the wind, birds, dogs, scraping, scratching, thudding, and myriad other noises that fell together in a heap of auditory sensation assaulting Amelia's ears. She felt the involuntary wrinkling of her forehead as if squinting her eyes could somehow diminish it. *This must be what Gabriel hears all the time.* But he could make sense of it. Somewhere in the cacophony, there were voices.

Joshua worked with the computer and began to isolate them. A woman was engaged in a phone conversation, extending apologies for canceling an appointment.

Beside Amelia, Gabriel made a groaning whine.

"What's wrong, sweetie?"

He shook his head. "Go back. It's not right. It's not right."

Joshua swiveled his head to face them. "What's up?"

"I don't know?" Amelia touched Gabriel's arm. "Gabe, tell me what's not right."

"Sounds wrong." The young man was rocking, shaking his head. "Not right that way." He pulled the earphones from his head and breathed a relieved sigh.

Amelia pulled off her own headset as well and watched her brother. He continued to shake his head and gave Joshua his side facing gaze. "Can't change sounds. Need to hear all the sounds. All the sounds, need to hear them all. Not right when you change them."

Joshua examined Gabriel. "He must mean the sound enhancement software. It's changing the sounds, canceling out part of what we're hearing. It helps us distinguish, but Gabriel's brain must process sound in a different way." He spoke directly to Gabriel. "Gabe, can you tell what the voices are saying without me changing the sounds?"

Gabriel's rocking slowed again. With his eyes to the ground and an ear toward Joshua, he nodded. "Need to hear all the sounds."

"I'm going to isolate your speakers to hear the raw sound and put the enhancement through ours." After a few moments of typing and moving the mouse on the console, Joshua dipped his head toward them. "Put the headsets back on and we'll try again."

The woman sounded like she was still on the phone, but along with occasional garbling and static, the conversation had a more conspiratorial tone. "No, they're in a meeting right now…Herschlag, Montclair, and I think they're waiting on Salzman …Something happened…All-day yesterday and today…That's right, all his appointments. He told me to put everything on hold until further notice…They've been coming in and out, mostly out. Then he tells me he's going to be in a meeting…That's the first I heard about it…He called it on his own…They're in the conference room between his and Montclair's office. You can't hear anything when they're back there."

"Ibbie," Joshua punched buttons on the console and the conversation ceased. "I'm retracting the mic. We need to get to that conference room. We might have caught a big break if that meeting's not over. Give me your best guess about which way I need to move."

Ibbie made a contemplative noise over the headset while Joshua readied the drone.

"Okay, mic's retracted, which way?"

"Try north, back the way you came. If I remember the blueprints correctly, there was a larger room that direction and that matches up with the window pattern."

Joshua worked the joystick and the image pivoted and headed quickly down the edge of the roof.

Ibbie continued. "Okay, that's the way. Keep going. You're almost there."

The copter eased across the roof. Joshua's eyes were fixed on the screen. In moments he had landed the craft and the mic was deployed.

Joshua turned to Gabriel. "Forget the enhancement. Gabe just tell us what they're saying. I trust you more than I do that software."

"…only ten people," Gabriel launched into the middle of

a conversation, "that tested positive last month. That's not gonna cut it, Norm. How long are you recommending that we keep the labs legal?"

A second voice spoke through Gabriel's mouth. "There was nothing breached. Thanks to our tight security, we were ready. We think it was one man initially that was trying to tap our phone trunking system, but we caught him before he could even get it open. We know he wasn't law enforcement by their exit strategy."

The first man spoke again, his language mixed with cursing. "How did one man get away from your whole security team?"

"One man initially I said. He had help on the getaway. They also apparently had running surveillance in the park on the other side of the creek. One of the vehicles was connected with a man and woman that the team contacted in the park, but the men thought they were civilians. The van was later involved in the escape."

Amelia began to shake as she listened. The men that were talking were just past the trees and across the large lawn. She tugged on Gabriel's shirt and drew closer to Joshua who climbed out of the truck and stood near her. She hated to hear the words coming from her brother's mouth.

"What do we have on those two?"

"Nothing. The only ones that got a good look at them are dead. The rest of the team got delayed cleaning up the mess. The responding state trooper was focused on the park, so it was a while before he came around to Steel street. At least the guys picked a place away from any residential areas so there were no witnesses. We barely got the vehicles out of there before the officer arrived. Once they called me, I made sure there was no way to trace anything that happened back to us. That's the reason I have a couple of tow trucks in the garage downstairs. I advocate for these resources so we will be ready for emergencies."

"Okay, then what did you find out about the car they

abandoned and the van?"

"The car was clean. The name it was rented under is fictitious. The rental agreement went through the end of the week, so we'll haul it in a closed truck and dump it somewhere in Oklahoma. The rental company will have to deal with it once it's found. They'll think it was involved in a wreck over there. We haven't been able to come up with anything on the van. It's vanished. We've scoured the whole town. It's too risky to go questioning people in the park. That would raise too many flags if anyone called the police."

The first voice was aggravated. "Someone tries to tap our phones and kills our men on the way out and you're just going to let it go?"

"I still have people checking. But we need to lay low. There is nothing connecting us with any of the events of that night and we want to keep it that way. My source inside the local law enforcement says the only report the police have of anything happening on this side of town is an unfounded call about some people chasing a man. When they arrived, there was nothing there but the roadkill we left on Steel Street. We don't want to do anything to make them think differently. We are a legitimate business that is concerned about corporate espionage. Naturally, we have tight security. But we don't want to look like anything new happened until this mess all blows over. And it will."

"Well that's comforting, but you're right about it being a mess. You made a big mess trying to catch these characters and they still got away. I don't mind extreme solutions if they get results, but we have a whole town scared to death, law enforcement on high alert and the only body count to show for it is on our side."

"Keller made some bad calls that night. He let the men get out of control. If you'll remember, I questioned hiring him. By getting himself killed, he saved me the trouble of getting rid of him. Chandler was a good man. Him, I regret losing. I am looking into everything that was done and I will find out where the breakdown occurred and either retrain or replace."

"Well, I guess you're already going to be replacing a few, aren't you? What are you going to do with the bodies in the basement?"

"Same as we do with Becker's used goods when he's through with them. They've been incinerated and the ashes are being disposed of chemically. They will go out the sewer tomorrow, indistinguishable from common sludge. There is no one to miss them, all of our special detail people are ghosts."

Amelia felt sick. The conversation was just what the team was looking for. She didn't dare stop Gabriel, but she felt like throwing up. After a moment of deep breathing, she prayed. *Help me get through this. We have to stop these people.*

Gabriel continued in the first man's voice. "So, are you saying we can get back to business?"

"I don't see any reason why not. It's a perfect time. Complaints about the validity of our lab results will be the last thing on the mind of the police for some time. Since DNA testing isn't regulated, it's a civil matter anyway."

"I'm glad you're finding a positive spin on this. I have a little greater concern over it. I don't want to be any more concerned, okay?"

"Understood." The Norm voice sounded quietly irritated.

"Okay, Bob. Since Norm and his steadily decreasing team have given us this wonderful hiatus from law enforcement scrutiny, we need to start getting some plans in place to get these lab numbers up. Our online sales are down again. We need to come up with a campaign that sells us over the big-name labs. With the price drop, no one can compete with us. We can't go so low we look suspicious, but we have to pull in more DNA profiles, especially positive ones. The supremacists are paying for targets. The Arabs are backing Becker's project, but the supremacists' money is what keeps our day-to-day operations going."

Norm had more input. "Speaking of Becker, this project

of his is the one thing we might consider postponing for a while. If anything goes wrong with that, it could lead back to us. That's the most dangerous thing we're doing."

Gabriel stopped talking. Amelia looked at him. He was still listening. Then he opened his mouth and the first voice came out, filled with menace. "Didn't you hear what I just said? I don't care what you think about Becker. Everyone at the main office thinks he's a genius and they are anxious to see the results of his work. As am I. I still wonder about the timing of this conference. Having his whole team out of town and everything put on hold right before the release has never sat well with me."

"It was his decision, but I did encourage it. Having some of the top DNA researchers in the nation absent from one of the biggest events of the year in that field was going to invite a lot of questions. My job is security. Part of that job is to keep us from looking suspicious in any way. This is risky enough without inviting scrutiny by acting out of character."

"All right, but there will be no more delays. Becker's due back on Monday. I'll give it that long. He set up everything before he left. We don't even need him here, but I don't want him to miss it."

"I'm just trying to do my job."

There was more silence and when the first voice spoke again it was obvious he was changing the subject. "Bob, I also want to work on our local sales. We need to advertise more over in Bentonville and Fayetteville, all the way down to Fort Smith. We've got to draw from a bigger area. Get our kits in every kind of store you can think of. But we also want to encourage walk-ins. Put that on our website. Do you have any data on the reach of our advance advertising for the grand opening of our ancestry research center?"

The Bob voice responded. "Not yet. It's too early. But I think that should reach a whole new customer base. There are still a lot of old-school researchers out there that want to pilgrimage to an actual site. If we promise them big enough results, they'll plan their vacations here. We're close enough to Branson, Missouri and that's a big attraction for that age group."

"That's exactly what we're looking for. We want to be open and friendly. The more people we can bring here in person helps the effectiveness of Becker's project. The further they travel the better."

"Hold on, Gabriel." Ibbie's voice in the headphones interrupted. "There's a golf cart coming around the north side. They're looking the whole building up and down. Might be a regular security check. They don't look stressed."

Joshua leaped back to the console. "I think we have enough. We can't risk them seeing the drone. Where are they? Can I move or will it draw attention?"

"Yes, go. You're still hidden by the wing that sticks out the back. Go quick."

Amelia watched Joshua ease the drone back from the edge which pulled the microphone cable with it. Once both drone and microphone were clear of the edge and safely out of sight of the security team's scrutiny, he retracted the microphone cable.

"Okay. Good. The cart's coming around still moving toward the other end. Moving past you now." After a moment, Ibbie resumed. "They went around the corner and checked the end. They seem satisfied with the building. Must have checked the front already. It looks like they're going to follow the lawn at the street and come down to the wooded border. We need to move. I think they're planning on going around the whole grounds. When they get to the back of the lot, they might see or hear us through the trees. Even with our cover story, we don't want to give them a reason to be suspicious. Better they don't see us at all. Bring the drone home. I'm coming down." The bucket lowered.

Joshua worked the controls, and the drone images began to hover again. He navigated the craft to the side of the roof away from the lawn where the security was patrolling. The cameras showed the roofs of the buildings across the street from DNAble. Keeping back from the edge and low to the roof, Joshua flew the drone the length of the building until he reached the east side which was close to the trees that the drone had first used to cover its approach.

The right-side view monitor showed human movement in the front parking lot. Two women were moving toward a car. Joshua pulled the copter back. Keeping as close to one of the air conditioning units as possible to mask any silhouette and sound the drone might present, he eased forward. The women were at a car that was parked within sight of his location. He didn't dare expose himself.

Joshua pivoted one of the cameras to show the gap between the trees and the building. Past that was the part of the lawn next to the trees at the back of the lot. Ibbie had said the security team was at the front of the lawn. Amelia saw the problem. The drone could not leave the same way it had come. The treetops would be visible to anyone on the lawn. Even going over the trees to get to the other side risked exposing the drone leaving the roof. Joshua voiced the problem to himself. "I can't cross high." The women were still chatting at the vehicle. "And I can't look for other options with these two in the parking lot."

The minutes ticked by. Amelia connected what Joshua had said about a ten-minute flight time and realized the stress of the situation. Ibbie was bringing down the bucket so she no longer had the security team in sight, but they were no doubt getting closer by the second. The women talked on. Amelia never imagined having a problem with the length of a female conversation. One of the women moved to the driver's door of the car and the other walked toward another vehicle further out in the parking lot. Both ladies appeared to be continuing their discourse as they moved apart. At last, they both climbed in their cars and drove away.

Pushing the drone forward, Joshua hovered just past the edge. Amelia followed his eyes to the view from the underside camera. There was a dumpster with a wooden fence around it. From above, she could see the grass around the fence had been beaten down where pedestrians had taken a shortcut into the woods.

The drone images shifted as Joshua moved it to the corner of the building. The screens indicated the craft was right at the apex of the corner where there were no windows. Amelia could see the asphalt below and suddenly it rushed toward her eyes. Just before the drone crashed, it swooped and flew level with the ground and zipped around the dumpster fence, following the trail into the trees. Joshua began dodging tree trunks and branches, following the footpath. He weaved around the obstacles as fast as he dared. The copter clipped leaves as it went.

"No!"

Amelia examined the screens and saw what brought the exclamation from Joshua. "Low Battery" was flashing on one of them.

Ibbie maneuvered the boom into place on the back of the truck and called quietly. "Do you think you can get it back before they make it to the back of the lot."

Joshua sighed in irritation but kept pushing the drone forward. "No, the battery's dying. That indicator was designed to give me enough time to bring it straight back, not run an obstacle course."

Ibbie jumped to the ground, pulled out the chocks and threw them on the back of the truck. "You've got to ditch it and we have to go. It doesn't store memory. Everything is transmitted to the console recorder."

Joshua's eyes darted back and forth, guiding his hand on the controls as he spoke. "If they find it, they're going to know this isn't your average drone."

At Ibbie's signal, Amelia and Gabriel jumped in the backseat while she climbed behind the wheel and addressed Joshua. "We gotta go."

Over Joshua's shoulder, Amelia watched the screens as

the drone slowed to a hover at a clearing in the trees on the opposite side from the DNAble property. Through the break in the branches, Amelia could see part of the park—the playground, the ballfield, the pavilion, and the duck pond.

The drone shot out of the opening. It buzzed the sloping lawn between the empty ballfield and playground. In the front view was the pond getting larger every moment. The copter was losing altitude. Green grass loomed like a hand coming up to swat the drone from the sky. Waterfowl scattered as the drone parted a clutch of cattails at the pond's edge. A glassy expanse of blue-green tranquility rapidly filled the forward screen. The front camera pierced the surface filling the view with bubbles. Wet darkness settled over the images as Joshua snapped the console lid closed and Ibbie brought the engine of the truck to life.

Chapter 9

Joshua let the disappointment of losing the drone wash out of him. By the time they were getting back to the street, he had stowed all the gear. He didn't want anything in view that might make them look suspicious. They had switched back to cell phone communication, and he let Marsha know they were coming out. They were all breathing easier as they left the trees.

Marsha answered him over the speakerphone. "Copy that. Everything looks…hold up, you have an L-E-O coming down the street."

Ibbie put on the brake, but it was too late. They were out of the trees and in sight of the blue and white police car before they could finish their collective inhale.

"It's okay." Joshua put a smile on his face. "Trucks come in and out of here to do work. We look the part. He won't even stop."

The police car stopped.

The lone officer in the car was sitting in the middle of the street looking at them through the windshield. Why would he be interested in them?

"Maybe we just surprised him." Ibbie tried to wave the officer on, motioning that they needed to pull out.

The officer pulled to the curb.

Amelia spoke from the back seat. "I know him. He stops by the farmer's market, sometimes."

Great. Joshua quickly opened his door. "I'll do the talking."

"I hope so," Ibbie said in her feminine voice while running her hand over her beard. She lowered her window and looked casual.

Joshua strolled toward the officer. He had a rule. He would never kill a law enforcement officer in a free country. Militia for wicked dictators yes, but not honest men tasked as guardians for their society. His mind began to run through scenarios to get them out of the situation without anyone getting hurt. Maybe he could turn the tables on the young cop and take control of the encounter. "How you doing, Officer? We got a report of an electrical outage, but all the lines back there look good. You haven't heard of anything being out up in this area, have you?"

The officer seemed to be caught off guard by the question. He glanced around. "No. Hang on." He keyed his lapel mic. "Base, Gosnell Six, have you had any reports of power outages?"

It took a moment for the female dispatcher to respond. "Negative, Gosnell Six. No outage reports."

Joshua gave the young man a smile and raised his hand in a gesture of gratitude. "Okay, thanks. We'll keep looking." He turned and headed back to the truck. Good. So far it was working. *Just get in your patrol car and drive away. We're not worth your time.*

Joshua caught Ibbie's eye and could see a subtle look of appreciation. The officer must be going to leave. Then her face changed.

"Sir, I'm sorry to bother you," the officer called after Joshua, "but can I ask you some questions?"

Joshua drew up and fixed his eyes on Ibbie. He couldn't let this man question the others. Ibbie might be able to pull off a man's accent, but he might recognize Amelia and Gabriel through their disguises. A conversation couldn't happen. He threw his smile on again and turned. "Yes, Officer?"

"You probably heard about the excitement we had the other night."

Joshua nodded. "Sounded like things got crazy for you guys. Thanks for keeping us safe."

"Absolutely, that's our job. Anyway, the Chief has us talking to everyone we can to find out if anyone has information we might not know already."

"I'm sorry. I was sleeping when all that was going on."

"We also got a call that someone was getting chased in and around the park. You didn't happen to see anything unusual when you were back in there did you, signs of foot traffic, or a vehicle going down there recently, anything like that?"

"No. Everything looked normal down there." Joshua became aware of Gabriel's voice. All he heard was the word Police.

The Officer canted his head toward the sound. Joshua extended a handshake to the cop. *Come on. Focus on me.* "Well, again, Officer, thanks for the job you do." Pumping the cop's hand, he smiled largely. "We missed breakfast because of this call out, so the guys are probably getting a little cranky." Joshua made a point of turning to gesture toward the truck so he could see what was happening while at the same time blocking the officer's view. "I better get 'em to lunch."

Ibbie closed the window with an innocent smile peeking through the beard. Gabriel's passionate voice was saying something about the police being good and they could help.

In the side of his eye, Joshua noticed the uniformed young man leaning around him to gaze at the truck.

Joshua turned back to him, all smiles. *Time to reverse it again.* "I'll tell you what, why don't we follow you to the best restaurant you know, and I'll buy you lunch." If he could just get the kid back in his patrol car, he could make an excuse when they got to the restaurant.

The suggestion captured the officer's attention. "I appreciate the offer, sir, but it's a little early for me. I would like to talk to your crew for a minute. It won't take long. You can understand with everything that's happened, the Chief's on us to talk to everybody." The young man started to move around Joshua.

The slam of a door drew both their attention to the truck. Ibbie stood outside the driver's side. She looked directly at the cop, tossed her hard hat on the ground, spun and ran.

The Police Officer glanced at Joshua who missed only half a beat. Throwing his hands in the air, Joshua made his voice sound frustrated. "I'm sorry. He must have another warrant. That guy can't stay out of trouble."

The word warrant touched the birddog reflex in the young cop. His head swiveled for an instant from Joshua to the hairy suspect sprinting down the trail behind the truck. Then he dashed after him with his hand on his radio mic. "Gosnell Six. I'm in foot pursuit of a possible wanted suspect just west of the DNAble building."

Joshua started moving toward the truck. He looked at Amelia, whose wide eyes swiveled as the cop passed by her window.

The officer yelled into his radio about the suspect heading into the trees just past an office complex. "White male, long hair and beard, wearing a baggy gray..." The cop was saying as he powered after his quarry down the rutted path behind the truck.

Amelia was fixated on the action. When Joshua opened her door, she jerked to face him with a startled expression. He took her hand and urged her out of the vehicle while speaking rapidly into his cell phone. "Rams Three, Rams Two is on the run as a diversion. Pick us up." As she got out, Joshua grabbed the console case off the seat beside her and set it on the ground near the front of the truck.

He motioned to Amelia. "We need to hurry. Get Gabe out and in the back seat of Marsha's car when she gets here."

As he grabbed the other equipment bag out of the front, Amelia ran by him on her way to the other side. His eyes scanned the interior of the truck. It looked clean.

"Don't leave anything behind. We're abandoning the truck." Joshua dropped his cargo and opened the hood.

Amelia yanked open Gabriel's door. "Gabe, get out. We need to go."

Joshua jerked a wire loose from the starter solenoid and left the hood up so it would look like they had been working on the engine. The locals would waste a little time on the idea that they might be coming back to repair or tow the truck.

As Gabriel crawled out, he addressed Joshua. "Why did you tell police officer that Rams Two had warrant? Warrant is for criminals. Rams Two is not criminal. Is Rams Two criminal?"

Joshua took a deep breath. He tried to put together a response that Gabriel could understand.

There was an aching realization in Amelia's eyes as they met at the front of the truck. "Is that why the cop chased her? You're doing this for us. If we hadn't…" She looked to where she had last seen Ibbie. "What if the officer catches her?"

Joshua gave her hand a squeeze. "We're not going to let that happen." He motioned Amelia and Gabriel to the car that Marsha squeaked to a stop on the street in front of them, the trunk lid already coming open. He snatched the hardhats off their heads and scooped Ibbie's off the ground and shoved them into the large bag along with his own.

Picking up the case and bag, he hurried after them, talking as he went. "No, Gabe, she's not a criminal." *I might as well just say it. He might not understand anything subtle.* "I lied to the police officer."

The impact of the statement moved across Gabriel's face, horror mixed with confusion.

"We're undercover. That's when you pretend to be someone else to accomplish your mission. It's not a lie for bad. It's a lie for good. You're right. He was a good officer. He was asking lots of questions just like he was supposed to do. But agents can't tell anyone they're spies. You know how people don't understand your autism? Being an agent is like that. People don't understand. Rams Two ran to protect us, so the officer wouldn't find out that we're spies. That's why I said she had a warrant, so he would chase her. Now we have to go pick her up, so she doesn't get in trouble. I wish I could have told the officer, but sometimes agents just can't."

Gabriel scowled but let Amelia hurry him into the car, where he fastened his seatbelt in silence.

Joshua threw the console case and bag in the trunk. Amelia collided with him on her way to the passenger side. He returned her smile as they danced around each other, and both dived into their seats.

Joshua spoke into his cell as Marsha synced the phone with the car's sound system. "Rams Two, we're in the car. Give me a pickup point."

Ibbie came over the vehicle's speaker system. "Don't know the streets. About four blocks northwest of where I started."

"She must be close to Orchard Avenue," Amelia announced from the backseat. "Go five blocks down and take another right."

"He's still behind me. There's a car in play or I would've lost him." Ibbie sounded out of breath.

"Rams Twelve, prepare for spy speed and be brave," Joshua called toward Gabriel.

They were all thrown backward when Marsha launched the car down the street. The blocks flew by until she slowed and swung wide for a quick right turn that laid all her passengers over in their seats.

Behind him, Joshua could hear Gabriel self-talking. He could just make out what he was saying despite the vehicle noise.

"Gabriel is agent. People wouldn't understand. Just like me. People don't understand. Gabriel is agent. Can't tell the police. Gabriel is agent. People wouldn't…"

He's gonna figure it out. He'll be okay. Joshua raised his voice hoping Ibbie could hear over the engine noise. "Where's the car that's after you?"

"Looks like a school ahead," Ibbie came over the speakers between gasps for air. "Gonna take the fence." She apparently had not heard Joshua's question.

"She's at Bachman Elementary." Amelia used the back of Marsha's seat to pull herself up. "Go two blocks, turn left… One block now," Amelia corrected as the first intersection winked by. "Take the—" Then they were leaning to the left as the vehicle slid around the corner.

"Next right," Amelia screamed.

Her voice worried Joshua. A quick glance back showed her looking white. She swallowed like she was trying to keep from throwing up. "You okay?"

She took a deep breath, "Street dead-ends at the playground behind the school," was all she could manage.

"Forgive us," Joshua grimaced toward her to indicate his regret.

"Just get to her," she told him.

Always thinking of others over herself. Searching ahead, Joshua saw a high chain-link fence and police strobes flashing. A car was suddenly in their path coming off the street to the left. Joshua braced his hands against the dash as he saw more red and blue lights flashing from the top of the car and his mind registered the words "Police" on the side.

Marsha stabbed the brakes briefly and then jerked the wheel hard left taking their vehicle behind the police car barely missing its rear end as it continued forward. The police cruiser turned onto the same street they were traveling, coming into the right-hand lane. Their car came up on the left side of it. Joshua could see the shocked look on the face of the cop behind the wheel. Playing the part of a good citizen who didn't mind the near-miss, Joshua waved him on. Marsha slowed.

Their roadway ended at the street that ran along the backside of the school. A police car was stopped in the street facing the fence, driver's door open. The young officer who had originally contacted them was bent over, searching for oxygen, with a steadying hand on the patrol car trunk. Another officer was inside the fence and heading toward the school. The unit they had almost hit pulled up beside the other patrol car. Joshua saw the young cop waving to the arriving officer and pointing toward the fence.

Using his hand to make a downward motion toward Marsha, Joshua indicated for her to decrease speed. "That's our boy. Go slow so he doesn't get a look at us." Joshua ripped off the fake mustache he was wearing. "Gabe, I'm going to take off your sunglasses so don't let it surprise you." He reached over the seat and snatched the shades from the young man's face.

Gabriel gave a yelp even after the warning.

"Amelia, you need to lose the wig."

"How do I get to the other side of the school?" Marsha asked.

As they eased forward, Joshua leaned his seat back to make himself less visible and looked toward Amelia to hide both their faces.

Amelia answered Marsha as she tugged the fake hair away from her scalp. "Turn left and go three blocks. There's part of the park you have to get past. Take a right and the road will curve around and take you over a narrow two-lane bridge that crosses the creek. Take a right after the bridge, then another right in two blocks. The school is about four blocks down." She looked in Joshua's eyes and gave a sheepish grin, trying to comb her hair with her fingers.

He half-turned toward Marsha. "Okay, turn on the glow, Marsh. Make sure you're the only thing they see."

The other woman sat erect, chest out, smile wide and directed her superpower toward the officers. She waved and gave her own perfect hair a toss.

Joshua turned back to look at the ratty-haired girl with the fake acne in the back seat. Funny how the heart worked. He preferred his view.

As the car approached the cops, Joshua stretched his arm like he was reaching for something and blocked the officer's view of Gabriel through the side window. Marsha turned left and Joshua timed his rotation back to the front to keep his face out of view. He prayed all his efforts had kept the young officer from recognizing any of them. In his side mirror, he could see both officers gaze after their vehicle for a second, and then they were back on the hunt.

Joshua determined to find the fugitive first. "Rams Two, what's your location?" After a moment, Joshua tried again. "Rams Two, copy?"

Once they were out of sight of the cops, Marsha mashed the accelerator.

Joshua rose and fell in his seat as the car bounced over the street. "Rams Two, if you can hear me, we'll meet you on the other side of the school." Then he muttered as much to himself as anyone. "She might be hiding and can't talk."

He saw the irritation in Marsha's eyes as they scanned the road for hazards.

When they turned onto the school's street, they again encountered red and blue lights flashing ahead. An officer was guarding the front of the school.

Marsha dropped the car's speed to a crawl.

Joshua tried again. "Rams Two, copy?"

Their vehicle crept forward.

Amelia leaned toward the front seat. "Let Gabriel try."

They were two and a half blocks from the school building. The park was on their right. Joshua motioned Marsha to turn left at the next street. She pulled over to the curb next to the privacy fence of the corner house, used her controls to roll down Gabriel's window and turned off the engine.

Joshua swiveled toward Gabriel. "See if you can find our lost spy."

As Gabriel began listening, Joshua unbuttoned the uniform shirt he was still wearing. He turned in the seat and reached toward Amelia. "Here, can you give me a hand? These uniforms are a liability now."

She took hold of his sleeve and he pulled his arm out. Her expression was troubled.

"Just keep praying."

Amelia nodded.

Joshua stripped down to the T-shirt he had underneath. He wadded the uniform and shoved it under the seat. They had been hustling since they left the DNAble surveillance. The exertion and stress had him sweating. Marsha looked at him with a wrinkled nose. He shrugged at her.

Facing Amelia, Joshua tugged on his shirt, pointed to the uniform top Amelia wore, made the motion of putting it under the seat, then faced the front again. He felt bad. Under her potbelly disguise, Amelia had to be sweating worse than he was. She would probably be self-conscious, but he couldn't help it. "They'll send a car back to the truck to recontact us and find out more about Ibbie. When we're gone, they will be giving out our descriptions. We don't dare look like that anymore." Without looking back, Joshua spoke to Gabriel. "Can you hear her?"

"She is on top of building."

"Is she all right? Does anyone know she's there?"

"They are looking on ground for her. They can't find her. One officer said to get dog." Gabriel went silent. So that was where things stood. She was trapped on the roof of the school and it was only a matter of time before they found her.

Amelia laid her bundle of clothing on his shoulder. "What are we going to do?"

Joshua took the items and put them under the seat.

Gabriel spoke in monotone. "She jumped off the roof."

Everyone perked up.

"She is brushing off, must be dirty."

"But's she's okay?" Joshua asked.

"She's walking now, now slow running."

"Can you tell which way she's going?"

Gabriel motioned away from them.

Marsha started up the car. "Is she still running slow?"

Gabriel howled. "Stop! Turn off car. It's too loud. Can't hear."

Marsha killed the engine.

His voice reverted to monotone. "A policeman is yelling at Rams Two."

"They've got her." Marsha sounded frustrated as she reached for the key. "We might have to fight our way out of this one."

Joshua stopped her with an upheld hand. "What is the officer saying to her?"

"Excuse me, ma'am." The voice was stern and deep. "Can you come here a minute?"

Joshua sighed in relief. "Okay, she got rid of her costume. Ibbie's smart. Let's see how this plays out." He encouraged Gabriel with a hand motion toward his own ear. "Keep going. Tell us what they say."

"She's running back." Gabriel canted his ear toward the school.

"Yes, Officer, I help you?" The Ibbie voice that Gabriel produced, sounded different somehow, excessively feminine.

Switching to the police officer, Gabriel's tone lacked some of the edge the man had displayed earlier. "I'm sorry to bother you, but it looked like you came from around the side of the school. Can I ask what you were doing back there?"

Gabriel mimicked an innocent little giggle from Ibbie. "I am running this way and I see all the lights. You were busy when I run up. I am sorry but police I like a lot. I could not help but do the looky-see." That was the difference. She was putting on a Latino accent. "I so sorry if I cause problem for your duty. I really like police officers, I no want to be problem."

"It's not that." Now all sternness was gone. "We are looking for a man that was seen around the school, and he might be dangerous. Did you see anyone when you were back there?"

"Dangerous." Ibbie's voice dripped the word. With a mock fearful tone, she said, "Nooo. I see no one." Then a coy flirtatious giggle again, "But, I give you confession. I only looking at you." She gave a little gasp, "Oh, I must hurry, go home. My husband, he be so angry with me gone so long. He always think bad, like I with some other guy. He so jealous." Then the impish voice was back, "I know. I give you my number and you call me, and I tell you if it okay for you to come over and question me more. Maybe you can take me to the police office and question me and then I meet all the officers."

The official tone was back in the officer's voice. "That won't be necessary, ma'am. I think I have everything I need."

"You no need question me more?" The pout was unmistakable.

"No, ma'am."

"You no want my number?"

"Not necessary. I'll let you go now."

"Oh, I got to hurry. Hector be sooo angry."

Gabriel spoke in his own voice. "She is running again. Fast now."

After they got Gabriel out of his uniform, they were able to drive right by the officer as Joshua gave a polite wave. They found Ibbie around the corner.

Her shirt was also soaked from her run in the hairy man disguise. As she went around the car to get in, Amelia slid next to Gabriel to give her spot to Ibbie.

"Thanks, guys." Ibbie closed the door. "Aren't we a happy party?"

Marsha reached into the purse she had next to her. "Okay, that's all I can stand." She pulled out a perfume bottle and began spritzing the air.

Gabriel batted at the spray like he was fending off a swarm of hornets. "Don't spray stuff. That stinks."

"Hey." Marsha looked at the red container. "This is Hypnotic Poison by Dior. Over $100 a bottle. One of my best weapons. They should sell it in a holster."

Gabriel looked like he ate a stink bug. "Smells like rotten pie."

The car broke out in laughter. After a moment, Ibbie sucked in air so she could talk. "Gabriel, you are my new best friend." She directed her voice over the seat to Marsha. "Sorry. Your best weapon just bounced off Superman over here. Got any Kryptonite in that designer bag?"

Gabriel reminded Joshua so much of Caleb, how his unique perspective caused people to take a step back and examine the world from a different angle. He had forgotten how much he loved those moments.

On their way back to the safe house, Joshua called to have the bucket truck towed to the lot of the company they had rented it from.

When he finished the call, Amelia spoke. "Well, you were right. These people really are using the DNA testing for something bad."

Joshua nodded keeping his eyes forward. "The way it sounds, it is every bit as bad as it was portrayed. But now we have a new weapon in the fight. Tomorrow we will put our plan into action."

Behind him, Amelia gave a tense exhale. "I don't know if I'm ready. Is this what your life is like all the time?"

Joshua reviewed the day's events. At least they didn't kill anyone. He clenched his teeth. What a great consolation.

Ibbie chuckled and answered Amelia's question. "No. Sometimes things go right."

Marsha started laughing. Joshua couldn't help himself, and the three of them began guffawing. Amelia joined in.

Her laugh seemed to fit naturally into the group. For Joshua it was like warm water, washing away some of the stain of the battle. But for how long? He thought of them going their separate ways when the mission was completed, and it caused an ache he didn't like.

Chapter 10

Back in the safe house command center, Amelia watched as Joshua nodded toward Marsha. "Tomorrow, you'll go first. Once we know security is buying your act, I'll follow." He turned his attention to Ibbie, Amelia, and Gabriel. "You guys will be in the surveillance van just down the street."

Joshua straightened in his chair. "Okay, we ran some tests last night, and the unit I attached to their phone system is working. We can tap into any line in the building."

"Wait a minute." Amelia sat up. The conversation that Gabriel overheard at the DNAble building came to mind. "When did you do this? I thought you tried that the night I…" her mind searched for what to call her involvement on the evening they met. *Oh, who cares.* "…rescued you." She gave a little grin, which everyone returned.

"That's what Joshua wanted them to think." Ibbie gave an eyebrow raise. "He was on his way out of the area that held the phone trunking system when he realized security was coming, so he turned around and made them think he was trying to get in." She narrowed her eyes at Joshua. "That little move almost got him caught." Her smile returned. "But it did convince them that the phones hadn't been tampered with. The unit he installed looks like all the other circuit boards in the system, so since they didn't think he got in, they didn't examine the system well enough to find the unit."

Joshua shook his head with his eyes closed and a smile on his face while listening to Ibbie's scolding and praise, then opened his eyes. "The cell phones were easier thanks to a friend at the cell company. Now we can monitor DNAble's landlines and the cell phone calls of most of the leadership. We were even able to identify the cell phones of some of the DNAble security personnel. Since we don't have a U.S. court's blessing on any of this, we'll never be able to legally use anything we get from it, but now with Gabriel on our side, we might be able to do more than just listen. This operation will go down in agency history. When this is all over, you two," he indicated Gabriel and Amelia, "will be famous. Of course, it will be limited fame since it will all be sealed with a need-to-know security clearance and we won't be revealing your identity." He showed his signature smile.

Amelia considered what he said, *When this is all over. What then?* "Somehow I imagine that everything your team gets involved in would be famous if it wasn't sealed." That brought another Joshua smile. Amelia could do without the fame. What she found herself wanting was more time to get to know the man in front of her. But she knew Joshua would be on to the next "famous" assignment…when this was all over.

Hours later, Joshua finally shut off the monitor displaying the blueprints for the DNAble building.

Ibbie gathered up the notes she had taken and headed to the door that led to the communication room. "I'm going to brief command on what we're doing." Ibbie closed the door behind her. Marsha excused herself to her room to prepare.

Gabriel gazed around the room, using the corners of his

eyes to follow those who were walking out. He had put on his headphones part way into the briefing. Amelia knew he had still heard everything going on in the meeting, but his mind needed more auditory stimulation and his ears needed a buffer from the intensity of the individual voices. In one of their deeper conversations, Amelia had come to understand that, for Gabriel, single sounds were like the drip of water compared to a waterfall of sound. Sometimes a constant little drop can drive you crazy.

Joshua walked over and sat beside Amelia. "Don't let us pressure you into doing this. I want it to be your decision."

She smiled at him and nodded slowly. "These people have to be stopped. I'm scared, but I have never felt so strongly about something in all my life. In James, it says that if you know you're supposed to do something good, you're sinning if you don't do it."

Joshua widened his eyes. "That's one of the scriptures I live by. But I didn't mean to put that kind of pressure on you."

"You didn't. God did, and I don't think either of us wants to argue with Him."

"I won't pretend I'm not glad because I didn't know how we were going to do it without you. We have tried to plan this so you and Gabriel will be safe. But please be careful." He gave her a warm smile. "It feels good to be doing something this significant, doesn't it?"

Amelia regarded him. "Is that why you do this?"

"It's a hard life. If I didn't feel what I am doing is changing the world, it wouldn't be worth it. And I certainly wouldn't be asking you to do it."

"What does your family think?" Amelia kept her eyes on the table as she asked it.

"Besides my mother, my sister is the only family I have left. She thinks I'm a shiftless bum traveling the world and working odd jobs. You can understand why I can never tell her what I do. We were not that close anyway." Joshua's face shifted into a memory. "She married a Wall Street millionaire and became an overnight socialite who has little time for anything else."

Amelia tempered the feelings she was having. *Listen to what he's telling you. The work he's doing is too important to get involved in a relationship.* "But your mother?"

Joshua sighed and put his attention back on Amelia. "I wish things were different. I would like to tell you things about myself." He was quiet for a moment. "I will tell you a story. You must never share this with anyone."

Joshua's words captivated Amelia. "I would love to hear it, but if you shouldn't…"

"It's all right. It doesn't violate my orders and I trust you."

The words wrapped around Amelia's soul like an embrace. To be trusted by this man who had such important secrets to guard seemed…intimate. Why would he want to tell her things so badly? She felt honored. While her heart hoped, she listened.

"My mother is a beautiful woman. She has such an innocent nature, like you. She had us children late, so she is nearly sixty now, but I never think of her as old. There were three of us kids. I was the oldest. Then came my brother, Caleb, and my sister, Rahab. Caleb was born with autism. I learned young how to help my mother care for him. We were very close."

Amelia tipped her head back in realization. "That's how you knew what to do with Gabriel. I think he can tell that you understand him. He seems to trust you already."

Joshua eyed Gabriel who returned a sideways glance. "Gabe reminds me of Caleb. It's been so long. I was surprised that it all came back to me."

Amelia felt her brow squeezing in preparation. "But your brother is…"

Joshua's face took on a peaceful sadness. "He waits for me in Heaven. He and my father were killed by two men that broke into our home when I was ten years old. My mother always kept a gun and she shot them before they could hurt the rest of us."

The horror struck Amelia full force. "Oh, Joshua," was all she could answer as her eyes filled.

"I know where they are and it's okay. I needed to tell you that. Being around Gabe brought back so many memories. It's been healing for me. The night I met you, I felt like I was able to do for you and Gabe what I couldn't do for Caleb and my father." Joshua rose and grabbed a handfull of tissues from the table, wiped Amelia's cheeks with one, and pressed the rest into her hands.

Amelia sniffed back the tears enough to speak. "My parents died on a mission trip to Mexico. While Gabriel and I were at the mission base, a mudslide buried the village they were ministering in, so I know about losing someone you love but also knowing that they are in a better place."

Joshua patted her hands. "I'm sorry."

She shook her head, not wanting the moment to become a sympathy session for herself. "May I hear your story?"

He leaned back. "Our mother taught us about our Jewish heritage and to love Israel. But she had come to understand that Jesus was the Messiah that every devout Jew waited for. She taught us to love Him more."

"I could tell you must be a Christian. I'm thankful you…are."

Joshua's face said he was glad she approved but he seemed eager to continue. "After the break-in, we moved and began going to a private school. Rahab became involved in all the social clubs and kind of became a snob. She spent most of her time with her stuck-up friends. I love my sister, but she was always a bit selfish. After my father and Caleb died, I think we spoiled her too much." Joshua had the look of regret. "The incident unnerved all of us. My mother became very protective and I began to feel like people were watching me."

He shook it off and continued. "My mother got me involved in drama at school. She made me practice pretending to be things I wasn't to total strangers on the street. She would stand nearby and act like she didn't know me while I convinced people I was poor or blind or handicapped. She said that being convincing was a useful skill. She taught me other things like sleight of hand and how to misdirect people's attention, looking for all the exits in a room the moment you walk in, how to identify people who were the greatest threats by the way they stood and acted, how to spot concealed weapons people were carrying, picking locks, evading and hiding, shooting. Unusual things for a young boy to learn from his mother."

And not what I was expecting him to talk about. Amelia was fascinated and a little confused.

Joshua raised one eyebrow at her. "We had so much fun. She made me promise not to tell anyone. And she taught me how to fight. Can you imagine a boy's mother randomly attacking him so he would learn to be on his guard? When I was a kid, that woman would suddenly grab me and throw me down. When I finally got good enough that I could break away from her before she threw me, she told me 'Well done.' Few words ever made me feel better. Then she took me to a man who taught me Israeli fighting called Krav Maga."

Amelia realized there was something she hadn't done. "I think you used that to save my life that night. Thank you. I guess I should also thank your mother."

Joshua gave a nod. "When I was a boy, I asked her where she learned to do all those things. She said she would tell me when I needed to know."

Joshua gazed at Amelia as if he was finally getting to the point. "One day, I needed to know. It was Sunday. My sister went to church with her friends, and my mother told me we were going to synagogue. That didn't make sense. The Sabbath was over, and we went to a messianic Christian church, not to the synagogue. The building was empty except for one man praying. As we approached him, he walked away, and we followed him into a side room."

Joshua paused a moment before continuing. "It was there

that I learned my mother had been an agent for the Mossad—an Israeli spy. The man bragged on her, telling how she had been one of their best honey traps. My mother blushed and made him stop when he told me what that was. My mother used to be a seductress that charmed men into Mossad traps where they were abducted to stand trial for crimes, recruited as spies, or eliminated if the security of Israel demanded it."

Joshua's eyes probed a memory. "That day, I learned many things about my parents that I didn't know, things that had been kept from Rahab and me. My mother cautioned me not to tell my sister because she feared, at that time, Rahab would not know how to handle the information wisely."

Joshua had opened chapters of his life to which few were privy. It caused a sensation that both enthused and concerned Amelia.

He went on. "They explained how in 1992 my father was a Russian nuclear scientist on loan to Iran. His expertise was crucial to Iran's growing nuclear program. Intel told them that father was interested in history and archaeology. Mother posed as a French teacher studying Persian history visiting Bushehr near where my father was staying. A 'chance' meeting was arranged with her and my father. Like most men, he was captured by her charms. But they were under constant surveillance. Mother contrived various ways to steal moments away from their watchers in a way that would appear natural. In those brief periods, my mother probed my father's heart and soul. What she discovered was that he was already disillusioned with Russia and their helping Iran. He realized that Iran's claim of pursuing nuclear energy for peaceful purposes was nothing more than a front to gain nuclear weapons, and it terrified him how they might use them. My father said he felt like he was helping to feed and grow a mad dog that would someday escape its cage. He wanted out but he was a man of science, not subversion. He later revealed that he had a dream about a beautiful woman that would help him. My mother was uniquely equipped to fill that role."

Joshua's eyes brightened with the excitement of telling the tale. "One night they proceeded with operation 'Mind Liberation' about which mother had briefed my father in their stolen moments. As they visited the Old City of Siraf in Bushehr, my mother made a show of needing to use the public toilet near the seaside in Persian Gulf Park. As the watchers crossed the park to follow my parents, most of them were systematically eliminated by Mossad agents. One of the Iranians caught up with my parents as they were crossing Khalij-e-Fars street between the park and the restrooms. As my father watched, my mother rammed her palm into the man's nose, drove a knee into his groin and spun him in front of an approaching car. With their pursuers out of the way, they fled down the rocks behind the restrooms to a waiting boat. Through the cooperation of the CIA, they were transferred to a larger vessel out in the Persian Gulf and eventually boarded a U.S. warship that was in the area as part of Operation Southern Watch to contain Iraq following Desert Storm. The ship took them out of the area. Of course, my father was madly in love with mother. During their trip to the United States, he amazed her with his brilliant mind and won her heart as well. The Mossad did not want to lose her, but my mother wanted to have children while she still could. They settled in New York with new identities."

Joshua stood, paced for a moment, then examined her. "They had run, but not far enough. The men that broke in that night were Iranian agents. They were sent to kill us all for revenge and a warning."

Joshua's eyes became misty. "In that synagogue room, my mother cried as I had never seen her cry before. She blamed herself. For the first time, I saw how much pain she had been hiding. She asked for my forgiveness. She looked at me and told me that she knew I would be safer if I knew the tactics of those who wanted to kill me."

The agony of that moment was in Joshua's eyes. "Then the stranger revealed the biggest shock of all. The man said they were impressed with my progress. I realized that all the times that I thought people were watching me, I had been right. He told me how impressive my grades were in school, especially in the sciences. That was thanks to my father. My fighting instructor said I was a natural master at the art. I began to realize that most of my life, all that my mother had done was preparing me for that moment. She knew her former life would always be a threat and it would be safer for me to assume that life as well. I would have the skills and the intel to protect myself and Rahab even after my mother was gone."

Joshua's expression took on the anguish his mother must have felt.

"The man reminded me that I would be 18 years old in a few months. He told me that I had a place in the Mossad if I wanted it. Israel needed good men, he said, because they had many enemies. It seemed to be the only option. I must confess that once the shock wore off, it excited me. I wanted to be able to protect my family."

Amelia pulled away the tears with the tissue.

Joshua eyed her. "My life must seem pretty wild to you, not very stable."

Amelia sniffed a laugh. "I don't think many people would consider my life very stable either. Gabe is my only family. We both live in a group home for people with special needs, and let me tell you it is chaos there half the time."

Joshua returned to the seat beside her and put his hand on her arm. "But you've done what you can to make a stable life for Gabriel. You prove there are many ways to have a significant life. I'm impressed."

The words were like a warm arm around her shoulders. "I appreciate that." She fumbled, trying to think of something to say. Give up this mad life of espionage and come live in the group home with us, didn't seem like the right call. *You're letting your imagination run wild. All he said was he's impressed with how you've helped Gabe.*

Joshua seemed to pick up on her awkwardness. "I'm

sorry."

"You didn't say anything wrong. Just a lot of memories. After my parents died, trying to get Gabe and me back together was the only thing that kept me going. I owe a lot to Gabe. He has a unique perspective on things. Seeing things through his eyes, or more often his ears, has kept me from dwelling on things I shouldn't."

Joshua's dark eyes were looking at her intently. It would have been intimidating if not for the warmth they conveyed. His hand slid down her arm and took her hand.

He smiled, soft and sad. "You deserve better."

Amelia felt her lips part slightly, but she had no words.

Joshua squeezed gently then released her hand and stood. Drawing back her arm, she looked at the floor. *You deserve better.* Better than what? Better than *her* life? Better than *his* life? What did he mean? Amelia felt her jaw quiver and she hoped he wasn't still looking at her.

"I'm going to fix us something to eat," she heard him say above her. "Are you hungry?"

She nodded and smiled, looking up.

His face was more lighthearted. "Okay, I better get busy." He grinned and tipped his head toward the communication room. "It's up to me because Ibbie and Marsha can't cook." His mouth and eyebrows both grinned.

Amelia slapped her thighs as she rose. "That is a pathetic cry for help if I ever heard one. I've seen the junk you guys have in that kitchen, but if I steal Marsha's smoothie veggies and use enough butter, there might be hope."

Chapter 11

The rest of that day and the next morning were filled with preparations. Amelia felt overwhelmed by the crash course she and her brother had received in the business of undercover activities. In a lonely vacant lot on the outskirts of Gosnell, the team wrapped up their final briefing before they split up in their separate vehicles.

"Do you think Gabe can do this?" Amelia searched Joshua's eyes for reassurance.

"You'll be there to help Ibbie guide Gabe. If he can understand what we want, I'm sure he can do it." He smiled and turned to Gabriel.

"You ready, Rams Twelve?"

Back and forth Gabriel swayed as he nodded. "Rams Twelve is ready. Rams Twelve can do it."

Joshua gave him two thumbs up which Gabriel regarded out of the side of his eye. Joshua briefed the group. "Okay, one last run-through on the overall timetable. In fifteen minutes, Marsha's taking the blue Honda to DNAble and she'll start her part. Ibbie will station the surveillance van on the street to the south. There is a view through the trees to the

DNAble building. Ameila, you and Gabe follow her in the Acura so you'll have a car in case you need it, but you two will be in the van with Ibbie during the operation. I'll be floating in the black Chevy, and once I know that Marsha's in place, I'll begin my part of the game." Joshua cast a positive expression to all the team members but lingered on Amelia. "God bless you and keep you safe."

Amelia could not help but return the warmth in his voice. "You too."

Marsha pulled into the DNAble lot. The building was impressive, but as usual, she was unimpressed. *You can paint the pigs and spray perfume but it's still a pigpen.* She was an expert at facades. The sneer she had inside made no appearance on her face. She beamed her perfect teeth at the edifice. Marsha was going to get her DNA tested to find out her heritage. Woo hoo. So exciting. Time to throw out the slop and see what comes running.

The sight of the blue on white "Police" emblem decreased the volume of her enthusiasm. She pretended to be admiring the architecture. It was the same officer that chased Ibbie. Marsha could see his intent face through the windshield as the cruiser progressed down the street. They should have seen that coming. Nothing motivated a cop like a suspect's escape. He was going to saturate the area with patrol until he caught the one that got away.

The cop was looking at her the way he looked that day when she drove by him. *Maybe he won't recognize me.* No holding her breath on that one. Unlike the others, she worked hard to be recognizable. It was the commodity that made her valuable in the part of the espionage economy in which she operated. She was already working out scenarios to quickly extract herself from a law enforcement contact. She wasn't having much luck coming up with one that didn't involve stuffing the cop in the trunk of his patrol car, something Joshua would never approve of.

The cruiser turned into the DNAble lot, the young officer looking like a dog on the hunt. The double-edged sword of Marsha's splendor was about to cut the other direction, and she was still short on a workable solution. She would have to waste the time necessary to convince him he was wasting his time. It was all a waste of time and she hated it. She considered hurrying into the building but the last thing she wanted was for him to come in after her. Having the DNAble people seeing her talking to the cops was risky. Better to get it over with in the parking lot.

Marsha turned away so the officer wouldn't see her talking to thin air. "Ibbie, we've got a problem."

Amelia sat in the surveillance van and listened to Ibbie relay Marsha's situation to Joshua. She realized the problem. If someone from the DNAble building saw Marsha with a cop, they might think something was happening that wasn't happening, which might affect what *was* happening. Things could get complicated quickly.

Beside her, Gabriel was fixated on the control and communication console that occupied much of the interior of the large vehicle. Amelia had finally made him understand that only Ibbie could touch the switches and buttons. He watched as Ibbie flipped a switch.

A police dispatcher was saying, "Copy, you're out at the DNAble building with a dark blue Honda Civic. Standby for listing."

Ibbie's eyes narrowed. "He ran her license plate."

Amelia started praying.

"Good morning, Officer." Marsha sounded completely relaxed over the speaker.

"I'm sorry to bother you." Amelia recognized Officer Conner Scott's voice from when they'd spoken at the farmer's market. He had seemed interested in her. "I'm Officer Scott with the Gosnell Police Department. I was wondering if I could ask you a couple of questions?"

"Sure. I've got a minute or two before my appointment."

"Didn't I see you driving this car over by the school yesterday?"

"Oh, you remember me." The statement carried just enough subtle tease. Amelia marveled at Marsha's ability to weaponize her sex.

Conner laughed shyly. "It's hard not to notice someone as pretty as you."

Disappointment stirred in Amelia. Conner's flirting had made her feel special at the time. She had even considered saying yes the next time he asked her out.

Marsha responded to Conner. "Oh, you're cute and sweet. I remember you, too. I hope we didn't get in the way that day. What was going on?" Marsha dropped her tone on the question like it was only between her and Conner.

Ibbie encouraged the interaction with a head nod. "Come on, Marsh. Make him forget his questions and get out of there before the DNAble crew wonders what's going on."

When Conner answered he sounded closer. "We had a guy run from us yesterday and since you were in the area, I thought you might have seen where he went."

Marsha must have closed the distance between them. "No. I was wondering what was going on. I'm staying over in Bentonville for a conference, and I heard about this DNA place. We came over yesterday just to see it and look around. We knew something big must be happening."

The dispatcher's voice came over the speakers from

Officer Conner's police radio and Ibbie's scanner, simultaneously. "Gosnell Six."

Conner sounded like he was stepping back. "Gosnell Six, go ahead.

The dispatcher gave a verbal code.

Ibbie straightened in the chair. She keyed one of many buttons. "Ram's One, did you hear that? Something's up. The cop's dispatch is cueing him."

Conner told the dispatcher to standby then spoke to Marsha. "Forgive me. I've got to take care of something real quick. Be right back with you."

Marsha's voice responded. "Can I give you my phone number and get with you later? I don't want to be late for my appointment."

"This won't take long." The sound of Conner's voice indicated he must be going back to his patrol car.

Ibbie blew out a breath. "For being young and full of testosterone, this kid's good. But that's not good for us. Must be something wrong with the rental plate on the car."

"What do you mean?" Amelia felt the tension of Marsha's situation.

"When the dispatcher has information she doesn't want to give in front of the person the cop's talking to, she gives a code so the cop can move away and get the info privately without alerting the suspect. We have descramblers for the police frequencies, and we keep up with the codes since they might mean trouble for us."

Trouble. Marsha was in the middle of it. She also had to know something was going on, but she sounded calm. What was Conner going to do? He didn't know Marsha. Everything was making her look more suspicious.

Joshua radioed his thoughts. "Okay, I won't move in unless I have to. It wouldn't be good if we're associated, and another stranger isn't going to help Marsha right now."

Ibbie brainstormed to Joshua. "Maybe Marsha can get him away from DNAble and we can give him a time out."

Amelia knew that didn't sound good. She grabbed the car keys off the control console. "I'm going. He'll listen to me. Gabe, stay with Ibbie." She heard Conner talking to his dispatcher as she left the van. She ran to the car and unlocked the door.

Ibbie leaned out the entrance of the van, her ear to what was coming over the radio inside while she motioned for Amelia to come back. She glanced around as if concerned about someone seeing the exchange.

Amelia gave her a look she hoped would convey her regret at disobeying. She prayed she wasn't making another mistake. She had to get there before Conner made a decision that would cause Marsha or Joshua to act. She couldn't believe they would hurt Conner, but she didn't want to find out. Didn't want Joshua to have to make that decision. They were only one street over.

As she sped into the lot, she saw that Conner was talking to Marsha again. She had the car door open and papers in her hand. What had his dispatcher told him? She saw him pivot sideways, so he could see the new car coming in and still watch Marsha. Recognition registered on his face as she pulled up in the slot right beside them and got out. "Sorry, I'm late. I was hoping you wouldn't go in without me. Hi, Conner. How's it going?"

It took the Officer a moment to respond. "You know her?"

"Sure." She smiled at Marsha and hoped it was convincing. *What name should I call her?* "She came in for a conference over in Bentonville." *Maybe he won't ask.* "We're going to get our DNA tested together. But I'm late. What's going on?"

Marsha answered. "Would you believe that the rental company put the wrong plate on this car?"

Amelia had no time to be scared. She kept going with it. "You're kidding." She gazed at Conner. "She's not in trouble, is she? That's not her fault."

Conner looked back and forth between them. "It happens. They deal with so many cars, they get mixed up sometimes. This is a Honda and the plate is for a Toyota." He seemed more relaxed. "The VIN matches a Honda to the same rental company so I'm sure it's fine." Conner furrowed his brow. "Where's Gabe?"

"Oh, I got a friend to watch him. Today is our big day out."

"I thought you couldn't go out because of Gabe?"

Amelia forced a smile. It was the excuse she always gave him. "I decided I needed a little me time."

"Oh. Well, maybe that's a good change." He glared at the car Amelia arrived in. "Where's your van?"

Amelia swallowed. "Sold it."

Marsha took Amelia's arm and grinned at her like the secret was out. "If you can't trust the police, who can you trust?" She turned to Conner like she was bringing him into the secret. "Now don't you tell anyone, but she's the real reason I'm in town. My company is treating this little girl in style while I'm here. Have you tried her jam? We're contracting to feature her jam in a new line of products. She's not going to need to be selling out of that old van anymore."

Conner regarded Amelia.

She raised her shoulders sheepishly. "No one was more surprised than me."

Marsha gave a start. "I almost forgot. Well, if that clears up the vehicle issue, we need to get inside." She gave Conner her full radiance. "Maybe we can get together sometime since you know Amelia." She tossed the papers on the seat, grabbed her purse, and slammed the door. "Come on, girlfriend, we're late. Nice to have met you." She pointed back at Conner as she ushered Amelia toward the building. "Officer Scott, right?"

Amelia gave Conner her own smile over her shoulder. "Good to see you, Conner." His parting gesture was half-hearted as he watched them walk away.

Chapter 12

Inside the DNAble building, the main lobby was bright and appealing. Marsha addressed Amelia at a volume loud enough to be heard without seeming like they wanted to be heard. She spoke in a perfect new accent. Each line was like Arkansas honey on a biscuit. "Can you believe the rental company got the wrong plate on my car? Wait 'til I turn it in. I didn't think we were ever going to get away from that cop. At least he was nice."

Amelia nodded as they made their way up to the front desk.

"May I help you?" The receptionist was a sleek, stylish woman in her thirties with a perfect smile.

Marsha went forward and spoke. "We're interested in getting tested to find our ancestors. Do you have some pamphlets we can look at?"

"Yes, we do." Suddenly the receptionist had an accent as well. Having seen Marsha in action Amelia knew this little actress had met her match.

The receptionist pulled out a colorful brochure from a holder on the counter. "This explains our services. The ancestry search is one of the most exciting things we do. It's a quick painless process and gives y'all an idea of your ethnic background, based on your genetic makeup."

Leafing through the pamphlet, Marsha leaned

comfortably on the counter and smiled at the receptionist like they were old friends. "Isn't this DNA stuff the most facinat'n thing. Since you work here, I'm sure you get the deluxe reading. Come on, tell us what you are."

"Oh, no. If you get tested, you'll get the same detailed results that I received. I knew we were Italian. That's what my mother and father always told us kids. But I found out that I actually have a lot of German in me. The profile DNAble provided led me to discover that I had a relative that was a famous German Ace pilot during World War I."

Marsha gave her hand a pat. "Just like the Red Baron. That is so special. Oh, I bet your family is so proud. What's your name, Honey?"

"Jessica Giordano."

"Oh." Amelia stepped closer. "That's derived from Hebrew."

The woman looked confused. "What do you mean?"

"Giordano, your last name, it has a background in the Hebrew language."

The receptionist's smile dimmed. "No, you're mistaken. Giordano is very much Italian."

Amelia smiled and nodded. "Of course, you're right. It's Italian, but I study languages. I guess I got it from my mother. Languages were special to her. Giordano is the Italian form of Jordan which comes from Yarden, the Hebrew word for the Jordan River that separates the countries Israel and Jordan. We have lost a lot of the history of our languages over the years, but that is one of the easier connections."

The receptionist's smile vanished. "You're wrong. I am European. My bloodline is pure and hasn't been contam…mixed with any…anyone from that part of the world."

Marsha eased herself between the woman and Amelia and faced the receptionist. "Just like I said. Your family must be very proud. Me, I want to find out something interesting and juicy about my history, maybe something scandalous that I can use to embarrass my mother."

The woman's smile returned.

Marsha turned, indicating Amelia. "My friend thinks she's French. I think she has some cannibal in her. You should see the way she eats a steak, practically raw."

Amelia gave a smirk.

The receptionist nodded. "Oh." She pulled out a clipboard for each of them. "If I can get your information, I'll have one of our ancestry specialists come and talk with you."

Marsha grabbed the clipboards. "We're so excited." They made their way to a corner while the receptionist waited on another customer that had come in.

Marsha filled out Amelia's form with fake information and handed it back to her. "Memorize this. It's you now." Her eyes strayed toward the parking lot. "Your cop friend moved out on the street, but he's still hanging around, so you can't go back outside. He probably wants to marry you since you're going to make your fortune in jam."

Amelia curled her lip. "More like he wants to marry *you*."

Marsha shook her head. "I'm not the kind of girl you take home to Mama. He was actually suspicious of me. I've got to up my game if I can't handle a little local boy. I'm sorry you're involved this deep, but I'm glad you came when you did, or I might still be out there." Marsha lowered her voice and spoke for the benefit of the cell phone open channel. "Ibbie, she's with me now. I can't extract her without looking suspicious. Besides, I think I want her around."

Marsha completed her own form. She clacked her clipboard together with Amelia's and held them up with one hand like she was showing Amelia something. They blocked the receptionist's view. She held out her hand behind the clipboards. "Let me see your phone." Marsha took the cell and smoothly hid it between her legs. She handed the clipboards to Amelia. "Memorize me, too." Taking up a magazine to hide her actions, Marsha retrieved Amelia's phone and pulled out the battery. She found the phone's unique ID codes on a label inside the battery compartment and quietly read them off to Ibbie.

Amelia crammed the information from Marsha's clipboard into her head. She used the mnemonics that her mother had taught her for learning languages. An overwhelming fear tried to creep in. *You need to get this right. Everyone is counting on you now.*

Marsha handed back her cell and took the clipboards. "Okay, Ibbie will be able to make yours work like ours. It's going to turn off and on a couple of times. When nobody's looking, stuff it down the front of your pants where it can't be seen. That way we can use mine to gain intel. Okay, let's get started. And don't worry—if all else fails, we'll shoot our way out."

The sun was streaming through the jeweled pieces that formed the DNA helix on the outside of the large wall of windows, casting prismatic colors over the room. A couple of other people moved around the lobby looking at the displays depicting the history and process of DNA research and use. Amelia tried to shake the image of bullets flying, glass falling, and people running.

Marsha stood and caught the receptionist's eye as she headed back to the counter. Pretending to adjust her clothing, Amelia stuffed the phone.

Taking the forms, the receptionist glanced at them and said, "Ms. Carlise and Ms. Braumley?"

"That's us." Marsha gave a giggly smile—the perfect slightly silly blonde.

The woman buzzed them into a door beside the reception area.

Joshua sat in his car on the street just south of DNAble.

He could see parts of the building through the houses and trees between him and the DNAble complex. Ibbie had the audio of everything taking place with Amelia and Marsha coming through his cell phone.

Joshua inhaled. "I don't like Amelia in there."

"I know, but I couldn't stop her short of shooting the tires out." She paused then resumed. "She did well. I think she and Marsh will make a good team. Marsh will keep her safe."

"She's not trained for this."

"But she's doing great. The way she put that receptionist on edge was perfect. I'm sure it helped make her believable. They're keying in on that. They might be thinking she has some hidden Jewish DNA. It's perfect."

Joshua didn't like it. He loved Amelia's caring heart, but it was always getting her into trouble. A thought came in his mind. *Or maybe God's using it for His purpose.* "How's Gabe doing?"

"He's all right." It sounded like Ibbie turned to look at Gabriel. "He knows his sister is on a spy mission and he's ready to help with his part. You're not scared, are you, Rams Twelve?"

"Rams Twelve is agent, Rams Twelve is ready." Gabriel continued the chant until Ibbie asked him to stop.

She addressed Joshua again. "I don't think we have a choice. We need to get things going."

"Okay. I'll stand by and move in when it's my turn. But let me know if anything sounds like it's going wrong."

Fifteen minutes passed. Amelia pretended to leaf through a magazine but watched Marsha out of the side of her eye. She was still unnerved by Marsha's warning. When the woman had first left them in the room, Marsha had thrust her phone at Amelia like she was showing her a funny on social media. She had caught on and pretended to laugh, but on the phone Marsha had written. "Don't say anything. We are on camera."

The other woman appeared to be scrolling through her cell phone as cool as could be. Amelia was trying hard not to squirm.

The door opposite from where they entered opened and a tall, burly-looking fellow entered, followed by a shorter man with oversized forearms that made Amelia think of Popeye. The big man spoke while the other man moved across the room. "Ladies, can I have you come with me? The facility manager would like to talk to you."

"Really?" Marsha kept her innocent smile. Amelia saw a brief swivel of her eyes to follow Popeye as he positioned himself in front of the exit into the lobby, but Marsha kept her main focus on the bigger man. "What about?"

"He just has some questions for you."

Amelia shuddered.

"Marsha giggled but it had a nervous flavor. "Well, I don't think we should. I mean we just came here to get our DNA tested. Don't you just, like, have us spit in a cup or something like that. Is this like a sales gimmick or something because I don't need any long-term commitments."

Big guy scowled. "The manager just has some questions."

"But you can't tell us what it's about?"

"He just has some questions."

Amelia could tell diplomacy wasn't the man's strong point.

Marsha motioned with her open palm like she was giving the bigger man a gentle push away. "That's okay. I think we'll just come back later." She turned and headed toward the exit.

Popeye didn't move. His large forarms were locked together across his chest.

Marsha smiled and stepped to the side to go around him.

The man's arms came down to the ready and he side stepped to block her way.

Marsha's voice expressed indignation. "What do you think you're doing?"

Popeye threatened with a hard look. "He said the manager would like to see you. You need to come with us."

Amelia pleaded. "Please, we really just want to leave." She hoped she sounded convincing.

Marsha turned away and took out her cell phone. As she started to hit the buttons, the Scowler wrenched it from her hand and held her by the wrist.

"Ow!" Marsha pulled against the grip in a girlish fashion. "That hurts."

The man let her go and rummaged through Marsha's purse, he jerked his head toward Amelia. "Get hers too."

The second man turned on her.

"I left my phone in the car." She needed something to bolster her story. "We can go out and get it. It's right out in the parking lot. Please don't hurt me."

Popeye patted her pockets. "She doesn't have it."

"Come on." Scowler tried to ease Marsha toward the door on the opposite wall. "You need to go upstairs."

Marsha grabbed one handle of her purse and didn't budge. It was obvious the man was surprised by the strength of her resistance. "I need my purse. It has my medicine and my," she paused for effect, "lady things. You don't want me to be without them. You saw I don't have anything dangerous in there."

The man relented and Marsha snatched her purse and walked toward the door. Amelia hurried after them, so Popeye would not have to touch her.

They found they were in a hallway full of closed doors with black signs proclaiming what lay on the other side, labels such as "Consultation," "Supplies," "Technician." Amelia tried to take in everything. They stopped in front of an elevator halfway down the hall. The sign on the door at the far end said, "Laboratory One." The elevator opened, and they were shoved on board.

"What are your names?" Marsha was demanding.

The men were silent.

She continued to bombard the duo with demands and objections until they got off on the second floor. Scowler herded them to the left and down another hall. This time, the doors were labeled with people's names: Jacobson, Fischer, Nousberger.

Scowler opened the last door. The sign said, "Conference."

The man pointed to the closest chairs positioned around a large table that dominated the room. "You wait here."

Marsha sat hard on one of the seats. She folded her arms, glaring at Scowler. Amelia took a chair beside her. The two men left and closed the door behind them. Marsha sat up and cocked her ear toward the door. There was the sound of jingling keys working the lock. Then nothing. Scanning the room, Marsha seemed to be satisfied they were not on surveillance. She held her hand out to Amelia. Amelia grinned as she fished the phone out of her pants and gave it to her partner.

Marsha made a production of wiping it off and then put it to her ear. "Okay, it worked. We're in." She paused, listening to Ibbie or Joshua, then responded. "It seemed like they bought it on our end. The guy that did most of the talking…Seth. Got it. I saw the lab on the first floor at the west end of the hallway, just like the blueprints showed." Another pause then Marsha asked, "Can you tell where they're at?" She nodded as she took in what the person on the phone was saying. "They locked the door, so I'll start working on that. The names are on the offices. We haven't seen a Norm yet. Let's hope it's not a nickname." She chuckled. "I guess that's true. Since he is the head of security, do you think his office could be downstairs? Okay, we'll start up here." Marsha's nodding became precise, single head bounces as if checking off a set of instructions. "Okay, I'll change and get started."

Marsha canceled the call and put the phone on the table.

"Well, it worked. They left us in this room, thinking the big boss wants to talk to us. They don't appear to have a clue that the voice giving them orders is not Herschlag. Your brother is good. The big security guy has my phone, and Ibbie can hear everything they're saying. Sounds like his name is Seth just like our cell phone contact said when he gave us the number. They took the elevator back downstairs, so no one on this floor should know us." While she talked, Marsha stripped off her top, turned it inside out, and slid it back on, revealing the official uniform of a Whistle Cleaning associate, complete with the slogan, "No one gets it as clean as a Whistle." Amelia watched as Marsha smoothed the final product of her outfit switch. There were no indications that a life grew inside her. She struck a modeling pose. "How do I look?"

Amelia acknowledged the form fitting top with a nod. "It fit's you…well, just like it did the other side out. You look too good for a member of a cleaning crew."

"I look good in anything. That's my business."

Amelia was confused. "I guess I don't understand why we didn't just come in as cleaning staff in the first place?"

"Sorry. I think we discussed that before you came into the picture. Everything in the building is done by key card access with keyed locks as backup in case the cards fail. All guests are screened and given a visitor card that only allows them access to the areas they are authorized to go. We wanted to avoid that screening. Ibbie's going to have her hands full with Joshua's cover story and since we don't intend on limiting where we go, we won't need their card. The only way to bypass the screening process was to come in as their prisoners instead of their guests. That's why we couldn't go willingly." Marsha gave Amelia a glance of approval. "You did good, by the way." The woman pawed through her purse, taking inventory. "All the security officers know is they got a call from Mr. Herschlag, who is listed as the CEO of the company, aka Gabriel, telling them to detain us and bring us upstairs for him to talk to and not to take no for an answer."

Marsha grinned. "But now we want to be friendly and move around freely, so we're Whistle Cleaners here to measure for a bid."

Amelia returned the smile. "Good. I think I like that a lot better than being a prisoner."

Marsha turned serious. "In this business, it's best not to get too comfortable with anything." Marsha's mind seemed to go to another place for a moment then returned. "Right now you're my helper." She assessed Amelia. "We'll have to make do with what you're wearing. Just look official and they'll buy it. You'll need something to look like you're taking notes."

The nervous feeling returned. Amelia needed to keep the humor going. "When we get done here, can we go clean over at my place? I'll have to be the supervisor over there of course."

Marsha's face expressed surprised appreciation at Amelia's banter. "Sure, if you want it to look like mine— Early American Messy. It would be worse, but I don't spend much time there." She scanned the room as if looking for something.

"I was hoping that since I've been shot at and chased through the town, at least I could get my apartment cleaned."

Marsha gave her a look of disbelief. "Are you kidding? We should charge you for experience like that. You hang out with us, and you can sell your skills to any covert agency in the world. Just don't pick the wrong side or we'll have to kill you."

Amelia raised her eyebrows. "Is that even a joke?"

Marsha shrugged. "Well…" Her eyes landed on something. She crossed the room and picked up a notepad and ink pen.

As hard as the woman was, Amelia couldn't help liking her. Putting things together, Amelia assessed Marsha. Her messy place and not being home much suggested she lived alone. Marsha had refused to admit she was pregnant, but Amelia suspected she was. She had said she would "take care of it." She wondered if the woman was facing something that no woman should face alone. "I guess the spy life doesn't leave much time for relationships."

Marsha headed back toward Amelia, eyeing her with amusement. "I thought a French girl could find romance anywhere."

Amelia pretended the remark didn't come as a surprise. "I guess…if romance is all you want."

"You must be holding out for domestic bliss, then?" Marsha handed Amelia the pad and pen.

Amelia took it, uncomfortably, her mind on Marsha's question. "I believe that romance only belongs in married life."

Marsha gave a sniff as she ripped open a hidden compartment on the bottom of her purse, which came away as a nylon holster containing a small black handgun. "Well, that sure doesn't sound very French." Hiking up her pant leg, Marsha strapped the holster to her calf. Drawing the weapon, she took a metal tube out of a pocket on the holster and screwed it on the end of the gun.

A silencer, Amelia guessed. She prayed Marsha wasn't going to have to use it. "Maybe you've been hanging around the wrong kind of French."

She canted the pistol. "Probably the wrong kind of people in general. Comes with the territory." She jerked the slide, sending a round into the air. As quick as a cat she caught the bullet on its way down.

Amelia jolted in surprise.

Marsha glanced her way. "Sorry. Just making sure there was a round in the chamber."

Amelia returned her mind to the conversation. Marsha's life sounded empty. "Isn't there any way a person in this line of work can have a family?"

Giving her a sly look, Marsha shoved the weapon back in the holster and pulled out the magazine. "Joshua's a good man. I'm sure you two could find a way." She mashed the ejected round into the clip, slapped it back in the gun handle, and pulled her pant leg over it.

Amelia straightened her shoulders. "What?"

"Oh, come on. Ibbie and I are still women. She told me you and Joshua seemed to have hit it off pretty well."

"I…he's nice."

Shaking her head, Marsha laughed. "If you define 'nice' as 'drool-worthy hunk,' yeah, I suppose he's nice." She pointed her finger at Amelia. "If you tell him I said that, I *will* have to kill you." "But I'm guessing to you, nice means potential family man. Now are we on the right page?"

With a look of disbelief, Amelia tipped her head back and shook it. The conversation had gone all the wrong way. She had wanted to see if she could help Marsha. "I guess, but maybe not the page I was—"

Marsha kept at it. "But you do like him, don't you…in a *nice* sort of way?"

Amelia looked at the floor and imagined Joshua as a family man. After a moment, she blinked her eyes and looked up. "None of this is worth talking about. My life has never been open to many romantic possibilities. And since, yes, my definition of nice is the second one, the possibilities don't look so *nice*, so we should just get back to work. Besides, I'm only half French."

"So you got a few things stacked against you. You need to take inventory of your assets. You have plenty of those. Map out a strategy and execute a plan. He won't know what hit him. I'm still woman enough to believe love can conquer all. It never seems to work out for me, but don't you give up, French girl."

"Thanks, but you can't give up something you never started."

Marsha gave her a smirk. "Oh, I think it's started, with or without you." Walking over to the table, she retrieved the phone and put it in her pocket. "But I wouldn't stress over it. There's every chance they might catch us and kill us. Then you won't have to worry about it." She picked up her purse and began fishing two thin items out from the seams. Holding them up she told Amelia, "Come on, I'll show you one of my best skills – how to pick a lock. That will take your mind off men."

Amelia followed her toward the door. "My mind wasn't… Why do you think it can work out for me but not for you?"

Marsha knelt in front of the door. "Joshua and me? Are you kidding? He wants the same thing you do."

Amelia watched as the woman went to work on the lock. "I didn't mean Joshua. Isn't there anyone else?"

"No one that matters anymore."

Amelia ached for the woman. "I'm sorry. I wish there was some way I could help."

The blonde stopped working the picks. "I know what's on your mind. You figured it out already and I guess you're right. I am pregnant. But like I said, things don't seem to work out for me. I appreciate your wanting to help, but I can't talk about it." Her fingers went to work again.

"Boy, this work does intrude on your personal life. Your baby doesn't have anything to do with your job."

Marsha's manipulation of the lock faltered again. "It wasn't supposed to. Like I said, I'll take care of it. Thank you for not telling anyone."

"Of course. But like you said, you're still a woman. Let me know if you need to talk."

The woman continued with her work. "Thanks."

Amelia was struck by the strange reality of the situation as she silently prayed for the pregnant covert agent who kneeled before her, picking a lock.

Chapter 13

In the surveillance van, Ibbie pointed at Gabriel like a director on a movie set. "Okay Rams Twelve, you're up again. Just like we rehearsed."

Ibbie punched the phone number on the keypad.

After a few rings, someone answered. "Hello."

Gabriel assumed the voice of the man that was obviously in charge during the exchange they had heard on the day they did their recon mission. "Norm, where are you at?"

"I'm still in the basement." The voice didn't invite further inquiry.

Ibbie sorted through a set of cards laid out on a console like a magician performing a trick. Each card had a printed message. She slid one in front of Gabriel.

"How's it going?" Gabriel's voice showed no signs that he was reading the question.

"Fine. We're almost through."

Ibbie shoved Gabriel another card. "Okay, listen. I forgot to tell you. A couple of girls are here from Whistle cleaners. They're looking the place over to give me a bid. With everything that's been happening, I thought it might be a good time to change it up a little. I was worried the old ones might be getting a little too familiar with the place."

Norm's voice was slow and precise. "It might have been a good idea for you to discuss that with me. Bringing in new faces makes security harder not easier. And cleaning crews are more likely to talk about what they see here if we drop them than if they are worried about keeping the contract."

Gabriel looked at Ibbie, who reached over and pressed the mute button for Gabriel's microphone.

"Say this: I don't like the way things have been going around here, but we can discuss it later. These ladies will just be here long enough to give us an estimate. Nothing's been finalized."

Ibbie released the mute and Gabriel repeated the lines word for word in the manager's voice.

Norm deliberated. "Do you have their contact information, so I can check them out?"

Ibbie had two cards to cover that: First card, "Of course." Next card, "I'll text it to you."

"Okay." There was suspicion in Norm's voice. "By the way, are we still on for lunch today?"

It was a test. Something wasn't sounding right to the man. Ibbie pressed the mute key. Would they have a lunch meeting? The seconds were ticking by. It was too close to noon. She couldn't afford a mistake. Maybe Gabriel should apologize and tell Norm he wasn't going to be able to make it. But what if they hadn't scheduled a lunch? Was the man lying to get Gabriel to agree to a conversation they never had? Ibbie didn't waste time wiping away the trickle of sweat running next to her eye. If she got this wrong, Norm might go looking for the girls. If they had made the lunch date and she said yes, that would prove nothing to the man because agreement would be the easy road. Ibbie licked her dry lips. Norm wouldn't take the chance of ambiguity. "Okay, say this…" She spoke quickly to Gabriel then unkeyed the mute.

Gabriel put in the same hint of confusion that Ibbie had

used. "If we had a lunch date, I don't remember it. Sorry, but I can't make it today. I already have a commitment."

"Sorry, maybe I'm confused. I remember now. I was thinking of someone else." Norm sounded apologetic.

Ibbie smiled. No lunch meeting. *You old gonif.* Gonif, the Hebrew term for a sneaky rascal, fit Norm perfectly. *We're going to beat you at your own game.*

She slid another card at Gabriel to wrap it up, "Also, there's a man from the head office coming down today. I want you to show him around, answer any questions he has. He's new. The bosses brought him in from the outside as a kind of trouble shooter. He hasn't been to this branch yet. Be helpful. We want to make a good impression. I'll text you his info. Okay, I'll let you get back to—"

Norm cut in before Gabriel could finish. "Why do you throw these last-minute things on me? We just got past a major security breach attempt and you're violating protocol. I feel like I'm being set up. What are you up to?"

Ibbie pressed the mute key. She looked at the ceiling, her finger poised to unmute. *Well, at least he believes it's the boss. We made him mad.* She looked back at Gabriel, "Okay, say this—the security problem is what's got the higher-ups concerned. That's your job, Norm. But it's my neck their breathing down. Tell them what they need to hear to feel we are back on track and there are not going to be any more problems." Then she unmuted.

Gabriel mimicked Ibbie's tone of authoritative menace as he repeated what she said.

The moment he finished, Ibbie ended the call. She blew out a breath and spoke to Gabriel. "Okay, now we monitor any outgoing calls he has. If he tries to call the boss to verify or follow up, we'll need to reroute it and let him talk to you again. You're doing great." She knew Joshua was listening over his phone. She raised her voice and tone to address him. "You heard all that. It sounds like he's buying it."

Joshua's cadence said he was calculating as he spoke. "In

a few minutes, the ladies will move out and see what they can find on the second floor. I'll move over to play my part. We'll keep things moving quickly and keep them off guard. If anyone calls about Marsha and Amelia, Norm will be tied up and won't be able to respond. He'll call Seth and talk to Gabriel again. Once I'm in, we'll find out where our best evidence is hiding. We'll be free-flowing a lot on this. Keep a close watch on Amelia. She shouldn't be in there, so keeping her safe needs to be a priority."

"This might be a good time to find out if she can fit into a life like this."

There was silence on the line. Joshua finally spoke. "We don't need to be testing her. When this is done, she and Gabriel have a secure life to get back to. We don't want to ruin that for them."

Ibbie rolled her eyes for her own benefit. "Granted this life isn't for everyone, but maybe that life isn't either. Aren't you the one that is always telling me, 'We live our lives waiting for God's next assignment?' Maybe you better let Him, Amelia, and Gabriel decide where they best belong." She gazed at the young man rocking beside her with a satisfied look on his face. "I know one person who looks like he was born to a life of espionage. It might be tough to pry him away."

Amelia watched as Marsha pushed open the door. It had taken her only a few minutes to pick it. She didn't hesitate but walked boldly into the hall. "Act like you know what you're doing," she had advised Amelia. "It's the best way not to look suspicious."

Amelia strode beside Marsha. She had found a clipboard on a table in the conference room and kept it poised, head up like she was ready to take notes. She had Marsha's purse, aka spy kit, looped over her arm. She hoped it didn't have a self-destruct feature. She felt exhilarated and terrified all at once.

One of the office doors opened and a middle-aged woman stepped into the hall. Marsha pointed at the windows with the partially extended end of the tape measure she had obtained from her purse before they left the conference room. "Make sure we get a count on how many we have on each floor. Make a note that we'll have to bring in a lift to get the outsides on this floor."

Amelia wrote, *lift for upper floor windows,* on her note pad. *Might as well keep it authentic.*

The woman said a brief hello and looked back at them again after she passed. Marsha had Amelia hold one end of the tape measure on the side of the window as she stretched it to the other. The woman went into a bathroom across from the elevator. Marsha let the tape suck back in and opened the door that the woman had come out of.

It was an office. Two other doors flanked the workstation in the middle. Marsha pulled one open—closet. She moved across to the other. As she nudged it inward, she said, "Oh excuse me, sir." Her voice put on its southern charm. "We're working on a cleaning bid. I sure didn't mean to bother you, but there was no one in the outer office. Do you know how many square feet you have in this room?"

Over Marsha's shoulder, Amelia could see a balding man looking over a pair of reading glasses and shaking his head.

She closed the door and handed the smartphone to Amelia. "We're going back inside and coming out with access to the computer system. Here is what you do…"

Amelia listened with everything that was in her.

When Marsha finished, she scrutinized Amelia. "You got it?"

Amelia nodded and brought up the camera app on the phone. She switched it to video and palmed it at her side.

Marsha opened the door. "I'm sorry to bother you again. Would you mind if we take a quick measurement of your room?" She moved in and held the door for Amelia, closing it when they were both inside.

The man smiled. "Go ahead."

Holding out one end of her tape measure she pointed Amelia to the far wall then stopped. "Honey, how you gonna write stuff down?" She turned her body to give her figure its best advantage. With a beguiling smile, she used her finger to beckon the man. "Would you be a sweety and lend a girl a hand?"

Taking in the view, the man came forward and took the tape. When he had it held to the wall, Marsha sashayed her way to the other side of the room. "So, what do you do here?" Everything about the woman—her voice, her movements, her smile—was alluring. She pulled the tape tight and called out the measurement to Amelia.

"I'm a controller."

Amelia wrote down the number as she inched backward to where she could see the computer screen sitting on the desk. Marsha turned and headed back toward the man. Amelia could tell it wasn't just the tape she was reeling in. "That sounds important. What do you control?"

The closer Marsha got, the more the strain on the man's shirt buttons moved from his belly to his chest. She came to within a foot and let her hand come right up against his as she pulled in the tape.

"Money." The man's voice was a little higher than Amelia suspected he intended.

Marsha tipped her head a bit and raised one eyebrow. "Really." She drew out the word. She leaned a large smile to within a foot of the man's face. "Just what every girl wants."

Amelia could see some type of spreadsheet on the screen. "We'll need to measure the other way, too." She knew Marsha would know why she said it.

Amelia watched as Marsha led the man around the room, measuring and flirting. She called out numbers to Amelia and made chit chat with the controller. The man was oblivious to anything but Marsha. After getting the basic dimensions of the room, she spoke to Amelia without taking her eyes from the man. "Do we need any more measurements?"

The spreadsheet was still on the screen. "Uh, maybe the window."

Marsha led her lamb to the window. "So, with all that controlling, do you ever get any time off?"

"Uh." The man faltered. "Sure."

With the man holding the tape on the bottom windowsill, Marsha stretched her form to reach the top. "I bought a pretty new dress, but I haven't had a chance to wear it anywhere." She called out the feet and inches.

The man stood up from the window. "That's a shame."

Did he get taller? The computer changed to the screen saver. Amelia called to Marsha. "We've got what we need."

Marsha took the measuring tape back but stayed in front of the man flipping it back and forth in her hand. "There's a restaurant I have been dying to try. I want to show it to you. You've got the internet, don't you?"

"Sure."

Marsha led the man to the computer. Amelia eased the phone into a discreet position where she could film the computer keyboard and started the recording. The man's eyes were so full of Marsha, he couldn't have noticed. Marsha moved the "Controller" into his seat of power.

He saw the screen saver. "My computer timed out. I'll have to log back in."

Marsha leaned her backside against the desk next to him and looked away. "Okay. I'll wait."

The man's fingers flew over the keyboard as he entered his account name and password. The spreadsheet came back on the screen and the man quickly downsized it and clicked on the internet browser.

Amelia nodded to Marsha who came off the desk suddenly looking at her watch. "Oh, no. Is it really that late? We need to go or we're going to be in so much trouble." She took the man's face in her hands. "I am so sorry." She turned to the desk and grabbed the man's business card. "I'll call you."

Snatching a pen from a holder, she thrust it at him. "Better give me your cell phone, also."

The man was flustered.

"Please hurry. We don't want to get in trouble." Marsha added an impatient bounce of her foot.

He grabbed the pen and scribbled his number on the card.

Marsha put her hand on the man's cheek and smiled. "I just love a man that's in control."

The two women hustled out of the room.

"Are you ready? I have two more numbers associated with a name."

Ibbie curled her fingers over the keyboard when she heard Marsha's voice in her headphones. "Go with them."

"Lawrence Shafman." Marsha rattled off the two numbers she had acquired from her new conquest. "He's the branch controller."

"Got it. We'll add him to the rest."

"We also have a video of his keystrokes logging into the DNAble network. Can you upload that and get me the login and password? We'll be looking for a vacant computer to use them. With that password, we should be able to speed up our hacking process.

Ibbie clicked at the keys as she talked. "Great. Be careful though. Joshua is concerned about the security manager. He sounds like he knows what he's doing and won't be easy to fool. Joshua will be trying to keep him busy.

There was ice in Marsha's voice when she responded. "Perhaps he's a candidate for an efficiency award."

"Who's getting an efficiency award?" Even from the one-sided conversation, Amelia knew what Marsha had been talking about with Ibbie, but that part seemed out of place.

Marsha put away the phone as she walked confidently down the hallway. "The security manager. He might be a problem. Sometimes we have to take strong measures when someone on the other side gets too good at what they do."

"Oh." Amelia suppressed her imagination on the topic. *Why did I ask?*

Marsha was scanning the names on the doors as they passed. The woman was a contrast. She was personable and pleasant. She was also deadly, and Amelia didn't like the way that made her feel. She had seen Joshua and Ibbie kill people and it was horrible to think about. But the woman she was following around seemed harder.

Marsha peeked her head into one of the offices and encountered an assistant. She asked if there was an office that had furniture in it but would not be in use that day so they could use it to measure.

They learned that a group the assistant referred to as Dr. Becker's team was at a conference. Those offices should be empty. They were down the hall and around the corner on the left. Marsha could probably get a key from security.

With a pleasant smile, Marsha had said, "Thanks, I'll look into that."

Ten minutes later, they stood in Dr. Frank Becker's office with the curtains closed, and the doors locked. It was composed of an outer room for an assistant and the inner office. They had passed an empty conference room on one side of the office and there was an outer wall on the other. Marsha gave a satisfied nod. "Very private. As tight as these rooms are, you could probably fire off a gun and no one would hear it. We shouldn't be disturbed." She went to the inner office and switched on the computer.

Amelia perused the room. Behind the desk was a bar with a sink and a small refrigerator underneath. Her eyes stopped when she came to the cabinet just above the countertop. She stared at the jam jars sitting on the shelf, each banded with the paper logo Amelia had worked so hard to design. "Jam de Monique," named after her mother. Nearby was a picture of a man receiving an award. It all rushed together in her mind and memories poured forth. The creepy old guy that stopped by her farmers market booth to purchase jam and stand too close to her. The subtle looks of disapproval he gave Gabriel. The jam stains on his shirts from him wiping his sticky fingers, shirts he wore outside his pants, so his belly didn't look so huge. How he would stand and glare at all the people as they enjoyed the park, like a wolf plotting over sheep in a pasture. But mostly the dark feeling she got whenever the man was near.

Marsha straightened over the keyboard and Amelia was thankful to be pulled back into the world of undercover activities. The DNAble logo and the company's login screen was on the monitor.

The blonde poised her fingers. "Okay, Ib, what's the account name?"

"Moneyman."

"Figures." The computer keys clicked. "And the password?"

"Capital I-c-o-n-t-r-o-l-t-h-e-s-t-r-i-n-g-$." Ibbie made an amused sound of realization at what it spelled.

"Not anymore, little moneyman." Marsha mumbled to herself as she typed in the pirated login. The DNAble logo filled the screen, covered by folder and program icons. Marsha ran through them. Her eyes brightened. "Ibbie, they have a central scheduling program. I found Norm. His last name is Salzman. She moved the mouse and tapped at the keyboard. "And he now has an appointment with Tanner Hughes in twenty minutes. I'm starting the data-mining."

Marsha took back her purse. Pulling a makeup case from the handbag, she removed one end where a USB cable was concealed. She held up the case. "Portable solid-state hard drive. It's huge. Should be able to get a bit of the good stuff. But I'll leave a little something behind that will keep us in touch, in case they get up to something else we should know about."

Amelia shook her head and smiled. "You have a lot of toys in that bag."

Marsha gave a funny twist of her mouth. "Yeah, it's a pickle. I don't have any room for my totty stuff. A girl needs things besides decoder rings and night scopes."

"You're from Britain."

Marsha looked up with just her eyes. "Where did you get that idea?"

"The way you say certain things and some of the words you use. I can also detect just a hint of accent you're trying to hide. Remember, my mother loved languages, and I have lived most of my life with a brother with super hearing. You start picking up on things yourself after a while."

Marsha's eyes went back to cruising the computer files as she spoke. "You could be dangerous. I gave you the 'might have to kill you' talk, right?"

Marsha's features were some of the most beautiful Amelia had seen, but behind them lurked something else. "Sorry. You know, you can be kind of scary."

"So can you. I'll make a deal with you. You don't get me killed and I won't kill you."

Amelia cocked her head sideways. "I'm not sure that makes sense from a timeline standpoint, but I think it's an offer I can't refuse. Deal. Can I trust you?"

Marsha raised her beautiful eyes again. "No." The eyes went back to the computer. "But fortunately, that doesn't stop most men from doing it. You, however, I'm starting to like."

Amelia's smile conveyed the warmth the statement produced. "Thanks."

Marsha nodded matter-of-factly. "Yeah, they'd have to give me a pretty good reason to kill you now."

Chapter 14

Joshua parked beside Marsha's Honda. As he got out, he stretched and scanned the DNAble building. Two stories and the ladies were on the top floor. Seth was probably on the first and Norm was in the basement by last account. Marsha's intel placed at least one lab on the first floor. With a natural move, he made sure his leather jacket was pulled down in the back to cover the Glock 19 concealed in a holster, tucked in his waist at the small of his back.

An attractive lady greeted him in the lobby. "Good morning. May I help you?"

There were four doors besides the entrance. From the blueprints, he knew the one on the wall to his right was a maintenance closet. The door on the far wall must give access to a part of the lab or a hallway outside of it.

Joshua approached the receptionist. "My name is Tanner Hughes. I have an appointment with Norm Salzman, your head of security." *Two doors behind the reception desk. One must lead to the waiting room and the other to the hallway where Seth took Marsha and Amelia. The waiting room would open into that hall as well.*

The woman moused on the computer at her station. "I see you here on the schedule. Please have a seat, and I'll let Mr. Salzman know you're here." She picked up a phone.

The lobby ceiling was at the top of the second story. The

front was glass all the way up. The second-floor windows overlooked the lobby, capturing the light pouring in from the two-story wall of sun—a striking display. The loveseat-sized chairs were comfort and function. Everything was designed to impress. *That way no one will doubt the information DNAble supplies in the end.*

The door behind the receptionist, which he had guessed went to the hallway, opened and a tall man in his forties came out. He was fit, other than a slight belly revealed by his DNAble polo shirt. "Mr. Hughes, Mr. Herschlag just told me you were coming." Joshua took his offered hand. "Welcome to Gosnell. I assume you brought in a company jet over at Drake. If I had known, I would have met you at the airport."

Ibbie nailed that one. An old gonif for sure. Still checking out every story. A jet at a small airport would be easy to confirm or deny. I'm not going to make it that easy. Joshua turned on enough of his New York accent to sell his character. "Are you kidding? They don't give me a jet. I came commercial. The airport between here and Bentonville— what's it called? Something that starts with an 'X.'"

"XNA."

"That sounds right." *I know you want to call the main office to verify me, but I'm gonna keep you busy, you old snake.* "Can we get out of the lobby, so we can talk?"

Norm led the way to the back area. The hall was behind the door as expected and halfway down the hall was the elevator. A mental review of what Gabriel's ears could determine about where the security officer named Seth had taken Marsha's phone told Joshua the security office should be past the elevator and around the corner to the right. Joshua made sure he let Norm go first.

Once the door closed to the reception area, Joshua made a show of verifying they were alone in the hallway and launched in. "I want to say up front that I'm sorry about this." Joshua put a regretful smile with the comment. "The big guys get a little jumpy when there is an incident, but I don't like to interfere with a local operation unless I have to. My goal here is to do a look around, a total view, so I can report back that everything is fine, and you can get on with the plan. A quick look at your stats said that you're on track here, and no one back East wants to mess that up. They just want an outside set of eyes on this for the peace of mind. I checked the news stations and papers when I got in. There's a lot of reports about what went on here. We want to make sure DNAble avoids any negative publicity."

"My men made sure of that."

"It looks like they did a good job. The only time the company name came up was during the commercial. Nice ad, by the way."

"I'll pass it along to promotions. Maybe I can get some of your business cards to pass around to the departments we visit."

Joshua pulled a business card holder from his pocket. *Another test. Something has this guy's alarms going off. I hope New York intel got the format right.*

Norm took the stack of cards that Joshua offered. He lingered on his examination. "I like the new design."

I'm not giving you anything. "Did they change it? I never look at the things. Just take what they give me. I've never been much of a card flasher. You strike me as the same kind'a guy. Get the job done. That's the best calling card."

Norm nodded and smiled. "Maybe I'm imagining things." He put the cards in his pocket. "Let's go back to the security office and get you a backstage pass."

Oh no. Joshua smiled to make sure his face didn't show concern. "Really? You're going to make me wear a security badge?" Joshua had planned on getting Norm to show him something else before they went to the security office. He wasn't ready for him to cross paths with Seth and risk the other security guard mentioning the ladies.

"Yeah, I was just talking to the boss about the need to maintain protocols in light of the incident. All visitors need to wear a badge. It won't take long."

The look on Norm's face said his mind was made up. Further argument would look suspicious. "Lead the way."

Following Norm, Joshua let his fingers snake under the edge of his jacket. He held them there for a moment, mentally rehearsing a fast draw of his gun, just in case.

Ibbie straightened in her chair. The headphones were around her neck. With three open cell phone audios going it was easier to keep them separate over the external speakers.

Keeping on top of things was essential now. Marsha was still running the data-mining program in the upstairs office. The miner was identifying relevant files on the DNAble network and copying them to the hard drive. She could hear the girls over Amelia's phone. They still had to install the spyware when the mining was finished. They needed more time.

Now, Norm and Joshua were headed to the security office. Over Marsha's confiscated phone, she could tell that Seth had not left the office. The other guard had gone back on patrol around the grounds, but Seth still occupied the room, occasionally clicking mouse buttons. If Seth and Norm had time to talk, the subject of the girls he had taken upstairs would come up and Norm's suspicions were alerted already. He could put it all together. Then Joshua would have both of them to contend with.

Joshua and Norm approached a door labeled Security

Office, and Norm took out his key card. Suddenly the door opened and a big man in a security uniform hustled out.

Norm came face to face with him. "Where are you going?"

"Mr. Herschlag wants me up in his office. I guess he needs to get a report done because there's some guy coming from the main office, and he has to have the report finished so this guy can take it back with him. He needs my statement."

Norm looked at Joshua.

Joshua juggled mentally. The real Herschlag would not know about Joshua being there. *It had to be Gabriel.* He gave a nod and shrug. "That's another thing they wanted me to do while I'm here."

Norm frowned. "No wonder he didn't seem himself today. Your office must really be jerking his chain over this. You know that's going to roll downhill on me."

Joshua looked at Seth who seemed to be engrossed in the gossip. He needed to get rid of him. Time to exert some authority. "You better get going so Mr. Herschlag can get his report done. Your boss and I need to talk."

Seth looked at Norm who nodded. The big man hurried down the hall and disappeared around the corner.

They had prevented Seth from mentioning Marsha and Amelia to Norm, but now he was going to talk to Herschlag. Marsha and Ibbie would have to stop that meeting. Joshua had no time to think about it. He had to come up with something to say to Norm. The man waited with a curious expression. Joshua took a deep breath. "Let's step inside." What could he say that wouldn't be proven false once Norm and Herschlag got together? They needed DNAble to keep operating normally with no knowledge they had been infiltrated. They still had to put a case together they could give to the locals.

Norm took his curious face into the office. Joshua closed the door behind them. He motioned to the chair behind the desk and seated himself in a guest chair. "Let's sit down."

Norm moved to the chair.

"Norm, how would you like to be running this place?"

The man's face did not move.

He's a cool one. "Here's the deal. The home office is concerned about this incident and the way things are going in general. My bosses aren't stupid. When they see the guy in charge pointing fingers at everyone else, they start doubting that guy is in charge. They are looking to make some changes. I came down here to get the lay of the land. When I see you are the one tapped to give me the tour, even after all the things your boss tried to blame you for, well that tells me who really gets things done around here."

Norm's head came up. That theme registered with him. The ground was fertile. The story had planted a seed of doubt concerning his boss.

"Then I see you checking me out, not being intimidated into shortcutting things, that impresses me again. I'm not one to waste time. It doesn't take me long to assess a situation. What I need to know now is if you're interested in moving up when there's an opening." Joshua purposely said "when" instead of "if."

The face stared back. Norm appeared thoughtful. Joshua tried to imagine what was going on behind the steel gray eyes. He might be wondering if his boss was trying to trap him. He had no verification that Joshua came from the home office. He didn't want to challenge Joshua in case he was telling him the truth, but the man wasn't swallowing the hook yet.

Norm frowned. "That's very disturbing to hear about Mr. Herschlag. I want to do what is best for the company, but Mr. Herschlag is my employer. Are you sure there is nothing I can do to help him get things back on track from the position I am in?" Before Joshua could answer, Norm stood. "It might be better if I show you our operation here before either of us make any decisions. Why don't you let me see your ID so we can get you a visitor badge?"

He was calling the bluff. He had not said no, and he had not burned his bridge with Herschlag in case it was a test. He would check Joshua out before he made a move he couldn't walk away from. When he got the ID, he would be on the phone to the New York office to verify what Joshua told him. Norm was being extremely efficient.

"Sure. I can understand your caution. I've got it right here." Joshua reached his hand toward his back.

"Marsha." Ibbie's voice was sharp and urgent over the cell phone's speaker and brought Amelia to attention. "Security guard Seth is on his way up to see Mr. Herschlag. We can't let that happen. He'll tell him about both you and Joshua. They'll know they have been talking to someone besides Herschlag, and this game will be over."

Marsha swore. "Okay." She looked at the computer and held her hands up in contemplation. She grabbed the cell phone. "I'm on it." She jumped up, heading to the door, firing instructions quickly at Amelia. "This door will lock behind me. Don't let anyone in. If they try…" She looked at Amelia her brow furrowed. She hurried back and looked at the desk phone. "Ibbie, the extension in this office is 6201. Call it and Amelia will put you on speakerphone, so you'll have audio on her location." She addressed Amelia again, "If someone is coming in, hide in the closet." Marsha's eyes had glanced briefly at a door on the other side of the room. "Ibbie will hear it and get you some help." Marsha stripped off her blouse, reversed it and pulled it back on as she talked.

Amelia took it all in, petrified. With Marsha, she had felt secure. Now things were going wrong again. *They got you through the last time. They know what they're doing.* But did they? They adapted, made things work, but what if this time it didn't? She tried to smile at Marsha.

The woman turned, shutting off the speaker on her cell

phone. She put it to her ear as she opened the door. "Okay, tell me what you told Seth."

And like that, Amelia was staring at the closed door. She took quick breaths. Going to the blinds, she peeked through, but Marsha had already rounded the corner.

The phone on the desk rang, startling her. She hurried over and remembered to search for the speakerphone button. When she pressed it, Amelia heard a jumble of conversations on Ibbie's end before the woman spoke.

"I've got you on speaker. I can't talk—too much going on. I'm muting my side, but I can hear you. Don't say anything unless it's an emergency." The noise on the line ceased.

Amelia sat, unmoving. Silence filled the room. Taking a long breath to slow her respiration, she eased herself back to the blinds, afraid to make noise. She had heard Joshua in the background of Ibbie's call, speaking to someone. *"Please, Lord, keep them all safe. Help us get through this."*

A feeling moved in. Amelia shivered. She remembered being sixteen, watching the social worker drive away from her new foster home. Gabe's face pressed against the car window looking at her. She didn't dare whimper, or he would hear her from there. Privately she had told her brother not to let anyone know about his hearing. She hoped he understood. Amelia told him things would be all right, but she had felt helpless. Not only had their parents been killed but also the other missionaries that were supposed to care for them if anything happened. Well, something happened that no one planned for. Their only other family lived in France, too old and with memory problems. She knew she was on her own and had no idea how to get Gabriel back with her.

Amelia's mind returned to the moment, but she still felt helpless. She wondered how Gabe was doing with Ibbie. It had taken her years to get the current situation arranged for her and Gabriel. Why was she jeopardizing it all to run around with a bunch of...? She couldn't even be sure of what they were. *Lord, You probably aren't going to let me in on Your plans here, are You?* She closed her eyes in regret of the sarcasm. She knew God understood. *I don't know why You're like that, but I want You to know it doesn't feel good.* She sighed. The hurt went out from her to the throne of God where it became sorrow for speaking to her Heavenly Father like that. *I trust You. You always know best.* Amelia prayed silently, trying to give her fears to God as she watched the empty hallway.

Ibbie wished she had Gabriel's ears. He sat beside her, but she couldn't ask him to listen to all the sounds coming from the speakers. He would hear it all, but he wouldn't know what to do. Each speaker emitted a separate audio feed from one of the three open cell phone lines.

As Ibbie muted the mic to the office where Amelia hid, she heard Joshua give Norm his identification.

From another speaker came the sound of Marsha skittering down the hallway to intercept Seth.

Norm's voice came over the speaker from Joshua's phone. "I'll get you a badge." A door opened and closed.

She heard the elevator as Marsha came to a stop in front of it, waiting.

Ibbie heard movement and then Joshua's whispered voice. "The extension here is 6300. Norm should be using a phone close to that if he doesn't use his cell phone."

Ibbie moved to the computer that received data from the hardware card that Joshua had installed in the hub of the DNAble phone system. The screen showed several calls in progress. Speech to text software was pulling out keywords and phrases from the conversations and displaying them briefly on the screen next to the call identifiers. It all looked like standard company business. She slipped on the headphones and switched the sound from the speakers to her headset. "Ready, Gabriel?"

The young man rocked in his seat. "Gabriel is Rams Twelve. Rams Twelve is ready."

Ibbie shook her head with a half-smile. "Standby, Rams Twelve." She reached over and straightened some of the cue cards in front of Gabriel, familiarizing herself with the locations of various ones she might need.

A computer beep indicated an outgoing call from extension 6302. Ibbie routed the call to her and Gabriel's headphones and let it go through. She kept their microphones muted so nothing they said would be heard by the people on the line.

Marsha's voice came over the other channel. "Can you call Seth back and have Gabe pretend to be Herschlag again? Tell Seth that he is getting to know my friend, and Seth is supposed to entertain me."

Ibbie unmuted the mic to Marsha. "Sorry love. I can't. I'm on another line already. You'll have to turn on the charm."

Marsha sounded bothered. "My charm wasn't very effective on this guy before. If he doesn't buy it, I may have to kill this—" Ibbie muted Marsha. She couldn't have the sound in the background while dealing with Norm's call.

The call connected and a pleasant woman answered. "DNAble corporate office, how may I direct your call?"

"This is Norm Salzman. Put me through to Keith Putts in your security office."

Ibbie grabbed a large index card and wrote "Keith Putts" on it.

"Thank you, Mr. Salzman. Please hold while I connect you to Mr. Putts' office."

The phone rang again. They were in luck. The receptionist transferred directly without telling Putts who was calling. Ibbie pressed a record button and captured the sound of one of the rings. The sound wave icon appeared on the screen.

Ibbie put Norm's line on hold and grabbed the recording of the ring and dropped it at the end of the indicator for Norm's line. She pressed the loop button on the recording leaving Norm to listen to the looped recording of the ring.

The real line quit ringing. "Mr. Putts' office." The woman was all business.

Ibbie grabbed a large index card on which she had earlier written Norm Salzman's name. She pulled one of the cue cards in front of Gabriel and put the index card with Norm's name after the other card. She pulled another card down and put the card with Keith Putts' name after that. Ibbie pointed at Norm's name. "In this voice." She clicked off the mute.

Gabriel read the cards. "Hi. This is Norm Salzman." And it was, at least his voice. Gabriel read on. "May I speak with Keith Putts?"

The woman's voice turned friendly. "Norm, how are you doing? You weren't even going to say hi to me?"

Ibbie hit the mute key. She had no time to curse her luck that had reversed so suddenly. She put together an idea. She looked at Gabriel, told him what to say, and unmuted the mic.

Norm's voice again poured smoothly from the young man's mouth, matching the friendly tone Ibbie had used. "I'm sorry. The line's bad on this end. You didn't sound like yourself. How are you?"

"I'm good. When are you coming up to see us again?"

Ibbie looked at the ring recording icon at the end of Norm's line. How long would he listen to the ring before hanging up?

She muted Gabriel's mic. "Say, 'I'm sorry. I've got something going on here. Can you switch me over to Keith really fast? I'll give you a call later and we'll chat.'"

Gabriel said the line when Ibbie unmuted.

"Oh. I'm sorry. Hang on." The woman sounded rattled, and the line went on hold.

Ibbie muted the mic, took a breath and spoke to Gabriel "When he comes on, listen just long enough to know his voice then nod your head at me. I'm going to switch you over to Norm's phone. I want you to use Putts' voice and say, 'Hey, Norm. Sorry about the wait. What's up?' Do you understand?"

Gabriel rocked back and forth looking unsure.

Ibbie bent down and looked in his face. He looked away and Ibbie spoke softly in his ear. "You're a great agent." She sensed she saw a smile form on his lips, but she had no time to be sure.

A male voice came on the line. "Norm, it's good to hear from you. How are things in Arkansas?"

Gabriel listened to his greeting then nodded. Ibbie switched Gabriel over to Norm's line and put Putt's on hold. *We'll call him back later and say we must have gotten disconnected. Okay, Norm. I hope you were patient.*

Gabriel said his line perfectly.

Norm sounded miffed. "Hey, Keith. I was about to hang up. Am I catching you at a bad time?"

Ibbie didn't waste time being relieved Norm hadn't hung up. She muted the mic, gave Gabriel his next line and unmuted.

"You know how it is." Gabriel now had Putts' voice down. "Always something. But I've got a few minutes I can give you. What do you need?"

"I've got a Tanner Hughes down here. He says he's from the main office. Do you know him?"

Ibbie had a card ready for that question. She pulled it in front of Gabriel, and he started reading. "He's a troubleshooter for the brass. If he's down there, it means something's up. He's got the ear of the big man, so it's always a good idea to stay on his good side. That's about all I can tell you about him. He operates outside of my influence." Ibbie slid the next card. "Listen, I need to let you go. I've got something going on here that I need to look into. Hope that helps."

"Yeah. That's what I needed to know. Sorry to bother

you."

She pulled another card, thankful she could use them. She feared Norm might notice the pause if she had to make up another response.

"Not a problem. We'll talk more when we're not so busy."

"Sounds good. Thanks. Bye."

Ibbie ended the call. She let her body fall back against the reclining back of the chair and blew out a breath. Pulling off her headphones, she unmuted the other speakers. She heard Marsha's voice midsentence.

"...telling you the truth. If you go in there, he is not going to be happy."

Marsha looked sweetly into Seth's face. Her southern drawl entreated him. "I told you, that thing before was a misunderstanding. We got it all worked out with Mr. Herschlag. But he wanted to talk to my friend alone. He told me to tell you he would call you later and you could work on that report then." She had her body between Seth and Mr. Herschlag's door. "Please don't ruin this for my friend. Mr. Herschlag said he might have a job for us, and he wanted to interview her first. Let's just go back to that room you had us in. Who knows, maybe we'll grow on each other." She put her hand lightly on the big guard's shoulder and pouted her lips. She had perfected the pose over the years—innocence and enticement bundled together.

And if he doesn't buy it soon, he's in a perfect position for me to drop him with a knee to the groin. Then I can slit his throat. Marsha's other hand removed a switchblade from a slot in her waistband and kept it palmed. The only thing that mucked it up was how to hide the blood and the body. If murder wasn't such a messy business, Marsha was sure there would be a lot more of it. It solved so many problems. She should probably just let Seth go inside and then she could shoot both him and Herschlag. The big boss's office walls should be insulated enough to cover the sound of silenced rounds. If she timed it right and dropped them in the right location, a tasteful area rug would cover the stains and enhance the décor. No one would question it. They could get the bodies out in a cleaning cart if they were folded right before rigor mortis set in.

Seth's phone rang. Marsha watched him as he talked, letting her face fall into her ditsy look. *That's probably Ibbie. She would call right when I'd worked myself up for a good kill.*

Seth fawned to his fake boss. "Don't worry, Mr. Herschlag, I won't tell a soul about any of this. No, especially not Norm. Seth nodded for a few more seconds and ended the call. "That was Mr. Herschlag."

"See I told you." Marsha put on her *I wouldn't lie* face.

"Okay, I'm supposed to take you back to the conference room. Lucky for you, he called."

"Yeah. Lucky for me." Marsha batted her eyelashes. When Seth turned to lead her to the conference room, she slipped the knife back in her waistband.

Joshua looked smugly at Norm when he returned. "So, find out what you wanted to know?"

Norm handed him an entry key card and an ID that said, "VIP Guest." "I run a tight ship, Mr. Hughes. What we are doing is too important not to. I hope you didn't take offense. I'm just trying to do my job well."

"Wouldn't have it any other way." Joshua rose. "Now, show me the rest of the place. By the way, how are your presentation skills? If the operation looks as good in person as it looks on paper, I might want you to speak to some of our backers. They want to know where their money is going. I want you to teach it to me just like you would to someone that didn't have any knowledge of the company's operation or the goals and objectives. Make me a believer, Norm. Make me a believer."

"Amelia." Ibbie's voice on speakerphone startled her, again. "Marsha's tied up with that security guard. You'll have to finish up the computer work. I'll walk you through it."

"Okay. Is Marsha all right?"

"If you call having to entertain that baboon Seth 'all right.' The faster you can get this done, the faster you can get Marsha out of that situation."

"*I'm* going to get her out of the situation?"

"Yes. First, tell me what's on the computer screen."

Amelia examined the display. "It looks like it's running a lot of things. There's a progress bar that says 93% complete."

"Good. We're getting close. While you're waiting, search around in the drawers there and find an envelope that can hold standard size sheets of paper. Make sure it can be tightly sealed. Get about twenty sheets of blank paper out of a printer and put it in the envelope. Leave everything how you found it when you're done. We don't want any evidence you were ever in that office. You should wipe off your fingerprints, but the most important thing is we don't want anyone to have reason to print the room."

"How's Gabe?" Amelia had never known Gabriel to be able to be away from the home for so long and do so well.

Ibbie chuckled. "We've created a monster."

In the background, Amelia heard her brother saying,

"Gabriel not monster. Gabriel is Rams Twelve. Rams Twelve is agent."

Chapter 15

The door opened and Joshua climbed the stairs to the viewing area of Laboratory Number One. The room had a sealed, glass-window view of the laboratory on the lower level. Glass enclosures divided the room below into several sections where various stages of the process took place. People moved around the lab wearing blue lab uniforms, protective gloves, and facemasks. Even with that level of protection, robotic equipment did much of the work to limit human interaction with the precious samples. Norm led Joshua through the steps of extracting the DNA for a sample, then processing it into a display that could be read by experts in the DNA reading rooms and entered into the computer database.

Joshua listened as Norm expounded. "With DNAble becoming the fastest growing lab, we have the unique opportunity to change our world. Over 26 million people have submitted to DNA testing. It's a popular gift item now. Did you get a chance to see our 'Give the gift that goes deeper than the heart' ad campaign?"

Joshua nodded. "It made DNA testing sound like the most

intimate thing you can do for someone you love. Better than a diamond."

Norm shared the smile. "We live in a narcissistic society. Everything is all about 'ME.' And there's nothing more 'ME' than DNA. At the rate it is increasing, within two years there could be over 100 million people who have their genetic information in commercial databases. We are currently in a position where it is possible to trace the relationship between most Americans, even if they have never taken a test. With that kind of power, it will not be long before we begin to see results in our mission to purify humanity. We are also taking aggressive steps to build DNAble's database beyond those people we test directly. We are tapping into the databases of the other major testing services in a couple of ways. We're offering a rebate to customers who have had tests from other labs, if they are willing to share the results with us. Since most ancestry experts say that having tests done in multiple labs increases the person's ability to find relationships with other people, a lot of people are taking advantage of that offer. While it doesn't give us as much information as collecting an actual sample, it is significant in helping build our picture of the human family tree. We have also invested heavily in developing friends on the inside of some of the other companies. That has enabled us to obtain data on people the other companies are testing. We have the largest database of human DNA information in existence. Though some of it cannot be shared with our customers, Becker is making use of it."

Joshua saw an opportunity to explore weaknesses in DNAble's security the team might exploit. "Is there any chance that might come back to haunt us? How are we protecting ourselves from someone finding out we have DNA information from people we didn't test?"

Norm smugly turned up one side of his mouth as if ready with that answer. "We are in the best of situations right now. That is why we are moving quickly before the climate changes. There isn't much regulation of the DNA testing industry. The business is so new and technical that the feds don't know what to do with it. They are also scared of its popularity. No one wants to be on the wrong political end of people not getting what they want. The FDA and FTC have done a little saber-rattling in our direction, but for the most part, they are staying out of our business. At the same time, there is enough outcry about potential privacy concerns that we can easily justify not cooperating with authorities." Norm gave Joshua a conspiratorial raise of his head. "We fight hard to protect our customer's privacy." He gave a sniff of a laugh. "Fortunately, the average person is more concerned with what the government might find out about them than they are with what we do with their information. I don't even think people have that much to hide. But it's the 'in' thing to hate cops and authority and that works to our advantage."

Joshua put on a concerned look. "I'm sure you're not getting too comfortable in that position though. What's your data security like?"

"We have our own onsite servers in the basement with limited access to them. We have one set for the legitimate testing business and another set for anything that is more sensitive. The latter is in a separate location that isn't even on the blueprints. That's where we have a large chunk of the company's money invested in what I like to call 'little brother.' That's the supercomputer doing Becker's number crunching. We know so much about people, sometimes it scares me."

Nodding to convince Norm that he liked what he heard, Joshua pressed on. "Who has access?"

"Herschlag and I have administrative access so we can supervise it. The working access is limited to Becker's group for their research. Members of his team put together the targeting reports for our outside teams to work on. The only terminals accessing those servers are in the server room and in the downstairs lab."

Joshua continued his satisfied look while processing the inward disappointment. *They were going to need access to the other server.*

Amelia stuffed in the sheets of blank paper. "Okay, the envelope's ready."

Silence. Her heart quickened. If she lost the connection with Ibbie she had no idea how to help Marsha. "Ibbie? Are you there?" Amelia glared at the phone. The light showed the line still open. "Are you there? I'm ready with the envelope."

"Seal it."

Amelia breathed out her relief when she heard Ibbie's voice. "Okay." She ran her tongue across the flap of the envelope and pressed it down with a quick swipe of her finger. "It's sealed."

More silence then Ibbie came back online. "Remember this. The envelope contains a report that Mr. Herschlag completed for Tanner Hughes. You will give it to Seth. You have not seen its contents. It was sealed when Mr. Herschlag handed it to you and told you only Tanner Hughes was to open it."

Amelia absorbed the information. "Got it. Am I supposed to go to the conference room now?"

"How is the data-mining going?"

Amelia glanced at the computer. "It says 'installing.'"

"It's putting our spyware on the network, so we can keep an eye on things remotely. Should be done soon. Gotta take care of some things. Stay put. I'll get back to you."

Amelia heard the jingling of keys in the hallway. Had Marsha gotten herself away from Seth? Her muscles tensed. *Marsha doesn't have keys.*

The speakerphone on the desk came alive with Ibbie's

voice. "Okay, what's the progress on the computer look like?"

Amelia silenced Ibbie by jabbing the button that turned off the speakerphone.

The noise in the hallway stopped. A shadow against the closed blinds turned its head as if listening. It had a manly size and shape. The person heard but apparently wasn't sure the noise came from the office.

Amelia looked at the phone. Pressing the speaker button would have hung up on Ibbie. Marsha hadn't counted on the speakerphone being a liability. Even worse would be for the phone to ring. *Take the hint, Ibbie. Don't call back.*

The computer popped up a box indicating the download was completed. Amelia closed the program, pulled the USB cable free from the computer and hit the shutoff key. She shoved the hard drive in Marsha's purse and slipped the bag in a bottom drawer of the desk. She didn't want anything to incriminate her if she was found. Marsha would be able to retrieve the purse later. The hourglass symbol showed the computer was thinking. She poked the button on the monitor and the screen went dark. The computer could do its thing without the display. *Don't leave any sign you were here.*

The shadow turned its head again then returned to the keys.

Amelia imagined Ibbie continuing to talk until she realized she was no longer on the line. In her mind, Amelia saw Ibbie saying her name with no response. *Please don't call back.*

The shadow selected a key.

Amelia glanced toward the closet Marsha had indicated. She feared the telephone would ring any moment. Spinning the phone around, she eased out the cable. Once she returned the phone to its original position, she made a dashing tiptoe to the closet door.

Behind her, she heard the key being placed in the lock.

She grabbed the doorknob but it wouldn't turn. The knob was big and thick. On the face of it was a keypad with indented numbers like a telephone. It needed a code to open.

The noise of the key in the lock stopped. The person was searching through the keys, trying different ones to see which worked.

Please, Lord. I don't know what I'm doing here. If it was really You that brought me into this, please help me. Amelia glanced around the room. The only other hiding place was under the desk. She headed toward it. The shelf was there, above the bar—her jam, the man's picture. Amelia froze. The full-size visage of the man was sitting in the chair. It was in her mind but felt real. The scene played before her eyes like an opaque movie. The man rose from the desk where her jam sat open, a butter knife laying across it. The dark threatened but something more bright and powerful pushed it down and held it squirming on the floor—just a feeling, nothing visible. The man wiped his sticky fingers on his shirt, walked toward her, and like that, the vision ended with the sound of keys jangling outside the door.

Amelia whirled, in fear that the fragile thought might leave her brain. At the closet door she ran her fingers across the keypad. On certain keys she could feel it, inlaid in the indents of the numbers—a hint of sticky. She started at the beginning and when her finger landed on the first tacky key, she pushed it. Then the next and the next until she reached the end. Taking hold of the knob she twisted and it turned. She shivered and pulled on the door. As it came away from the frame, it felt unreal, like it could be her imagination. The feeling dissipated as the opening widened.

A metal panel confronted her. *This isn't a closet.* She nearly screamed when the metal slid aside with a mechanical hum. It took a moment for her to realize she was looking into a private elevator.

A glance over her shoulder showed the door still closed. That would not last long once the person got the right key. Amelia hesitated for a second then slipped inside the elevator and closed the outer door.

She stared at the wood grain before her. The metal door started to close. The noise and the fear of being trapped inside the strange apparatus overwhelmed Amelia. She put her foot in the door to stop it. The door pushed against her shoe and wedged it against the side of the elevator entrance. A warning bell began to chime. The elevator held her foot fast in its grip. In a panic, Amelia jabbed at the buttons at the side of the door to get it to open. The button with the "L" beside it lit up, but the door continued its warning. With a mighty jerk, she freed her sneaker from the metal grip. The chime stopped and the door continued its interrupted course and sealed her in.

Amelia felt a lurch, in the elevator and in her emotions. The elevator car descended. She examined her enclosure. Where was it taking her? The "L" button was still lit. On the same panel was an emergency stop switch. She reached for it but hesitated. Would it also sound an alarm?

The elevator continued its descent.

Looking up, she wondered if she could hide on top of the elevator as they did in the movies. There appeared to be a hatch in the ceiling, but it had a keyed lock and was out of her reach. The car continued moving. It was a two-story building. Had she gone past the first floor?

The elevator stopped. She jerked when the metal door moved out of the way. She was staring at wood grain again.

Amelia considered the door. She had gone down. Whoever had been trying keys to get in Becker's office must have heard all the noise she had made. Was that person calling to have her intercepted on this floor or could they make the elevator return? If she was inside the elevator when either of those things happened, she would be trapped. Staring at the door, she wondered what was on the other side? She couldn't hear anything. *You can't afford to panic like that. Act like you know what you're doing.* Amelia took the handle of the door in her grip. She took a deep breath, squared her shoulders, lifted her head, and pushed it open.

Marsha sat across from Seth looking fascinated with his tale about his mercenary training in Guatemala. She wished she had kept her knife handy to cut out his tongue. *I need to get back to Amelia. What are you doing, Ibbie?* She watched Seth's Adam's apple move as he talked about how there weren't any women in the group because it was too dangerous. *One quick kick would crush his trachea and shut him up.* She would have liked to have seen him in the camp she went to when MI6 first loaned her to the Israelis. *You wouldn't last the first day on an Israeli mission.* Israeli women knew how to fight, and the men respected them.

Seth's phone rang. Marsha smiled patiently as the man responded with several 'Yes, sirs' and then hung up. Her face conveyed disappointment that Mr. Herschlag needed Seth to handle an important matter. She held the look until the door closed behind him leaving her alone in the conference room. The jingle of Seth's keys indicated he was locking the door. *After all our time together and you still don't trust me?*

She pulled out her own phone and addressed Ibbie. "It's about time."

"I know. I've been busy. I've got a lot of conversations I'm monitoring. But listen. I've lost contact with Amelia. The phone went dead and now she's not picking up." Ibbie sounded concerned.

Marsha was already kneeling before the locked door with her picks in her hand.

As Amelia opened the elevator compartment door, she saw a desk with a large computer monitor and an empty chair. Behind it, the walls of the office were glass with a view through to a room full of white. There were countertops with shelves above and doors and drawers below, all white and sanitized looking.

She saw no one in the rooms. Amelia let out her breath.

While the office was ordinary, the walls were not. White beams framed the sealed glass about five feet apart, resembling an aquarium with no water or fish. A tight door led into a smaller glass-enclosed area, like an airlock prior to the main room. Several spacesuit looking outfits hung on hooks with the backs open down past the waist so someone could step into them. Helmets with large clear face shields sat on one end of a white counter. The other end housed a sink for cleanup prior to entry into the sterile world.

Inside the main room, there were white machines on the counters that resembled large desktop computer printers, but they were different somehow. Some had round hatches. Likewise, items that resembled refrigerators sat around the room, but they gave the impression something sat inside more important than milk and baloney. Finally, some color registered. On some of the countertops were clear plastic encasements—smaller aquariums within the aquarium. Ultraviolet lights revealed racks of test tubes inside with lids of red, blue, green, purple and several other colors. Red LED numbers displayed on the white tops covering the clear enclosures. Boxes and bottles sat on the shelves above the counters, and their labels also expressed various hues. Still, everything about the room screamed, "Don't contaminate me."

She tried another door on the sidewall of the office. It was locked. There was a black box on the wall next to it that she guessed was a card key reader. She looked back at the open door to the elevator compartment. The inside sliding door was also open. If she didn't close the hinged door, maybe the sliding door would also stay open and the elevator couldn't return and the door in the office above would stay locked. But would that be an indicator that someone had taken the elevator down? She decided to leave the door open, hoping no one could follow her. The office afforded no hiding place. The door to the "clean" room had a metal handle with no lock and no card entry.

Amelia crossed to it and stood, staring at the handle. *Alarm or no alarm?* She visually searched the edges for anything suspicious but had no idea what to look for. Through the glass, she could see across the room to several doors with large windows. Maybe one led to an exit or at least a place to hide until Marsha or Joshua could find her.

Would they try to find her, or had she become a liability? Would they leave her? Why had she ever imagined she could do this? She wasn't one of them. *Please, God. I need to get back to Gabriel, and I don't want to let Joshua down. This is so important and I'm messing up.* What if someone caught her? They would kill her. No, they would do worse. *I don't know if I can stand torture.*

Amelia felt tears forming in her eyes. Images of another closed door flashed in her mind. A professional sounding female voice spoke on the other side. "The girl is troubled. She feels responsible for her brother now that their parents are gone, but she is not equipped to care for him. The agency is not asking you to take on the boy. He will go to a special facility. In between the meltdowns, he's been nearly unresponsive since we took custody of him. The Mexican authorities said he was the same with them. The only trouble you'll have with the girl is that she will try to find ways to get her and her brother back together. But the sooner both of them get used to living separate lives, the better it will be. We can't let her ruin her future trying to care for someone who will never progress past where he is now. She's a bright girl, but at her age, she needs to concentrate on her education and having fun. Transitioning from the homeschooling environment she was raised in will be enough of a challenge for her. I understand her parents were conservative Christians. She must have been very restricted."

Amelia clenched her teeth and her eyes, trying to squeeze out the memory. She was not that girl. The feelings of helplessness stabbed at her like a knife-wielding assailant. The years in foster care separated from her brother, watching the toll it took on him, working jobs after school, saving every penny for the lawyer to fight for custody of Gabriel. She tried to bring her mind back. Focus on the good, working at the restaurant, showing them she could cook, getting the job at Gabriel's home, finally winning the fight for Gabe.

But Amelia couldn't focus. The bad thoughts elbowed their way in. What if she didn't make it out? The godparents she had chosen for Gabriel would take care of him, but she didn't want him to have to go through that kind of shock again. They had worked so hard to build a stable life. Why had she jeopardized that?

Amelia shook out her hair, tossing the memories with it. She grabbed the handle and pushed the door open.

No alarm…that she heard.

She struggled into one of the suits hanging on the wall, managing to make the oversized garment work by adjusting straps that were built in. The straps pulled the suit closed in the back and fastened in the front. She grabbed a helmet from the table and slipped it over her head, tucking her hair inside the neck of the suit so it wouldn't show. Then she hurried through the next door into what she decided must be some type of laboratory. The suit was not airtight, and a few moments after entering the room Amelia distinguished a lingering odor that brought back memories of high school lab classes when her foster family put her into public school.

She moved between the countertops and devices until she stood before one of the doors. Peering in the window, she jumped. A face stared back at her.

Joshua stretched as he spoke to Norm. "I think I need a bathroom break. You have any coffee around here?"

"That sounds like a good idea." Norm yawned.

"Great. If you have a packet of creamer and a couple of sugars that would make it even better."

"Should be able to manage that. I'll see you back in my office. Your card will get you in my waiting room."

In the bathroom, Joshua checked to be sure he was alone and put his earpiece in his ear. "How is everything going?"

He recognized stress in Ibbie's voice that others wouldn't detect. "Amelia's out of contact."

"What?" Joshua had trained to manage the unexpected, but panic rose in him. "What happened?"

"They were working on the download and the install, but Marsha had to leave her to stop Seth from talking to Herschlag. I was keeping contact with Amelia through a DNAble line, but the phone went dead, and I can't get her back."

"Okay, I'm breaking it off with Norm. Where was she when you lost contact?"

"Slow down. I knew you would want to know, but don't make me sorry I told you. Marsha is heading that way. Remember, your job is Norm. Marsha will take care of Amelia. Think about it. Norm hasn't gotten any calls or messages. I think if she had been caught, they would be alerting him. She probably got scared and is hiding like Marsha told her to do."

Joshua ran it through his mind. *Please, Lord. Let that be it.* "Okay, but I still want to know where she was when you last talked to her."

Ibbie didn't answer.

"You seem unusually concerned about my ability to act appropriately." Joshua tried to keep the anger out of his voice.

"I know you better than anyone. I can tell Amelia's different. I know you can handle things, but there is nothing wrong with an agent keeping an eye on her best partner. If I lose you, I want it to be because you and Amelia are making a better life somewhere not because you were distracted."

Joshua didn't know what to say. It felt like Ibbie could see a running narrative of what had been going through his mind the last few days. "I shouldn't have brought Amelia into this, but I hoped Gabe would give us the edge to make this go smooth. We should have aborted when she went into DNAble."

"I don't think Amelia would agree with that. She decided to be a part of this because she saw that it was something worth doing. I heard what Norm told you. You and I know getting access to that other server needs to be your priority and Amelia would understand that too."

He let the anger drop. She was right. It felt like something was gripping his insides, but he had to get back to the mission.

Ibbie's tone softened. "But just in case, you should know where Marsha is headed. They were doing the download in an office belonging to Frank Becker. It's on the second floor, west end. I'm guessing it is the same Becker that Norm told you about. Marsha found out he was away for the day, so the office was supposed to be empty. Now that I have access to the DNAble network, I looked up Becker. He runs a project called 'The Ultimate Answer' but there's no information for it. I had a thought, though. Remember what Hitler called his plan to exterminate the Jews?"

"The final answer to the Jewish question."

"Yeah. Sounds ominously familiar doesn't it?"

"Sure does." All Joshua could think of was Amelia in the middle of it. "How far away is Marsha?"

"She should be at the office by now."

"I've got to get back to Norm. Text me the moment she

finds out anything."

Marsha stopped at the door to Becker's office and listened. She heard nothing. *She's probably hiding in the closet. Someone probably walked by and spooked her.* The reasoning didn't satisfy Marsha. Amelia seemed too smart to be hiding for no reason.

She quietly put her picks in the lock and had the door open in less than a minute. Pulling the gun from her ankle holster, Marsha entered the room. It was dark just as she and Amelia had left it when they had been in the offices. There was nothing in the outer room that said anything had changed there. She didn't take time for a thorough search or risk someone in the inner office seeing her before she got the drop on them. Her concern pulled her toward the place where she had last seen Amelia. Moving to the doorway of Becker's office, she peeked around the frame a little at a time, scanning the room in small chunks as more of it came into view. There was the desk. The hard drive was gone, and the computer was off. The door to the closet was open. The frame around the lock was broken. But it wasn't a closet. There was a metal panel behind the door. *That wasn't on the blueprints.*

Something popped behind her. Her instinct tried to turn and engage the threat, but it was too late. Her muscles locked up and she felt herself falling as the first wave of pounding painful electricity coursed through her body.

Amelia relaxed when she saw that the face staring at her

belonged to a child. The toddler stood in the middle of a surface covered in white vinyl mats. The little one stared up at her with a mix of fear and anticipation. She couldn't tell if the child was a boy or a girl. The sparse hair was wispy, making it look bald. Amelia judged the features to be more feminine. It wore what could have been a plain white dress, but the gown looked clinical and unisex. Still, Amelia found herself thinking of her as a little girl. The top of the girl's overlarge head showed veins through the olive skin. Her thin frame had a malnourished appearance.

Amelia glanced around, still alone. Who was caring for the child? Trying the door, she found it unlocked. As Amelia opened it, the child's eyes widened, and she quickly tottered, half dragging a malformed leg, to a mattress on the floor in the corner and threw a blanket over herself. Amelia tried the handle on the other side of the door. It was locked on the inside. She took a rolling chair from under a counter and used it to wedge open the door. Stepping inside, she could hear the child crying across the room.

Amelia called softly to the toddler. "It's okay. I'm not going to hurt you."

When the little one heard her voice, she cried louder.

Another voice made Amelia jump. "Leave her alone, you monster."

Amelia spun around. No one.

"I know what I say means nothing to you…" The high-pitched voice sounded muffled. It must be coming from one of the other rooms. "…but I'll keep telling you. You're monsters, all of you. She's just a baby."

Amelia moved the chair and followed the sound.

"The fact that you don't care makes you even more of a monster. You know it's true. It's not okay no matter how you try to justify it."

Amelia passed two more of the doors. The voice came from the last room. From her angled view of the door's window, she saw movement.

"You'll rot in hell for what you're doing. It doesn't matter why. It's not right. It doesn't matter what you think, you're going to find out. You hear me? It doesn't matter."

The window came clearly into Amelia's view. She drew in a breath. A wrinkled face glared back at her. Large, angry eyes sat between tiny ears on an abnormally large upper head. The bottom of the face was smaller with a little hooked nose and equally petite chin. The face looked ancient, but something in the puffy eyes projected the fire of youth.

The individual inspected Amelia through the clear plastic of the helmet that Amelia wore. "You're new. What pile of dung did they find you under?"

The statement flabbergasted Amelia.

"What are you staring at? That pretty face won't last you long. At least my ugly is on the outside. I can close my eyes and still see the kind of ugly you are."

"I'm not..." Amelia stopped. *How much should I tell...* Again, Amelia felt she saw something feminine in the mouth and cheeks, but it was harder to tell through the wrinkles and sagging skin. "I'm not going to hurt her."

The person in the window examined her while processing the statement. "Then what are you doing here?"

Amelia decided to change the subject. "What's your name?"

The face darkened and the eyes glistened. The person's protruding Adam's apple constricted in a swallow. The eyes blinked and then drilled Amelia with a stare as the squeaky voice spoke. "You have no feelings at all, do you? It doesn't matter. The fact that I don't have a name doesn't say anything about me. It says something about you. It makes it easier for you if you don't name us, doesn't it? Just like you don't name a chicken you're going to butcher. You can call me a number all you want. It doesn't mean I'm worthless."

The emotion in the odd voice touched Amelia. "No one gave you a name? What do people call you?"

The face jerked as if Amelia had struck it. The eyes gave

Amelia a deep examination. "You really don't know anything about us, do you? Who are you?"

Amelia reached under the hood and wiped her eyes. She looked around. The suit wasn't protecting her. It was meant to keep her from contaminating the room, but she didn't care anymore. She pulled off the helmet and let it drop on the floor.

The individual behind the door scrutinized her.

Amelia moved close to the glass, batting her lashes at the tears. "You really don't have a name?"

The person spoke flatly. "Primary Subject Sixteen. But all my friends just call me Sixteen." The statement projected obvious sarcasm.

Amelia shook her head. "That's all they call you? Didn't you have a name before you came here?"

"What do you mean, before… Who are you? Do you even work for Becker?"

"No." Amelia deliberated before saying, "I am just inspecting the work here."

Primary Subject Sixteen sneered. "Inspecting?"

"Yes. I need to know what's happening here. Tell me what they have been doing to you. Maybe I can help."

The face took on a wary but hopeful expression. "Can you get us out of here?"

Amelia didn't know how to answer. She didn't know if she could get herself out. "I can't promise anything right now. I'm here with friends but I got separated and I…don't know if they can wait."

"Does Becker know you're here?"

"Who's Becker? All I know about him is his name."

Primary Subject Sixteen's face dropped out of sight so all Amelia could see were the large eyes over the bottom of the glass and she realized the person had been standing on tiptoes. The eyes narrowed as if in pain. The individual looked back at Amelia. "Open the door. I'm not talking through this glass anymore."

Amelia reached for the handle, but it was locked.

Sixteen's face moved close to the door. Eyes fixed on Amelia. "There's an extra deadbolt. The keys are in the drawer below the centrifuge."

Amelia looked around. "What's the centrifuge?"

"That square white machine with the two blue knobs sitting on the bench over there." Sixteen pointed behind Amelia.

Amelia got the keys. Sixteen watched her carefully. Focusing on the deadbolt above the doorknob, Amelia inserted the key, unlocked it and turned the handle. The door was yanked inward out of her hand. Amelia turned, stunned as a form clad in the same type of white gown as the little girl raced across and grabbed a glass bottle from a countertop. The bottle shattered against the edge of the counter, and Sixteen whirled to face Amelia with the jagged remains pointing at her. The person looked like a deranged ancient old woman the size of an emaciated 10-year-old. The bald head suggested she could have been stricken by cancer. The gown hung tilted on the body that was too thin to keep it straight. The loose white fabric heaved with the figures breathing, and Amelia could hear a wheeze at the end of each respiration.

Sixteen bared thin crooked teeth and the squeaky voice sounded nasty as it said, "Don't move or I'll cut you."

Chapter 16

Ibbie listened through the phone in Marsha's pocket, her guts twisting with each groan from the woman that was her partner and friend. It took everything to focus and run through her options in her head. She couldn't call Joshua. He would have to extract himself from Norm and get upstairs somehow without arousing suspicion. Then how would he engage the man without endangering Marsha, himself, the mission? If something went wrong, they would never get Amelia out. Only one person was in danger right now. They needed to get into the basement lab and if Joshua had to leave Norm now, that might not happen. Many more lives depended on exposing DNAble. She had to keep the mission first. If she acted too quickly, made an error…*Please forgive me, Marsh.*

The pop had been a taser. She knew the sound. Whoever, the attacker was, he had not wanted to kill Marsha…yet. Ibbie needed to find out what was going on. She kept her microphone muted and listened. The taser had kept firing past the standard five-second cycle, so she knew the person operating it had been continuously pulling the trigger to keep Marsha down. She heard what were probably zip ties being used to restrain the incapacitated woman. *You're real brave. Tase her from behind and then zip tie her while she can't move.* Finally, the taser had stopped and so had Marsha's moaning.

"You are alive." A man's voice spoke. Ibbie heard him moving, perhaps picking up something from the floor. The slide of a semi-automatic handgun was activated, and a round hit the floor.

It must be Marsha's weapon. He checked to see if it was loaded.

"If you want to stay that way you will be quiet."

Ibbie heard the man searching Marsha. The sounds found their way to where the phone was stashed, and she heard the thumps and rustling against the microphone. Quickly she sent some remote commands to the phone. The audio became clearer as the phone left the pocket. It made a thump as the man laid it on something nearby. Ibbie sent more instructions to the phone. She heard the man moving around.

If he was part of DNAble security, he would be calling for backup. He wasn't behaving like local law enforcement. Must be Fighters for Israel. *So, you're here already and you're inside.* He had gotten past them and DNAble. *You're good. Now, what's your plan?* The FFI's usual course of action was to destroy the building with explosives. One lone man on the inside wasn't making sense. Ibbie waited and listened to see what she could learn. *I am so sorry, Marsh.*

The man spoke again. "You do not work for DNAble. Who are you?"

Marsha responded. "I do work here. I'm in the office down the hall. I saw someone go in here and I got my gun from my purse to find out what was going on. This office is supposed to be closed. There are so many workplace shootings a girl can't afford not to be packing."

The taser fired again and Marsha let out a whimpering sound of pain that vibrated with the spasms of her muscles. Ibbie knew what it felt like. She had been tased before and had felt the cascading waves of pounding, stinging pain going back and forth through her body like an electric fence on steroids.

The cycle ended. "And yet you had to pick the lock to enter. Your beauty may turn some men's brains to mush, but surely you would not expect me to believe that? I need you to call your friend that went down the elevator and have them come back up."

Marsha took deep breaths. "I wish I could call my friend. The security guard took my partner's phone. They've been chasing us, and we got separated. The truth is we're private detectives working on a lawsuit case against DNAble, but we got caught. If you let me go, I'm outta here before the cops show up. I am guessing that you scared my partner when you came in here and he went down the elevator. He's on his own now."

The man mused over Marsha's statement. When he spoke, he sounded speculative. "A quick and effective story designed to get someone other than a DNAble security member to let you go. So, you deduced I'm not security and you quickly fabricated a story to account for you having skills and being armed but something that would make you of no value to me."

The voice paused. "Far too much talent for anything local. FBI undercover perhaps. That would explain the rescue tactics. When you came in, you didn't search this room well enough which allowed me to tase you from behind. Your bearing tells me you are experienced. Why would you make that mistake? You were obviously looking for someone who would not be a threat to you but was possibly in danger. You therefore assumed if there were hostiles involved, they would be openly confronting that individual and not hidden. You were moving quickly, willing to take the risk of not searching, which says you were concerned with the person's welfare. So, a rescue mission involving a comrade with whom you were no longer communicating."

Again, the man seemed to be thinking. "But if you were

FBI, I think you would have identified yourself by now since I know you don't work here. No reason to endure the pain if a tactical team is on the way to save you. You would be better served to go into negotiation mode and stall for time. No, I think your secret is much bigger. The only part that rings true is that you lost contact with the person that took the elevator. And that is unfortunate. My plan hinges on me using that elevator. Every other way requires key cards that I do not have access to. They also require me to pass areas where I am much more likely to contact employees that might inform security."

Ibbie heard the man moving around again. She heard the sound of a chair being pulled closer and someone sitting in it. The voice continued. "But it is a waste of time for me to pursue who you are. It doesn't matter. You are apparently part of some covert operation targeting this place. That is good. We want the same thing. There is no reason I shouldn't share my plans with you. I hope it will make a difference because regardless of who went down that elevator, we need to find a way to communicate with them and tell them to return it. If you will help me with that, I will give you the time you need to leave the building before I destroy it. I intend to leave a pile of rubble where this building used to be, but I have no reason to harm you since I am convinced you are not a part of this organization. If we can get the person that went down to come back up, we can go our separate ways."

Marsha swallowed and exhaled. "What's so important about that elevator?"

Ibbie closed her eyes at the pain she felt inside. *Good girl. You're trying to get information for me, in case he... You know I'd help you if I could.*

More silence from the man before he spoke. "I see no advantage for you to ask that question unless you truly do not know." Another pause. "Since you are in his office, I must assume you know the significance of Dr. Becker's role here."

"This was just an empty office for us to work in." Marsha was so good. Being honest but not telling too much. Trying to draw the man out.

"Perhaps I do have the advantage of having spoken with him personally. Sadly, he will not be here today. In fact, he will not be returning. He had a tragic accident. Fortunately, I obtained his keys before his demise. Interesting that he did not trust the key card system. Did you know that? Kind of a paranoia he had. One of many his demented mind contained. Obviously, you have demonstrated that locks are not so reliable either."

The man gave a sigh and continued. "Perhaps there is someone else you can call that might help us with this little problem." The phone was picked up again. Ibbie heard the rustle against the microphone as the man moved it in his hand.

"Let's you and I come up with another way to reach your friend. My bargain to let you live depends on it. You are so beautiful. I do not want to kill you. I think I can spare a few minutes. Think hard, please." The rapid clicking of the taser returned and the sound tore Ibbie's heart out.

Amelia's shock must have registered on her face because Sixteen's voice softened. "I don't want to hurt you, but I'm not going back in that room, ever."

Amelia watched the pointed shards of glass that Sixteen wielded. "I'll never make you. You don't have to be afraid of me."

"You're right you won't, and you better be afraid of *me*."

Amelia examined the tiny hand that held the broken bottle. It was shaking.

Realizing she had her own body bent forward with hands in a defensive position, Amelia straightened and lowered her arms. "I'm not afraid of you because I don't think you're the type of person who would hurt someone for no reason. I understand that people have hurt you, but I'm not one of those people. I didn't know if it was safe to tell you, but the truth is I'm not supposed to be here and if the people that work here find me, they will kill me. We need to help each other and maybe we can both get out of here."

Sixteen made a noise of acknowledgment. "I could tell you didn't belong here." The old woman looked tired. She let out a resolved exhale. The thin vein-covered arm relaxed but still clutched the broken bottle. The other hand reached out and used the counter for support.

Sixteen's eyes widened suddenly. She spun around with renewed vitality and rushed to a cabinet behind her. Glancing at Amelia, she laid the broken bottle on the counter and pulled out the bottom drawer. With effort, Sixteen lifted the drawer until it came free from its guide and slid completely out of the cabinet. Reaching into the empty space below where the drawer had been, she pulled out a book. The leather cover displayed a cross. She leafed through it and then held it to her chest and sighed. She put it gently below her nose. "Still smells like herring and onions." A tear made its way down the withered cheek. She wiped it away and looked back at Amelia. "If you think you can help me escape, I'm ready to listen. So, who are you really and what are you doing here?"

Amelia inhaled. What did she have to lose—besides time which she might not have much of? "I'm going to give you the quick version because they might already know I'm here, so we have to hurry. I'm helping a group that wants to get evidence against DNAble so they can stop what they're doing. But I almost got caught in Becker's office and had to take his elevator down here. Now, I'm trapped here like you. Is there another way out?"

Sixteen scrutinized Amelia's face as if trying to see inside her and determine if she was lying. She scrunched her forehead one last time then spoke. "I'm Eve. That's the name I call myself when no one else is here. I've never gotten past this outer lab area, so I don't know about a way out after that.

All I know is everyone except Becker leaves out that door each day." Eve pointed to her right.

Amelia felt glad her impression was correct about Eve being female. She walked to the door and the old woman watched, still holding the Bible. Of course, the handle was locked. There was a card reader on the wall to the right. "There wouldn't be a card around here to get us out would there?"

"If there was, I would have been gone a long time ago. Why do you think there's a deadbolt on my door? I've gotten this far too many times to count. Don't bother trying to take the card reader apart or break a window. They won't break and it sets off the alarm."

Amelia raised an eyebrow at the woman.

Eve shrugged. "Just keeping you from wasting time on ways that don't work. Want some more? The walls are solid even above the suspended ceiling, the heating ducts go to that mechanical room over there which there is no way out of." Eve's eyes followed her own memories around the room. "If you try to use acid from that chemical cabinet over there to melt the locks, it just burns your hand." She displayed a scar on her palm. "There's nothing here to make explosives. There are some things that burn, but if you go crazy and try to burn up everyone in the place including yourself, the sprinkler system puts the fire out and they come and wrestle you to the floor and put you back in your cage." Eve's bottom lip quivered. Her eyes had stopped moving and she stared vacantly off into her imagination. "And then they reinforce your cage and install the deadbolt and cut you off from the computers and the internet." She held the Bible closer. "And you're more trapped then you ever were before."

Amelia squeezed back her own tears and started to move toward the woman.

Eve snatched the bottle from the counter and the snarl returned to her voice. "Don't."

"I want to help you. You were alone when you tried

before. We are going to get out of here."

Eve's gaze fell to the floor. "Not always alone." When she looked back at Amelia, her red watery eyes said she was about to reveal even worse pain. "One of the people that worked here felt sorry for me and started letting me out of my cage when the rest of Becker's crew wasn't around. He was a Russian computer programmer named Ivan, and he often worked late into the night. He had become a Christian and stopped believing in what they were doing here, but he was too scared to leave. He gave me this Bible and taught me about God and Jesus."

"Ivan." Amelia gave a scrunched smile at the curious irony. "That's the second DNAble employee that has a name with Jewish roots. I don't think they know their linguistic history very well. Ivan comes from the Hebrew 'Yehohanan' which means 'God is gracious.' In English, we say it as 'John.'"

Eve pondered a moment. "He certainly was God's gift to me. He showed me how to use computers to get on the internet. He couldn't believe how fast I could learn. That's one of the good things my DNA gave me. I don't know if Becker meant to do it or if it was God's joke on him. With Ivan's help, I taught myself to read and went through everything they had on these hard drives. I started to understand what they were doing to us. He gave me his password to get on the DNAble network. That's when I started to think maybe Ivan was right. What Becker was doing to us was wrong. I mean, I trusted Ivan, but I supposed he didn't understand. He was a genius with computers but kind of simple about other things."

"My daddy used to say something." Amelia wished she had Gabriel to speak it in her father's voice. "Listen for the simple things. The truth is usually there."

Eve gazed at Amelia like she had handed her the key to her cell all over again. "Ivan talked like that. He read me Luke 10:21 in the Bible where Jesus says, 'I thank you, Father, Lord of heaven and earth, that You have hidden these things from the wise and understanding and revealed them to little children.'"

"He sounds like a good man."

"He…was." Eve said the word "was" with significance. "We prayed together. He prayed that I would be able to leave this place. He said we could not tell the police or try to contact anyone through the internet because DNAble had spies all over. But he said he was going to find a way. I always believed they just fired him, but after what you said they would do to you..." She looked at Amelia. Her shoulders sagged and the broken bottle hung loosely at her side. "…They probably killed him, didn't they? If they would hurt babies, they would do it to other people wouldn't they? He didn't forget about me. It wasn't possible for him to keep his promise." A mix of emotions shifted across the wizened face. She looked up at Amelia. "But now you're here. Maybe I'm not supposed to die in this place after all." The white gown fell even further to the side as the thin shoulders jerked in a sob.

Amelia became aware of how much time had passed. "Listen to me. We already have a way out." Amelia looked around the counters and through the glass wall into Becker's office. The elevator was still sitting there, open. "No one has come for me yet. The person that I was running from when I came down in the elevator must not have known I was there, or they would have been here by now. We can go back up the elevator. Do you know when the people who work here will come back?"

Eve also looked into Becker's office, composing herself with a breath that sounded hopeful. "The normal staff are gone. They were talking about going to a conference, but they took a lot of stuff out of here, so they may be gone for a while. Seth came in and fed us just before noon, so he won't be back until dinner time. He doesn't like being in here. I can tell."

"Then we should wait a while longer to be sure the person in the office is gone and then take the elevator back up."

"How do we get out of the building?"

"I told you I'm not here alone. My friends already have the way out planned. They don't know where I am right now. In fact, they are probably worried. I hope the woman I was working with didn't come back to the office looking for me and walk into something."

"I hadn't considered the people here hurting other people before you came, but now I am sure you're correct. They would probably hurt your friend."

Amelia reflected on Marsha. "Actually, it might be the other way around." She smiled at Eve. "The people I came with are professionals. My brother and I are the only amateurs."

"Oh." The skin on Eve's forehead lifted accentuating her lack of eyebrows.

Amelia gave her a sheepish expression.

Eve showed a feeble smile. "Hey, I'm out of my cage and there's an elevator waiting for us. I'm not complaining." The smile evaporated. "But if we get caught, you need to know that I'm not going back to that cage. I don't have long left. I want to die someplace besides in there."

Amelia noticed Eve running her thumb over the surface of the broken bottle she still clutched. *So, she is sick.* There were a thousand questions she longed to ask the old woman. But there wasn't time. She turned toward a computer on one of the counters. "We need to get a message to my friends so they will know I'm okay, and they'll need to figure you and the little girl into our exit plans."

"You don't sound like an amateur."

Amelia realized she had repeated the language she had heard Ibbie use in some of their planning. She shrugged. "I'm on the learn-as-you-go plan with this career track. You should have seen me last week."

"How long have you been doing this?"

Amelia bobbed her head back and forth pretending to calculate. "Since last week."

"Okay, but it's not just Chloe…" Eve's face projected a hard sadness. "That's what I named the little girl you were talking to. I refuse to call her Test subject 54." The skin on Eve's forehead scrunched up. "I don't know *your* name."

Amelia looked up from where she had seated herself in front of the computer. "I don't think the people I'm with would want me to say."

"It's okay for you to be the only one that knows my name, but I can't know yours?"

Amelia let out a sigh. "I'm sorry, but these people already know your name, so they won't be torturing me to get it. But they don't know mine. If you're caught, it might not be safe for you to know it."

Eve looked introspective. "They've been torturing me since I was born. Be nice if it was for a reason next time."

Amelia's fingers stopped typing out the message she was creating for Ibbie. She looked in Eve's hard lashless eyes. "We're getting out of here and nobody's being tortured anymore. My name's Amelia."

"Well, Amelia, before you send that message, you need to tell them there will be an extra six for your exit plans."

Ibbie's torment at Marsha's pain lingered even after the taser had stopped. But a flagged message displayed by the spyware on the DNAble computers seized her attention.

EXPLOSIVES, BOMBS, DEATH TO AMERICA, PLOT TO TAKE OVER THE WORLD was the subject line of an email from a generic DNAble account being sent to comments@flyonthewall.com. She read on. SORRY. THIS IS RAMS ELEVEN. I DIDN'T KNOW HOW ELSE TO CONTACT YOU. I'M HOPING THE COMPUTER WILL THINK A MESSAGE WITH THOSE WORDS IN IT IS

IMPORTANT ENOUGH TO WARN YOU ABOUT. SORRY I HAD TO HANG UP ON YOU, BUT I SUDDENLY HAD TO AVOID SOME COMPANY. I AM USING THE EMAIL ON THIS COMPUTER TO SEND THIS TO A CONSPIRACY THEORY WEBSITE I FOUND ON THE INTERNET SO IF THEY DO TELL ANYONE ABOUT IT, NO ONE WILL BELIEVE THEM, BUT I AM HOPING YOUR SOFTWARE WILL PICK IT UP AND YOU CAN FIND OUT WHICH COMPUTER I'M ON AND SEND ME A DIRECT MESSAGE AND GET US OUT OF HERE. I'LL TELL YOU WHO THE US IS WHEN WE CAN TALK DIRECTLY.

Ibbie muttered to herself. "There you are." She sat back shaking her head then turned to Gabriel. "Your sister is one resourceful little cookie." *Why did I send Marsha after her? She can take care of herself and now Marsha is the one in trouble.*

Gabriel looked off to his side and rocked back and forth. "Amelia is Gabriel's sister. Amelia is not a cookie. Amelia is an agent."

Ibbie put on a pleasant expression for Gabriel. "She is. Remind me to put that agent in for a commendation when this is all over."

Gabriel rocked. "Gabriel is good agent."

Ibbie examined the expectant look. "Remind me to put you both in for a commendation."

A hint of a smile registered on the swaying face. "Commendations are for good agents."

It wasn't long before the cloud over her thinking returned. "I have a feeling this 'us' she's talking about is going to complicate things even more. But there is another good agent that needs our help. Your sister sounds safe for the moment. I've got to work on the other problem." *Hang on Marsha. I'm trying to come up with something.* She pulled up the program to send a text to Joshua. *What am I going to tell him?*

Joshua's phone gave a chirp. He smiled at Norm and read the message. WE FOUND OUR MISSING FRENCH POODLE. SHE MANAGED TO GET HERSELF LOCKED IN THE CELLAR. WE'RE TRYING TO FIND A KEY TO GET HER OUT, BUT SHE IS FINE. SHE HAD A LITTER WHILE SHE WAS DOWN THERE. MORE PUPPIES TO CARE FOR. ALSO, THE COMPANY WE WERE EXPECTING SHOWED UP. M IS ENTERTAINING HIM. I HAVE BEEN THINKING A LOT ABOUT THAT TRIP DOWN SOUTH. I THINK IT WOULD BE BETTER IF YOU WENT ALONE. I'LL MAKE THE CALL. SEE YOU WHEN YOU GET HOME. LOVE YOU.

Cellar? She must mean the basement. How did Amelia get in the basement with…a litter? I can't take Norm there for him to find Amelia. She's right. I need to go there alone. The "company" must mean Fighters for Israel. "Him" tells me there's only one. What's Marsha going to do with him? This operation is out of control.

Norm watched him.

"Excuse me. If I don't answer this, she'll keep bothering me." He finger-typed a rapid reply. LEAVE HER DOWN THERE TO CARE FOR HER PUPS. I KNOW WHERE THE KEY IS. CALL LATER. Joshua gave a sigh and shook his head. "My wife. The things she gets into. Always some kind of drama and chaos going on at our house. Now you know why I work so much. Who wants to go home to that?"

Chapter 17

Tears fell from Amelia's eyes as she looked at the five children that she and Eve had released from the rooms. Each little body twisted in some way by heterogeneous deformities. "You mean they experiment on all of you?"

"They told us that's what we were made for. When I was little, I believed it was important and an honor. Even when it hurt, I imagined I was doing something good. That is the way they made it sound. But Ivan told me Becker didn't make me. He said God created us no matter how it happened."

"What do you mean, how it happened?"

"Becker works with a DNA altering technique called CRISPR Cas9. When I could escape from my room at night, I used to study it to try and understand what I was. CRISPR made it easier, cheaper and more accurate to alter DNA. I read where the scientific community condemned altering the human DNA that could result in traits that could be passed on to offspring because they still didn't understand DNA well enough to assure the outcome. But that didn't stop Becker. He was willing to take the chance. I found his research notes on the server and read them. Becker had one main obstacle to his plan that he had to solve. Because humans take so long to mature and progress through their lifespan, he wouldn't live long enough to fully understand the results of his experiments. That's why scientists experiment on fruit flies. They live their whole life in a couple of weeks, so the results of the experiment over the entire lifespan of the creature can be realized quickly." Eve surveyed the group of children. "We're Becker's human fruit flies."

Amelia started to understand. "How old are you, Eve?"

As if the question had caused the result, the old woman moved to a chair and eased herself onto it with a pained expression. She looked at Amelia. "I'm 3 years old." Amelia realized her look of shock was evident because Eve smiled to ease the pain she had caused. "Dog years can't hold a candle to us."

"What did he do to you?" The last of the question came out in a sob.

"He did the opposite of what most people are trying to accomplish. Have you ever heard of progeria?" When Amelia shook her head, Eve continued. "It's a rare syndrome that causes children to begin to age rapidly starting in the first year. It only happens in about 1 in 4 million births so it's not surprising that you haven't heard of it. Most kids with progeria don't live past 13. But that wasn't good enough for Becker. He isolated the progeria genes and used CRISPR to alter human embryos to produce a super progeria. I was one of his first successes. I have outlived all my…" The old woman put on a mock smile as her eyes misted over. "What do I call them? My siblings? We began in a laboratory and were implanted in a host mother. I never knew her. From hints in the notes, I think they used young runaways and took us at term by cesarean."

An awful question came to Amelia. *I wonder if those girls are alive.*

Eve's face changed when they made eye contact. "They couldn't allow them to live, could they? If one of them talked, it would ruin everything." Eve pondered for a few moments. "Whoever my mother was, she sacrificed everything to have me."

Fear and anger converged in Amelia as she listened to Eve.

The elderly three-year-old swallowed. "I'm the last of the original subjects. The rest aged and died in about a year. That was Becker's goal—a life lived in a year. For them, the seasons of life were January to December. I was the anomaly of the group. They worked hard to keep me alive." Eve looked at all the children. She ruffled the light wispy hair of the closest little girl. "You know why they have kept me alive so long?"

Amelia didn't think she wanted to hear the answer.

"Becker needed a steady supply of new subjects. Even though I have lived over the year, I still pass down the DNA for a year-long life span." The woman used her twisted arthritic hand to gesture toward the group of kids. "These are some of my children."

There was no way to miss the significance of the word 'some.'

Eve pointed to a wall of steel refrigerated lockers with rows of two by two doors. "Some are there. Awaiting..." She broke down as she said, "autopsy." After a moment, the wrinkled face hardened again. "And the rest have been disposed of. Becker didn't let them live what little life they had. He wanted to know the effect of the genetic changes he was implementing at the various points in the aging process. But I have resolved in my mind that perhaps the ones that they terminated...listen to me. I'm talking like them. If you call a child a number, if you call murder termination...I guess you can do almost any unthinkable thing if you just rename it. The procedures they did without pain medicine were the worst to listen to. They didn't want to risk the sedative influencing the results. It is also hard on the liver and kidneys, so they didn't want to risk damaging their subjects. Pain didn't seem to be a problem."

"But how could you have so many children in three years?"

Eve put on a sarcastic smile. "Oh, I'm too valuable to risk to a pregnancy. Surrogates are used to carry my babies. Since we were to be his breeding stock, Becker altered our DNA, so our ovaries contained more eggs. I'm also given treatments that bring more of them to maturation and faster. They continuously strap me down and take eggs from me to fertilize and implant in a surrogate." Eve paused. "I read about human trafficking rings. Is that real? I don't know what to believe on the internet."

Unfortunately, Amelia knew the answer to that one and nodded.

Eve hung her head. "I wanted to believe Ivan when he said it would be better when I got out of here."

Amelia needed to keep her hope alive. "It will. It's not all bad."

Eve came back from her mental wandering. "Anyway, I think that's where they get the girls to have my babies. We both already guessed what they do with them after they are no longer good as host mothers. The births happen somewhere else, but I think it's nearby because they bring in new babies regularly.

Amelia remembered Norm telling his boss about disposing of bodies in the basement. She felt numb. She could honestly say that she rarely hated anyone. She knew Jesus condemned hatred. But she struggled with her anger against the people behind DNAble. *God, how could You let this happen? I don't understand. How can You let someone like this exist?* Eve made her realize how much evil she ignored in the world. The Nazi war crimes against the Jewish prisoners, the experiments that were done, they had seemed far away, having nothing to do with her. *We're letting it happen again, aren't we, Lord?* She wasn't prepared for anything like this. "What are the experiments about? Are they trying to eradicate the Jews? Are you Jewish?"

Eve had a strange expression. "No…I mean yes, I think ancestry-wise I might be Jewish, but that's just to justify it. I have heard Becker talking. If I lie next to the vent and am really quiet, I can hear him and the others talking in his office. The people paying for all this want to destroy the Jews. He calls them the Islamists and the Supremacists, and it sounds like they are using both. I think he is telling the Islamists that they will blame it on the Supremacists and the Supremacists they will blame it on the Islamists. But Becker is all about what he calls an evolutionary assist."

"Assist?"

"He is trying to alter the human genetic structure to force evolution."

"You mean like making a perfect human?"

Eve turned both hands toward herself. "Do I look like the perfect human? No, what he does causes more defects and a lot of the babies die early. It has something to do with 'putting pressure on junk DNA.' I read a lot of articles on the subject, trying to understand what they were doing to us. Ivan used to bring me books from the library that I kept hidden with my Bible. Back in the early days of genome research, a lot of DNA didn't appear to have much use to the function of the organism. The scientists that believe in evolution decided it must be 'junk' leftovers from years of evolutionary mutations. More recent articles admit they have found that the 'junk' parts do seem to have a purpose, but we don't understand them all yet. Ivan said that when people don't understand what God does or why He does something, they make up stories."

Eve shook her head like she was trying to make sense of it. "He told me people that believe in evolution are trying hard not to believe in God. It must be true because now some evolutionists are saying that junk DNA must play a major role in evolution. Everyone would be laughing if it wasn't people with Ph.Ds behind their names saying it." Eve forced a grin. "I guess the key is to sound intellectual when you're completely contradicting yourself and everyone will accept it."

Amelia smiled to encourage her, but she didn't like the topic.

"Anyway, Becker wants to cause an evolutionary jump. Evolutionists acknowledge that the fossil record does not show gradual evolution. There are fish fossils and mammal fossils but not any half fish, half mammal fossils. That is an oversimplification, but you know what I mean. Species just suddenly appear in large numbers without any genuine transitional species. Even Darwin admitted it. Rather than consider rethinking their conclusions and being open to the idea that things were created all at once, they have a lot of different theories as to why the fossil record shows a sudden explosion of species. One of them is that evolution happens in jumps. That's what Becker believes, but he thinks we have hit a plateau in evolution and the earth isn't going to sustain life long enough to make our next evolutionary jump. He plans to help it by accelerating random mutations in human DNA worldwide. It's complex and hard to explain, but how it affects us is that he needs lots of test subjects to perform his experiments." Eve paused, thoughtful. "At least he did."

Amelia noticed the alteration in her voice. "What do you mean?"

Eve shook her head as if considering an unanswered question. "Everything changed a couple of weeks ago. They stopped the experiments and started packing up samples and files and downloading things from the computers. These," Eve indicated the children again, "were the latest test subjects." She ruffled Chloe's hair. "I'm glad they don't understand yet. The accelerated aging does not begin right away. They still have the innocence of toddlers but that will change rapidly now." Eve looked back to Amelia. "They arrived last week, a couple of days before the team left for the conference, but the researchers didn't seem that interested in them. They took blood, fluid and tissue samples from them, but they did it even rougher than usual, like they were in a hurry. I used to hear lots of sounds. Now all activity in the basement seems to have stopped and everyone is gone."

"Maybe they were shutting down." Amelia knew that wouldn't be good for Joshua's evidence quest. "Do you think they could have run out of money?"

"I don't know. Becker always talked like there was an endless supply as long as they thought he was working to genetically eliminate the Jewish race. He could tap into the money of the rich Muslim radicals and the white supremacists. And neither group would care what he did to his test subjects if they were Jewish. That's how he was able to create us—his own little population." Eve put on her sarcastic face again. "He owns us because he made us, so he can use us for the 'greater good of humanity.'"

Amelia pushed down her anger. "If that's the greater good, then humanity isn't worth saving. Becker's insane. Don't judge the rest of the world by him."

Eve's face beseeched Amelia. "Is that true? Most people would think this is wrong?"

Amelia couldn't believe Eve had to ask. "Of course. Only evil people would do this."

Doubt inhabited Eve's face. "Since Ivan is no longer here, I don't have anyone to ask." Eve shook her head like she was trying to get her mind around the new idea. "It seemed like some people believed that things like this were wrong, but I see the news on the internet, and a lot of people can do awful things, even to children." Eve gazed at the little faces around her. "What about abortions? Are those real? People really do that, kill babies before they're born?"

Amelia joined Eve's contemplation of the children. "Some people do."

Eve shook her head. "On the internet, they talk about it just like Becker talks about us. They call the baby a fetus, like that makes it okay. And don't they use their parts for experiments like they do in here?"

"No, I don't think they…not legal…" Amelia's insides felt sick. "I guess I'm not sure. Maybe some places but most people—"

Eve interrupted. "They say there's a debate. It seems like a lot of people think it's okay." The old woman took in a breath and reached out touching each little head in its turn. "When I first read about it, I realized those babies are like us, trapped inside a small space, dependent on what other people decide to do with them." Her eyes pierced Amelia then looked at the floor. "I've never been outside of here. Ivan was the first person that made me feel like I was worth more than something to experiment on. He also said most people were good. I want to believe that, but it's hard sometimes."

Amelia struggled to answer. "Well, you can't believe what you see on the news and the internet. At least I hope not. People can get really messed up and believe crazy things, but I think most good people are just too busy with their lives and their families. They don't have time to get on the internet and talk about it."

"I hope that's true."

Amelia felt unsteady in her emotions. Memories of working in the crisis pregnancy centers came back to her. Her mother had been so passionate about the subject that when she and Gabriel had time, they liked to volunteer at the local center. How many times had the girls told her stories about being pressured to abort their babies? Turning her concentration back to the computer she said, "If my friends would ever get back with me, maybe we can get out of here and you can see for yourself." Inside she was trying to cast off her own troubling thoughts. *God, I don't want to believe the world is this evil either.*

Marsha lay still, thankful for the relief, but she couldn't afford to waste her time. Her wrists and ankles were bound with zip ties and a third zip tie fastened those together. She lay on her side like a hogtied calf. The man was good. He didn't make the mistake of putting her hands behind her where she could pull out the taser darts that were lodged in her back. Her hands were in front where he could see them and having them fastened to her feet made running, or even standing upright, impossible. *I have to admire him. He knows what he's doing. This one's going to be hard to kill.* There was no way for her to strike a flattering pose, and she doubted overt flirtation was going to work on him anyway. The man was obviously a professional. *Be subtle. Get to know him.* He was also the epitome of tall, dark, and handsome. *Okay, Mr. TDH, let's talk.* "If I did help get you down to the basement, where are your explosives? If you had any, you would be using them on that elevator."

The man raised an eyebrow in her direction. He was over six feet. Under other circumstances, Marsha would have liked what she saw. He walked to the elevator, careful not to tangle the copper taser wires. He placed the taser on the floor and began to examine the metal door. "The explosives are already in place. Part of a last resort escape plan for the leadership of the organization. Becker explained it to me." The man cast Marsha a look of approval. "He didn't have your pain tolerance."

I wonder if my baby can feel it? The consideration was spontaneous. Marsha had not consciously let it enter. She never would. It concerned her that she would think of it at a time when she needed all her mental resources to save herself. She didn't have time to be thinking about a bunch of cells that were basically a parasite feeding off her body. Caring for someone besides herself was how the parasite got in. So much for birth control. It didn't seem to be a thing that could be controlled. She should have had a hysterectomy like she had considered. She couldn't explain her apprehension about it, then or now.

Turning back to the elevator doors, TDH expounded on what he had learned from Becker. "They wired the place in case they needed to get out fast ahead of the authorities. Once they were gone, they could destroy all the evidence with a cell phone call. There must be something incriminating in the basement, something that you can't take with you on a portable hard drive. It was not relevant to my needs, and I was worried Becker might not be man enough to last before I got the information I really needed." TDH peered approvingly at Marsha. "Or woman enough."

Woman enough. Marsha couldn't stop the doubts coming to her mind. Amelia had jokingly questioned her womanhood. What did it matter to Marsha? She didn't need to be a woman unless it was an advantage. Her womanhood was a tool. She liked that this attractive killer appreciated her for her skill even though he didn't seem to mind looking at her either.

TDH examined the ceiling above him. "Unfortunately for Becker, his partners didn't trust him with the code that needs to be entered after the call is made. I didn't believe him at first. Used up a whole taser battery before I was finally convinced. Two men named Herschlag and Salzman are the only ones that can set it off."

Marsha made a pretended stretch of her muscles and felt for the knife in her waistband. "If the evidence will be buried in the explosion, why would you want to help them do that?"

The man turned his harshly handsome face toward her movement. He reached in his pocket, held up the knife she was looking for, and grinned. "Evidence is only useful if there is someone to stand trial. I intend to relieve the state of that burden."

Marsha tipped her head back in acknowledgment of her switchblade in his hand. "Sounds reasonable, but how are you going to get the code?"

The handsome stranger slid a tall stool in front of the elevator. "I'm not. Becker told me there is one central call receiver that sets off the detonator. I will replace the phone in it with my own."

"So, you do plan on being elsewhere when the place goes up."

Standing on the stool, he pushed a ceiling tile out of the way. "Of course. Were you thinking I intended this to be a suicide mission?" He shook his head. "Not my style."

"You're putting a lot of trust in what Becker told you."

"He was appropriately motivated. After my taser ran out, I had to get creative, but I have an active imagination."

Marsha sniffed a laugh. "You'll forgive me if under the circumstances I don't indulge mine to picture what you came up with."

The man tipped his head out of the ceiling. "You disapprove?"

"Are we talking about Becker or are we talking about me?"

The man dropped down off the stool with a thud and dusted off his hands. "Surely you don't think I would do that to you?"

"Well, considering our history so far and the fact that you're about to bury a lot of innocent employees with the bad guys in this scenario, it could make a person a little doubtful that you would hesitate to do awful things to a defenseless woman."

"I'm not that sure anyone here is innocent any more than I think you are defenseless. And you should know that you can't get sentimental about life and death in this business." The man forced his hand behind the edge of the door and leaned back, pulling hard at the steel. He stood up and scowled. "When you cut out a cancer, there is sure to be some good tissue damaged." He glanced back at Marsha. "You are not Jewish. You would not understand. Jewish people can no longer afford to be reactive. Never again can we afford to let our fate be decided by courts, summits, or tribunals. We need to take steps to make sure no one will dare to move against us for fear of their lives. It is all that such people understand. It is the only thing that guarantees our survival."

Marsha stretched again. "Honestly, I can't argue with that. I believe in that kind of direct approach to a problem. But a girl's got to keep the odds stacked in her favor. You'd better also. If you're going to take on the world, you'd better have the support to back it up. If you tick off the United States, I think you're tossing away Israel's best ally."

The man gave the door a last look and ran his fingers around the edges. "My people have been taking on the world for thousands of years. I am afraid we can no longer trust the U.S. There are too many voices in your country that seem to hold anti-Semitic views."

The man picked up the taser and talked as he walked back to Marsha. "Even if they would never wear a swastika or bomb a synagogue, they support policies that allow people who hate us to gain the advantage and then claim we do not even have the right to protect ourselves. Even as your president speaks favorably toward Israel, others in your government are supporting sanctions against it in the U.N. Israel has been the United States best ally, but your country no longer remembers that." He squatted next to her and looked in her eyes. "So pretty. You wouldn't have any explosives, would you?"

Marsha smiled sweetly at him. "Normally, I would, but this operation didn't call for any such fun. And I never said the United States was my country."

The man gave a light chuckle. "How many men have gotten lost in that smile?"

Shrugging her shoulders, Marsha added a little pout to her lips. "I'd be satisfied with just one more."

"I'm sure." He examined her. "Let's see. Would you stab me or shoot me?"

Marsha returned the scrutiny. "Of course, it would depend on what scenario presented itself, but if I had to make the choice, I would have to go with the gun. I don't think it would be safe to let you get too close." She gave a little wink. "For a lot of reasons."

"Flatterer. But as pleasant as this conversation is, it is not getting me into the basement." He gave Marsha a regretful smile. "No help?"

"Sorry. Under other circumstances, you understand."

The man sighed deeply. "Then I must kill you and your friend when he comes back up. Are you sure?"

"If you're just going to wait anyway, why not have company? You could always kill me later. Maybe, I'll think of some way to get you to the basement while we wait. I can be pretty good company. Give me a chance."

"I think that might be dangerous." His mouth took on a thin pressed smile that conveyed regret. "For a lot of reasons."

Laying the taser on the floor out of her reach, the man put his hand to the back of his waistband where he had placed Marsha's handgun. "I feel the same way. I would not want to use the knife on you. This will be quicker and less painful. I hope it is some comfort to know that I will always remember you."

Joshua put the coffee that Norm handed him to his lips and tipped up the cup, pretending to take a sip. Out of habit, he let just a taste onto his tongue, searching the strong flavor for bitterness or burning that might indicate a drug, not that he intended to really drink any of it. He detected nothing out of the ordinary. "So, all we have left is a look at the basement."

Norm wrinkled his forehead and nodded. His face looked like he had a pleasant idea. "Maybe we can cut out of here after that. I assume you're staying over in Bentonville. Since you have nothing to go home for, you might as well take in a little of the Northwest Arkansas night culture."

Joshua held up the coffee in a toast of approval. "Lead me to that basement and let's get this done. The board wants my report pronto, so I don't have much time to spare, but if we hurry, I can run back to the hotel and get something sent, and we can meet up somewhere later. I'm impressed with what you've done here, Norm, and my report's going to reflect that."

"I appreciate that, Tanner. We all know what's at stake, and I for one plan to work hard to bring about the change that we all envision." The man's face held a conspiratorial hint. "Of course, there are things that I would have done differently, but you work with what you have and keep pressing toward the future we all see coming."

"Good attitude, Norm. I think that is the kind of thinking that the board is looking for. Show me what great things you are accomplishing in the lower levels." Joshua smiled as he watched for the man to move. With his peripheral vision, he targeted the retractable key card holder and its metal clip that was slid over Norm's belt.

Marsha looked directly at the man as he brought the gun out. A new feeling was running through her. She had faced death before, but it had been on the run, in the heat of the battle. Not staring at her through gorgeous eyes. She wasn't going to make it easy for him by closing hers. The tall man's handsome face was calm. She decided she had never seen anything uglier.

"I can get you to the basement." Ibbie's voice came through the phone's speaker causing the man to instinctively jerk the gun toward the phone he had sat on the nearby table. "Don't hurt her and we can work this out. You're right. We want the same things."

The man looked back at Marsha and the corners of his mouth turned up. "It doesn't appear you have lost all communication after all."

The air went out of Marsha's lungs. She felt a strange quiver in her stomach. She was alive but she knew beyond a doubt that the man would have killed her. She knew because it was what she would have done.

Norm moved to head toward the door.

Joshua timed his own advance to collide with the other man sending coffee onto his pants on the other side from where Norm's key card dangled. At the same time, Joshua feigned trying to bring his other hand up to catch the coffee and used it to connect with the key card holder, sliding it from Norm's belt and flipping it as far behind him as he could.

The other man's attention was held by his efforts to wipe away what coffee had not already soaked in.

"Oh, man. I'm sorry, Norm. What a klutz move that was." Joshua turned as if looking for an item to help. "Let me get you something." He saw the card holder lying on the floor and dashed toward it in his pretend search. He struck the holder with his foot and sent it out-of-sight under the nearest armchair. He turned again and located a box of Kleenex on a side table and brought it to Norm.

The man took it and began wiping the wet stain.

"I owe you a pair of pants. No doubt about it. I am so sorry."

The irritation faded from Norm's face. "Don't worry about it. It happens."

"Have you got a change?" Joshua dipped his head toward the offended area on Norm's pants and added a small laugh. "That coffee couldn't have picked a more conspicuous place to land. Please forgive me, Norm."

"Yeah, I've got a suit in my office for important meetings." He added to the laugh. "I would have been wearing it if I had known you were coming. But Herschlag sprung it on me, out of the blue. Give me a few minutes."

Joshua gave him an elbow bump. "Sure you trust me?" He grinned at the man while he reached down and snatched his empty cup from the floor and held it up. "I promise to skip the coffee until I can buy you something stronger later." With an easy toss, he landed it in the trash can.

"You got a deal." Norm went to his office closet, pulled out a garment bag and excused himself to the bathroom.

Joshua hurriedly dropped to the floor. "Ibbie, I have the key. When Norm returns, I need Gabe to talk to him as Herschlag and tell him there is someone hiding in the trees outside. I'll tell him to handle it because I need to make a phone call." He ran his hand under the armchair and fished out Norm's card key and holder. "Ibbie?" He shot a glance toward the door. Norm would need the card to get back in. He hoped he wouldn't notice it was missing before he got to the bathroom and came back for it. Fortunately, the bathrooms were not locked so he wouldn't need a card there.

Joshua laid the card that Norm had given him beside the one he had just stolen. "Ibbie, are you there?" Thankfully, DNAble made its card keys separate from its ID cards so the cards were identical except small identifying numbers and Norm's had more wear. Joshua pulled a pair of scissors from Norm's desk drawer and scratched at the places on his card that coincided with the worn parts of the older card. He made it look as much like Norm's card as possible. Then he switched the cards, so his card key was on Norm's holder and he pocketed the other man's card. *That should get me into the basement server room.* He was sure the visitor card Norm had given him would not open such a high-value area. "Ibbie, I need you to answer. You need to make that call as soon as Norm gets the card, so he won't look at it too carefully."

No response.

Now, what could have happened? He eyed the door again, then placed Norm's card key holder just under the coffee table near where their collision had occurred. He made sure it was easy to spot. *Okay, Norm, maybe it's going to be me and you.*

Chapter 18

The monitor came alive in front of Amelia. A popup box displayed, THIS IS RAMS TWO. THERE WILL BE A BOX ASKING YOU TO GIVE ME PERMISSION TO TAKE OVER THE COMPUTER. CLICK YES.

Amelia went through the steps, a video conferencing software loaded and Ibbie's face appeared on the screen.

Ibbie examined Amelia and the area behind her. "Who's with you?"

"This is Eve, and these are her children. Becker was using them to experiment on. We can't let him do it to them anymore. We have to get them out of here before he comes back."

"It doesn't sound like he's coming back. Remember the ones we told you about, the Fighters for Israel? One has Marsha prisoner and I need you to help her."

"Me? What am I going to do?"

"I can't talk long. You're doing great. But this guy might really kill someone if we don't do this carefully. So, stay calm and listen close."

Stay calm? An undercurrent of panic ebbed beneath the

waves of her emotions and Amelia had the nebulous impression that her unalienable right to scream was being denied her. But Marsha was more important, so she forced her ears open as wide as her eyes.

Marsha watched as Mr. Tall, Dark and Handsome stood up and stepped back from her. She gently curled into a seated position and the man said nothing. She knew he was considering his options. He would be concerned that Ibbie was stalling.

And she must be. She heard the man's plan to blow up the building. It was just what they didn't need. The FFI would take credit for the act so they could send a message. Fear was the commodity they traded in. Even though they were not tied to the Israeli government in any way, all the public would hear was the 'Israel' in their name. The Islamists and other anti-Semitics would capitalize on the chance to rail against the Israelis. The terrorists would use it to spread their propaganda and justify the attacks they planned.

Of course, the man would not kill her until he heard what Ibbie had to say, but she could see the wariness in his eyes.

Tall, Dark and Handsome backed away from Marsha and scrutinized the room as if he might see beyond it to determine the extent of this new threat. "I am listening. Make it quick and of course you realize if you are trying to trick me it will not go well for your friend here."

Ibbie's voice was hard. "And you need to understand that I hold the power to inform the DNAble security team, local law enforcement, and the FBI of your location and your plan if anything happens to her. Remember, suicide is not your style."

TDH looked at the phone. His face said he was

calculating. "You listened to your friend in pain but choose only now to intervene." His head came up as if he had reached his conclusion. "The success of your mission is that important to you. You do not want the authorities involved. Your position is no stronger than mine."

"Our mission is complete. Now we want to extract our team. We are in the way of you getting in, but you are in the way of them getting out. That is the only problem we have. Surely, we can work that out without anyone getting hurt. I have a proposal. Leave the woman in the outer office with something to cut herself free and put her gun nearby—I assume you have one of your own. Then go into the inner office and lock yourself in. I will send up the others on the elevator. They are unarmed, untrained civilians. They will get off and you can get on."

The man shook his head. "That will not work. I will keep the woman's gun. I have no guarantee of what is coming up in the elevator. Your friend said one male went down. Now you are saying that more than one will come up. If she has a gun, I might have guns to the front and the back of me. Why is there more than one person coming up?"

"She lied to protect the person that went down. It was only one female. We are rescuing prisoners. DNAble was experimenting on Jews in the basement. One adult and five children. With our female civilian contact, there will be seven people coming up. You will see they are not a threat to you."

TDH took in a breath. He peered at Marsha. "The woman stays with me as cover until I can assess what is on the elevator. I will have a gun on her and if it is not exactly as you say when the elevator comes up, I will begin by putting a bullet through the back of her head. If all is well, your contact and the prisoners will go out of the inner office and close the door. Once I am in the elevator and it closes, the others may come in and free the woman. You will be out. I will be in."

Marsha knew that Ibbie would have started negotiating high, knowing the man would counter. But why was she sending up the elevator at all? It must be Amelia's only way out. Did she really have six others with her? Again, sensations came without her consent. Marsha wanted to live. Not since she left London had she wanted it so much. But more than that, she wanted Amelia to live. It wasn't anything she could explain. "Don't risk anything for me."

At Marsha's words, the man's eyes darted to her.

She risked him thinking it was some code between her and Ibbie, but she had to say it. She had worked with Ibbie enough to trust what she was doing, but she didn't deserve life at the cost of someone else—someone who hadn't done the things she had done.

Ibbie's voice sounded displeased. "That puts everything in your favor. What is my guarantee that you will not clear your way by killing everyone once the others bring up the elevator?" She was ignoring Marsha's comment.

TDH had his eyes on Marsha again. "As you said, you have the ability to give me away to security. I have no assurance you will not do that once your team is out of the building. I will be outnumbered with only your word that these seven other people are harmless. I will be taking the greater risk. What advantage would it be for me to kill the others with you still in play and able to report me?"

The phone was silent.

The man walked to the door and cracked the miniblind enough to look down both directions of the hall. Like a mouse in the cat's parlor, he appeared to be listening. "I will not wait long. You are making me nervous."

Ibbie's voice came on. "All right. I will do it your way, but understand that the only reason that I am doing this is to get all of our people out alive. If you do anything to jeopardize that outcome, I will tell everyone where you are and share the video of you that I took when you first took out the phone. You are like us, I think. You depend on anonymity. I may not have the power over your life that you have over my team members, but with that video I can end your life as you know it."

Walking to Marsha, the man took a phone of his own from the cargo pocket of his pants. He squatted and took several pictures of Marsha. "Now we are even. I guess we were destined to be linked. I was right, your face will always haunt me." He cocked his head toward the phone. "Give me a moment. I will let you know when you can send up your friends." He turned back to Marsha and whispered in her ear. "I hope she is not lying. I really want you to live."

Joshua smiled at Norm's knock on the door. He let him in. "Card not working?"

Norm reentered the outer office with a scowl on his face. "I can't find it."

"Did you leave it in the bathroom?" Joshua had been ready for the discussion.

"No, that's where I noticed it was gone. I had it when we came…there it is." Norm scooped up the badge from where Joshua had planted it.

Joshua put an apologetic look on his face. "It must have gotten knocked off in our collision. I am sorry, Norm. I've been flying all over the country, and it must be catching up with me. You're looking snappy in that suit, though."

Norm examined the clip on his holder. "I guess I'm going to have to get one that fastens around my belt. Be bad if I lost this." The man fingered the card.

"Well, we better hustle if we are going to get out of here early." Joshua slapped the other man good-naturedly on the back.

Norm looked up from the card and smiled. He shoved the clip back on his belt. "Okay, I'll take you on the tour of Becker's freak show. Prepare yourself. Some of the things he is doing down there are necessary but not pretty."

"I'm about results, Norm. Sometimes you gotta break some eggs, right?"

"Well, Becker's breaking a different kind of egg down there. Wait 'til you see it."

Norm led the way out of the office. Joshua followed, thinking about what was going to happen when they came to a door Norm's card no longer opened. *Where are you, Ibbie?*

Marsha watched TDH return from the elevator. "There. I disabled the safety for the outer door that I broke. Now the elevator should be able to operate with that door open." He returned her gun to the back of his pants and pulled two more zip ties from the cargo pocket opposite from where he kept his phone. "We are going to make an adjustment. I am going to get close and personal for a moment. Please don't see this as your opportunity. I will by no means be off my guard. I have the highest respect for your skills. If you did get a hold on me, I might be forced to kill you to get free. Besides breaking my heart, it would make my relationship with the woman on your phone a bit awkward. I could find myself having to shoot my way out and your friend on the elevator might get hurt."

"You really know how to charm a girl."

"Finally. I was beginning to think you weren't talking to me anymore."

"It's hard to say much under the influence of electricity."

"You were still beautiful."

"Thanks for saying so. A girl could start wondering when all she hears are death threats. It's good to know you still care."

Ibbie spoke from the phone. "We could trade endearments and threats all day long. Let's concentrate on making this work, so we can all survive."

The man looped a zip tie around Marsha's upper left thigh. He looked in her eyes. "Your friend really is the epitome of 'three's a crowd.'"

Marsha returned the gaze. "Maybe we'll meet someday under different circumstances."

A sly uplift of TDH's mouth said he didn't miss the menace in her voice. He slid another zip tie in the loop that encircled her wrist and fastened it to the one around her thigh. The switchblade snapped open in front of Marsha's face. She remained stone-faced. She had seen it coming and knew he wasn't going to kill her at that moment. The man used it to cut the zip tie that attached her wrists to her ankles and tossed the used tie to the side. Putting the knife away, he got up and lifted Marsha to a standing position, which the new arrangement allowed. Marsha still had limited ability to move her hands since her wrists were still bound tightly together and fastened to her thigh. "There. Now you will make a better shield."

"I always like to be useful."

He moved Marsha, lifting her almost completely off the ground with just his arms. He slid her feet lightly across the floor and seated her on the corner of the desk. She turned her head to watch him and realized his strategy. He stood behind her, making her a shield but positioned himself where he could drop behind the desk for cover if needed. The elevator was at an angle to them. When the door opened, anyone inside would have to peek around the corner of the elevator to see them. The man pulled open a Velcro area on the front of his pants and pulled his own gun, a larger model Glock than Marsha's, from the hidden holster. His weapon also had a silencer. The man turned and spoke to the phone. "Send up your friends."

Amelia and Eve coaxed the little ones into the elevator. Eve spoke lovingly to them and they reacted to her voice, trying to take hold of her legs, some only managing to touch her. The old woman caressed each head in turn. "When I was able to get out, I used to gather whichever children were there and hold them and sing them to sleep."

Eve ran her hand over the wispy hair of the children. "That was almost a generation ago." She spoke in a volume only for Amelia. "Those are gone now. Since they stopped me from escaping, all I have been able to do for these is talk to them and sing." Eve struggled to hold the tenderness in her sorrowful face.

The children turned their oversized heads toward the only kind voice they had ever known. "This is the first time I have touched them."

Amelia reached and squeezed her arm, causing the little ones to press even tighter to Eve. She drew back as Eve comforted them.

Amelia spoke slow and quiet. "They know their mommy."

Eve blinked her eyes several times and nodded.

"Ready?"

A look of peace came over the little woman. "No matter what happens, we will be leaving here."

Amelia breathed in, straightened her back, and touched the button. The lurch of the elevator car caused the children to huddle again.

Marsha could sense the man tense when they heard the hum of the elevator starting up the shaft. She turned toward him, letting her hair fall off her shoulder. "Take care. My friend is harmless. She's not even in the business. Don't hurt her."

"Perhaps. But I don't trust the woman on the phone."

Ibbie's voice was quick to acknowledge. "Then you understand why I don't trust *you*. But I will not do anything to threaten the young woman who is coming up or those that are with her. I am trying to make sure there are no mistakes that might get someone hurt."

"Quiet." TDH snapped.

The elevator reached the top. Marsha heard the man moving back. He was distancing himself from her, so there was no chance she could interfere with his shot. The panel slid open. Marsha saw shadows shifting against the side of the door.

Amelia stuck out her head.

Marsha tensed. *Don't do things so suddenly.* But TDH did not react.

Amelia's face brightened at the sight of Marsha. Then her eyes widened, and she jerked her head out of view. She spoke from inside the elevator. "Don't shoot."

TDH's voice boomed. "Throw out your weapons."

"We don't have any."

"Then show me just your hands."

"There's too many of us to show all our hands. I have children in here. Don't point that gun at them." Amelia sounded disturbed. "I don't want you scaring them."

TDH huffed. "Just you then." His voice was sharp. "Put your hands out first and then walk out alone. If anyone else comes out, I will shoot them."

There was a gasp from the elevator. Marsha could hear small whimpering sounds along with someone trying to quiet them. A child's crying started up and more joined in.

"Please, stop it." Amelia sounded on the verge of tears herself. "You're scaring them. Listen to them. You can tell they're just children. I'm coming out."

"Hands first," TDH barked.

"Easy." Marsha said it slow, hoping to help maintain calm. It was all she dared. She didn't want to add to the man's stress level.

A set of hands peeked out past the edge of the elevator. Slowly Amelia moved into view. She shifted her hands to stick straight above her head and walked until the man stopped her with a command. He directed her to turn around slowly, had her lift up her shirt both front and back to show she had nothing hidden there. Obeying the man's commands, Amelia pulled tight any of the loose areas of her clothing until the man was satisfied she was clean. Then he had her lay face down on the floor to the side of the elevator with her arms out. She cried and pleaded for him not to hurt the others. Her entreaties joined the cacophony from the elevator.

Marsha risked turning to face the man. "Just remember you're a professional. There's a lot to be lost by a mistake at this point."

The man allowed his eyes to stray in her direction. Suddenly, he jerked his focus to something over her shoulder. His two-handed grip stiffened, and the barrel of the gun snapped to attention. Marsha swiveled her own gaze forward. A small wrinkled hand was waving around the edge of the elevator opening.

"Do you want us to come out?" The voice was high and cartoonish. "The children are scared, and I am afraid some of them might try to run and hide. I can't come out without them. They won't understand."

The man scanned and evaluated. "How many more

adults?"

The voice hesitated. "I think…I'm the only one you might consider an adult."

The man's eyes narrowed.

"They've been experimented on." Amelia spoke from the floor. "They're all young but they age fast. Eve is the only one who can really understand what's going on." Desperation filled her words.

"Okay, Eve, then…you come out and keep your hands showing. If you have children with you, they can come out, but if I see anything I don't like, I won't take time to negotiate. Slowly. Keep your hands visible and show me there is no one crawling behind the children. Don't think I won't take the shot."

A tiny body darted out circling to connect with the figure attached to the hands that were being presented. Marsha clenched her teeth. One of the hands grabbed instinctively at the little one and pulled it closer. *Too much movement.* A large head appeared as the person leaned to comfort the deformed looking toddler. The other hand moved. Marsha couldn't breathe, fearing any moment for the gun to fire behind her. The group came forward. *Too fast.* The hands were no longer being displayed. They were holding back little forms that rushed around to take hold of the white oversized nightgown draped over the one that must be Eve. The little figures looked almost inhuman, but their actions were definitely childlike, displaying the ungoverned fears of ones that had no idea how to react to the situation. They hovered around Eve, trying to keep hold of the only thing familiar. Marsha wanted to place her body between the churning mass and the gun, but she dared not move. She could sense the man's frustration. It was just what he warned against. The swirling bodies made it impossible to confirm no one was behind them, low crawling, waiting for a shot at TDH.

Marsha was out of her element. Unable to move, fight, return fire. She watched helplessly, hoping for something to intervene, something that had the power she lacked. She didn't know to whom she was appealing but a pleading went out from a part of her beyond her conscious control. *Please.*

"Eve, lie down with them." Amelia didn't move her arms but spoke to the haggard-looking little old woman. Then she told the man, "Let her lie down with them." She addressed the tiny woman. "Sing to them, Eve. Just like you used to do."

The woman's face showed discomfort as she eased her bony body to the floor. She reached out and tugged gently at the children, urging them to her. Her eyes were wide as she looked past Marsha to the gun that was no doubt searching for a target. Her voice was high and squeaky as she began to sing. "Lullaby, and goodnight, in the skies stars are bright. May the moon's silvery beams, bring you sweet dreams."

The little ones followed Eve's lead, gathering on the floor around her, each trying to find a part of her to lay their head against. As they moved to the floor, the area behind them was revealed to be empty.

Amelia joined Eve in the next verse of Brahm's Lullaby. "Close your eyes now and rest, may these hours be blessed. 'Til the sky's bright with dawn, when you wake with a yawn."

Marsha turned to a rustle behind her. The man was gone. A shadow crossing, brought her head around to see him swinging out wide on the other side of her, coming around the desk. He had his gun on the elevator and was clearing it inch by inch as the soft singing continued.

"Lullaby, and goodnight, you are mother's delight. I'll protect you from harm, and you'll wake in my arms."

TDH eased forward, gun up, sighted over the group of tiny bodies gathered around the shriveled woman.

"Sleepyhead, close your eyes, for I'm right beside you. Guardian angels are near, so sleep without fear."

The man let the gun relax in his hand as the last of the elevator was exposed to his view. He looked down at the group of strange children, heads nestled against Eve. Some of the eyes were already closing.

Marsha let out a breath of gratitude. Again, she didn't know to whom. Eve and Amelia's voices had quieted to a gentle coo.

The man walked to Amelia and her singing stopped. TDH reached down and took her by the arm and helped her rise.

Marsha slid from the desk.

"Stay there." The man pointed his weapon at her. He took a handful of Amelia's hair. Forcing her head back, he pulled her toward the elevator.

"You said you would let them go out to the other room."

The phone came alive with Ibbie's voice. "What's going on?"

Marsha addressed the man. "You don't need her. Just take the elevator and let us leave. That's what we agreed."

TDH winked at her. "Trust me, love. There's nothing between her and me. I still don't trust your friend. I can't take you. That would make things too tedious. Never knowing when you might make a move on me. Love's dangerous that way." The man stepped inside the elevator, keeping Amelia in front of him and the gun on Marsha. "I can tell you weren't lying about this one. She's a lamb. Don't worry. If I make it out, I'll bring her with me." He pulled Amelia in with him.

"You're breaking our agreement. Just because you go down that elevator doesn't mean you won't have me to worry about."

TDH wrinkled his brow, "Let's not part on that note. That's exactly the reason I need this little insurance policy." He broke his aim at Marsha just long enough to jab at the elevator buttons.

Ibbie pleaded. "Please, don't do this."

Some of Eve's children were whimpering again.

Amelia tipped her head against the hair pull and looked at Marsha. "Get Eve and the kids out of here. They're scared. That's what you have to do."

The man spoke. "Good advice. You all have plenty to do. This motivates the woman on the phone not to interfere with me until I get out safely with this pretty little package that you all seem to care about." The doors slid shut.

Marsha whirled around and jerked a desk drawer open a few inches. She dropped, bending her knees with her bound hands beneath the thin edge of the drawer. Exploding upwards with her legs she caught the zip tie around her hands on the edge and snapped it clean, raising the desk off the floor so it came back down with a thud.

She heard a squall from the floor as the babies came awake. Eve and the children were staring at her as she viciously sucked air through her clenched teeth. She looked away and snatched out the middle desk drawer.

Ibbie interrogated Marsha. "What's going on? Did he take Amelia?"

Marsha grabbed a pair of scissors and sliced away the rest of her restraints.

"Rams Three, talk to me."

Anger swelled through her like a violent storm. Anger at the man for what he had done. Anger at herself for caring so much.

"Rams Three!"

And anger at whomever she had been stupid enough to be crying out to.

"Marsha, report to me now!"

"Yes! He's gone down the elevator and taken Amelia. Why did you send her up here? She would have been safer in the basement."

"Maybe, maybe not. Joshua is trying to get down there without Norm. He's going to have his hands full as it is. I was hoping he wouldn't have Amelia to worry about as well."

"Well, that worked out really well, didn't it?"

"You think it would have worked out any better with you dead?"

"Maybe. It doesn't matter now. I'm on my way to the basement by another route. Where's Joshua? We'll do better against this guy together."

"You're not going there."

"Oh yes, I am. You traded her for me. I'm not leaving her with him."

"Marsha, you have a more important mission now. Eve and the children are your priority."

Eve had managed to quiet the little ones again. At Ibbie's words, she glanced at Marsha.

Marsha softened her voice. "Listen, I know you're scared, but I'll come back for you when I know Amelia's all right." Eve nodded.

"Marsha, there's more to it than a rescue. We came here on a mission to get evidence. That evidence is right in front of you. It's better than what's on the server in the basement that Joshua is after. Amelia and I talked about it. She knew the risk. She didn't trade herself for you. She traded herself for Eve and the kids. And not just because of them. She traded herself for the mission. With their testimony, the authorities can easily get a warrant for this place and the server in the basement. Your most important mission now is to get Eve and her kids safely out of here. You're going to have to trust Joshua…and Amelia. She's not the lamb your boyfriend thinks."

Chapter 19

Joshua had stalled all he dared. He had Norm take him back to the DNA lab on the main level, coming up with a few questions that began to sound more contrived as he went. He couldn't risk Norm's suspicions returning.

Now they were on their way to the basement and ever-tighter security. Joshua thanked God that the card he had given Norm opened the elevator. He had taken a chance on that. A little sleight of hand inside the elevator had gotten them past the card reader that turned on the button allowing access to the restricted basement. Timing a casual lean of his hand next to the card reader at the same time Norm had placed his card against it, had given Norm the impression that his card was working. He had Norm's real card palmed, and the reader beeped and turned green.

The elevator was descending. Joshua gave Norm a smile. "I hear Becker's a genius. Is he quirky like most of them?"

Norm held his answer for a moment, and his face said his mind had turned to deeper considerations. "He has some strange hang-ups. I don't always know what they have planned. Mr. Herschlag insists on managing that part of the operation."

"What's your opinion about his work?"

Norm shifted uncomfortably in response to Joshua's inquiry. "You'll see the test group he's created. It's disturbing, but he says it's accelerated the experimental process."

The elevator stopped. Joshua continued his probe. "What's next on his timetable?"

"He says he's ready for a field test. It's scheduled. Most of it is beyond my college chemistry but it sounds," another pause from Norm, "like it could be pretty far-reaching. I'm surprised Herschlag hasn't briefed your office about something that big."

Joshua made a conscious resolve not to falter in his step. *Slow down. Don't excite his suspicions again.* Leafing through his mind for responses, Joshua pulled out his best option. "Another reason I'm here. The main office feels a little out of the loop as well."

The elevator opened and Norm stepped out, walking briskly. Not far down the hallway was a gray heavy metal door. Next to it was a card reader. Outwalking Norm and trying the palming trick was going to look suspicious. Norm arrived at the reader. He pushed his card toward it. Nothing. He moved it closer, but nothing happened. Norm drew back the card and started examining it.

Gabriel fidgeted and looked at the floor. "Where did Amelia go? Gabriel wants to talk to Amelia." Worry wrinkled his forehead. "Amelia should not go with bad man. Where's Amelia?"

"It's okay, Gabe. Amelia is a good agent. She'll be okay. I am going to have Joshua help her. He will bring her back."

"Joshua is good agent. Joshua will bring her back."

"That's right. But now I need you to help Joshua get to Amelia." Ibbie unmuted the sound from Joshua's phone but not the mic. Norm's voice was talking. "I don't know why this card's not working."

Ibbie explained what she wanted Gabriel to do and dialed the phone.

Norm's phone rang.

Joshua tensed but recovered to take advantage of the interruption. "Let me see your card while you answer that. We've been having trouble with some of ours up at the main office. Let me see if I can get it working. I hope I didn't mess it up with that knock I gave it."

Norm was looking at the phone with concern. "It's Herschlag." He pulled the clip that held his card from his belt and handed it to Joshua as he pressed the screen and put the phone to his ear.

Joshua turned to the card reader, his back to Norm. He unsnapped the plastic strap and removed the card from the retractable cable on the clip. Pretending to examine the card apart from the strap, Joshua kept Norm's real card concealed in his other hand. *The call should be from Ibbie.*

Norm twisted his face in irritation. "Get Seth on it. He can handle that." He listened, continuing to scowl at the voice coming over the phone.

Joshua prepared to perform another magic switch. Like a card dealer, he held a high card and a low card. If Gabriel's Herschlag impersonation could succeed in sending Norm on an errand, he would snap the low-level card back on the clip. *Send him somewhere he won't need his card, Ibbie.* Joshua hoped his job offer hadn't puffed Norm up so much that he decided to blow Herschlag off. If that happened, he would have to put Norm's real card back on the clip.

The scowl deepened. "What kind of assignment? I need to be in the loop if I am to manage security. If you keep circumventing my authority and using my men for…"

Joshua could tell Gabriel's Herschlag had taken over the conversation, and Norm's face said he didn't like what he was being told.

Joshua caught Norm's attention and made a sweeping motion with his hand and whispered. "Humor him. I'll solve this."

Norm worked his mouth in frustration then said, "Okay. I'll grab Moser to go with me." Norm made sure the call was ended. "Sorry. He's been strange since all this happened. I'm not sure he can take the pressure. I think he's trying to make me the fall guy and move Seth into my position. Now he's got Seth doing his own errands and not telling me what they are."

"He was the one that called Seth away earlier wasn't he?"

Norm acknowledged with a nod and a frown.

"I can see what you're up against. For now, just make him happy. I'm going to call and brief the board about this. This is the kind of division we can't afford right now. It's obvious we need to make a change here before it gets out of hand."

Norm's expression said he was liking what he heard.

"But they don't want the changes to be disruptive or erode confidence. The timing and method have to be right. We can't dismiss Herschlag and let him walk away with what he knows. Do what he asks and then take a break. Someplace public where they know you and will verify your alibi in case there is an accident that needs investigated. We don't want the new manager starting under any cloud of suspicion."

Norm adopted a slight smile, not enough to appear over eager but pleased none the less.

Joshua dropped the next hook while the other man was chewing on the bait. "This will need to be an extremely private conference call. Do you have somewhere that has limited access, so I won't be disturbed? Someplace that afterward, I can invite Herschlag and no one will interrupt us?"

Norm considered the question. His smile returned. "Come on. I think I have the place."

Joshua followed. It was working. Only one wrinkle still had his pulse tapping a warning beat. Where was Amelia?

The man had hesitated at Becker's office, examining the airlock and the white suits. He had become even more suspicious when Amelia told him that he didn't need one because it was only to prevent contamination. He had opened the door and pushed Amelia in, telling her to stay just inside. He watched her, door closed. When his canary showed no signs of distress, he entered himself. At his command, she walked ahead of him. They had stopped frequently for him to scrutinize her health. By the man's comments, he believed that Ibbie had Amelia set a trap for him. As they progressed, he had relaxed. Then he had set about searching the lab for open doors.

Amelia winced at the pain of the zip tie the man had applied to her wrists during the elevator ride. "I tried that. And Eve has been searching for a way out for at least two years. All you have done is trap yourself. We might as well go back up the elevator."

The man sneered at her. "You have a very negative attitude."

For the first time, Amelia looked him over. "What's your name?"

"You don't need to know."

Great, another anonymous person. "Do you know what they do in here?"

Mr. Anonymous scanned the lab. "You mean what they used to do in here?"

Amelia shrugged. "The woman you talked to on the phone said you were planning on setting off explosives that are here in the basement. If you destroy this place, it won't hurt my feelings. You saw Eve and her children, how they're deformed and aging rapidly. That's what this place is for. They performed experiments on them."

"I'm glad you agree with my mission, but don't assume that makes me trust you."

"I didn't say I agree with your mission."

The man forced Amelia forward while he searched the ceilings. "That doesn't show much loyalty to your friend Eve."

"Eve wouldn't agree with your mission either."

The man put the gun away. With another zip tie from his pocket, he fastened her bound wrists to a metal shelving rack.

Amelia rested her fingers on the edge of a shelf to keep the pressure off her sore wrists. "It doesn't bother you to kill all the people in this building?"

Mr. Anonymous was on a chair doing an overhead press with a ceiling tile. "Not at all. It's simple self-defense."

"They aren't attacking you."

"Some attacks are more subtle than others. Those are usually the most insidious and dangerous. They are attacking my country and yours. Don't you love your country?"

"My father always said to never love things. Love God and love people but not things. I think the United States is a great country because it gives people the freedom to do that. Life has been hard for me and my brother sometimes, but I think it could have been much worse somewhere else."

"So, if someone was trying to destroy the U.S., wouldn't you want them stopped, even killed if necessary?"

"Is it necessary?"

"I think so." The last of the statement came out as a grunt as Mr. Anonymous pulled himself up and into the ceiling.

Amelia raised her voice to reach his lofty position. "The group I'm working with doesn't think it's necessary. They think it's going to make things worse. And by the way, Eve already tried to get out through the ceiling. She said it was all blocked off."

A stream of dust rained through where Mr. A. had removed the tile. The supports in the ceiling creaked from his movements. "She is correct." The man's breathing said he was working intensely at something that produced noises of metal on metal. A thin, four-inch square, metal plate dropped through the opening and clanged on the floor.

"Then what are you doing?"

Mr. A. eased himself down from the ceiling. "I wasn't looking for a way out just yet."

"What are you looking for?"

The man faced Amelia. "Wires."

"What wires?"

Moving his tongue around in his mouth in deliberation, Mr. A. shrugged. "Wires leading to explosives."

"Eve looked for something to make explosives and didn't find anything."

"Your friend wouldn't know what she was looking for. But they are there, enough to destroy this section of the basement and bring what's above it down also. I'm glad to see Dr. Becker wasn't mistaken. I am sure there is enough in the rest of the basement to destroy the building and everyone in it."

"You speak rather calmly about killing all these people."

"Killing is part of my job. When I have to do it, I do it well."

"Ib…the woman on the phone said you were going to kill the blond-haired woman upstairs."

"I'm glad it didn't become necessary."

"You say necessary a lot. Doesn't life have any value to you?"

"Everyone dies eventually. Most people aren't doing much living anyway. I might as well get it over with for them." The man dipped his head as he said, "Your blonde friend would have been an exception, but I can't afford exceptions."

Amelia gave the man a hard look. "Just because you have the power over someone's life doesn't mean you have the right to take it. Only God decides that."

Mr. A. half-smiled. "He hasn't intervened yet. So perhaps He feels the same as I do."

"Perhaps He's keeping count of things you'll have to answer for someday."

The man briefly uplifted the corners of his mouth and abruptly the switchblade was in his hand.

Amelia drew a quick breath before fear took the ability from her.

The blade flashed by her head and cut the tie that attached her hands to the rack. "Let's go." Pulling her by her arm, Mr. A. forced her to the nearest exit. He produced a set of keys, opened the door and pushed Amelia into the hallway.

Joshua examined the area where Norm had left him. It was a large utility room. At the far end was a door labeled "Heating." Closer to him were pipes that appeared to make up the beginning and terminating points of the plumbing and sewer utilities of the structure. Several 55-gallon barrels were grouped around a floor drain and what amounted to a large commercial garbage grinding unit that was attached to the largest of the sewer pipes. Strong acidic odors assaulted his nose. It was not a room for someone with a weak stomach.

God had answered his prayer. The door to the utility room was the final entry that needed the higher clearance card. The last trick he used to keep Norm from discovering the card switch had been stretching it. When the card Norm had didn't work, Joshua had told him that it was the same trouble they had been having at headquarters. He told Norm that he learned if you banged on the corner of the card reader it would make it work, and he had demonstrated with Norm's real card palmed and it had opened the door. Joshua thanked the Lord for blinding the security chief's eyes.

Norm had been gone long enough to be back on the elevator. "Ibbie, are you there?"

Ibbie was apologizing the moment she came on the line. "Sorry, I know I left you hanging, but there has been a lot going on. I had to keep you muted."

Joshua opened the door and checked the empty hall. "Is…are Amelia and Marsha okay?"

He made sure the card he had stolen from Norm would get him back in the utility room.

"They're alive but there's a lot in play, so let me run through this quickly to catch you up. Ibbie explained the events that led to Amelia being back in the basement with the FFI.

Joshua let go of the breath he had been holding. He needed to center on what was going to help Amelia now. "Okay. Then he's down here with her. I'll start looking. Do you have any contact with them?"

"No. Marsha's got the phone. All I know is the elevator leads to the lab and this guy has Becker's keys, so he might be able to get anywhere he wants. He told Marsha that Herschlag and your boy Norm have the basement wired to blow up the whole building if they need to get rid of the evidence. They can set it off with their cell phones, but this FFI guy plans to replace the phone in the call receiver with his own and blow it and kill everyone."

"Well, we can't let that happen."

"Be careful. This guy's good and he won't think twice about killing anyone he has to. He told Marsha he's not here on a suicide mission, but I don't think he likes to lose. If he gets desperate enough, he might detonate while he's still inside. You need to get yourself and Amelia out and I'll work on Marsha and our human evidence. That's not going to be easy with six kids."

"Where are the explosives?"

"I emailed the blueprints to our bomb techs. They came up with the places that they would plant them to bring the building down. There are a lot and to miss any one of them would be disastrous from a mission standpoint. I debated bringing in the FBI. But we wouldn't know who we're dealing with. If Herschlag, Salzman, or this FFI guy suspect anything, they could blow the place before we could stop them."

Joshua deliberated. *I won't be able to find all the explosives and disable them. I have to find the FFI and stop him. But even if I stop him from switching phones, that still leaves Norm and Herschlag with the ability to blow the building if something goes wrong. I have to find the call receiver.* "Where did you send Norm?"

"To check on some suspicious people on the walking trail in the trees north of the building. I was able to see him and another man leave the building on a golf cart headed for the woods."

Great. Norm is already out of the building. All it would take would be for him to see Marsha getting the children out. Even if he couldn't stop them, if Norm finds out their incriminating experiment is gone, he'll take off and self-destruct the place. And Amelia is somewhere in the basement. Judging by the hallways that he and Norm had traversed to get to the utility room, the basement appeared to be a labyrinth of large and small rooms with a maze of corridors connecting them. "Pull up those blueprints. I need you to guide me."

"Okay. Just remember I am dividing my time between you and Marsha. Getting the children out has become mission crucial. Be careful what you get into. You're not going to have much help down there. A rescue will be a lot more complicated than just eliminating the threat."

There was no hesitation in Joshua's mind. "You do what you have to do for Marsha, but I have a crucial mission down here as well. I got her into this. I'm not leaving her behind."

"I know. I wouldn't want you to." Joshua heard Ibbie take in a preparatory breath. "Any more than I would want you to leave any member of the team behind." A lightness returned to her voice. "It's just that I'm not going to be there to save you and that worries me."

Joshua made a smirking sound. "Cut the apron strings, Ma." he snickered. "You in an apron. I'd like to see that."

Ibbie answered with a similar sound. "Go rescue the jam maker and you never know what might happen."

Amelia decided to say something. "I think this zip tie is damaging my wrists. My fingers are tingling but that's all I can really feel."

With a broom he had obtained in a janitorial closet, Mr. A. lifted a ceiling tile in the hallway they traversed and examined what was above it. "That's possible. If we make it out of here alive, you might want to have them checked."

He certainly has a way of putting things into perspective. "You don't care, do you?" *God, help me. Tell me what to do. I know You brought me into this for a reason.*

The man motioned her forward with the broom in his left hand. One of his guns was in his right, which hung at his side. "Not a luxury I often have time for in this business."

Amelia hurried to keep ahead of him. She feared what he would do if she slowed him down. He was keeping her in front as a shield. "What makes a person become like you?"

"Do you really want to have this conversation?"

"Are you scared to explore what you are?" Amelia clamped her mouth shut. *Where did that come from?*

"I know what I am. I am an operator capable of accomplishing things outside the norm because I place my mission above all else."

"Even above people."

"I am committed to the survival of *my* people. The rest of the world has been trying to destroy Israel for thousands of years."

"Why were you going to kill the woman upstairs?"

"A better question might be why I didn't kill her. She might yet prove to be a problem for me. It might have been a mistake not to have put a bullet in her head before I left her. But had I done that the woman on the phone might have made good on her threat to send the security after me. It was a risk either way." The man snickered. "I would probably have less trouble with the security guards." He was quiet for a moment. "In the end, perhaps I violated my own code because I did not *want* to kill her. It is rare to find someone like myself. Especially one so clever and beautiful."

"How can you call her rare, clever, and beautiful and say you should have put a bullet in her head in the same breath? The team I am with feel the same way about Israel. They are trying to accomplish the same things, but they haven't let this work completely take away their humanity. You had Marsha tied up." Amelia let her friend's name slip out but was too upset to care. What did it matter? "What kind of code allows you to kill a bound woman?"

"A code of expediency." Mr. A. sounded severe. "She has the potential of complicating my mission…and my life perhaps." The man halted and fell silent.

Amelia froze with her back to the man and wondered if she had gone too far. Was he pointing the gun at her, preparing to make his next move of expediency? He was silent so long that she ventured a look at him. He examined the ceiling with no apparent intention of pushing up a tile. He looked different than he had thus far. Almost vulnerable. Again, she said something before she realized it. "You sound like you're falling in love with her."

Mr. A. lowered his eyes to meet Amelia's and grinned.

"See what I mean? Nothing but complications with that one. It was a mistake not to kill her."

Amelia felt a chill. "You *could* kill something you love, couldn't you? Are you going to kill me?"

A dark contemplation passed through his eyes. Then he smiled. "I have nothing to fear from you."

Amelia considered the statement. "So, what you're saying is I'm not attractive enough to tempt you and I'm not skilled enough to be a threat." The chill deepened. "I guess when you say someone is not worth the bullet, you mean it. I don't think I could have even imagined that level of callousness."

The man smirked and shook his head. "I could shoot you if it would make you feel better."

Numbness hardened Amelia. "I don't think it matters what I feel. You'll shoot me the moment it's convenient for you. And I don't think it has anything to do with your mission." Her emotions vacillated. *Amelia, shut up! Are you trying to get killed? Don't challenge him.* Tears trickled from her eyes, and she wiped them wondering if the movement would lead him to react, but unable to stop herself.

The corners of the man's mouth started to turn up but seemed to get confused. He thrust the broom upward, pushing up a tile.

Amelia stumbled back a step.

The man glanced at her then fixed his gaze on the ceiling. He seemed to stare into the dark hole longer than before. Quietly, he lowered the tile, then motioned forward. "No more talk."

Getting Eve and her children out of the building was proving to be difficult. Marsha ran through the ideas she and Ibbie had already rejected to see if her new proposal presented any of the same problems. *We can't call in a disturbance, bomb threat, or fire because the police would be dispatched and Herschlag or Salzman might worry about being exposed and set off the bomb. Whatever we do has to be common enough not to draw suspicion.* "Taking out a couple of babies at a time in a wheeled trash cart could work. I've got on my Whistle Cleaners outfit already."

Ibbie didn't take long to bring up an objection. "We'd have the same problem as we had with my idea of trying to put them in shipping boxes. The babies are going to cry, and someone will hear them on the way to the pickup vehicle. It doesn't matter if it's a parcel delivery van or a garbage truck."

"But I wouldn't be taking them past the receptionist. I would go out the back door to the dumpster. Eve could be with each load I transport and keep them quiet in the halls."

"Then you would have to leave some in the dumpster and Eve would have to go back for the next ones. They are going to squall the moment they are away from Eve. I think babies crying in a dumpster are going to draw attention. Besides, think of the things they'd be putting in their mouths."

"Okay, yeah, you're right. I wasn't thinking. The crying would be a problem, but honestly, are we really worried about how sanitary the operation is at this point? These kids have got to be tough with everything they've been through."

Eve was staring at her with an astonished expression.

Marsha gave a sheepish scrunch of her cheeks and waved off the woman's concern. "We'll give them an antibiotic or something once we're out."

Eve apparently wasn't convinced. "They might choke on something."

Ibbie chuckled. "I know it's not funny, but this is like that riddle with the rowboat, and the hen, grain, and fox."

Marsha sniffed a laugh. "I know what you're talking about, but I heard it with a wolf, goat, and cabbage. Even without someone eating something else, I always wondered how the man kept the wolf and goat from running off when he left them alone."

Ibbie's laugh continued. "Well if it had been you, I guess you would have just thrown them in a dumpster."

Marsha turned her back to Eve's scowl. "Okay, forget the dumpster. But, regardless of how we get out, I think we are going to need a cover noise."

"Like what?"

"Something to mask babies crying."

"Well, that depends on who's listening." The mirth was still in Ibbie's voice.

"Why would that be?"

"Because if you're the mama, you can hear your baby crying over anything. It's a superpower."

Marsha lifted her eyebrows even though Ibbie could not appreciate the gesture. "And, exactly what would qualify you to make that statement?"

"Hey, I'm not saying I know how the trick is done, but I've seen the magic. I lived with my aunt, remember? She had kids."

"Sorry. I didn't mean to bring that up."

"You didn't. I did and I'm fine."

Marsha hustled past any guilt she might have felt. "I think we have established that I am the reigning novice on children. Now, can we figure out this problem?"

"According to my mama, nobody really knows anything about children until they've had a baby of their own."

Why is everything about babies? Marsha was sick of the word. She wanted to finish this mission and take time off and make sure she would never have to worry about babies again. She wanted to talk about anything but the topic that was on the table. "Back to the cover noise."

"Okay," Ibbie hesitated. "We've already established that anything with a siren is too risky. Some kind of heavy equipment maybe?"

"You'd have to rent it and get it back here. I don't know if I have that kind of time."

"Sorry. I considered that too, the moment I said it. What am I thinking? I have the sound expert sitting next to me. Gabriel," there was movement on the other end of the line, "What noise would you make to hide baby cries?"

Over the phone, there was a baby's cry.

Marsha was amazed. "Is that him?"

"Yes." Ibbie laughingly spoke over the wail. "No, Gabe, I want a noise to hide *that* noise."

The sound changed into the noise of another baby and then another.

"Is he making all of those at once? That's uncanny."

"I'm *watching* him, and I don't believe it. He's moving his mouth all around and varying the tone to make it sound like it's coming from different places in the room."

"Like a ventriloquist throwing his voice." Marsha had to raise her own voice.

"Exactly. I don't think he understands. Stop, Gabe. It's too loud."

The sudden end to numerous babies crying hit Marsha like a punch. She grabbed her stomach at the emptiness. She felt like something had been ripped from her. She couldn't breathe and wanted to scream, to attack the threat but there was nothing there. Jerking her head around, she looked into Eve's wide eyes. Was the strange woman feeling the same thing? Was it what a mother felt? Marsha shook her head. Must be hormones. *I am not a mother.*

"Gabe," Ibbie spoke slowly. "I don't want you to cry like a baby. We need a noise that we can use so people won't hear *Eve's* babies crying."

Gabriel's voice came through the phone. "When babies cry people don't hear other babies cry."

Ibbie was still chuckling. "I guess he's right about that. We need to have a baby convention in the lobby, and no one would notice a little more crying."

Marsha shook her head to unclog her thinking. "But if Gabriel stands in the lobby making that noise, I think we'll have other problems, like how to keep the police from taking him away for an evaluation or an exorcism."

"Keep thinking. Let me know if you come up with anything. Right now, I need to help Joshua."

Marsha started to put the phone away but stopped. "Wait a minute." The sight of the babies gathered around Eve entered her in a different way. Beyond their value as evidence or their importance to the mission, she wanted to protect them. A voice—an impression—someone, was speaking inside her again. Like a callus being ripped away, it opened a hidden part of her—an instinct ancient, powerful…maternal. A scene played in her mind. "Ibbie, those riddles we were talking about earlier. Remember what the answer was?"

There was silence for a moment before Ibbie responded. "The man had to take some of the animals back and forth, didn't he?"

"Maybe that's our answer, too."

Chapter 20

"Rams One, you there?" Ibbie's voice came through the earpiece that Joshua had put in.

As he hurried to the next corner in the hallway, gun aimed in front, he whispered into the mic so he wouldn't give his position away. "Copy."

"Sorry to leave you, but I think Marsha and I might have a plan to get our little bundles out of the building. Our CIA contact still can't involve himself, but he has set up a meeting for me with a local independent operator to handle one of the details. The local won't be any help in the hands-on component so don't expect any additional firepower. He said this guy deals with unusual needs, and I guess that's what I'm after."

"I'll let you deal with that. I've got to focus here. Can you tell my position?"

"Nothing beyond placing you in the building. The floors above you are blocking the satellite. I've got limited GPS. We'll have to run it blind off the blueprints. Keep giving me landmarks you're seeing."

"While you were talking to Marsha, I found some of the

explosives in the plumbing room. There was only a wired detonator attached to them, nothing that could receive a cell phone signal. The FFI's intel must be right—there's only one receiving unit that will accept the cell call and then send the signal through the wires to set off all the other explosives. While you were working with Marsh, I traced the detonator wire from the explosives that I found in the plumbing room to this hallway. It's enclosed in red conduit, so in the rooms with open ceilings it's easy to track. This hallway has ceiling tile, but it should be running right above me. The FFI will be doing the same thing, following the conduit. I'm moving west, and I've come about five meters from the plumbing room. I'm at a corner."

Ibbie made a pensive noise. "That's not in the plans. I'm betting we're going to see even more structural deviations. They probably made a lot of changes after the final inspection that they didn't want to share with the city planners. These prints won't help a lot."

Joshua whispered in the mic. "I'm going silent." He swung out wide around the corner and did a slice-the-pie search, slowly moving laterally so each movement revealed the next slice of the new hallway around the corner. Then he broke the silence. "There are two doors on the west side of the hallway, one about the middle and another about five meters further down. Give me the distance and direction to the next possible explosive location. I'll do the best I can to relate that to the layout I'm seeing."

"The tech guessed they would take out a column support approximately eight meters northwest of you. From these blueprints, you should be able to see it across a large open area, but if you're at a corner, they've divided it up and probably enclosed the column in a room."

"I'll guess that location is somewhere behind the first door I'm looking at. I hope the FFI hasn't made it this far. I need to find that call receiver before he does so he won't be able to trade it out with his. If he does that, he will be able to detonate anytime. I won't be able to rescue Amelia without risking him destroying the place before I can stop him."

Ibbie took a breath of concern. "But if he hasn't made it here then it could mean he already found the receiver. Maybe we should back off and not push him, take him down when he leaves the building. I'm going to have to leave you and work with Marsha to get Eve and her kids out. Maybe you should pull out and set up surveillance outside. Try to take him down out there. If he detonates, at least you and Amelia won't be inside."

Joshua ran the option around in his mind. "It leaves a lot in his hands. He still has to get out without security catching him. If he's caught, he might detonate. He might decide to leave Amelia in the building. I have him somewhat contained down here. We don't have the resources to cover the outside well enough. And if he has the detonator and something goes wrong on the takedown outside, all this has been for nothing if he destroys the place." Joshua rotated his shoulders at the stiffness from keeping his weapon up and ready. "I think our best scenario is still to stop him before he finds the receiver. That's what I'm going to pray for. God is in control of this whole thing. I'll do my part and let Him do the rest."

Ibbie's breathing came through the microphone for a moment. "Okay. You know I don't have your faith, but I guess I'll be praying for that also. If God can make this work out, maybe I'll have a little more."

Joshua sighed. "Funny thing about faith, it kinda works the other way around." He made a scan around him. "I'm getting ready to move up."

Gabriel and I will be out of the van and off the air. Please be careful. I lost my father, my mother, and my sister. You're like a brother to me. I can't afford to lose any more family."

"After all these years you finally adopted me."

"That happened on that first day I had to pull you out of that mud pit. I felt responsible for you. I don't know what else to do with myself but look after you."

"Don't worry. Self-preservation is top on my priority list."

"Hmmm. That might have been true in the past, but I think there might be someone else slipping into that number one slot in your mind. You're going to have to be double sharp now. I want you back, but I don't know if I could stand to see you broken-hearted."

"I'm not sure it would be the right thing for her. You're right. Her heart's more important. I might make it through this and still be broken-hearted. I am not sure I should even pursue it."

Ibbie snickered. "Like you have a choice. You'll be telling her you love her the first chance you get."

"Women think they know everything."

"You are outgunned in this argument, brother. You better go pick a fight you're up for. I'll see you back in the van. Rams Two out."

There was a click on the phone. He put it away and took out the earbud. He never felt as good when Ibbie wasn't on the line. Now, Amelia pervaded his mind. Ibbie was dead-on. He had to be double sharp.

Joshua fast-walked to the first entrance. He crouched to the side of the door and prayed no one had heard his approach. If the FFI had Amelia as a shield, he didn't know what he would do. *God help me. Protect her. Please, more than anything ever, I'm asking this. Help me do this right and not make any mistakes. She shouldn't be in the middle of this. I shouldn't have brought her into it.* He needed to move before someone decided to put a round through the wall. The sheetrock wouldn't stop a bullet. He reached for the knob, then stopped. The FFI would expect him to crouch beside the door on the knob side rather than reach across the door. He eased his body to the other side of the entrance.

When Joshua tried the latch, it was locked. He would have to use the key card and it was going to make its usual beep sound when he did. But there was no other option. Taking out the card, he held it to the card reader. The indicator sound seemed to be exponentially louder than before. The tone lingered in the silence of the hallway. As he rotated the door handle, his imagination made the tiny, metallic sounds inside the latch feel like he was raking a tin cup on a metal fence. He eased the door ajar, examining everything he could see as the opening widened. Too late, he heard the rattle above.

Crash! Something metallic hit the floor. The door had been boobytrapped to knock something over if it was opened.

Smack! Smack! Sheetrock flew as two holes appeared on the other side of the door where he had been moments earlier.

Joshua faked a yell like he was in pain as he jerked his head to see the wall on the other side of the hallway. Two holes, low and behind him.

Smack! Smack! The shout worked. Two more holes opened up near the bottom of the wall to finish off the wounded. The bullets chewed up the floor where Joshua's body would have been and ricocheted to the opposite wall.

As fast as the bullets themselves, Joshua's mind drew a line back to the wall beside the door. He imagined the angle the bullets would have taken and carried it out in his brain tracing it to an approximate location in the room beyond. Throwing open the door, he targeted the spot he estimated as the shooter's location by the angle of the shots. A tall man was coming toward the door, gun aimed at the other side of the opening. Joshua hesitated, making sure Amelia was not with him. Shock registered on the man's face, and he leaped behind a shelving unit as Joshua fired.

Pulling back and putting the door jamb between him and the shelving units where the man was hidden, Joshua scanned the room for Amelia. He didn't want to hit her by mistake. He was looking into a large storage area. Pallets of items were lined up in an open area that ran from the door to the other side of the room. To his left were row upon row of shelves that occupied a quarter of the huge room. *What has he done with her?* "Amelia!" He yelled hoping she could hear him and let him know her location.

Clang! A round impacted the metal frame.

"Joshua, I'm here." Past the pallets and a parked forklift, Amelia's eager voice yelled out of a dark doorway in the opposite corner of the room.

The warehouse was well lit by banks of overhead lights. The only other illumination was a single fluorescent fixture that lit the hallway. Joshua noticed the bank of light switches next to the door where he hid. The hallway light was probably on a different circuit that he couldn't shut off with the switches. He fired a round into the ballast on the fixture in the hall. With a spark, the light went dead. A swipe of his hand over the switches plunged the warehouse into darkness.

Joshua dashed into the dark, heading for the image of the nearest pallet that was burned in his mind when the lights went out. A volley of silenced rounds resounded in the room accompanied by the varied sounds of the items they struck. He thanked the Lord none of them was him. His outstretched hand struck the boxes that were stacked on the pallet, and he ducked behind it. A bullet struck nearby.

The shooting stopped. Joshua listened. He wished he had Gabriel's ears, but at least he was no stranger to the dark. The blackened room had nothing on the remote cave in Cyprus where he had trained. He had learned to fight in dark, cramped quarters to prepare for possible combat in the underground hideouts of the ISIS leaders in Syria. If the FFI was a former Kidon assassin, he might have received the same training.

There was a scrape of a shoe. Joshua cautioned himself. *Don't be deceived by sound.* He had learned even small sounds can echo. You might think it is coming from one direction when it really comes from another.

Lifting one of the boxes on the pallet, he determined it was light enough. Grabbing it by one of its flaps, he swung the box in a high arc toward the shelving and jumped to the next pallet as the box crashed from a shelf to the floor. He stopped and listened. The FFI would be doing the same.

Joshua's eyes began to detect the tiny glow of an LED on the charging unit of some tool on a bench along the wall to his right. He inched forward always feeling first with his free hand to make sure he didn't collide with anything. He could just distinguish the next pallet and moved behind it. He hoped he wasn't hiding behind anything flammable or explosive. He listened.

His eyes were adjusting, magnifying the visibility provided by the LED. That meant the FFI was getting the same benefit. Joshua was too close to the light. He feared his movements would be seen. The shelving units behind which the FFI had hidden were still obscured in darkness. He could see the ends of shelves but could only look down the closest row. It was a dark tunnel the glow didn't penetrate. The FFI could be at the end of it with a gun pointing his direction. Joshua remained perfectly still. The tiny light from the charging unit was becoming a beacon, casting the shadow of the pallet onto the floor as his eyes embraced the darkness. *Help me, Lord.*

Joshua heard the rustle of cloth against something. It sounded like it came from down a shelving row to his left. In the glow, Joshua examined the area around the pallets, using his peripheral vision since it was better in low light situations. Nothing moved. The FFI must be in one of the rows between the shelving units, maybe moving to get Amelia and use her as a shield. He wanted to work his way across the open area and get to Amelia, but it felt too much like a setup. Would they both be trapped when he got there? He didn't want her in the middle of an exchange between him and the man. Better take him out here in this large room where no one else would get hurt.

As he searched for options, Joshua's ever-increasing sight revealed another door near the workbench where the red glow came from. On the wall beside it was another set of light switches. He decided to take a risk. Easing out, he stayed low, keeping the pallet between him and the shelves, shifting his head to pick up any sign of his adversary. His gun was toward the row of shelving where he had heard the movement, but his head swiveled, searching for the other man. The LED glow gave him a slight impression of the pallets and the forklift in the open area of the room and the closest end of each shelving unit. The blackness engulfed the rest of the shelves. Moving to the light switches, he let the glow guide him. He scanned the room one last time for the FFI. If the man was where he had a line of sight to Joshua, what he was about to do was suicide. But he needed an advantage to stop his adversary from reaching Amelia.

Joshua crouched beside the door and faced the floor. He clamped his free hand over his eyes and with the back of his gun hand, he flipped the light switches on. He didn't dare look to see if they came on. He couldn't afford to search for the FFI. All he could do was wait for the eternity that it took for a few seconds to pass. He kept his eyes squeezed tight, hand covering them, maintaining the precious adjustment his eyes had made to the darkness, hoping a bullet didn't find him. *That should be enough.* He swept the light switches back off. Someone ran into something.

Joshua's hand came off his eyes and he immediately moved to the shelving unit where he heard the noise. Gun forward he crept down the row. His peripheral vision picked up the shelves on each side, something his opponent should not be able to do after the lights had ruined his night vision. He pressed forward, exploiting the advantage. More noises came from the right, like hands feeling their way along the shelves, touching boxes. The first set of shelves ended, forming a walkway crossing the rows. In front of him, the row continued between the next set of shelves. He could go right, left, or forward. He saw nothing down the walkway. His vision was improving even more in the deeper darkness between the shelves.

There was a clang and a rattle. Further in and to his right. Joshua moved toward the rattle, following the walkway. He decided the sound came from about two shelves over. He came to the row and turned. A flashlight blazed from above. The beam of brightness pierced the dark of the row next to him and swept his way. The FFI was on a top shelf and had a flashlight. Joshua fired at the light then flattened himself against the shelf. A bullet struck the floor beside him at the same time he heard the silencer.

"Now that you've done me the favor of giving away your position, I would be a little more careful." The man's voice sounded surprisingly calm. "The explosives are just above my head. You wouldn't want a stray round to bring this part of the building down on the young lady in the next room."

"Joshua?" Amelia's voice was filled with new hope.

He was already discovered so he returned the plea. "I'm okay. Are you?"

"He hasn't hurt me. I'm praying he won't hurt you. I'm praying he will see this is not the right way."

Another round pinged off the rack above Joshua's head causing him to drop even further behind the shelves.

The man called down to him. "I, on the other hand, do not find myself in need of caution about firing on you. You might want to consider backing out and letting me finish my job. I'm willing to do as the lady says and not hurt you if you will let me finish my mission."

Joshua evaluated his predicament. Ibbie had said the next explosives should be on a supporting column. The shelving unit that the FFI was on must be on the other side of the column. Joshua's rounds wouldn't penetrate such a pillar. The man had known better than to use his flashlight without something to hide behind. He knew Joshua would shoot at the light. Instead, he had deliberately made the noise to lure Joshua to him. The FFI had taken the high ground with the column as cover and the danger of the explosives to make Joshua reluctant to shoot. The C4 he found in the other room shouldn't go off if struck by a bullet, but firing indiscriminately could hit the detonator and wasn't a good use of ammo either.

Joshua realized the man couldn't move from his position without sacrificing his cover. Joshua would hear him if he climbed down. The light was fixed on the shelving above, waiting for him to move. The plywood shelf exploded near his head and he felt a sting in his shoulder. He moved back from his position as another round tore through the shelf, further away.

Joshua felt his shoulder. He winced as his fingers came to a long splinter sticking out of his shirt. It didn't feel deep enough or big enough to endanger him. He pulled it out, ignoring the pain and tossed it away. Flattened against the shelf, he crept backward until he reached the end of that set of shelving and moved around the corner. It was a much better position. Any round from the FFI would have to penetrate the shelving at an angle and also go through what was on the shelves.

Joshua accessed his options. The man's flashlight would eventually go dead. But it would take time. Things were still moving upstairs with Ibbie and Marsha and eventually Norm would get suspicious. A long standoff wasn't an option. If he moved into the row on the right or the left to get back to the door, he would be an easy target. With his back pushed against the end of the shelf, he examined the racks across the walkway in front of him. Boxes of varying sizes held their places on the shelves. Joshua dropped and slid onto the lowest shelf, pushing boxes outward until some moved onto the floor. Low crawling, he cleared the cardboard obstructions like a snowplow down an alley. The boxes made little noise as they moved off the shelf and into the aisle. In the dark, he doubted if the FFI could see what was happening. A few of the boxes were heavy and left the shelf with a scrape and a thud, but still, the noise was only enough to speculate on. It was the FFI's turn to wonder where Joshua had gone.

As he reached the end of the shelves, Joshua noticed the light sweeping down the row beside him. When he moved out a box, a round struck near his hand. He had been discovered. He hurried to the end and crawled out.

The pallets were in front of him and he ran to the nearest. The light was sweeping back and forth. He timed his advances, so he was moving in the dark from pallet to pallet until he reached the forklift. It sat with its forks still under a pallet. He slipped around to the side that put the pallet and forklift between him and the FFI. Joshua used his phone screen to examine the controls. It was electric, similar to the ones they used to load their equipment on transport planes.

When Joshua turned on the power and raised the forks, the light jerked quickly his direction. A round rang a tune on the metal above him, but the pallet absorbed most of the gunfire. Driving in reverse, Joshua kept the cargo between him and his most attentive audience. The rounds had ceased. They were having no effect. The man was saving ammo or reloading. The flashlight went out and the room went black again. Joshua clicked on the forklift lights.

He steered around the pallets and came to the door Amelia had called from. He wanted to jump out and run in and hold her, but he couldn't. Instead, he yelled into the open door. "I'm okay. I love you. Stay where you are."

"I'm zip-tied to a shelf. I can't go anywhere. What do you mean you love me?"

A bullet zinged off the metal cage on which the lights were mounted. Joshua aimed the pallet at the shelving unit that stood between the unit the FFI was shooting from. With enough speed, he should be able to tip the first unit into the next and topple the FFI's perch. A second shot knocked out the light leaving only one. Joshua grabbed one of the boxes and used it to jam the accelerator to the floor. The forklift sped forward toward the FFI's position. The other light shattered, and the blackness returned.

Joshua leaped from the vehicle, but in the dark, his landing was poorly executed. His feet hit the pavement before he expected, and he couldn't catch up with them. He went down at the same time he heard a crash followed by the rumble of boxes falling and hitting the cement with a heavy thud followed by another. He was able to absorb the fall with a forward somersault and came back on his feet only to stumble over a pile of boxes that had been ejected from the load. He rolled again and this time he stayed on his hands and knees to orient himself. His gun was gone. Someone kicked a box near him and started to stagger by.

Joshua targeted the sound and hit the man in the shoulder like a football blocker. Something went clattering to the ground. It felt like he tackled a wildcat. An elbow connected with the side of his head, rattling what was inside. He shook it off and wrapped up the arm in a lock. The arm twisted out, and he felt a hand at his windpipe. Striking upward he cleared the hold before it could crush his trachea. Hands came at him again. He blocked and parried, struck and punched. The other hands were doing the same, both striking out in the dark, searching for targets and escapes. He landed a knee somewhere low and produced a groan from the FFI. A well-placed elbow to his midsection brought a groan of his own. Joshua had an arm again and was pulling it in for a joint lock when he heard the click of a switchblade. He brought his leg up to block his torso and felt a sting go into his thigh. He thrust out with the leg and took the knife from the grip that held it. His foot connected with the man's chest and he felt his opponent go backward. Joshua grabbed for the knife in his leg, but it was gone. His hand was wet and sticky. He jumped to his feet despite the penetrating pain from his wound. Flinging blood from his hand, he moved to the sound of the man sucking in air and pulling himself to his feet. Joshua had him again, around the neck. The FFI dropped, twisting and clawing his arm away. The slippery blood made it hard to grip. A punch connected on Joshua, but the FFI never got his arm back as Joshua wrapped it up and threw his legs around the man, taking him back to the ground. The exertion made the wound in his leg feel like it had been stabbed again. The blood let the man slip his arm free and he began repeatedly ramming his elbow against Joshua's wounded leg. Joshua tried to block the blows, but the pain made his leg grip loosen involuntarily. The man spun away from the hold. There was the sound of a handgun skittering across the floor as the man fumbled to retrieve it. Joshua grabbed a box, threw it and rolled as fire spat out of the gun barrel and lit up the room.

Chapter 21

Ibbie didn't like leaving Joshua without phone contact, but they both needed to stay focused. Hopefully, the little gift she sent him on his phone would help. The plan she and Marsha put together required some things that would take time to collect. She had to keep herself from thinking about what might be happening to Joshua and Amelia in the basement.

A little shopping trip would take care of the props. The picture that Marsha sent her would help her calculate the size she needed. But she also needed something to fit inside what she was about to buy. Finding the right one was going to be harder to do. She might have taken on an impossible task. If Joshua was with her, he would be telling her that the Lord Almighty likes to deal in the impossible. *God, everything depends on You helping me get the right one and fast.*

Amelia heard the sound of stumbling and panting, approaching the door. "Joshua?" She breathed out his name, hoping. The person was feeling along the wall in the room just outside the door. The lights came on in the next room, the room where Joshua battled Mr. A. "Joshua!" There had been so much shooting and loud crashes, and…Joshua had said he loved her. He had to be alive. If he had won the fight, then there was no reason not to answer. "Joshua!"

It seemed like a long time, but it was probably only a few minutes before she heard someone running toward the door. Again, in a hushed tone, fearing, hoping, she called, "Joshua?"

Mr. A. came through the entry, the knife in his hand. His face was bruised and scratched, and his clothes were a tie-dye of bloodstains. He locked the knob and slammed the door. Hurrying to her, he sliced the zip tie. Amelia stared at the blood-covered blade. Mr. A. grabbed her sleeve and wiped the knife with the cloth between his thumb and fingers. All she could do was stare at the smeared impression of the blade on her shirt. When the man grabbed her and forced her toward the exit on the other side of the room, she finally looked at him.

"Where's Joshua?" The question came from her quivering mouth like a plea.

"Dead." Mr. A. expelled the pronouncement like it was the final blow.

Amelia's mind wasn't ready to accept anything close to that word. "Liar."

"I stabbed him and shot him. He's crawled off somewhere to die, but I don't have time to search for him. When I blow this building, it will be his tomb." The man was more intense than he had been earlier. As they reached the other door, his breathing slowed. "Good fighter, though. Awfully good." Mr. A. seemed less invincible.

Putting things together in her mind, Amelia confronted him. "Is that why you locked the door?"

"I never takes chances that I don't have to." Mr. A.

glanced back. "Going after him might be what he wants me to do." The man pushed Amelia through the door. "But it won't matter soon. I'll give him a fitting burial. That will be my final tribute to his honor."

"If you kill him, you will have killed the best of the country that you say you love. He is trying to stop these people and keep Israel's name out of it. All you're going to do is make people associate your act of terrorism with the State of Israel."

"I don't have time to discuss this now." Mr. A. was hustling, dragging Amelia by her arm, following the path of something high in the open ceiling. They moved from room to room, traveling across the width of the basement. He stopped in another janitorial closet and found a mop. They came into a hall with a suspended ceiling. Sliding a chair from the room they had just left, he stood on it and pushed up a tile. The man gave a frustrated exhale and looked down one length of the hallway and then turned and gazed in the opposite direction.

Amelia took the opportunity to resume the conversation despite the risks. She was fighting for Joshua's life. "What if you're wrong?"

The man cast a perplexed look in her direction. "If I'm wrong it won't do me any good to keep going. I'll have to start over and go the other way."

His comment surprised Amelia for a moment. *Thank you, Lord.* "That's all it takes, a willingness to admit you're wrong and start over. God's ready to forgive."

Confusion flickered across the man's face. With a smile, he lowered his head, raised it again and gazed at Amelia. "I appreciate that rather than wanting to see me dead, you think God might be trying to turn my life around. But I was talking about the detonator wire I'm following. I either go right or left. I'm sure this wire goes in a circuit through the basement. One way leads to the call receiver and the other takes me in the circuit back to where I started. If I choose the wrong way,

I'll have to come back here and go the other way. The receiver might be in the next room, either direction, or it might be ten rooms away. But, like the old joke says, 'It's always in the last place you look.'"

The humiliation Amelia felt was dulled by the realization that the man was not having second thoughts at all. He was still on his mission to kill everyone in the building including Joshua. She wanted to cry but realized that wouldn't do any good either. She was also at a crossroads—despair or trust God.

The man was moving her again. He chose left.

Marsha hated waiting, not knowing if Amelia and Joshua were all right. Ibbie had her hands full. She couldn't bother her. Marsha had everything ready on her end. She had found a janitor's wheeled trashcan in a closet and brought it back to the room. At Eve's insistence, she had made Becker's office into a playpen, removing all the dangerous objects and placing them in the outer room. She photographed everything before moving it so they could return the room to its original state. That seemed less of an issue considering what they knew about Becker's status, but still. She found a few soft things to serve as toys for when the babies awoke. Apparently, it was nap time. The little heads each rested on whatever part of Eve they could connect with.

While she worked, Eve had given her some of her background. Marsha suppressed the feelings that wanted to surface in response to the story. She couldn't afford emotions and she didn't particularly care for them either. The protective feeling had passed. It was replaced by irritation that bordered on anger, which she couldn't explain any more than the earlier feeling.

Marsha demanded that her mind behave. She pondered Eve's situation, trying to think of something further to discuss to distract her mind from the slowly passing minutes. Considering Eve, with all the tiny bodies around her, Marsha let out a frustrated breath. There seemed to be only one topic. "Are these your children?"

"Yes. They share my DNA even if I didn't birth them."

"So, they're test-tube babies or something?"

"You want to know the process? They strap me down and take eggs from me and fertilize them in a petri dish full of a nutrient medium. About five days later, when the baby is still only a handful of living cells, they implant them into a surrogate female—is that what you're asking?"

Marsha gave an affirmative nod. "Who's the father?"

"I don't know."

"Maybe it's Becker. Guys like that are arrogant enough to want to spread their poison."

Eve glowered. "My babies aren't poison."

The night she was raped, Marsha felt like she was taking in poison. Even though she consented to the act…*consented?* Sacrificed was more accurate. The General's bed was the altar. Marsha must have been quite a distraction for him to dismiss all his guards just so they could be alone. She always had that to be proud of. What a legacy.

How could you have been so reckless, Dylan? I told you, you wouldn't get out of the mercenaries' compound alive. Reckless was her letting Dylan become more than a partner. If it had been anyone but Dylan, she would have let him die in that hole before she would have given herself to such a man. But she would have died for Dylan. She wished she *had* died. *I should have stolen the General's gun and tried to shoot my way out then Dylan and I could have died together.*

Would he have died with her? She might have still been the distraction that let him escape the impossible situation he had gotten himself into. He certainly escaped their relationship. She should have known he wouldn't make the same mistake as she had, crossing the emotional line with another agent. He kept his lines more firmly drawn. She was going to have to deal with her little problem alone.

Marsha stared at Eve and the gaggle of tiny bodies around her. "They forced you to supply your half of the DNA. It wasn't consensual. Why do you feel such a responsibility to these…?" A tragic little face opened its eyes at the sound of the raised voice. Marsha silenced herself and looked away.

Eve's dejected reply was almost inaudible. "Are we that ugly to you?"

Marsha regretted not facing her, but she felt too awkward to turn around. "I'm sorry." She left her back to the shriveled little lady. "But you can't expect every woman to carry the child of a rapist."

Eve was silent.

Marsha wanted to examine her face, but an internal struggle still kept her from turning. *Since when have I not been willing to face someone?*

"You're one of those aren't you?" Eve's voice sounded monotone and lifeless. "Does Amelia know?"

Marsha hardened herself enough to face Eve again. "One of what?"

Eve stared at the floor. "You murder babies before they're born."

"It's not a baby. It's a fetus, a blob of tissue." Marsha clenched her teeth to control her volume. "You can't murder something that's not alive."

"When you were talking about it being a rapist's baby, it sounded like you considered it more than a blob of tissue, as if it had a destiny."

Marsha set her jaw. *Don't lose control.* She spoke calmly. "A destiny I don't want to be a part of."

Eve put a protective hand over the little ones closest to Marsha. "You can't convince me Amelia knows about this. If she did, she never would have had us come up the elevator with you here. Are you going to kill us?"

"No! Of course not. I'm going to protect you." The stunning effect of the question rattled Marsha. "Amelia knows I'm pregnant. That doesn't have anything to do with…" Marsha paused, realization flowing in.

Eve scrutinized her as if she had just walked into the room. "You're talking about *your* baby." The woman's craggy finger pointed.

Glancing down, Marsha saw her own hand resting against her stomach. She found herself nodding. A sensation moved up from her insides. Nausea overwhelmed her. She searched the room and spotted what she desperately needed. Dashing to the trashcan, she emptied the contents of her stomach.

Ibbie pulled her car into the parking lot of the deserted baseball diamond. Gabriel had his head half-turned to the window, the warm sun shining on his face through the glass, his headphones over his ears. She had planned on turning around and continuing her search through the park when she saw what she was looking for. Through the trees that separated the empty lot in which she was parked from an equally empty volleyball court, Ibbie saw a girl sitting on a bench next to another parking lot. The girl, with her eyes glued to a cell phone, was way too young. She looked to be about twelve. *What are you doing out of school?*

She was the right size. Ibbie's search for a tiny woman had been fruitless. Every adult female she had seen was too large. And who knew if an adult could be convinced to help without a lot of questions? *I don't want to use her. She's only a child.*

Childhood. It was a relative concept. Ibbie remembered herself at that age. She had no memory of her father who was killed in the First Lebanon War, but she wanted to be like him.

At twelve, she was running through her neighborhood in Sderot, playing army in the bomb shelter near her home. Her mother encouraged it so Ibbie would not have far to go when the sirens went off. The concrete structure had been painted with animals and smiling children in bright colors to dim the reality.

Running to shelters at the wailing sound of the warnings was part of daily life until the day the policeman came to the shelter after the sirens stopped. She remembered asking why she couldn't go home, demanding they let her go to her mother, all the time realizing what must have happened, refusing to believe it. She knew lots of people that had been wounded by the rockets that were fired from the Gaza strip. Everyone in Sderot knew. That day, it became real. That day, her childhood ended.

As Ibbie watched, a vehicle pulled into the lot near the girl with its tail end facing Ibbie and its driver side toward the girl. The car was loud, and a playboy bunny sticker covered most of the back window. A muscled male arm hung out the passenger side and flicked an unfinished cigarette onto the gravel. The late teen male driver got out and motioned to the girl. His shirt was too tight and his pants too loose.

Ibbie's senses came alive. *I don't have time for this.*

The girl put her phone away.

Ibbie bristled. *Don't even think about it.*

Hopping over the cable that separated the grass from the lot, the girl walked toward the male.

The driver had left the car running and his door wide open. The passenger drew in his arm and rolled up the darkly tinted window.

Evaluating the girl, the driver spoke to the pre-teen, motioning his hand up and down toward her adolescent figure.

She smiled at his comment and tipped her head in shyness.

The driver began a slow adjustment as he talked, putting the girl between him and the open car door. His head made a nonchalant sweep of the area. There was no one else around.

Ibbie jammed her car into drive as she gave a long blast of its horn. The male jerked and finally saw Ibbie's vehicle. He was turning back toward his car when Ibbie left the baseball lot heading for the volleyball area and lost sight of the scene behind the trees. She picked them up again when she was on the road. The male was back in the car and it was leaving the volleyball lot, spinning its tires in the gravel. The girl was in the same place she had been and was looking confused. Ibbie caught the car's tag as it pulled onto the street and headed the other direction. She jotted it down as she pulled up to the girl who stepped back.

Ibbie spoke to her through her open window. "Crawl in, I'll take you home."

"I'm not getting in there with you. I don't know you."

Ibbie raised her eyebrows. "You were about to get in that car with that boy."

"No I wasn't."

Ibbie shook her head. "Maybe that's not what you were planning, but let me give you a tip. When you see someone get out to talk to you and they leave their door open that means they're not planning on being there long, and when they get back in they might be thinking about taking something with them. You were about to be that something." Ibbie considered what to say next. "I've studied a lot about abductions." She decided it was best not to mention how many she had pulled off herself. "Why do you think he took off so fast when he knew I was watching?"

The girl looked the direction the car had gone and back at Ibbie. Her eyes widened.

Ibbie evaluated the situation. *If you scare her any more, she'll never get in your car or tell you where she lives. I don't have the time to follow her and I can't leave her here knowing that car is trolling the park.* She needed to take the girl with her, at least for now, and there seemed to be only one way that was going to happen. The girl was the perfect size. Maybe she *was* the right one.

It had taken plenty of persuasion and challenged Ibbie's patience, but they were finally in the surveillance van. Ibbie turned to the girl in the seat behind her who had identified herself as "Savannah." The sweats fit perfectly over the basketball shorts and T-shirt she wore. She pulled the hood around the girl's head, so her face was obscured by the covering. "You're a rebel, remember? You always wear your hood in the hood."

"Nobody says 'hood' anymore. And I wouldn't wear this anywhere. What kind of study did you say this was?"

"It's to test people's reaction to young children. But we have to prevent bias, so we have to conduct the study undercover. You're sure you don't know anyone that works at the DNAble building?"

The girl shook her head. She stared at the $100 bill Ibbie had given her when she climbed in the van. She seemed contemplative.

"You get another one of those if you do a good job. But you have to wear the hood and you can't tell anyone about this. We don't want to influence the study before it's done." *The chance of her keeping her mouth shut is probably zero but if I can get a day or two of quiet out of her, it won't matter after that.* "And don't forget. I'm nice but there are bad people out there. Don't ever get in a vehicle again with anyone you don't know."

"That's a little hypocritical don't you think?"

"Yes, it is but I'm desperate. I need someone who's the right size."

"Okay, then it's going to cost you another hundred." When Ibbie narrowed her eyes, the girl looked aloof. "Hey, you came to me."

Ibbie raised her eyebrows. *This kid's not as gullible as I thought. Eve's not the only one that has been aged beyond her years.* "That's gratitude considering I just saved you from getting abducted."

The girl lifted her chin. "That was your duty as a good citizen. This is business. It will cost you another hundred, so I don't leave and tell everyone."

Don't you blackmail me! If you weren't a kid, I'd... Ibbie gave the girl her pleasant face. "We'll see how well you can act. When we're finished, I'll give you another $200 if you do it right."

"Okay, but you better not stiff me."

Gabriel rocked in the front passenger seat. "Not nice to argue. Not nice to be ungrateful."

Savannah gave Gabriel a look over. "What's wrong with him?"

This kid's lucky she's Eve's size... This country needs mandatory military service starting at twelve. "What's wrong with *you*?"

"Nothing."

"There's nothing wrong with him either. He's just different. It's good to be different." Ibbie muttered under her breath, "For some people, any difference would be an improvement."

"What?"

"Just thinking out loud. Hand me those sacks back there." *Okay, God. Joshua is counting on You...and I guess I am too. Why else would I think this is going to work?*

The girl pulled several shopping bags from the floor behind her seat and looked inside. "What's with all the dolls?"

"Real looking, aren't they? Why didn't they have these when I was a kid? Not that I played with dolls, but...Anyway, I'm about to explain that part. First, I'm going to teach you a skill everyone should know." Ibbie wrapped a doll in a blanket from one of the sacks.

The girl looked dubious. "Okay, what is it?"

Ibbie smiled angelically. "How to hold a baby."

Marsha sat on the floor, leaning against the desk with the trash can between her legs. Her breathing had slowed since the nausea had ended.

Eve stood over her, holding another tissue, just in case.

Marsha gave her best effort at a smile. "Thanks. I think I'm done."

The old woman used her offering to wipe Marsha's sweating brow. The children leaned around both sides of Eve and studied her.

Marsha's feelings were flipping on her again. Taking hold of the woman's wrinkled arm, Marsha gave it a squeeze. "I'm sorry. I'm the one that's full of poison. I wish it would come out as easy as my breakfast."

Eve's bobbing head gave the impression it might fall off. "Trust me. I know. But I believe it works about the same way. You have to be sick of it enough to let it go."

Marsha turned her cheek to the cool metal of the desk. "With all you've been through, how have you survived?"

"Survived is all I have done sometimes. But I know that God's standing by with a divine trashcan ready to take the junk I have inside—when I finally decide to give it up. My challenge has been putting it where it belongs instead of spewing it on people."

Marsha regarded Eve. This was getting even weirder. She felt like the unknown entity she had been talking to might be using the strange woman to talk back.

Ibbie's voice came over the phone. "Are you guys ready? I think I have what we need."

Marsha forced herself to her feet and tied the trash bag she had used. "We'll be on our way in a minute." She went to the small refrigerator built into the bar behind Becker's desk.

Marsha grabbed a soda out of it, popped the top, tipped it back, and began to gargle.

The wheeled cart holding the 55-gallon trashcan clacked down the main hallway on the first floor of DNAble. Marsha hummed a cheery tune to mask the small noises the babies made despite Eve's efforts to keep them quiet. Crammed in the can with a trash sack covering them was not a calming experience. *Don't cry until we get to the lobby.*

Marsha worried about Eve's children they left behind. The office was relatively soundproof as TDH had proven by all that he had done to her there. There was no one in the rooms down that wing. They must all be at the same conference. Still, she worried. She found herself begging they wouldn't be hurt or be found. She couldn't rationalize what difference it made, but she also asked that they not be scared.

Who was she even talking to? That worried her as well. What was this part of her that kept surfacing, causing her such concern about others that she was…praying? What were Eve and her children to Marsha? It was Amelia that started it all.

Everything was in disarray—Ibbie and Joshua involving Amelia and Gabriel in the operation, Amelia finding Eve. Marsha liked executing a strategy. Sure, nothing went perfectly, but you flowed within the plan. Joshua often maintained that they were part of Someone else's plan—like the controller that believed he was in control but wasn't. That was the part she didn't like.

A restroom door opened in front of Marsha and a man emerged. Smiling at him, she hummed louder. Pretending to adjust the janitor tools in the plastic caddy fastened around the large receptacle, she stretched her body between the man and the top of the can, as she passed him. She knew he would be doing a double-take and watching her from behind. As long as he was fixated on her, he wouldn't care what was in the trashcan. She always turned heads. It was her way of hiding in plain sight. Everyone believed she was one thing when she was another. She was beginning to wonder what she really was.

Ibbie led the way into the DNAble lobby, wearing the motherly dress she had picked up at the thrift store downtown. She didn't want her clothes looking too new. She was patting the baby doll on her shoulder. Behind her, Gabriel carried a doll wrapped in a blanket like a real baby. Savannah followed with a doll of her own. Gabriel emitted small baby fussing noises, enough for three. Ibbie glanced back at him in that motherly way and ascertained that he was holding the doll as she showed him to mask his mouth movements.

The professional woman behind the desk rose at the sight of the procession.

Ibbie recognized the look as anything but motherly. *That's right, sweety. Your worst nightmare.* She sauntered up to the woman. "Hi. My name's Misty Dawn Chandler and I want one of those DNA tests." Ibbie hoped she had done well enough with the makeup to lighten her olive complexion and hide the mark from the airbag. Before the receptionist could sink too deep into the recognition that Ibbie's Israeli features didn't match her name or the southern accent she was using, she launched into her story designed to distract. "You see I had triplets but no one in my family ever had triplets and no one in my husband's family ever had triplets and so now my mama tells me I was adopted but nobody can find the records and I need to know who I am and where these triplets came from." Ibbie didn't have to look toward the door that opened, she knew it would be Marsha entering because it was Gabriel's cue. A baby's cry seemed to emanate from the bundle that Savannah held.

The receptionist's dumbfounded eyes brightened, and she

waved at Marsha. "Oh, hi. Mr. Herschlag called down a little while ago and said you were going to be our new custodian. That is so strange how you needed a job and there it was."

Marsha acknowledged the woman. "Funny how things work out."

Ibbie brought her back to their conversation with a silly giggle and her free hand touching the woman's arm. "I mean I know where my triplets came from, but I want to know if I have a rich relative out there that might be gonna die soon and leave my babies anything because I want them all to go to college, ya know?"

Marsha crossed the room and entered the restroom. The crying grew in volume.

Ibbie gave a frustrated look. "Oh, there goes little Martha Mae. Savannah, take her in the bathroom and see if she needs changing." Ibbie patted her own bundle of joy. She could tell the cooing noises came from Gabe, but she knew he was forming the sounds so the acoustics in the room would make it sound like a baby in Ibbie's arms, from the receptionist's point of view. Likewise, the crying moved away and accompanied Savannah into the other room.

Ibbie pulled the woman back into her bizarre narrative. "So, my mama says I was born in Missouri, but up there they got closed records about adoptions and they say I can't find out who my mother was so my Elmer, that's my man, he says someone at work got one of your tests and found his half-brother he didn't know he had so I figure I should get one so you can tell me who my mama is." Ibbie ad-libbed the story with the receptionist trying to interject but failing.

Behind her, the sound of a baby's cries emerged from the restroom. The crying gradually closed in behind her. She could tell the sound was slightly different than the noise Gabriel had produced, and she hoped the woman wouldn't catch it. The receptionist looked over Ibbie's shoulder.

When she turned, Ibbie appreciated that she had her back to the receptionist so the woman couldn't see the shock that certainly inhabited her face. Martha Mae had grown. *Uh oh. I should have gotten bigger dolls.* Ibbie made a quick sidestep to block the woman's view. She spun Savannah, who was starting to say her line to the effect that the baby didn't need changing. Making sure the child's head was covered and her body was hidden behind Savannah's she aimed them toward the front door. "Savannah, take that child to the car and put her in her seat. She's mak'n so much noise, mama can't talk to the nice lady."

With Savannah on her way, Ibbie turned back to the woman. "They sure grow up fast don't they?"

She allowed the woman to get a word in. "Yes, they do. Now, Ms. Chandler, we would be happy to provide you with a test. While we can't guarantee you will find what you are looking for, we know you will be amazed at the results. We have had many people find relatives to connect with and learn family history that had been lost to them."

"See, that's what I need to do, find one of those rich lost relatives."

The woman gathered some forms and a clipboard. "I don't know if you will find any rich…"

The crying was growing louder again but Ibbie knew it would be Gabriel this time. He was sounding exactly like the noise Eve's child had made. He had known to adjust his sound effects to match the real cries.

Savannah was back. She was coughing as she tried to say her next line. "Mama, she must have been just gett'n ready 'cause she's… (the girl made a sound like she might throw up)… messy now."

Ibbie whirled to meet her. Savannah had swapped out Eve's baby for another doll from the van. An odor assaulted Ibbie's nose, making her eyes water. She had provided Savannah a spray can of foul-smelling bathroom odor from the joke section at the dollar store to add to the realism. She must have used the entire container.

The receptionist gagged.

Ibbie cringed when Gabriel's sound effects faltered as he succumbed to the smell.

Gabriel's lapse allowed a faint cry to be heard from the van, letting everyone know that Eve's baby wasn't liking being in the van alone.

Fortunately, the woman had retreated into the side office for a moment to choke in private.

Ibbie took a breath before she could say her next part. "Well…*cough*…take her…*cough*…to the bathroom…*deep breath*…and change her." Maybe the girl's mistake was divinely inspired. Ibbie glanced over her shoulder. The woman was still overcome. She likely hadn't noticed the weight loss baby Martha-Mae had suffered during the trip to the van and back. Ibbie whispered to Savannah, "Get the next one out," as she made a hurry-up gesture.

Savannah was in the bathroom and out again with another size-shifting child. She called out, "I forgot the diaper bag," as she headed outside.

We might have to recruit this girl. She's doing well.

Gabriel's crying and cooing were back on track when the woman emerged from the office with a tissue covering her mouth and nose. "Perhaps I need to give you a moment to tend to your children."

Ibbie made a dismissal gesture and returned to patting her doll. "Naw. Savannah knows what she's doing." *But remind me never to let her loose with a can of pepper spray.*

Marsha emerged from the restroom pushing her trashcan with her hand covering her mouth. She leaned over and coughed a few times as she crossed the lobby. The original plan called for her to make a comment about needing more trash bags as she wheeled Eve back to get the rest of the children. Under the circumstances, there didn't seem to be a need to make excuses for her leaving the room. The glare she gave Ibbie when she was behind the view of the receptionist was also not in the script.

Ibbie covered her own grin with a pleasant smile to the

woman. "I'll take those forms over to the table and fill them out." Savannah was on her way back to the restroom, doll on her shoulder, diaper bag in hand. As Ibbie headed to the table she caught Savannah's eye peeking from under the hood and gave her a wink. The girl looked like she was enjoying herself. *Two babies out. Three more to go.*

Amelia jumped as Mr. A. dropped the ceiling tile and swore. He had chosen the wrong way. They could see the lab through large glass windows. They were back where they started.

The man muttered. "Why would they put it at that end? The lab and everything important is this way." He inhaled sharply and released a sigh of resolution. "Come on. Back the other way."

Exhausted and in pain, Amelia didn't care what he did to her. "Please, can you take this zip tie off my hands? They're hurting. They've been hurting for a long time. If you can't find somewhere inside of you that cares about that, then there is something deeply wrong with you. I'm not your enemy. Your enemies are terrorists. They hurt innocent people to get what they want. They hide behind women and children. But look at yourself. That is exactly what you're doing."

Mr. A. grabbed her arm and yanked her in close.

Amelia felt her lip quiver, making her words sound weak. But she said them anyway. "If you're not different than the people you're fighting, then why fight them?"

The man stared at her. She didn't look away. Amelia realized she had faced demons like his before. They had tried to keep Gabriel and her separated. They had tried to break her down to self-destruction after her parents died. God had kept them from annihilating her. The ones inside of Mr. A. were no different. They couldn't do anything God didn't let them, and she trusted Him. Even if this man was going to kill her, she trusted God.

Mr. A. clicked the switchblade open. Amelia clenched her teeth. He sliced through the zip tie. She closed her eyes at the relief, flexing her fingers and rubbing her abraded wrists.

The man let go of her arm and walked back the way he had come.

Amelia trailed behind him.

He stopped and turned on her. "I've let you go. Why are you following me?"

"I'm not. I need to help Joshua. He's that direction." The man started to turn, but Amelia had more to say. "And maybe I can help you, too. I don't want anything to happen to you either."

The man stood for a moment without turning around. Then he took off walking quickly without comment.

Amelia hurried after him.

Chapter 22

Marsha was practically running down the hall. She needed to get back to the other babies. Putting her hand under the trash sack, she touched Eve's head. "Hang on." She wheeled the cart around the final corner in the hallway.

All Marsha saw were two big hands latching onto the cart and stopping it. Her momentum propelled her into the plastic container as it impacted a body that was over twice Marsha's weight.

Eve let out an involuntary "Uhf."

Marsha looked up into the eyes of Seth.

At Eve's sound, he ripped the trash bag out of the can and jumped back in reaction to Eve's face. "What the…? How did you get out here?" He looked up at Marsha and grabbed the cart again. "What's going on? Where have you been?" He ran his eyes over her Whistle Cleaners shirt. "You're a janitor?"

Marsha sighed and put on her sweet voice. "Seth, you're just not keeping up." She sidestepped and jerked the can, rotating it out of the man's grip. Pulling the cart past her, she snatched the broom from the tool holder as the can and Eve rolled down the hall away from Marsha and out of danger.

Spinning the broom like a fighting staff, Marsha leaped at Seth. He threw up his right hand in reflex. She rotated the broom handle and powered it into the outside of the man's arm, driving it inward and sweeping away his defense. Reversing her momentum, she brought the end of the broom smashing across Seth's face. The man staggered backward. Marsha flipped the cleaning implement and switched her hand placement in one move. She thrust the bristle end between Seth's legs and brought the handle horizontal as she leaped forward and around the back of the man. The broom locked up Seth's legs and twisted them out from under him. He fell on his back with a thud. Flowing through the move like she was sweeping the last of the dirt out the door, she spun the broom and jabbed Seth in the solar plexus, bringing what defense reflex he had left to his stomach. Several quick thrusts to the head put him out.

Bending over the big man, Marsha felt for a pulse. He was alive. *Oh well. Better for Eve. She's seen enough death.* She relieved Seth of a gun in a waist holster, his cell phone, and his key card.

Looking up to check on Eve, she saw the little woman standing in the trashcan, eyes wide, mouth open, mesmerized by what she had seen. Hurrying to her, Marsha felt the urge to give her a comforting embrace.

Eve threw up her hands and pulled back.

Marsha stopped in shock. "It's okay. I'm not going to hurt you." She looked back at Seth. "And I'm not going to let anyone else hurt you either."

After a quick glance around the corner, Marsha put the trash sack over Eve, and they hurried on to Becker's office. In a few moments, they were inside. One baby was whimpering.

Leaving Eve with the kids, Marsha took the trash can and returned to Seth. She laid the can on its side and maneuvered Seth's upper body into it. Throwing his legs over her shoulders, she pushed and pulled until she had the container upright with Seth inside. Once she was back in Becker's office, Marsha used an electrical cord from a maintenance room to hogtie Seth and fasten him to a closet door. He wouldn't move any time soon. She also covered his mouth with packing tape.

Standing back to survey her work she smirked at the man. "Be thankful no one's tasing you." She frowned at the unconscious form. They couldn't leave him behind to tell what happened. Joshua had told Ibbie that they were going to have to get Herschlag out and hold him until after the locals could raid the place. Seth would have to go with him. *But how am I going to get you out of here without anyone knowing?* She let a smile spread across her face. *You, I can put in the dumpster.*

Ibbie had been stalling by asking ridiculous questions about the forms. She could tell that Gabe was getting tired of providing the sound effects for the occasion and Savannah was getting impatient for her next performance. *Where are you, Marsh?*

She texted her partner. YOU OKAY?

In a moment, the response came. ON MY WAY. HAD TO VISIT WITH SETH A MINUTE.

Really. I wonder how that went?

It wasn't long before Marsha came through the door. Almost immediately, a baby was crying. The receptionist looked at Ibbie, reminding her that it was her baby that Gabriel threw the cry into this time.

Ibbie patted her doll's bottom. "Savannah, could you go in the bathroom and mix some formula in a bottle so I can feed Bobby-Joe."

Savannah obediently picked up the diaper bag and headed

for the bathroom. The restroom door had just shut behind Marsha.

Ibbie directed a comment to the receptionist. "I better make sure she gets it right. I'll take him to the van to feed him and make sure he doesn't need changing."

The woman nodded. "Perhaps that would be best."

Ibbie held up the forms. "I'll be back to finish these."

"Take your time."

Marsha had one of the babies wrapped up in the doll's blanket, ready for Savannah to take out. She looked up when Ibbie came in. "These babies are a lot bigger than the dolls. You sure this lady isn't going to notice?"

"She might this time since we don't have Savannah's stink bomb to cover us. You better go out and distract her somehow."

Marsha furrowed her brow. "Did you have something in mind?"

"I'll leave that up to you."

Giving a sigh, Marsha took Ibbie's doll and put it in the trash sack at the top of the trash can. Removing the bag, she revealed a tiny bald woman, who looked ancient. The woman held a small toddler who had a large head. Marsha took the child from the woman who then picked up another baby that was sitting beside her in the trash can. Wrapping the little one, Marsha handed it to Ibbie.

With a real baby on her shoulder, Ibbie leaned into the trash can and held her hand out to Eve. "Glad to meet you. Soon this will all be over."

Eve took her hand. "I've waited all my life." Her smile made her wrinkles glow.

The baby was crying, wanting Eve. It seemed all the poor woman could do to heft the other baby, but she reached out a hand and stroked the child that Ibbie held. The baby calmed. Relieving Eve of the child, Marsha helped the frail woman from the trash container. Eve took the baby back and went into a bathroom stall and closed the door.

Marsha tossed the sack of dolls in the now empty trash container. "Here." She held out the hard drive that contained the data mining. When Ibbie took it, Marsha added, "I also got a little present for you, courtesy of Seth." She handed Ibbie a key card. "This might come in handy for whoever executes the warrant on this place. Clone it and send it back in with the girl. Give me a couple of minutes with Ms. Congeniality." She pushed the cart ahead of her out the door.

Ibbie turned to Savannah as they both bounced crying babies. "I'm going to add a little extra to your wages. You've done well." She smiled sheepishly at the girl. "I have to tell you that I wondered about you when we first met but I guess Someone else knew what He was doing. I couldn't have asked for anyone better."

The girl was beaming. "Sorry I was such a jerk at first. I was worried. I didn't trust you, but I didn't want to pass up the money." Tears came to the girl's eyes.

Ibbie probed. "What's wrong?"

"My mom's been sick and lost her job. I know it sounds like some kind of con, but it's been…" Savannah wiped her face on the baby's blanket and wrinkled up her nose. "Ooo! Is this the blanket I…?" She sniffed lower. "No, this kid really does need a change."

Ibbie cackled for a minute. "But what were you going to say…about your mom?"

The girl shook her head like she was starting over. "My mom…she's been praying for grocery money. That's what she's always done. Her prayers always work. Every time we're down to our last bowl of cereal, someone gives us something or we get some money we didn't know was coming. Mom never asks anyone for anything. It just happens. Ever since my dad left, I've been kinda mad at God, so I didn't want to believe it was Him. I figured we had used up all our luck this time because nothing was happening. I was thinking about taking off—seeing if I could find my dad and make him give my mom some money. He owes her after everything he's put her through. So I skipped school and was sitting in the park trying to find him through people we used to know when that car came up. I know it was stupid, but I was mad. I would have done it, if I hadn't met you. And now we have grocery money. It's like it was all planned. Crazy, huh?"

Ibbie reached out the arm without a baby and gave her a squeeze. "Not crazy at all. I've got a friend like your mom. You were an answer to his prayer. I was the one God needed to convince. I guess we'll both have to have more faith from now on. My friend tells me that we're supposed to have the faith first, but God must have known we both needed a break this time."

Savannah nodded.

Ibbie jerked her head up. "We better get out there. Marsha's probably tap dancing by now."

When Ibbie pushed open the door, she heard Marsha say, "Let me look at the back of it one more time."

The receptionist turned her head in the other direction.

Marsha handled some strands of her hair and mouthed in Ibbie's direction, "It's about time." To the woman, she said, "I just love the way it lays. I am so going to switch stylists." The look she gave Ibbie said, 'and maybe partners too.'

Ibbie and Savannah hurried out the door with their larger bundles.

The man stopped in front of Amelia and gestured toward a door. "That's the way to where I last saw your friend. It winds through a few rooms. You'll have to find your own way. I can't afford the time."

Amelia turned toward the door then turned back. "What are you going to do?"

"What I came here for."

"Please don't do it. With Eve's testimony, we can show what DNAble is doing. They're guilty of murder. They won't get away with that. Ibbie said law enforcement can get a warrant and arrest everyone and seize the evidence. Help Joshua and we might be able to arrest people in New York and other places. But if you blow up the building, some of the evidence will be lost and all of the big dogs will get away. Plus, your organization will be associated with Israel and the world will blame them. You're going to cause a lot of problems for the country you say you love."

"Israel already has problems. Our leaders are cowards. They refuse to act when our nation is surrounded on all sides by people that vow to destroy us. Hamas rains rockets on us almost daily. I am doing far less than what happens in my country. You haven't dug women and children out of the rubble of an exploded building."

"You're right. I haven't. But if you do this, an innocent family member could be learning what that feels like tomorrow. If Israel gets blamed for a terrorist act on U.S. soil, think what ammunition it will give to all of Israel's critics. Ibbie says the team has everything it needs to do this the right way. Let it work. If it doesn't, you can always do this later."

The man stiffened. "No, I can't. I have Becker's keys. The explosives and detonators are in place. All I have to do is change out phones. If your plan fails, none of that will be available to me. I might be able to blow a hole in the side of the building at best. My window will be closed." The man contemplated. "And your plan won't work either. Becker was supposed to be back tomorrow. His body will not be found, but when they are not able to contact him, they will know he is either dead or has betrayed them. Either way, they will destroy the evidence. Your window will be closed before you can do this raid of yours."

Amelia felt like she had been punched in the stomach. Everything they had done would be for nothing. "Then at least help me get Joshua out of here. Help me find him and help us get out before you set off the explosives. Please!"

"I'm going to do my job. You can help your friend. That is the best I can do. Be thankful for it." Mr. A. turned and followed the deadly wire in the ceiling.

Amelia called after him. "Thank you. I'm grateful for what you've done…I just know you could do more. I pray that one day you will be free from whatever is stopping you."

The man straightened his shoulders and hurried on.

In the van, Ibbie worked to quiet Eve's children as she handed the last doll to Savanah. "It has been a pleasure to work with you."

Savannah took the toy.

Ibbie pulled the key card cloning device out of a cabinet in the back of the van and made a copy of Seth's card. She gave the original to Savannah. "Tell the janitor lady she dropped this." Ibbie winked.

The girl nodded and turned to the toddlers in their car seats. "This wasn't really a study or anything. It was more important than that wasn't it? Did we, like, save these babies from something?"

Ibbie examined the pre-teen. The girl waited for the answer—hopeful and expectant. Ibbie put her hand on the thin adolescent shoulder. "There are some things so important that they can never be mentioned. Things that not only save lives, they save nations and stop horrible evils from happening in the world." Ibbie paused to let what she said sink in.

The girl looked like she had won the lottery without even buying a ticket.

Ibbie went on. "Some of the greatest heroes never get any recognition. They don't do it for that. But they know this world is a far better place because of their service."

The girl hardly reacted as Ibbie took the doll from her hands and wrapped it in the last blanket.

"Yeah. So, like, do you do Snapchat or anything? My mom even has a Facebook account if that's better."

Ibbie's smile was pressed and hardened from all the things she couldn't say. "We never met. This never happened, no matter what you hear or see. If you see me somewhere, even on television, no one can ever find out you recognize me. It won't be safe for either of us."

Savannah lowered her head, and a frown took over.

Ibbie put the bundle in the girl's arms and squeezed it in place. "But I will never forget you."

The light slowly came back to the young face. It shifted to concern. "What do I tell Mom?"

"Tell her God answered her prayer." Ibbie put an envelope in Savannah's hand. "Tell her a lady you never met before gave you some money and told you God wanted her to do it—because that's what I'm telling you. There's enough in there to get your mother to the doctor right away and plenty for groceries. You earned it. Call the phone number on the card. The person will make arrangements to take care of you and your mother and her medical bills until she can work again."

Savannah grabbed her in a hug.

Ibbie squeezed her then motioned toward the DNAble building. "The janitor will wait until she knows you made it out. Go straight home and don't let anyone know you have that money until you give it to your mom. Don't tell anyone about this, not even your friends." Ibbie winked. "You never know who people really are."

Savannah nodded conspiratorially.

Then Ibbie put on a stern look. "But seriously, be careful."

Savannah rolled her eyes. "I know."

"You better. I have high hopes for you. Work hard in school. Don't get in trouble. Get going. That janitor's waiting."

Savannah lingered. "So, tell Gabriel it was good working with him. That's really cool what he can do." She gave an embarrassed smile. "And tell him to stay different." Savannah clutched her baby and jumped out.

Ibbie reached out and caught her arm. "When you get older you might want to consider the CIA. Don't be surprised if they know your name."

The young eyes widened in wonder.

Marsha listened just enough to the receptionist's prattle so that she could respond if necessary. With an absent gaze, she watched as the sweatsuit clad teenager entered, trying to console the baby on her shoulder. It was amazing how from where she and the receptionist stood the sounds that Gabriel made appeared to come from the bundle she carried.

The girl came toward them with her hood tipped toward the receptionist just enough so her face couldn't be seen. She handed Seth's card to Marsha. "Here, you dropped this."

Marsha took the item. "Thanks. Don't want to lose that."

The girl trotted off toward the bathroom waggling a bottle in their direction. "I gotta fill this. My mom says that we're going to have to go, but she'll try to come back when she doesn't have the babies."

From the corner of her eye, Marsha saw the receptionist's happy smile and nod. Once the girl was in the restroom, the woman spoke. "Thank my lucky stars. I can still smell that stench. Something's wrong with a kid that smells like that. It'll take the rest of the afternoon to get that smell out of here."

Marsha nodded but didn't mention that she had the offending blanket in a tightly sealed bag in her trashcan. After a few minutes, she heard the bathroom door open, and the figure in sweats reemerged. Marsha shifted to block the receptionist's view of the last expanding baby. She made a comment about the woman's lovely handbag and drew her attention in that direction with a point. Gabriel turned to leave, still patting his baby. The crying went out the door, grew faint, and ended as they both got into the van and it drove away. Marsha waited for the final act as the receptionist went on about the purse.

Savannah came out of the restroom, wearing basketball shorts and a t-shirt. Her air was confident, and she gave a happy wave as she took off out the door and frolicked her way down the sidewalk.

"Where did she come from?" The receptionist's perplexed gaze followed the teen.

Marsha responded like it was of no concern. "She came in earlier and went straight to the restroom. Probably heading home from school and got desperate. I think it was when I was messing with your hair. You must have missed her. Well, I better get back to work. Don't want to get fired my first day on the job."

"Okay, well, come back again and we'll talk. Then we won't have the white trash to worry about. There ought to be a law against those kinds of people reproducing. I'm glad I never plan on having kids. That was disgusting. Families like that are a strong endorsement for birth control." The receptionist grinned at Marsha.

Marsha gave a polite head raise in response. She wanted to slap the woman. She was surprised she didn't consider doing something worse. Her hand went to her stomach and for the first time in ages, she felt like crying. Instead, she moved her hand to the janitor cart. "Speaking of trash." Marsha moved around changing out the bags in the office receptacles and around the receptionist's desk.

The other woman went to gather up the forms where Ibbie had left them.

While the woman was across the room, Marsha pulled out the bag from the trash right behind the receptionist's normal position. She removed the tightly sealed trash sack from her large trash barrel and, holding her breath, she tore open the bag. With sly execution, she dropped the contents in the receptionist's trash can and put a new trash sack over it so it wasn't visible. Leaving the top of the bag loose to allow plenty of airflow, she let out her breath and hurried to the door that led into the inner part of the DNAble building. She waved to the woman, who had made it back to her position. She gave the receptionist a wrinkled nose smile. "Enjoy the rest of your afternoon without all those nasty babies."

The woman was just starting to cough as the door closed behind Marsha.

Ibbie got the verification from Marsha that Savannah was clear. The van was well away from the DNAble building. She looked in the rearview mirror. "Okay, you can uncover your head now."

Eve removed the sweatshirt hood. She looked out the window with wariness. "I can't believe it. You're sure they can't come and stop us? There's no way for them to take us back?"

Ibbie reached back and squeezed her tiny hand. "I'm sure. This is a free country, more or less. There are still many places in the world where you might have to worry about that, but not here, not now. I'm going to hand you off to some agents who are going to take you to a safe place. You tell them what you and the babies need, and they'll get it. You'll be safe and the kids can run around and play while the agent takes your statement."

Eve gazed at all the toddlers who were also seeing things they had never seen before. "We're really out. We're free." She started crying.

Ibbie fell silent. She had taken people out of oppressive countries before. She had freed prisoners. But all of them were coming back to the green grass and blue sky that they had once known. Eve had never seen it before.

Eve sniffed and wiped her nose on the oversized sleeve. "I never believed it would really work. I just walked out. When the girl gave me her clothes and said I was just supposed to walk out with my baby, I didn't think it was possible. Not really. But it worked. They thought I was her and I just walked out." She turned and looked back, but DNAble was no longer in sight. "Will she get out? There's no way they can stop her?"

"She's already out and on her way home. They have no idea she helped you or that you are even gone. And it has to stay that way until we can use your statement to get a warrant. Once people know what they did to you in there, the DNAble people will be the ones in the cell. They can see how it feels."

"When you were talking to Amelia, you said you didn't think Becker was coming back. What did you mean?"

Ibbie hesitated. *I guess there's no reason not to tell her.* "We think Becker is dead. The man that took Amelia back to the basement said he killed him. We have no reason to doubt the claim."

Eve contemplated her feet for a moment. Her voice was a whisper. "Funny, I'm not happy he's dead. I'm just glad he can't hurt anyone anymore." Eve's face said she was moving on from the topic. "What will happen to Amelia? Is someone helping her?"

"Yes. Another agent is in the basement trying to rescue her."

"Only one?" Eve looked over her shoulder, distressed. "If people think this is bad, why can't a lot of people go in and stop all this and save her?"

"That's one of the costs of having a free country. There are limits on what government agencies can do." *Especially when you're not even supposed to be operating in the country.*

"In the United States, everyone is considered free until it is proven that they should not be. We have to show evidence. That's why we need you. With your information, law enforcement can get a warrant to go in and stop this. Before these people can be held accountable for their crimes, there has to be a trial. Do you know what that is?"

Eve looked out at the world. "I have read about it. But I have read about everything I am seeing now, and it's not the same as I imagined, even from video on the internet. How long will a trial take?"

Ibbie considered the U.S. legal system. "Sometimes it can take a long time."

Eve sighed. "I don't have a long time."

"I'm sorry. I know there must be many things you want to do. It won't take all your time. There will be plenty of time for you to live your life." *Oh, Ibbie. Why did you say that?* She gave Eve a look of regret. "I'm sorry. I wasn't thinking."

"It's all right. Please don't be afraid of being frank. The one thing I don't have time for is dishonesty. But who does? Ivan told me no one ever has plenty of time. And he was right. I mean, he's dead and so is Becker, but I'm still alive. It's ironic, isn't it? Time doesn't matter. It's what you do with it."

"What do you want to do with your time?" Ibbie watched Eve in the mirror.

A look of joy overcame the wrinkles. "I've done what's important already. Ivan told me that preparing for the next life is all we're really here for. I gave my life to Jesus." Eve gazed behind them. "I did that in my cell. I guess freedom is a relative thing, isn't it?" Taking a deep breath, she sat back in her seat and looked out the window. "All I want to do now is hold my babies." Eve reached into her sweatpants and pulled out a Bible. Her wrinkles got wrinkles as she grinned. "It's the only way I could bring it with me and still carry my baby. This belonged to the only friend that I had in there. I just want to read this to my children. They will soon be able to understand it more. I want them to keep learning about God because they don't have long either. That's all I ever hoped for. Is there a place I can do that?"

It was all Ibbie could do to drive the van through her liquid filled eyes. "We'll find one." The light coming in her own window seemed brighter. "Maybe I could listen when you read."

Marsha used Seth's card to let herself into the basement hallway. She saw no cameras. There had been one at the top and the bottom of the stairwell. She set aside the broom that she had used to sweep her way down the stairs. For anyone watching the monitors, the speed of her descent would look like shoddy custodial work, but she hoped they wouldn't consider it their job to police the maintenance staff. She eased out the gun she had taken from Seth but kept it hidden behind her leg. If she met someone, she could still play the janitor role if she wasn't pointing a gun in his face when she encountered him. But so far, she was right—the stairs were the road less traveled. Hopefully, the broom had been enough to account for her presence there. Even though the elevator might appear more normal, she didn't want to risk meeting someone that might recognize her as Seth did. She couldn't keep collecting DNAble employees like rare reptiles. The dumpster would only hold so much trash.

Amelia and Joshua were her priority…along with stopping TDH, of course. Nothing mattered if he was able to succeed.

Horrible images were trying to claim her mind for their own and she had to kick them out before they distracted her and caused her to make another mistake. She needed to get back to herself—her hard, ruthless self. The one that always put the consideration of her own survival and success above others.

The image of TDH stood in her mind just as he had stood over her earlier, gun in hand, ready to take her life. The picture merged with something in her subconscious. There was a blurring, a melding with someone else. It was herself she saw, superimposed over the man's calm face. He was her. The same indifference to life. She knew why TDH did what he did. She saw herself there, and she never wanted to be there again. She couldn't go back to that. Something had come alive in her, the most important part, and she didn't want to lose it. In fact, she wanted to share it…with someone like herself. She wondered if TDH would listen.

She had to find a middle ground. The job was important. She had to do it. But she was determined never to let the new Marsha die again. It had started with Amelia. She wanted to talk to her some more. She had to. The hope was in her mind again…like a prayer.

Amelia rushed through the rooms in a panic to find Joshua. *Please, Lord, let me find him. Let him be okay.* After backtracking from a few wrong turns, she arrived in the large room. Joshua had last spoken to her from the forklift. She headed toward the machine. Moving boxes and debris, she searched. Wait…blood on the floor. Amelia let out a squeak of a scream. *Stop it. He's not here. That means he moved. He's alive.* She followed the stains, a smear that way, drops over here. They crossed the room and led her to the doorway on the other side. A handprint on the frame made her jaw quiver. She wanted it to be his hand so she could take hold of it and pull him to her. She stifled the feelings and moved past.

In the hallway, droplets led her to the left. Was it a lot of blood? She didn't know. How much could he lose before…

He's moving. Just follow.

At the end of the hall, into another room, through there, then another door, blood on the handle. Where was he going? He needs to stop, save his strength. *Please, Joshua, don't use yourself up before I find you. Just stop already. Does he know what he's doing?*

Amelia grabbed the handle. It was locked. She yanked at the door. Squeezing her eyes shut, she let her head drop against the hard metal. *Lord, Please. He said he loved me. I love him. Please don't let me lose him now.*

There was no answer. Amelia drew back and slammed her body into the door, over and over. She was twelve again, locked in the counseling room at the Child Protective Services listening to them take Gabriel away. She was trying to beat that door down as well.

Then her mother's voice had come to her from the other side. "Stop, Amelia. Let God do the hard work." Everything had stopped. There was no sound from the other room. The voice had stunned everyone. *Gabriel.* It was something her mother always told her when she was frustrated and trying too hard. Like a voice from heaven, Gabriel had called out to her in her mother's voice. She couldn't let him say it again and give away his abilities.

She called back to him through the door. "I'm okay Gabriel. It will be okay. You're right. God will help us. Go with them. I'll see you later."

And God did help her, through her patience and hard work—the work she could do. She knew how to cook, thanks to her mother. Amelia worked at it until she was an expert. She proved herself responsible, and they let her visit Gabriel. And wouldn't you know it, the home needed a cook. God did what she could not do.

Amelia stood before the locked door, quiet, listening. She heard Joshua's voice in her mind. *I love you. Stay where you are.* It was his last words to her, and it seemed to be God's words to her now.

Amelia shook her head and cried. She looked to heaven. "Lord, I can't just sit here and wait. He might be..." She was telling God things He already knew. *Okay. I'll wait. Please, hurry.*

"Amelia." The voice came from behind her, a hushed, elated exclamation that scared the wits out of her. She jumped and spun around as Marsha grabbed her in a hug. It took a moment for her heart to settle back into place before she could appreciate the woman's presence.

Amelia clung to Marsha squeezing enough reassurance from the contact to keep on standing. She poured out the briefest version of what had happened between her and Mr. A, her dread over Joshua, the blood trail, everything right up to the locked door in front of them.

Marsha furrowed her brow. "I saw the blood down the hall. That's how I found you."

Amelia pointed out the smear on the handle. "I know he went this way, but the door's locked. Amelia brightened and gestured. "But you can pick it."

In a moment they were standing inside a room with a desk, computer and a staircase that led upward. There were two other doors in the room, one to the left and one straight ahead. Amelia scanned the floor. There were blood spots in every direction, toward both doors and the stairs.

Marsha put two fingers to her eyes and pointed to the staircase. She motioned for Amelia to stay put and started up the steps, aiming her gun upward.

As Marsha disappeared around the corner of the stair landing, Amelia huffed. She needed to do something. Joshua needed her help. She tried both doors. They were locked and there was blood on both handles. She ached inside but took a breath of resolution. *Okay, Lord. I get it.*

Chapter 23

Ibbie took the man's hand as he reached out of the vehicle's window and identified himself.

"Professor Reuben Welch." His wide form filled the seat of the large passenger van he drove. The unruly mat of gray hair on his head brushed the van's ceiling liner. Round, ruddy cheeks and a bulbous nose joined the professor's friendly smile, giving him a warm appearance. "In such a situation, there is no need for me to know yours. Our mutual acquaintance told me what you needed. I believe Providence is with us because the institute is not far from here and I think it is the perfect place for your friend and her children. It is run by a couple who love kids and there is plenty of room and a unique learning environment for them to explore their new world in safety. The FBI can come there to interview…what is her name?"

"Eve. It sounds perfect, Dr. Welch. I know your reputation in the intelligence community. I'm grateful to be able to send them with someone I can trust to protect them. I wish I had more time for this handoff, but our mission is at a critical place. I need to get back to support my team. Thank you for helping us."

"On the contrary, I thank you for being willing to take on this mission. You are an answer to our prayers."

The comment surprised Ibbie. "Your prayers?"

Turning his attention upward, the professor said, "For His own purposes, God has chosen to connect me with intelligence sources independent of any of the clandestine agencies of governments. Those sources have been following the suffering caused by the organization you are investigating. My group is not equipped for the type of operation your team is attempting, but we have been praying for intervention from people like yourself. We understand the need for covert strategies to impact what official government channels are unable or unwilling to address."

"I appreciate that, Professor. I hope I can come and visit Eve after this."

"Certainly, anytime. And bring your team. Perhaps we can discuss more about these topics." He pulled open his door. "But I know the tight timetable you are on. Let me meet your unusual friend."

The handoff had taken too long but at the same time had gone too quickly for Ibbie. She watched Welch drive away with Eve and her kids. It was like sending her child off to school, only worse. She was so thankful she would be able to see Eve again. Because, as Eve said, she didn't have long…

Okay, that was enough. She needed to get back to work.

Ibbie looked over to Gabriel. The young man rocked, holding himself with his arms as he swayed. He looked a little pale. "How are you feeling?"

"I want Amelia. Amelia needs to take Gabriel home now."

Ibbie rubbed his shoulder but he pulled away. She pulled out her phone. It was still silenced from when she and Gabriel had been playing their various parts. "I'm sorry Gabriel. Sometimes being an agent is hard. You don't get to sleep like you want. You don't get to eat like you want. You don't even get to be who you want. I hope this will be over soon and you can get back to being Gabriel."

The young man's rocking stopped. "Gabriel likes being an agent. Gabriel is a good agent."

Ibbie mindlessly logged onto her cell. "Yes, you are. But sometimes even a good agent needs to rest."

"Amelia will take Gabriel home. Gabriel will sleep in his bed and then Gabriel will come back and be an agent again."

Ibbie gave him a fond smile as she scrolled through her messages. "We'll see."

"Gabriel needs to be an agent." The rocking started again. "Gabriel needs to be an agent."

"Okay, Gabriel. Shhh." Joshua had sent her a text. She hoped the satellite photo she sent him of where the cell phone antenna cable entered the building had led him to the call receiver. The idea had come to her when she thought about not being able to see Joshua's GPS signal. If Salzman and Herschlag wanted to detonate remotely, they would want to make sure the cell phone would be able to receive the signal all the way in the basement. A cell phone antenna on the outside of the building would be the answer, and they probably would put it as close to where the detonator was located as they could.

She read Joshua's message and sat straight up in the van seat. This couldn't be happening. He couldn't be serious. Her heart began to rev up. *No way, Josh. You can't ask me to do that. You can't.*

Ibbie switched to the audio communication side of the device. She had to warn Marsha.

As Marsha reached the top of the stairs, she could hear a

humming sound. It was faint. There was an opening where the stairs stopped that was darker than the staircase. It emitted some light, but it was dim. All she could see was a wall through the open doorway. She would have to go left to get into the room. Straining her ears, she still could not determine the sound. She reached up and took out her earpiece and put it in her pocket. Still not distinguishable, but at least she could hear better.

Marsha paused on the top step, took a breath, and dashed into the room. There was a movement to her left. She whirled that direction, gun up.

Amelia sat at the desk. God was teaching her patience, again. She wished He had chosen a better time.

She bumped the desk accidentally causing the computer screen to come on. It wasn't a screen saver or password entry box. The computer must not be connected to the DNAble network.

A program was running. The title at the top was, "THE ULTIMATE ANSWER." Below that was the heading, "RELEASE DATE AND TIME." It was today's date, less than two hours away. That sounded ominous.

Amelia read some of the headings that had numbers after them.

DISPERSING FAN SPEED
WIND SPEED AND DIRECTION
ESTIMATED DISPERSION DISTANCE PER
MINUTE
HUMAN TARGET ESTIMATE IN ZONE

There was a video window under the last heading with the words LIVE FEED in the corner. Amelia examined it and after a moment, recognized it as a video of the park behind the

DNAble building—her park. The view was similar to what she had witnessed from Joshua's drone only it was stationary. From the angle, Amelia deduced it must be from the tower on the DNAble roof. There were small red squares moving in the park. On closer examination, she saw the squares were highlighting people enjoying the ballfield, the playground, and the lawns. As more arrived, the HUMAN TARGET number increased.

Ibbie hit her hand against the dash. Why wasn't Marsha answering?

Gabriel spoke up. "Not good to get mad. Not good to hit things."

"I know. I'm sorry, Gabe."

Ibbie read Joshua's text message again. GET MARSHA OUT. LEAVE AREA. FOUND CALL RECEIVER THANKS TO YOU. ABOVE SERVER ROOM. DID WHAT I COULD. NOT SURE CAN STOP FFI. STILL HAS AMELIA. WAITING FOR THEM. TRY LAST TIME TO SAVE HER. IF CAN'T, TAKE CARE OF GABRIEL. THIS IS MUCH WORSE THAN THOUGHT. SOMETHING HORRIBLE HAPPENING SOON. HAD TO USE PHONE TO HACK INTO THE SERVER. BATTERY ABOUT DEAD. HAVE COMPUTER DOWNLOADING LARGE FILE TO CLOUD. HAS EVERYTHING WE NEED. YOU/MARSHA GET DATA TO RIGHT PEOPLE. IF I DON'T MAKE IT, YOU BEST PARTNER COULD EVER HAVE. TRYING VOICE MAIL TO EXPLAIN.

Marsha relaxed. The movement wasn't a threat. A metal container with large glass windows sat against one wall of the room. It was the source of the humming. A glow emanated from behind the glass, illuminating a churning liquid. There was a large pipe coming from the top of the container and going into the wall, which Marsha determined must go to the outside.

As she advanced on the vat, she changed her mind. It didn't really look like liquid. She moved closer. The glow from inside the glass was just enough to illuminate the room. but she decided her original call was right. Something was moving inside. Staring into the container, she began to distinguish what she was seeing. It wasn't something moving. It was a lot of somethings. Thousands, no, maybe millions, of tiny insects swarmed behind the glass. *Did they get in through the pipe?* No. She could see through the vat's window, up to where the pipe was sealed with a louver type closure. By the hardware and wiring on the outside of the pipe, Marsha determined it could be opened electronically. A conduit ran from the pipe's opener through the floor and apparently into the room below. She focused on the nearest insects and worked to identify the familiar-looking forms.

Shivering, Marsha felt like something was crawling on her neck and she swatted at it, but nothing was there—the power of suggestion tricking her. She hoped there wasn't an opening in the container. Who in their right mind would have a huge vat full of mosquitoes?

Amelia felt sick. The words HUMAN TARGET were imprinted in her brain. Her horrific imaginations were interrupted by a key turning in the lock across the room. She ducked beneath the desk.

From her hiding place, Amelia looked through a slit. Mr. A. came in to view. He went to the door on the opposite side of the room from the stairs, opened it with a key and went inside.

Amelia made her decision in a split second. She shot out from under the desk, raced across the room and put her foot against the door so it stopped an inch from fully closing. She panted for a moment. Fearing Mr. A. might see the door hadn't closed and push it shut before she could get in, she pushed it open and stepped inside. Behind her, she heard Marsha's voice call her name from the stairs.

Mr. A. was a little way into the room. He whirled at the sound of Marsha's cry and rushed back, shoving Amelia out of the way and slamming the door just as Marsha hit it. Mr. A. pointed a handgun at the door like he might shoot through it but didn't. Lowering it, he spun on Amelia with a harsh expression.

Turning from him, Amelia fled down an open area along the wall the door occupied. When the man didn't pursue her, she stopped and glanced back. His attention had transitioned to a rapid scan of his surroundings. Amelia accepted the advantage of not being worth his time.

Not far into the room began rows of interconnected metal racks that were filled with stacks of computer-like components. Wires sprouted from various types of ports and crawled like vines across the hardware to other connectors.

The man began grabbing things to barricade the door.

With regretful confidence in Mr. A's skills, Amelia realized Marsha would not be getting in that way.

Cold air poured over Amelia from a vent in the ceiling, but the room was warm overall. The racks of electronics were generating a lot of heat. She scanned the floor. Finally finding what she was looking for, she set off toward one of the aisles between the rows of metal racks.

Ibbie deliberated as she thumb-typed through to get the voicemail Joshua left. He had found the call receiver. He must have beat the FFI to it, but what had happened to him? If he was doubting his ability to stop the FFI, he might be injured.

When she finally got the message to play, Joshua's voice sounded weak and raspy. "Ibbie, I'm in the server room. I can't talk long. My phone's dying. I sent you a text, but I also wanted to send you this message since I might not make it out. I'm sorry to do that to you. I know how you will feel, and I feel the same way about you, but we always knew this might happen someday. Please take care of Gabe."

Joshua took a deep breath. "Listen, this server array is huge. The amount of data they have in here is mindboggling. They have enough information that they can extrapolate the DNA profiles of people who have never taken a test by going through their genetic relatives who have taken one. They can link anyone in the United States and a lot of the world with the data they have.

But when I started data mining, a file popped up from a guy named Ivan. It was like there was a program that was watching for anyone digging for dirt on DNAble, and when it saw what I was doing, it handed me this file. This Ivan guy explains everything, all the bad stuff that DNAble does, giving specifics. I think this guy might be the one that was feeding us intel. There's evidence that DNAble hacked the other major DNA test providers. He shows how they use the data to target latent Jews, and it includes names of people that have been eliminated and how it was done. There's enough evidence on my upload to cinch the case against all the DNAble players, if it matters anymore.

Here's the scary part. This thing's a supercomputer. Ivan explains that Herschlag and the DNAble Corporate people believe Becker is using it to isolate what they believe are undesirable characteristics in the human genome, such as the DNA that results from a Hebrew heritage."

There was the noise of Joshua shifting in pain. "But what he's really been doing is calculating how to change human DNA to produce the most mutations in the shortest amount of time. He thinks he's going to speed up evolution.

"Becker's team made a major breakthrough in what Ivan calls a 'retroactive gene drive.' It's a way to alter a live human's DNA using a virus. This gene drive makes this DNA dominant in a way that it replicates itself like cancer in the human body. In a few years, it will completely alter the individual to produce incredible amounts of genetic mutations. Ivan speculates it will cause sickness, bodily deformities, and mental abnormalities of all kinds. Any offspring these altered individuals have will carry the same traits and produce more mutations, if they survive, which Ivan thinks is doubtful because almost all mutations observed in DNA result in negative consequences to the species, in the end. Ivan speculates it could completely wipe out the human race in a decade or two." Joshua paused. Ibbie could hear him taking several breaths.

There was an ominous tone of deep concern in his voice when he continued. "This isn't just a crazy idea. They have already loaded the virus into millions of mosquitoes. I saw them. Becker even double-crossed Herschlag. He has a computer program set to automatically make the release. I think Becker's team went to the conference to be out of the area when it happened. They have it set up to automatically release the mosquitoes from this building in about two hours. If it happens, it could completely change the human race, starting right here. And I doubt if anyone can say for sure what we would change into. Becker didn't even know and he didn't care. His god was evolution and he was willing to sacrifice everything on that altar.

"I don't have the tools to dismantle the release apparatus without risking the mosquitoes escaping. I'm scared to pull wires without knowing what they do. I've temporarily neutralized the explosives, but I'm rethinking that. I am going to rest a moment and then try to pack enough explosives around the vat to destroy it and every mosquito inside. I want you guys far away when it happens. If I fail, Gosnell might be ground zero of something unimaginable. In that case you'll need to get out of the country, and the U.S. military might have to seal off this area and do something radical."

Joshua didn't seem to be finished. "Something else is going on. I had to pick my way into this room. Norm's card wouldn't work on the card reader. Also, the phone in this detonator looks like it has been changed out lately. I am guessing Norm no longer has the ability to set it off. I think Herschlag was locking Norm out. I'm going to hang out here until the FFI arrives and see—" The recording ended. The battery must have died.

Ibbie wanted to hit the dash again but restrained herself. She looked at the DNAble building through the windshield. Everything had changed. Her contact at the CIA had taken a risk to help them. He had made the arrangements for the FBI to interview Eve without mentioning where Ibbie's team was from. Now she would have to call him back and convince him that they were facing a threat big enough for him to jeopardize his career, and she didn't have time to do much persuading. They had Eve as confirmation, but it was still asking a lot. If help came at all, it would never happen in the window they had.

There had been a few times in her career that Ibbie resolved she might have to sacrifice herself for the mission. And if Joshua was right, this was the most important mission she had ever faced. She reached into her pocket and took out the clone of Seth's key card. It should get her in the back door and the basement.

Facing Gabriel, she took a deep breath. "Gabe, I'm sorry, but I have to ask you to stay in the van while I try to help Amelia and the others."

The young man did the Gabriel rock as he shook his head. "Gabriel can help. Gabriel is a good agent. Gabriel will go too. Gabriel will help Amelia."

Ibbie let out a breath. *Now, what am I going to do?*

Marsha examined the entrance. *What were you thinking, Amelia?*

It had sounded like something had been wedged against the steel-clad door. She would have to go back in the hallway from where she came and try every door in every room hoping there was another way in. *God, why are You doing this to me? I know I've done a lot of things wrong, but You know Amelia. Let me help her.*

She stopped, took a deep breath. *"Please."*

Amelia worked her way to the back of the room. Just a tiny drop of blood here or there. It was so much less than it had been. Was that good or bad? Mr. A. hadn't noticed. He was still in a hurry to follow something else. Amelia didn't care. She had one purpose. *Please, God, let me be right.* Every time she tried to help, she only got in the way. But she couldn't just wait there with Joshua possibly injured and needing help. It wasn't possible. Her heart wouldn't let her.

At the back wall, the blood trail seemed to go two ways. To her left, Amelia heard metallic scraping like someone was dragging something across the floor. Probably Mr. A. It was the direction he had gone. There was double the blood that way. *Joshua must have gone that direction and come back.*

Amelia went right and hurried down an aisle along the back wall of the room, which was wider than it was long. She came to the sidewall of the room and turned right again. In about the middle of the wall, there was a door where the trail ended. She pulled it open and sucked in a breath that she did not exhale for several heartbeats. In the dark closet, Joshua lay on his side, a bloody smear marked the area where he had been leaning with his back against the wall before he fell over. Amelia's knees weakened. She dropped beside him, needing to touch him but fearing to touch him. She was suspended, being torn apart by the emotions of hoping he was alive and fearing he was dead. Both brought the realization of how much she had come to love him. She reached out to Joshua and to Heaven. *Please, Lord.* Her hand touched the skin of his bicep.

Like a snake strike, Joshua's arm came up and knocked her hand away.

Amelia sucked in for a scream that never came.

Flipping over, Joshua had both hands out in a defensive posture until he realized who she was. He immediately collapsed back to the floor.

"You're alive," was all she could manage through the tears.

"Yeah, but I guess I passed out for a minute." He looked at her as if realizing the significance of her presence. "You can't be here. You need to get out of this building and get far away." His pale face showed defeated resolution. "We don't have much time before Becker's mosquitos are released."

"Mosquitoes?" Amelia examined Joshua. *Maybe he's delusional.*

Joshua nodded. "There's a whole tank full of them…up the stairs in the next room." He glanced at his watch. "How long have I been out?"

He seems coherent. "What are they for?"

"To alter the human race."

Well, mostly coherent. She bent down trying to examine his eyes. "With mosquitoes?"

Joshua stood, steadying himself on the wall. He continued to scrutinize the hands on his timepiece like they were out of focus. "We've got less than an hour. He switched his attention to Amelia as if he had just heard the question. "Yes. They carry a virus that alters DNA."

Amelia put it together. "Becker's experiments. He's trying to cause evolution." The live feed video came to her mind. "The timer is on a computer in the next room. It's counting people in the park and labeling them as targets." She realized something else. "The Ozark festival. It's today. The park should be packed by now."

Joshua was nodding but stopped and closed his eyes in despair at her last statement. "I need to stop it. I'm going to have to blow up the vat." Moving a mop bucket, he lifted an electronic device from the corner. "I've got to use enough C4 to vaporize it. There's a risk it will set off the other explosives. This building might still come down." Joshua was digging in his pocket. He took Amelia's hand and squeezed. She felt him pressing an entry card into it. "This card will get you out the back door. Ibbie should still be in the van with Gabriel. I want the three of you to get as far away from here as you can."

Amelia shook her head. "I'm not leaving you."

"I'll follow if I can, but I want you out of the area. If this doesn't work, there will be nothing we can do for the people in the park. We'd never get anyone to believe this much less evacuate them in the time we have. If even one mosquito escapes, it could be devastating if it or its offspring bite anything. You have to take care of Gabriel. He's your main responsibility. Ibbie will help you."

She looked in Joshua's face. It was a blur through the tears. "I can't get out. The other man is here. The one you fought. He has the door blocked."

Joshua moved toward the closet entrance. "I'll get you out."

Amelia stepped in front of him, hands on his arms. "You can't. You're weak and injured and he knows how to take advantage of that. Please, Joshua."

"Joshua!" Mr. A's bellow came from across the large room. "I know you're here, and I know you have it. Where is he, Amelia? That's why you came in here isn't it?"

At the sound of the man yelling his name, adrenaline pumped into Joshua's body. The pain fell behind his resolve. Taking hold of her arms, Joshua tried to move Amelia out of the way.

She grabbed him in a hug.

The unexpected warmth of her body reminded him of how cold he had been. He couldn't bring himself to pull away from her. The strength he had mustered suddenly felt useless.

Amelia breathed into his ear, her breath warm. "Don't fight. God's working on him. He let me go so I could find you. But if you try to fight him, he's going to have to win. I can't stop the mosquitoes without you. I don't know how to do that. You need to be alive. Gabriel is safe with Ibbie. Right now, I'm with you. Let me help."

It was like the breath of God in his ear. Never had he felt the Lord speaking through a human being as powerfully as that moment.

Amelia let go and darted out of the closet.

"Amelia, what are you going to—" Was all Joshua got out before she closed the door on the rest of his question. He stood in the darkness, vulnerable, helpless. Reaching deep into his faith he prayed.

Amelia ran toward the front of the room, to the door where she entered. She didn't care what the man did to her. She reached the end of the row and turned.

Mr. A. came out from a row between her and the entrance. He smiled. "You run loud but not fast."

Amelia let her shoulders drop. "Please, just let us go. He's hurt. All I want to do is get him out of here."

"You may only want to leave, but Joshua is still trying to win. He has the detonator and without it the explosives are worthless. I need the detonator."

Amelia straightened. "This isn't about winning. This is about life and death, not some game. Joshua is trying to keep you from killing all these people you don't even know. And there's more. Becker has a horrible plan that could change the human race. You're on the wrong side. You don't have to do this. Just stop."

The man frowned and took a step forward.

Instead of retreating, Amelia stepped toward him. She probed his eyes. "I think you were a good man once. I think you started out doing what you believed was right. But you've lost yourself."

Mr. A. tipped his head back and sighed.

Amelia ignored the look. "You had to do hard things. It didn't feel right, so you had to close off part of yourself. That's the only way you could be so indifferent to life. You don't dare think about it, feel it. The guilt would be too much."

The man smiled. "Guilt is something other people put on you. I have no guilt because I don't accept it."

"That's a lie."

The man's head made a slight move back from the force of Amelia's statement and the smile dimmed.

"We all have guilt. We either let Jesus deal with it or we make up lies just like that one, so we won't have to face it. Then we attack anything or anyone that tells us differently. Even if that person is saying it because they care."

Mr. A. returned her gaze. "So, you care, do you?"

"Yes, I do."

"And so do I."

Amelia and Mr. A. both jerked at the sound of Marsha's voice.

The man smirked but did not turn around. "I knew you would be the death of me."

Marsha didn't leave the cover of the row of racks she hid behind. "If I wanted to be the death of you, I could have killed you several minutes ago. But I still don't trust you. Use your left hand to take out your gun and put it on the floor. And my gun." Marsha took in a frustrated breath. "And my knife."

The man complied and placed the weapons on the floor.

Marsha still didn't move. "She's right, you know. Something's wrong with us."

Mr. A. studied Amelia. "She makes a convincing argument." He glanced over his shoulder toward Marsha. "But your method still seems a bit more persuasive."

Marsha deliberated before speaking. "I don't think so. It doesn't matter much if I get you to put down a gun if you still want to kill me inside. Something's been working on *my* insides in a big way. You couldn't have changed that part me, even if you shot me."

"If I wanted to kill you," the man's tone softened, "I could have done it when you were tied up."

"I think I have my partner on the cell phone to thank for that, not your compassion."

A tender expression took over the man's face. "You think I don't know about open channel cell phones for covert operations? I knew someone would be listening on the other end of your phone and I had to get them to talk. I could tell you weren't going to help me," The man twisted his head toward Marsha again, "even if I killed you, which I wasn't going to do. But I had to put on a good act so your friend would believe it."

Marsha lifted her head at the words.

Boom! A gunshot resounded through the room. Mr. A. arched his back and grimaced.

In horror, Amelia snapped her eyes toward Marsha. The other woman crouched, head swiveling in search of an attacker.

Mr. A. ran directly at Amelia. She screamed as he grabbed her around the waist and propelled her between the nearest racks. He released her, and her hand was bloody where she had touched his back.

The sound of Marsha's pistol came from out in the room. Then again. It was getting closer. Marsha came around the corner and almost collided with Mr. A. who was leaning with his hand against a rack, gasping for breath.

"You've been shot." The concern was evident on Marsha's face.

Mr. A. nodded. "Think it clipped a lung." His knees sagged.

Marsha grabbed him and eased him to a sitting position with his back to a rack. "I've got at least one shooter. I have to deal with that." She beckoned with her head for Amelia as she put her pistol in the back of her waistband. Taking Amelia's hands, she put one on the front of Mr. A's shoulder and the other in the middle of the widening bloodstain on his back. "Push hard."

Amelia nodded.

With a serious expression, Marsha added. "And pray…please."

Standing, Marsha positioned herself at the corner of the rack where she could look down the front wall of the room toward the direction from where the shot had come. Glancing toward the other end of the row they were hiding behind, she appeared conflicted. Did she fear an attack from that direction also? With her gun back in her hand, centered, ready to swivel either way, she faced the rack, watching each direction out of the sides of her eyes. Her expression had hardened. Amelia knew she was evaluating how to take out her target.

Marsha concentrated on the threat. She didn't look at TDH. She didn't dare. The pain of seeing him lying there would distract her. The wound was bad, but she needed to forget that. *Please, don't let him die. I need to…* What she needed to do was focus before the shooter took them all out.

The gunman must have come in the same entrance she had found at the other end of the room. She didn't have a good position. She couldn't stay there having to watch two directions and wait for the shooter to come. It gave him the advantage. She also wanted to take the battle away from Amelia and TDH.

Marsha dashed to the next row of racks, gun forward, then swiveled to check the space between the racks. Seeing it clear, she sprinted down the row to the back of the room. She eased out around the corner, gun up. There was a man, assault rifle in hand. Marsha fired and heard the man give a pained curse. As she ducked behind cover, the items on the end rack nearest her tore apart in a barrage of bullets.

When the shooting stopped, a voice called out, "Norm, I'm hit."

So, there were at least two of them. The one she shot looked like Seth's partner, Popeye, whom she had met when she and Amelia had first been taken inside DNAble. Norm Salzman must also be there. He didn't stay away like he was told. No one was answering the wounded man. That meant Norm must be advancing and didn't want to give away his position.

Marsha turned her gun toward the other end of the row. If anyone came around the corner, she was an easy target with nowhere to go. If she tried to move out into the aisle along the back wall, the man with the assault weapon might shoot her despite his wound. Better to attack the target that was coming after her.

Rushing down the row, back to the front of the room, she was ready to shoot anything that poked its head out. As she approached the end, she hugged the rack to her left, swinging wide on the corner from which someone would be coming. Little by little she brought more of the aisle into view. A large, middle-aged man was in the aisle, ducking behind the third rack down from her. Marsha didn't take the shot. He was already behind cover and she didn't have rounds to waste. He surely saw her. So, they both knew where the other was.

"She's two rows ahead of my position." A voice yelled from where the man would be. "Okay, the rest of you move up."

She didn't like the sound of that.

Chapter 24

Amelia realized she was still clenching her teeth from when she heard the rapid-fire gunshots. She had learned enough to know it wasn't Marsha's gun. But she had hope. Marsha had hit one of them. Amelia reasoned that if they knew Marsha was down, they would be saying so. She must still be in the fight.

Amelia's mind was swirling. *Is Joshua okay?* She wanted to go back to him, but she was afraid to take her hand away from Mr. A's wound. She listened for any sound that might indicate the shooters were close. She knew Joshua wouldn't stay in the closet when he heard the shooting.

Mr. A. was taking in painful breaths. Something inside her said there were spiritual battles going on that were more important than all the others.

"Can you talk?"

"Not much."

"Is there anything else I can do?"

The man gave a slight shake of his head.

Amelia knew of one thing. Just what Marsha had asked for. "Lord, please do not let…this man die. I don't even know his name, but I am begging you to have mercy on him."

The man whispered. "Hevel."

Amelia adjusted to look in his face. "Is that your name?"

Another breathless nod.

"Hevel. That's the Hebrew form of Abel. It's a good name. He pleased the Lord with his offering."

Again, a nod.

"Hevel, I don't want you to die, but if you do, I want you to be with God in heaven. Faith in Jesus is the only way that can happen. Would you be willing to accept that?"

"I am Jewish, not Christian." It took all he could to say it.

"You can still be Jewish. Jesus is the Jewish Messiah. Your ancient ancestors just missed that. They wanted a Messiah to save them from their enemies, but the worst enemy they had was their own sin. Abel knew that it took a blood offering to atone for sin. That's why he pleased God. Even back then, God was getting the world ready to understand the sacrifice that Jesus would make. Jesus fulfilled all the Hebrew prophecies about the Messiah. I am not asking you to not be Jewish. Just understand that Jesus is the Savior you have been waiting for and accept Him."

Hevel tried to smile. "You take my breath away…with your proposal."

Amelia turned up the corners of her mouth, but she doubted if her eyes were fooling him.

"You changed my mind. Did you know that? After I let you go…I texted my contact…told him…I was going to wait…let everyone leave…before detonating."

Hevel's appearance stung Amelia's heart.

"Now…I won't even…do that…Joshua wins…Have to do it…his way."

"You're talking too much. Just rest and think about what I told you. That's more important. You don't have to speak to talk to God." She leaned down close to his ear. "But thank you. You won a bigger battle." Amelia's arm was aching from putting pressure on Hevel's wound.

Boom! A gunshot filled the room. Then another. All too loud to be Marsha's.

Hevel pushed himself up on his arm. "I need to get my gun."

"You can't."

"I must. She needs—"

Gunfire burst in their direction. A form loomed around the corner of the rack. Amelia threw up her hands, trying to fend off what was coming. Hevel fell back with a groan. Two hands clasped Amelia's, the figure dropped to her level and she saw Joshua's face.

"What happened?" Joshua examined Amelia. "Are you hurt?"

"I'm okay but he's been shot."

Joshua's haggard face showed his joy at seeing Amelia mixed with confusion and worry. He addressed Hevel. "You're the man that shot me."

Amelia intervened with a head shake. "It's okay."

Hevel strained for enough air to speak. "Sorry. So much…I wish I could start over."

There was no hesitation from Joshua. "We were both fighting for something. We'll give it to God and sort it out later." He transferred his attention to Amelia. "I heard Marsha. Where is she? A man took a shot at me when I was searching for you. What's going on?"

"She went that way." Amelia pointed, curving her finger to indicate how Marsha had gone around the rack. "She's after the man that shot him. But I heard more people, and there was a lot of shooting."

With a wheeze, Hevel spoke. "She is fighting my fight. I don't think…my contact…pleased with my decision. Knew it was…someone in DNAble. Didn't care then. He must be the one that shot me. Making sure I didn't talk."

Joshua furrowed his brow. "We thought you were with Fighters for Israel."

Hevel gave a slight shake of his head. "I told

them…would do this job…when I heard what DNAble was doing. Someone contacted FFI…with this intel…so I…communicating with that person. They knew too much…not to be on the inside. They wanted everything destroyed…but they wanted to know exactly when."

Joshua continued the thought so Hevel wouldn't have to. "Someone wanted out and didn't want any evidence left behind. That's probably who we're fighting now. I think I know who. Do you have a weapon?"

Hevel shook his head and pointed into the open past the end of the racks. "Two guns on the ground…out there, if…can get to them."

Joshua gave a couple of quick peeks around the rack. His breath came heavily at the exertion, "I see them."

There was a shot that sounded like Marsha's pistol and a man groaned.

Joshua's eyes widened.

Another voice. "Carson's down. I don't know where the shot came…Whoa! How'd she…Watch yourselves. She's jumping across the top of the racks. I think she's behind us now."

"Good girl." Joshua dashed from the cover of the racks.

A petrified gasp escaped Amelia's mouth.

Yet another voice yelled, "Reynolds, she might be coming your way. Don't let her out the door. She's—"

Gunshots from where Joshua had run cut the voice off. The firing of the gun came closer and Joshua was with them again.

The last voice resumed. "One of them at the back just got the guns off the floor. Everyone get it together. We've got 'em way outnumbered. Four of you go back and take care of the girl behind us. The rest of you move up on the ones at the end."

Panting, Joshua tucked one gun in his pants and eased the other around the metal shelving taking aim as he went. *Boom!* He fired a round. A shot came from the direction he was targeting, hitting the wall behind them. Joshua put two more rounds toward the enemy and held his position.

Amelia could see the pain on his face.

Hevel grabbed the rack and began pulling himself up. Amelia hurried to assist.

He looked at her through watery, painfilled eyes. "I have lots of sin…if Jesus…" His chest heaved as he tried to suck in air. Looking directly at her—he nodded.

Amelia squeezed his arm and returned the nod.

Holding out his hand he told Joshua, "If you trust me."

Without taking his eyes off his target, Joshua transferred the gun to his left hand and reached behind his back. Pulling out the second gun, he handed it to Hevel.

"Do you mind? The other one's mine." Hevel wheezed air.

Joshua sucked in a breath and made the switch. "I need to get her out of here. She needs to try and stop something that Becker set in motion. Nothing we do here will matter if we don't do that. I need to get her out that entrance over there."

"He barricaded the door." Amelia gave Hevel a 'sorry-for-tattling' look.

Hevel's return smile was weak. "It can be easily removed…but you'll be in…the open." His chest heaved. "I cannot run…but I'll lay down…suppression fire."

Joshua gave a painful sigh. "Trade me places."

When Hevel was in place, Joshua told him, "Let's let 'em know there's more than one of us. Fire when I fire." He turned and told Amelia, "Stay here." Hurrying to the other end of the row, he put a shot toward the enemy. Hevel followed it with a round of his own. They fired another round each and Joshua came back to them, looking pale. "That should slow them up a little on their approach and buy us some time."

He pulled something from his pocket. "Here take this."

Amelia took the smartphone he offered.

"I'm going to get you back in the room where the computer is counting down for the release. My phone's dead, but it has a built-in USB for charging and connecting." Joshua reached to the phone she held and flipped out the connector to which he was referring. I want you to plug it into that computer and use it to contact Ibbie. I need to tell you about the mosquito release mechanism so you can pass on the info to her. We don't have much time. Listen carefully."

Amelia nodded. She knew her face must show how scared she was.

"The mosquitoes are in a glass tank in the room above where you saw the timer running on the computer. There's a clear plastic tube that goes through the wall to release the insects to the outside. The opening from the tank to the tube is sealed with louvers that are kept closed by a magnetic latch. The louvers have a powerful spring. If you cut power to the magnet, the louvers snap open so you can't stop the release by disconnecting the power. I'm sure it's powered off the same backup circuit as these servers, so it should stay closed even if the other power is off."

Hevel fired a couple of rounds and they both flinched.

"The mechanism is all welded, heavy-gauge steel, so you're not going to disable the hardware without power tools or a cutting torch and there is no way to get to it without letting the mosquitoes out." There are fans on the floor of the vat to force the mosquitoes up and out the tube when the louvers open. The tube's big enough for a person to crawl through, so it's too big to seal in the time we have. Any crack would give our little friends an easy exit."

Amelia licked her dry lips but tried to take in everything he was saying even if she didn't understand it all.

"The electronics to the louvers and magnet are behind a panel on the outside of the tank. I couldn't get into that, but cutting wires should be a last resort. If you accidentally break the circuit, the louvers will open. I'm sure the timer is designed to cut power to the magnet when the times up. The safest way to defeat the system is to stop the timer or keep it from cutting the power. As long as there's power to the magnet, the louvers will stay closed until we can find a way to flood the vat with insecticide. Maybe Ibbie can connect to the computer through my phone and crack the password to shut off the timer. Do you think you can explain that to her?"

"I hope so. I'll try."

"You'll do fine. Ibbie will be able to help with the right questions."

Joshua paused. "I didn't get long to study it. Someone else might see something I missed. But we have to be careful. It's better to blow up the entire thing than to risk one insect escaping. But I've got to get to the explosives, which are on the other side of this room. If I can get to Marsha, we might be able to work together and take out this security team and clear the way."

Joshua turned his back to Amelia. "We need to move. Grab hold of my belt and don't let go. Keep up and keep behind me. If I go down, just lie there like you're dead until you can make a break for cover."

Amelia's jaw quivered as she took a grip of the leather at his waist. She wanted to say she wasn't ready, but she knew there wasn't time to be ready.

Joshua took a deep breath and admonished Hevel. "Those shots won't stop them very long. They'll be coming at you around the other end of the rack."

"Too bad. I'll be busy here…won't have time for them."

Joshua nodded to Amelia then spoke to Hevel. "Say when."

Hevel reached into a cargo pocket and brought out a fresh magazine and traded it for the one in his gun. He put the other away in a different pocket. Amelia's heart thumped two times in her chest and Hevel said, "When," and fired a round.

Joshua pushed forward as Hevel fired another and another. She held onto Joshua as he moved sideways, his gun searching for targets. As they moved laterally and forward, they came to where they could see down the row in front of Hevel's position. A man with an assault rifle was moving forward to get to Hevel's row.

"Down the row." Amelia didn't want to say more for fear of distracting Joshua.

His gun snapped in that direction and fired several rounds sending the man retreating behind the rack he just left. He shoved his rifle out and fired blindly in the row as Joshua pulled her forward behind the cover of the next racks.

Marsha prepared to die. She wasn't going to make it out of this one. Her gymnast trick across the racks would only work once. They would be ready next time. She heard gunfire on the other side of the room. She hoped it wasn't for TDH and Amelia. She had taken the pressure off them for a moment but now she was surrounded.

She had too many sins to confess, and she figured God knew them anyway. She had just told Him that she wanted things to be right between Him and her and asked Him to take care of the details. She figured He was God. He ought to be able to do that in the middle of a firefight.

Any second a couple of rifles would come around the corner. The cowards were sure taking their time. She would use her last round on the first one and the second one's barrage would tear her corpse to pieces. Her body had served her well. Too well, probably. She was going to be an ugly, bloody mess when they finished with her. No one would be ogling her beauty then. The DNAble crew would flush it down the sewer.

I guess that's not what You're interested in anyway, God. I'm counting on You to make sure I'm with You when they do all that. She placed her hand on her belly. She had changed. She had been looking forward to being a mommy. Taking her eyes off her gunsights for a moment, she whispered to her stomach. "Sorry little one, but we're going to a better place together. I would have loved to be able to have you, you know, bring you into the world or whatever. At least He kept me from being the one that killed you." That's what gave her hope to believe. She never would have changed on her own. If He could do that, the idea of a Marsha being in Heaven didn't seem so farfetched.

She wondered if TDH was still alive. He had looked bad. *God, I know I don't have any right to ask for special favors, but could You change him too? I would love to get to know him better, up there.*

She heard a noise from the end of the row. Her eyes snapped up to her gunsights again.

Ibbie motioned Gabriel to hurry down the DNAble basement hallway. The earlier gunshots had helped her zero in on where the action was, but that was the only good thing about the sound. Even though the FBI might be on their way, it was up to her team to stop the release and extract themselves if they were going to get out. *Please don't let us be too late.*

She didn't worry about the possibility of an explosion. If the concrete overhead came down on them, they'd never know what hit them. Buried alive didn't sound good, so she didn't let her imagination go there. That was the secret she had learned long ago. Take what comes. Creative thinking was only advantageous for tactics, not potential death scenarios.

Ibbie stopped and pulled back around the corner. The door ahead was guarded by an armed man. She counted it as a significant indicator they were in the right place. Time to put the creative thinking to work. By the full-auto gunfire she was hearing, they were outnumbered and outgunned. They needed something to even the odds. Joshua was in there. She knew him well. What could she do to shift the advantage to their side, considering what she knew about him?

Behind her was the door to a utility room. It was in the right location...*I wonder.* She moved past Gabriel and opened the door—and smiled.

Chapter 25

Joshua pushed forward. His focus was narrowing. Amelia had spotted the man coming after Hevel. He was glad she was there but wished she was far away. The pain from the bullet wound in his side had become a background roar in his senses. He had no time for it. How long could he go before it took over?

He had been wounded before, but he'd never had to keep going so long and so hard afterward. He prayed he could make it. Prayer had also become a background thought in his pounding head, just the knowledge that God was there, listening and in control, even if he didn't know how. If he could just get to the door. He knew nothing after that.

"They're moving on the north side of the room." The voice must be the man with the rifle. A face peeked out and ducked back as Joshua and Hevel both landed multiple rounds where his head had been. A gun poked out in the same location, but before it could fire, Joshua pounded the site with several shots producing a growling cry and the noise of the gun clattering to the floor.

"They're heading for the north door!"

"Don't let them get out!"

Hevel put a round into the leading edge of each row just to discourage any brave heart that might want to take a chance at moving out to charge them.

They were at the door. A four-wheel rolling cart and a computer workstation that resembled a hat rack were wedged together against the nearest rack to block the door from opening. Joshua boot-kicked the workstation where it connected with the cart, dislodging it.

"Joshua!" Amelia screamed. Rounds struck the door at the same time Hevel released a multi-round volley.

Spinning, Joshua saw a man pulling his wounded buddy behind cover. *Good job, Hevel.*

Hevel was changing magazines. *Good man.* He jerked open the door and pushed Amelia inside.

Amelia was screaming again. "Hevel, look out."

Joshua spun. Several men ran by the far end of the row down which he could see. Their rifles were aimed forward as they moved to converge on the other end of the row Hevel was in. He sighted at them through blurry vision and emptied his gun. It was too late. They all made it past. Joshua had not risked carrying extra ammo in his undercover mode. He dropped the useless handgun and turned to Amelia. "This door will lock. Go contact Ibbie." He slammed the door and swung around to face the action. Making eye contact with Hevel, he thrust a pointed finger in the direction of the assault. The last thing he saw was Hevel turning to face his attackers before the lights went out and the gunfire started.

Marsha blinked and her gunsights were gone. Everything was dark. Something metal clanked against the end of the rack. She jammed her gun in her waist holster, grabbed the top of the rack and with a skillful mount was on top of the row of metal when the first rifle blazed into the row, shooting blindly. She didn't even bother with him. She was after the others that would be staging one row over. She made a quiet rotation over the rack and dropped to the floor under the cover of the gunfire. With one hand sliding along the rack and the other out in front of her, she rushed to the end of the row, illuminated only by a tiny light here or there on the server electronics.

Her outstretched hand struck someone's back. He started to turn in surprise, but Marsha's arm snaked around his neck in a chokehold as she planted her foot in the back of his knees and pulled him backward. He grasped madly for her, but she slammed him down and his rifle clattered to the floor.

The metal of his partner's rifle struck the rack as he whirled toward the sound. Marsha left the man on the floor and spun to the other side of the row.

"She's over here," was all the other man got out before Marsha put her last round right where his voice came from. Clanking and footfalls pounded her direction. No time to get the guns. She was already over the rack and into the next row.

Ibbie walked beside Gabriel in the dark. While they were still down the hall, Gabriel called out to the guard, "What's going on in there?"

"Norm? How did you get out here?" The man's voice sounded puzzled. "Someone killed the lights."

Gabriel continued the ruse. "I came out the other door. Too much shooting in there. Hurts my ears."

"What?"

They strolled up, still just shadows to the man. Gabriel said, "Let me see your gun."

The man hesitated. Then they heard the rifle come up.

Gabriel changed to Sean Connery. "Let me introduce you to my friend."

Ibbie rushed forward until she felt the metal and stock in her hands. She twisted the man's arms with the leverage of his own gun, threw her hip into him and tossed him over to the floor, forcing him to let go of the weapon.

He gave a grunt and she followed the sound with the butt of the rifle.

Marsha heard Norm yell, "Check the rows on either side. She'll be trying to move on top of the racks again. Nobody get on the racks. Everybody be listening. If you hear any noise up there, sweep the top with full auto. Keep her pinned down and we'll get her."

Well that's not very nice. Marsha flattened herself against the row. She heard boots at the end. The tiny lights were starting to light up the place. The servers would be on some type of generator or battery backup on a separate circuit. The boots were coming down the row from each direction. If she moved, she was dead. She would soon be dead one way or another. She could at least take out one if he got a little closer.

Before she could act, she heard a grunt from the man to her right and he hit the floor, making strangled noises. Someone had him—*Joshua!*

The man to her left rushed forward to help his partner. It must have looked like the rack next to him came to life as Marsha climbed him like a tree, spinning, locking her legs around his neck, casting her body weight into the spin and throwing him to the floor. She somersaulted, scooped up his rifle, ripped off a couple of rounds to end the threat and landed back to back with Joshua. "Where have you been?"

Joshua's breath came in ragged gasps. "Taking it easy 'til you showed up. You're all supposed to be out of here. Now we're all…" He didn't finish.

"You okay?"

"No, not really."

Norm yelled. "Follow that sound. Don't go into the row. Keep cover and cut them down in the crossfire."

Norm yelled again. "There by the south wall. Move quick. They're running."

The sound of boots moving away almost drowned out Norm's protests. "Who said that? Who's talking?"

Joshua and Marsha hurried to the front of their row.

Someone called out, "Norm, what's going on?"

"I don't know. Someone else is trying to sound like me. Find them."

From the back of the room— "That wasn't me. Don't listen to that."

Norm's voice. "That's him. Follow that sound. Shoot him before he can get away."

Boots headed toward the first voice. "That's not me. Don't anybody shoot. Go to the other voice."

Joshua and Marsha slowed to a creep and headed toward the front door.

Marsha heard her own sultry voice from the far corner. "Come on over here boys and I got something for you."

Norm's voice came from the back again. "That's her. Move in. Fire on that corner."

Too late, another Norm yelled. "That's not me."

Several weapons fired on the corner from where the fake Marsha had spoken. Joshua and Marsha went to separate rows. Each targeted the blaze from a weapon that they could see, ending those threats. When their targets dropped, they moved to another location.

The gunfire stopped, and Norm's voice was yelling. "Stop shooting."

The other Norm. "There he is again. Get that guy. Be

watching for someone who looks just like me and don't let him get away."

There was no answer from the first Norm.

A man called out. "Norm where are you? There was no way out of that corner. How'd she do that?" It was the last thing he said as Marsha opened up on the voice, and quickly changed position.

There was whispering at the back of the room then the Norm voice spoke. "Listen up. We're shooting each other. Everyone sound-off with your name, so we know where everyone is."

"Riley."

"Jones."

That one was close. Joshua skulked away to dispatch him.

Norm's voice bellowed. "Riley, stay where you're at and I want Jones to come to you so we don't make any more mistakes. They must be hiding. We need to get together and do a team search. Come on, let me hear the rest of you."

"Edwards."

"Skinard."

Marsha slinked toward the Skinard.

As she moved on Skinard, Jones called out. "Riley, I'm coming over to you. Don't shoot me. We need to stick together so they can't pick us off in the dark. Like Norm says, we need to form a team."

The sound of Jones's voice had been enough to cover Marsha putting Skinard down with a rifle butt. The voice stopped after he hit the floor. Marsha knew that Joshua had already dealt with Jones. It had to be Gabriel and his amazing hearing. Following the sounds, he would know where each man was. He was throwing his voice, paving the way for her and Joshua to walk right up on the men, calling out to cover the noise of their attack. She was sure Gabriel would call to Edwards, and it would mean Joshua was removing Riley from the picture. Then they could both pay the last man a visit.

As she entered the room, Amelia froze at the sight of the churning insects. Ibbie hadn't responded, so she had left Joshua's phone plugged into the computer. She wanted to see them for herself. She knew it was too late. The timer said they only had 27 minutes.

Amelia had not wanted to stay at the computer, watching the targeted rectangles milling all over the park. Her park. She fixed her eyes on the louvers. If she hadn't met Joshua, she would be there—in her park—when they opened, and the fog of parasites descended on it.

Faces of other vendors that she knew, regular customers, children playing—they hung in her mind like portraits of friends and family. Amelia shuddered. She clutched her arms around herself and rubbed at her shoulders, imagining the bites. What would it be like to have her DNA altered—the blueprints of who she was changed and twisted? Her insides knotted. Amelia envisioned the mutations Becker wanted to produce running rampant. The miracle of the perfectly synchronized collection of organs and systems that was the human body reduced to random malformation. Not an exception, but the norm. Perhaps the very essence of humanity—lost. All in a quest for what didn't exist. There was no evolution in the world. Zero times zero was nothing. What Becker's demented brain was about to produce was devolution—the end result of viewing life as only a collection of cells. If that's all it was, why even bother. Even Becker's twisted soul knew there was something more. Some kind of demon had to have possessed the scientist to cause him to tamper so flippantly with something so sacred.

Amelia stared at the louvers that sealed the bottom of a rectangular housing that was mounted in the top of the tank, just as Joshua had described it. Soon they would snap open. Examining the bottom of the vat for the fans that Joshua mentioned, she saw them through the clouds of swirling insects. On the outside of the vat, a small set of steps led to a sealed access door with a handle to get inside the tube. Probably to service the louvers. The tube was clear, and Amelia could see the top of the rectangular housing protruding into it.

She shivered at the image of anyone in the tube when the louvers opened. They would be the mosquitoes' first meal, taking in the person's blood and leaving the virus behind. Plenty of blood to use for reproduction. The making of millions more, each carrying the disease. She could not help imagining the horror of the louvers opening and the fans coming on. When that happened, the top of the housing would be like an open container without a lid and the mosquitoes would come pouring out like the evils from Pandora's box. Staring at the top of that box, Amelia realized…she knew that size.

Marsha rendered Edwards unconscious with a carotid neck restraint. She noticed Joshua did not even attempt to help. She could hear him, bent over gasping. She heard him whisper, knowing Gabriel would hear him. "Where's Norm?" *Good thinking. Thanks for not yelling and making us a target.*

Gabriel yelled across the expanse. "Bad man tried to get out door. Rams Two has him on floor."

How poetic. Marsha wondered if Gabriel even realized it rhymed.

Ibbie yelled, "I have him hogtied at the back door.

Marsha heard Joshua kneel and then collapse on the floor where he called out. "Ibbie, did Amelia get a hold of you?"

"No, of course not. I silenced my phone for all this. Where is she?"

Joshua's watch lit up. Marsha followed the light and was at his side as he yelled. "Get the lights back on. We've got 25 minutes before the release."

"What release?" Marsha took his arm as he was forcing himself up. "You gonna be okay?"

"Not if the tank that's housing Becker's mosquitoes opens up. None of us will be okay."

"I saw those. What's that all about?"

"No time for a full explanation. The mosquitoes carry a virus that alters human DNA, and it could change humanity as we know it. We've got to stop it, but it will take a miracle."

"I'll pray."

The room blazed with light.

Joshua turned and looked at her as he blinked at the brightness. "Since when?"

"Never mind. I'll pray. Like you said, there's no time." Marsha wondered about TDH, but Joshua's statement had established the priority. She was alive. It was a miracle. Marsha knew it was. Maybe God had something planned. "What else do I need to do?"

"Ibbie and I will get as much C4 as we can. You've got an electronic engineering degree. Go see if you can help Amelia do anything to stop the timer."

Chapter 26

Marsha saw Joshua's phone plugged into the timer computer. *Where's Amelia?* There was no time to find her. Marsha's search for passwords around the workstation was fruitless. She started the password cracker, but she wasn't optimistic it could work in the time they had. Hoping for better luck with disabling the electronics, she dashed up the stairs.

Still no Amelia. Examining the mosquito tank, Marsha saw the panel that housed the electronics. She was going to need a set of screwdrivers, some needle-nose pliers, and a sharp knife. Surely, she could find some back in the server room.

Joshua watched Ibbie lay the detonator she had obtained from the closet on the table. Jumping onto the tabletop, she hoisted herself into the ceiling that gave access to the explosives and call receiver.

Laying the assault rifle he had acquired during the shootout on the table surface, Joshua glanced at Norm, who watched the interaction from the floor where Ibbie had sat him against the wall. His hands still appeared securely tied in front. Joshua didn't like that his legs were free but when they needed to move, they needed him ready as well. Unzipping the backpack, he had talked Gabriel out of, Joshua emptied its contents onto the floor.

Gabriel stood nearby, staring at his items, rocking. "Gabriel's bag. Gabriel's things. Not nice to touch other's things."

"Gabe, agents have to help each other. We need your bag." Joshua didn't have time to explain, but he certainly didn't have time for Gabe to have a meltdown. "This is an emergency. We'll get you a better bag and better things when we're safe." Joshua felt lightheaded. He had to focus if they were going to get the explosives out in time.

Gabriel turned his head and closed his eyes. "Other—"

"Gabe, please. This is the most important thing. We're in danger. Please just let us do this before we talk about other things."

Gabriel turned his head and looked past Joshua to the empty row leading to the back door. "Most important thing. Don't talk about other things."

Amelia remembered passing the kitchen for Becker's prisoners when Hevel was dragging her around, so she found it quickly. She was right. It had heavy commercial grade equipment. She had grabbed the two items she needed and was back at the room where the computer timer was located. She glanced at the timer as she went by. Eighteen minutes.

This was going to be close. Hurrying up the stairs, she found the mosquito room empty. The shooting had stopped. *Why aren't they here yet to help?* Fear served up the worst-case scenarios, and Amelia returned the volley with hope. Maybe it was God delaying them. There was no one to prevent her from trying her madness. It might be tight to work in the small space, but if she was inside when the others got there, it would be harder for her friends to stop her. Amelia climbed the small ladder that led to the maintenance door. She opened it, crawled in, and turned the handle, sealing herself inside the tube above the churning vat of insects.

Marsha bounded up the steps, screwdriver and knife in hand. She couldn't find pliers, but she would have to make do. She was running out of time.

She hadn't seen the others to see how far along they were. The tools had been right at the front of the room. She had heard them talking at the back, but she couldn't make out what they were saying. A quick check-in at the computer informed her that she had fifteen minutes left. They'd better hurry. She wasn't confident in her ability to stop the timer.

When she came into the room, she zeroed in on the panel and began attacking it with the screwdriver. She had the plate removed when she heard the noise that drew her attention to the top of the vat. The metal cover slipped from her fingers and clanged on the cement floor.

Joshua grabbed the second wad of C4 that Ibbie handed

down and shoved it in the backpack. He checked on Norm again.

The man caught Joshua's eye. "You're jeopardizing us all by wasting the time to move the explosives. Put the detonator back and let's all get out of here and blow the place. You obviously know what they're doing here. You never should have derailed my bomber. If you would have just stepped back and let him do his job, we all could have walked away from this."

Gabriel was moaning. "Don't talk about other things." His body swayed, eyes locked onto the way leading to the back entrance into the room.

Joshua's vision seemed blurred on the sides. *Just have to do this last thing.* He looked into the ceiling and took the next handful of C4 from Ibbie. "We have to go. We're out of time."

"Yes, you are. Don't move, any of you." The voice came from behind him, where Gabriel had been looking.

Joshua turned to see a tall, heavy man snap an assault rifle in his direction.

The man yelled toward the opening above Joshua. "Whoever's in the ceiling show me your hands or I'll open up on you and the ones down here." Ibbie only had her handgun. Because of his position, there was no way for her to see the man to get a shot.

"Okay." Ibbie stuck her hands out of the opening.

Norm addressed the man. "Herschlag, I'm glad you're here. Shoot 'em quick. They got the drop on all of us. Don't trust 'em. Shoot them all. They're trying to blow the place up."

The man narrowed his eyes at Norm. "What were you saying when I came in?"

Norm pushed himself up the wall so he could stand. "It doesn't matter. Now that you're here I don't have to lie anymore. I was trying to stop them, but they've taken out all my men. There's more of them in the next room. Shoot them before the others get here."

Joshua considered grabbing for his gun, but he saw suspicion in the look the man gave Norm. There might be room for some negotiation. Get the man talking and off guard before he made his move. "We're not trying to blow the place up. That's what he was doing. Norm and Becker both double-crossed you. In a few minutes, Becker's machine is going to release a virus that will destroy everyone in the area, not just Jews. He wasn't waiting, and he knew it was going to get you, too. We are trying to stop it, but we are almost out of time."

Norm joined the debate again, talking fast and moving closer to the table. "He's right about Becker. But they're not on our side. They're trying to bust us. They have the detonator. We need to put it back and get out of here and blow everything before that release or we'll be implicated in this whole thing. It's over. There's nothing left to do. Just shoot them and let's get out of here before it's too late."

The man's eyes darted from Norm to Joshua.

Gabriel started wheezing, making whistling gasps for breath that grew ever louder.

The man turned the gun toward Gabriel. "Shut up." Herschlag shifted his gaze to Joshua. What's wrong with him?"

Norm was shouting over the noise. "Don't trust him. He can talk just like other people. He's some kind of—"

Joshua saw something come out of the side row just behind Herschlag. It was Hevel, closing in on the man, his own wheezing and movements covered by Gabriel's sound. Joshua lunged to get Gabriel out of the line of fire. Hevel's hands scooped up under the rifle, driving the gun barrel up as the man pulled the trigger. Joshua took Gabriel to the floor as bullets tore into the ceiling above them, just to the side of Ibbie's position. The weapon continued back, making a rut in the overhead tiles as Hevel flipped the man backwards. The big man hit the floor hard, losing his grip on the gun. Hevel collapsed, pulling the rifle in tight to himself and gasping for breath.

Another sound brought Joshua's attention toward the table. He rolled off Gabriel, who was batting at him. Norm had the pistol grip of Joshua's rifle in his bound hands and was trying to swing the barrel toward Ibbie. Two shots from the ceiling made Norm drop like someone let go of the puppet strings.

Joshua heard another struggle.

Herschlag was up and trying to wrestle the gun from Hevel. The big man started kicking the helpless Hevel who clung to the rifle while his mouth gaped like a guppy.

Joshua poured all his strength into a scramble to the rifle lying by Norm's body. Negotiation was over. Lives depended on the minutes they had left.

Hevel's grip failed and Herschlag jerked the weapon free.

Joshua snatched up the other rifle.

Herschlag righted the gun in his hands, swiveling it toward Joshua as his finger went for the trigger.

Joshua had already pulled his and fire blazed from his barrel, destroying the other rifle, the hand that held it, and the man behind it.

Looking at his watch, Joshua realized the chance to blow up the mosquito tank by itself was gone. They couldn't get the explosives installed in time. Grabbing the detonator, he looked into the ceiling at Ibbie and tossed it up to her.

Gazing back at Joshua, she nodded.

"Install your phone in the call receiver. I know your number."

Joshua knelt by Hevel.

The man still struggled to find his breath.

"We're out of time. We'll have to do it your way. I need your phone."

Hevel's head made a weak nod. Joshua took the phone from his pocket. He clasped the other man's hand. "Good fight."

Another nod, stronger than the last.

Joshua stood and dialed Ibbie's cell number as he crossed

to the table. Again, he looked into the eyes of his partner for so many missions.

She smiled sadly at him. "I'll stay up here to make sure everything goes okay. If it does, I'll hug you in heaven."

His finger moved to the "send" key. He stopped. He wanted to die holding Amelia. He wanted to stand with her in this world one second and in a better world the next. He had just enough time. With the strength he had left, he struggled toward the door and yelled behind him. "I need to tell the others."

Ibbie responded in monotone. "I know."

Marsha ignored the gunshots from the other room. Through the clear walls of the tube, she could see Amelia. "What are you doing? Get out of there."

Amelia held a rectangular metal object and a wide roll of plastic wrap. She ignored Marsha's demands and struggled in the tight space to pull another length of wrap across the face of the object.

Marsha considered trying to go in and pull her out. If she did, it would cost her the precious minutes she had to disable the timer. She couldn't bring herself to even think the motto, "mission first." It was Amelia, not some obstacle or distraction. Marsha looked at the wires. It wasn't even another agent in the tube. It was Amelia. There were six wires of various colors.

A quick glance revealed Amelia pulling more of the wrap over the metal item. "Please come out. I don't think I can do this in time." Marsha felt tears building up. It wasn't fair. She had questions for Amelia, talks they were going to have.

Focus on the task. The red wire should be power, the green—probably the ground wire. She had no time to wire a bypass, but it looked like the circuit was normally closed and the circuit board was probably set up to release the magnet only when it got a command from the computer timer.

Amelia pulled more plastic, adding another layer.

The blue wire was probably coming from the computer. That sounded right. Blue, computer—made sense. She tried to trace the tiny copper imprints on the circuit board, but she couldn't see the other side. Grabbing the blue wire, she wondered how long she had—a minute, less. She had lost track of time.

If she waited too long and the timer went off, the fans would come on and force a cloud of blood-sucking, DNA altering demons into the tube with Amelia. She would never be able to open the door to get her out without exposing all the rest of the team to the parasites. If she went in after her, the timer would probably go off while she was inside and she would miss her chance to save the people in the park, and she and Amelia would both be lost.

She tried to focus on the wires, but her eyes were a sea and the waves were crashing on her cheeks. "I love you, Amelia."

The door burst open. Marsha swiveled her head to see Joshua entering the room. She watched his eyes fasten on Amelia, his finger poised over the key of a cell phone. His eyes went to his watch.

Marsha jerked the blue wire and as the anguish poured from her throat, she heard a click, then a clunk. The magnet released, and the louvers opened.

Amelia had ripped off the last layer of cling wrap that she hoped would provide a tight barrier over the top of the rectangular opening that she had recognized as just the size for an 18 by 24 cake pan to cover. The heavy pan should push the wrap that was stretched around its surface firmly against the louver opening making an almost airtight seal. She heard Marsha yell then she heard the clunk of the magnet release. Marsha's yell turned into an anguished scream. It was too late.

Amelia flipped over expecting to face a flood of evil insects. But the fans at the bottom of the vat had not engaged. Instead of being forced out of the vat, the mosquitoes that had been right at the opening drifted through the louvers and rose upward. Everything slowed to a crawl in Amelia's perspective.

Spinning the pan in her hands, she swung it toward the opening. But she watched the pan fall onto the mouth of the rectangle like it was moving through water. Amelia's eyes seemed to possess microscopic vision. She saw three huge mosquitoes shoot out from under the pan, carried outward by the air pressure produced by the pan's descent.

The pan hit the opening and Amelia held it there, wanting to be sure of the seal. Her breathing, which felt slow to Amelia, was pouring out the carbon dioxide that acted as a beacon for the blood-lusting predators now in the tube with her.

One landed on her arm. Amelia's hand flew toward it in slow motion. Her adrenaline enhanced vision saw it ready its proboscis for the thrust into her skin as she flattened it under her palm. Its brother moved in for a bite to her face. Amelia swatted at it, sending it riding the wave of air her flailing hands produced. Another whined by her ear, moving around to attack her exposed neck. Amelia pivoted, bouncing her head off the plastic side of the tube. Slowing her defense, she undulated her hand, matching the evasive maneuvers of her foe and slammed it into the ceiling. Turning, Amelia searched for the remaining adversary. She saw it, drifting at her left. Behind it, on the outside of the tube, were Marsha and Joshua's horrified faces. They were the backdrop against which Amelia smeared the last assailant.

Chapter 27

<u>Months later…</u>

Amelia looked out the sliding glass door of her new home. The pristine Oklahoma woods opened up for an expansive view overlooking Lake Gallant. The setting was everything that Dr. Welch had said it was. The Hollenbeck Institute owned much of the property around the lake. The construction crews were working hard to maintain the natural beauty of the area while they transformed the land into what Dr. Welch and Talisa and Luke Sanders envisioned—The Hollenbeck Research and Exploration Center for People with Special Needs and Special Abilities. The name was a little long, but she liked it. It gave no indication of the other purpose the institute served and only a hint of the amazingly gifted people Dr. Welch was recruiting—people like Gabriel.

She couldn't believe how good God had been to her. To be married to Joshua, to have a home of their own, and to be a part of something so significant, had never been a part of her dreams.

Talisa had explained a little of how the institute began. She had given her a book that someone had written called "Seeing Beyond" that she said was about the events that started it all, but things had been so crazy she had barely gotten into it. Talisa had explained that while the book told the story of the bizarre situation that brought her, Luke and Dr. Welch together, it really centered around her sister Janie and their friend Teddy. Dr. Welch's role in the global intelligence community was classified and therefore not included in that book. Until Amelia understood it all, she was happy to have a home and be part of an organization that valued her unconventional family.

Dust and equipment noise rose over the trees on the lot next door. Despite it all, Ibbie was sleeping in. She was excited to tell her about the construction crew's current project.

As if her thoughts had produced her, Amelia looked up to see Ibbie wander into the kitchen. "There you are. How did you sleep?"

"Like a stone. That was an exhausting trip." Ibbie looked at her watch. "I'm still on Israeli time. She looked around and found the wall clock. "Wow, did I really sleep that long?" She stretched like she was stiff.

"You needed it. Are you ready for breakfast?"

"No. I'm bloated from all the junk food I ate on the trip. Now that I'm more awake, tell me how the kids are doing."

"They miss Eve, but Talisa's sister Janie and her boyfriend Teddy have been teaching them how to swim. Well, Janie really. Teddy tries but it's not his best skill. The kids think he's great though. You should see them in the water. It's pretty funny."

Ibbie's smile was tender. "Built-in babysitters. I don't know how this place could be any better."

"So, Joshua tells me that was your last debriefing."

"The last. I am now an official employee of the Hollenbeck Institute. It feels odd."

"Has the director finally gotten over losing another agent?"

"I think he's satisfied. He said Welch has assured him the institute will be willing to loan us to the agency for special projects. It opens his budget up, so he can bring on some new recruits, but he can still have access to our experience if he needs it—best of everything for him." Ibbie swiveled her head in awe. "Your place is beautiful. I can't believe they finished it so fast."

"They have their own dedicated construction group and plenty of money. That dust cloud is your place they are putting up just as fast. I'll take you over to see it later." Ibbie looked out the glass doors to where Amelia pointed.

"I'm still in shock. They must have money to pay for this kitchen. I've seen chefs on TV that don't have it this good. That must have been some meal you cooked them."

Joshua came into the kitchen. "It was. Dr. Welch is a connoisseur and Luke Sanders just likes to eat. I think they offered me the position just so they have more chances at Amelia's cooking." He shoved Ibbie with his shoulder as he passed her.

Her hand came out and jabbed at his side as he danced out of her reach.

Gabriel came in, trailing Joshua, and Ibbie broke off her attack to give him a squeeze.

Amelia grinned. "When Dr. Welch said he wanted to introduce us to the co-founders of the institute, I just wanted to make a nice dinner for them. I didn't know it was going to be part of my resume."

Joshua crossed to the other side of the kitchen. "As soon as we committed, Talisa Sanders called and said Amelia needed to decide how she wanted her kitchen because she was going to send over their architect and money wasn't a problem."

Before Joshua got too deep into his praise, Amelia decided to change the subject. "Right now, along with your place, they're working on a special facility just for Gabriel."

Gabriel looked sideways at Ibbie. "Going to hear all the sounds."

"From all over the world and satellites, apparently." Joshua pulled an apron from a set of hooks beside the pantry. He walked over and handed it to Ibbie.

Amelia took a large colander of cherries over to the sink.

Ibbie transformed. "Are those cherry's? Are we really going to do it?" She was a kid ready for her first pony ride. "It's about time. My partner has monopolized your every moment." She made a production for Joshua of tying the apron around her khaki pants. "I've hardly had a chance to get to know you."

Joshua put his hand on his chin and looked Ibbie over like he was evaluating a show horse.

She missed a swipe at him but got him with a snap kick to the rear as he spun away, all while continuing the conversation. "I have been looking forward to this all the time I was in Israel."

Joshua smirked at Ibbie's apron. "Me too."

He was out of range so Ibbie sneered and flipped the apron his direction. "I love cherry jam. You said you had a special recipe?"

Gabriel pawed through the items on the huge center island.

Amelia gave a head tip in his direction. "Trust me, by the end of this you'll know the recipe because Gabriel will repeat it throughout the process. He's used to helping me."

Gabriel turned and said. "On fait de la confiture?"

"Yes," A smile moved onto Amelia's face like a warm wind sweeping away clouds. She translated her brother's question into a proclamation. "We are making jam."

Joshua leaned against a counter with a look of satisfaction. "My mother had a blast speaking French with him when she was here." He sighed. "It was like something came back alive in her. Gabe is so much like Caleb."

Amelia turned from washing the cherries and smiled at him. "When we made jam, my whole family would speak French. I'm glad we can keep that tradition alive with your mother. I really love her. It will be like having a complete family again."

Joshua looked lovingly at Amelia. "Once mom gets her place in New York settled and all her stuff packed up, she'll be back. All the intel says there's no longer a threat to Rahab, so Mom feels like she can leave. Rahab's husband has plenty of security anyway. Dr. Welch has promised to use the institute's resources and connections to keep an eye on her. That's better than Mom can do by herself and she realizes that." He turned to Ibbie. "Mom will stay with us until they get your house finished and then they'll start on her place. Dr. Welch is excited. He says they need people with covert skills and intelligence connections to complement their more unusual team members."

Amelia had a pleasant feeling. "I can't wait 'til your mom gets moved in. They call it a team, but it's more like a family around here."

"We're a family that has a lot of work to do." Joshua began putting out fingers to illustrate the task list. "There are a number of the overseas DNAble conspirators and members of Becker's team that we have yet to identify. If we move on the ones we have without knowing who and where the others are, we risk some of them disappearing." Joshua kept expounding. "And the FBI wants us to help them go after the traffickers that were supplying Becker with his surrogate mothers. Teddy and Janie are narrowing that down, but it will take Gabe to pinpoint them."

The cherries were clean. Amelia carried them to the island. "Okay, that's enough about work. We need to have a little fun."

Ibbie sent a sarcastic grin toward Joshua and gave a shoo with her hand. "You are no longer needed."

Joshua wiggled his head and gave a humph sound. "Well,

while you three play, I'll check on how the tracking of Becker's team is going."

Ibbie gave a smug look of disinterest. "These things do not concern us." She lifted her head in conceit and smoothed her apron. "We are making jam."

Gabriel turned his head sideways and stared blankly at the floor, silencing everyone with a perfect French accent in a high octave. "Le miracle de la confiture."

Amelia closed her eyes, tipped her head back and breathed deeply. "Oui, Maman."

She opened them to see Ibbie smiling at Gabriel. "Was that your mother's voice?"

Amelia shuddered slightly and nodded. "It was something she would always say. The miracle of jam." Putting her open hand over her misty eyes and then turning an outward palm to them she said, "I'm sorry."

Joshua's face turned to concern as he started toward Amelia.

Ibbie stepped over and took her in an embrace. "You have nothing to be sorry for." She pulled back, keeping her hands-on Amelia and motioning her head toward Joshua. "How do you say, 'Get lost' in French?"

Joshua spoke first. "Va-t'en." His eyes requested verification from Amelia. "Oui?"

Amelia gave a little laugh. "That would work."

Using a mock French accent, Ibbie told him, "We don't care if you know how to say it, we want to see you do it."

"Okay, okay." He waved his hand over his shoulder and disappeared into the other room.

Ibbie winked at Amelia. "Sorry. I know he's cute, but he's taking up my jam time."

They giggled together.

"Confiture de cerises aux amandes," Amelia said with glee.

Gabriel translated, "Cherry almond jam."

Ibbie waggled her head and licked her lips.

"First freeze spoons." Gabriel stood erect and spoke as if quoting from a cookbook.

Amelia opened a drawer and took out a handful of the prescribed silverware. With Ibbie keeping a curious eye on her, she placed the selected utensils in the freezer and explained. "For later sampling. A cold spoon will cool the jam quickly, so we can check the consistency."

"Preheat oven." Was the next step according to Encyclopedia Gabriel.

Amelia eyed Ibbie. "Do you know how to preheat an oven?"

Ibbie looked insulted then smiled. "I've heated a few frozen pizzas in my time."

"Pardonne-moi." Amelia returned the smile and pointed across the kitchen. "250 degrees," she said as she opened the packages of jam jars.

"So," Ibbie spoke as she went toward the oven, "did you grow up in France?"

"No, right here in Arkansas."

"How did your mother get here?"

"My father brought her. He went to France as a sort of self-made missionary. He had three passions in life. The first was Jesus, the second was organic farming and he found the third when he went to France to work on an organic fruit farm and share the Gospel. Her name was Monique Paulette Delacroix. It was 'le coup de foudre.'" Amelia gave a couple of eyebrow raises. "Love at first sight. She was selling jam in the same farmer's market where my father's employer sold his fruits and vegetables. My father said he spent all his money buying jam just so he could talk to her.

"When the season was over and it was time for him to go back to the United States, he begged her to be his wife and she happily agreed. But he only had enough money for his own plane ticket. The village gathered a collection to pay for my mother's fare." Amelia grinned and shrugged. "Les Français connaissent l'amour. The French know love. When my father was packing up, his room was full of jam. He gave it to the villagers as gifts. He said it was only fair that since he was stealing the artist, he should leave the art behind."

Ibbie blinked her reddened eyes. "The miracle of jam," she said dreamily.

"Oui," Amelia gave a sideways nod. "Le miracle de la confiture."

Ibbie breathed out heavily, "Let's make some."

Later that afternoon, the aroma of the warm fruit filled the kitchen, encouraged by the large spoon that Ibbie swept through the bubbling pan.

Amelia looked over her shoulder. "That's looking just about right."

Scowling into the depths of the thick liquid filled with cherry pieces, Ibbie seemed to be searching for the mystery of life. "How can you tell?"

"Easy." Amelia gave a nonchalant shrug. "Watch for it to start jamming."

"So, the jam is ready when it's jamming?"

"Exactly."

"How many times does it take before you can tell jamming when you see it?"

"Just listen."

Amelia could tell her playful tone had Ibbie on guard and the other woman eyed her suspiciously. "What am I listening for?"

Amelia put her ear over the pan. "When it's jamming, you'll hear the music."

Ibbie gave her a shove and joined her in a laugh. "I bet your family had a lot of fun in the kitchen, didn't they?"

Amelia slowly nodded at the memories. "I think that's one of the reasons I love jam making so much. It brings them to life again. Mamma would oversee everything while Daddy told bad jokes. We would sing French songs and Daddy would get Gabriel to make the sounds of different instruments."

Ibbie looked wistful. "I remember my mother and older sister cooking and laughing together. I was always outside, outdoing the boys. I wish I'd known how much I would miss it when it was gone. Or that the evil that my people live with would so easily find our kitchen." She looked at Gabriel. "If only he had my mother and sister in his memory. I would love to hear them again." She frowned at herself. "Sorry, I'm sure it hurts just as much for you." Ibbie squeezed Amelia's hand.

Amelia used her free hand to pat the hand that rested on hers.

They were both quiet.

Joshua burst into the room. "We have to go."

Amelia struggled to keep pace with Ibbie as they rushed down the corridor. "Where are you?" She listened to Hevel's response in her earpiece. She could hear Marsha's painfilled whimper in the background. Hevel ended his transmission with, "Hurry."

They were almost there. *Please, Lord, let us make it in time.*

Ibbie reached the door first and put her shoulder against it, causing it to swing inward, making a way for Amelia to pass. They spotted the contact they had been told to look for. The woman looked young.

Ibbie motioned Amelia to go on without her. "I'll watch for the guys."

Amelia followed the young woman through the next two doors. The room was bright. She spotted Hevel. His face displayed beads of sweat and worry lines around his eyes.

Then she saw Marsha, behind him, on her back.

Marsha's hand made a tight, quick motion, beckoning

Amelia to her, before clasping the side of the bed again. "Oh, thank You, God. Amelia, I need you. Hevel is driving me crazy. You have to help me breathe before the next contraction. He's not doing it right."

Amelia put her hand on Marsha's back, and for the next two hours they struggled until the doctor came in and authorized the big push. In another thirty minutes, he pulled Marsha's baby girl into the cold light of the world and laid her at her mother's breast. It had already been decided that her name was Eva. The nurses remarked how much Eva resembled her father as well as her mother. It touched Amelia that he did not dispute them.

After some bonding time, the nurse took little Eva for a bath and evaluation while Hevel doted on his bride. Marsha's tangled blonde hair was matted to her head in some places and stuck out in others. Her exquisite curves were muted by added pounds and adorned in a generic hospital gown, and her sweat-soaked face was highlighted only with a motherly glow. Amelia remarked that she had never looked better. Hevel agreed.

Even though the medical staff had not been told, Hevel had expressed concern to Amelia, over the past months, about what the taser might have done to the baby. God was merciful and the doctor came and announced that Eva appeared perfectly healthy.

Amelia left Marsha to rest and hauled her own exhausted body to the waiting area. Joshua had arrived with Gabriel. He sat talking with Ibbie while Gabriel stood nearby, gently rocking. Joshua and Ibbie rose and approached her in anticipation.

Amelia reassured them. "She's beautiful, just like her mamma." Amelia heard the same small noises that Eva had been making. She realized the sounds were coming from Gabriel and turned a questioning expression toward the others.

Joshua looked guilty. "I kind of had him tell us what was

going on. Sorry. We couldn't stand not knowing. He's been doing that ever since Eva was born."

Ibbie pleaded their case. "It was too adorable to stop him."

Amelia looked to Heaven and tried to keep the smile off her face. "You two with your new toy. I guess I'm going to have to give up trying to keep this professional because every time I turn around the three of you are up to something."

When Eva was ready, the nurse brought her to the window of the nursery for everyone to see.

Joshua nodded approval. "We start her training tomorrow."

Amelia narrowed her eyes at him.

"Next week, then."

The next morning, mother and baby were released. Joshua pushed Marsha in the wheelchair, Hevel carried Eva, and Amelia toted the tools for their next assignment—bottles, diapers, and toys. The way the couples had bonded since their double wedding put a glow in Amelia's heart.

When they were alone in the hallway, Marsha let out a breath. "Well, that hurt as much as a being taser shocked over and over."

Joshua cringed and slapped Hevel on the back. "Ouch. She's not letting that go is she?"

Hevel shrugged. "Some debts you pay with money, some with labor…" He sighed. "Others are more costly. I have a lot to atone for."

Amelia grinned at him. "May your offering be acceptable."

They made their way to the third floor in the opposite wing, far from the feeling of new life in the maternity ward. When they entered the room, Gabriel eyed them from where he sat by the window with headphones over his ears.

Ibbie stood from where she sat beside a bedridden figure.

It took Amelia a few tries to wake Eve. "You have a visitor."

The eyes eased their way open and the face brightened in a weak smile.

Marsha took Eva from Hevel and came forward. "We accomplished our extraction mission and brought the liberated captive to meet you."

Ibbie motioned Marsha to her chair so she could lay Eva in front of the shriveled figure.

Eve stroked the tiny head with a bony finger. "She's beautiful. I never got to see my own babies when they were this little. So precious."

Marsha leaned in close. "Today she is alive because of both you and Amelia, so her name is Eva."

Eve's eyes twinkled with moisture and she patted Marsha's hand.

Marsha went on. "I have been reading about the patriarchs in the Bible, how they blessed the next generation. I would like you to bless Eva for me."

"I'm the youngest one of all of you. How did I get to be the matriarch?" Eve's tiny mouth made her grin look more mischievous.

Amelia leaned in. "You showed us age doesn't matter. What else could we do? We took a vote."

Eve struggled to lift her head. "I would be honored." She placed her hand on Eva's tiny knit hat. "Little one, in the name of Jesus Christ, may God bless you and give you peace. May you know how wide and how long and how high and how deep the Lord's love is for you. And may your life and your words draw others to Him." She looked around the room. "May you be a blessing to your family and friends as they will be to you. May your days be lengthened and full of life and love." She paused and looked into Eva's face. "But may you never be happy enough or live long enough to forget God."

They spent a while longer visiting and stood when Eve started nodding off. Ibbie assured her that she would bring all the kids around that evening for Bible reading.

As they walked down the hall Ibbie addressed Amelia. "How is the new treatment coming?"

"Good. She's tired right now but the doctors have hope the therapy might gain her another year. Then we'll see. It's day by day. They're going to start the kids on it next month. But that's going to happen at the institute. The Sanders have an exclusive contractor building a specialized medical facility. They're working on the ICU first. Once it's done and Eve is stabilized, we're going to move her over there."

Ibbie let hope brighten her face. "Now that I am going to be around, I hope I can help. I looked into some of the new Israeli breakthroughs. DNA research is progressing all the time and it's not all like Becker's brand. Who knows? It sounded promising." Ibbie dropped her head. "Let me take that back. I know Who knows." She pointed skyward.

Amelia brightened. "Well, there are lots of miracles going on. Eve's expenses shouldn't be a problem. The institute's legal team is taking on her case. They have been in communication with the court and the U.S. Attorney, and they think they can get the court to release some of the frozen DNAble assets into a trust fund for Eve and her children. Until then, the institute is taking care of everything. If there is any money left over, Eve can use it to help the Christian crisis pregnancy center she's been visiting."

"As soon as we get settled, we'd like to volunteer there." Marsha looked at the bundle in her arms. "Wouldn't we?"

Ibbie came around so she could look in Marsha's face. "So you're not going back to Israel? Does that mean Welch has talked you two into coming on board as well?"

Marsha looked up at Hevel.

He turned his hands out as if offering himself. "I have burned my bridges and am happier for it. I have nowhere to go and nothing to do. My love and I agree that it would be best for us to join you."

Marsha sighed in resolution. "Don't think it means I like you or anything. It was necessary." She let her British accent loose. "That piker in finance at Legoland won't give over about my wardrobe and makeup expenses. I need to work for someone who can afford me." Marsha's smile lingered but her eyes said she had turned serious. When she spoke, the Brit was safety tucked away again. "I also want to work where everything is centered around God. I need that."

Amelia gave her a shoulder pat. "Having lived there for a few months, I can tell you Dr. Welch and the Sanders are committed to that. They also will make sure you can raise a family while you work for them."

Enthusiasm crept onto Marsha's face. "That sounds refreshing." She gave Amelia and Joshua an inspection. "So how is that working? Are you getting plenty of time to get to know each other?"

Joshua blushed. "We are, and now that Ibbie is back, she and Gabe will be hanging out with the kids more, so Amelia and I will have some newlywed time." Joshua grabbed Gabe in a squeeze around his shoulders. "The clincher for us to take the offer was that Gabe likes the institute. It's populated by unique people. He fits in well."

The embrace caused Gabriel to twist his neck toward Joshua while keeping his eyes to the floor. Joshua gave him space again to remove the pressure, but a satisfied look lingered on Gabriel's face.

Amelia grabbed onto Joshua's arm and leaned conspiratorially toward Marsha. "The institute is putting us up in a luxury suite in the Villa Florentine in Lyon, France when we go to meet with the Interpol representatives to help plan this DNAble roundup. So it's not all life and death."

Beside them, Gabriel spoke in his mother's French voice. "Mets-moi comme un sceau sur ton cœur, comme un sceau sur ton bras. L'amour est fort comme la mort."

Joshua tipped his ear toward him. "I recognize that from

the Bible, don't I?"

Amelia had her eyes closed. "It was one of my mother's favorite verses from the Song of Solomon." She translated. "Set me as a seal upon your heart, as a seal upon your arm, for love is strong as death."

Joshua mused for a moment. "I remember the passage in First Corinthians that says, 'Death is swallowed up in victory.' He looked pleasantly at Amelia. "Love is stronger. He wins in the end."

If I say, surely the darkness shall cover me; even the night shall be light about me. Yea, the darkness hideth not from thee; but the night shineth as the day: the darkness and the light *are* both alike *to thee.* For thou hast possessed my reins: thou hast covered me in my mother's womb. I will praise thee; for I am fearfully *and* wonderfully made: marvellous *are* thy works; and *that* my soul knoweth right well. My substance was not hid from thee, when I was made in secret, *and* curiously wrought in the lowest parts of the earth. Thine eyes did see my substance, yet being unperfect; and in thy book all *my members* were written, *which* in continuance were fashioned, when *as yet there was* none of them. How precious also are thy thoughts unto me, O God! how great is the sum of them!
Psalm 139:11-16 (KJV)

In this book, several characters have an encounter with
God.
Getting your life right with God is the most important
decision you will make, the greatest experience you will
have, and the most life changing event you can encounter.
It is not about religion; it is about reality.
There is truth and this is it.
Without Jesus you are a slave to sin, it will destroy you
in the end, and there is only one thing you can do about it.
When you truly give yourself over to God through Jesus
Christ everything changes
You will have the power to weather everything else this
world and the powers of hell can and will throw at you.
You can endure until the end and spend eternity with
God.
The Bible is where to go for the answers.
Start with these scriptures and have a sincere talk with
your Heavenly father.

**For no one is put right in God's sight by doing what
the Law requires; what the Law does is to make us know
that we have sinned. But now God's way of putting
people right with himself has been revealed. It has
nothing to do with law, even though the Law of Moses
and the prophets gave their witness to it. Romans 3:20-
21(GNB)
We are made right with God by placing our faith in
Jesus Christ. And this is true for everyone who believes,
no matter who we are. For everyone has sinned; we all
fall short of God's glorious standard. Romans 3:22-23
(NLT)
They are made right with God by his grace. This is a
free gift. They are made right with God by being made
free from sin through Jesus Christ. God gave Jesus as a
way to forgive people's sins through their faith in him.
God can forgive them because the blood sacrifice of Jesus**

pays for their sins. God gave Jesus to show that he always does what is right and fair. He was right in the past when he was patient and did not punish people for their sins. And in our own time he still does what is right. God worked all this out in a way that allows him to judge people fairly and still make right any person who has faith in Jesus.
Romans 3:24-26 (ERV)

Brothers and sisters, my heart's desire and prayer to God on behalf of the Jewish people is that they would be saved. I can assure you that they are deeply devoted to God, but they are misguided. They don't understand how to receive God's approval. So they try to set up their own way to get it, and they have not accepted God's way for receiving his approval Christ is the fulfillment of Moses' Teachings so that everyone who has faith may receive God's approval…If you declare that Jesus is Lord, and believe that God brought him back to life, you will be saved. By believing you receive God's approval, and by declaring your faith you are saved. Romans 10:3-4 & 9-10 (GW)

My friends, what good is it for one of you to say that you have faith if your actions do not prove it? Can that faith save you? Suppose there are brothers or sisters who need clothes and don't have enough to eat. What good is there in your saying to them, "God bless you! Keep warm and eat well!"—if you don't give them the necessities of life? So it is with faith: if it is alone and includes no actions, then it is dead.
James 2:14-17 (GW)

Don't miss book one, Seeing Beyond. Get it here

Acknowledgements

To God Most High. You are my everything. Thank you for the gifts you give.

Thank you, Rebekah, my wife, friend, and best editor. You are always sincere in your evaluation of my product and your encouragement of my craft. Bless you for taking the time and the punishment of my whining to spur me on to better works.

Thank you Kwinn and Calista Wyatt for your honesty as well. Without it this book would have been so much less. May the time and money you invested return to you in the Lord's blessing.

To my beta readers in alphabetical order:

Mary Jane Blackburn
Alicia Callahan
Laura Coen
Ray and Natalie Hines
Lucinda Hyatt
Linda Johnstone
Jeanette Nelson
Billie Thompson

Kathy Thompson
Calista Wyatt
Kwinn Wyatt

Thanks for digging out the weeds. May you be rewarded with a bountiful harvest in whatever garden the Lord has you plant your seeds.

We are grateful to all the prayer warriors who have interceded for this book, we could not have done it without you.

More About Kent and Rebekah Wyatt

Kent Wyatt was born and then he died. Wait a minute, I'm getting ahead of myself. (Whew! I'm glad I put that part in because, for a second there, I thought I was dead.) Now that you know the beginning and the ending of my story, let's go a little closer to the middle...

Actually, my novels are "our" novels, produced by the team of Kent and Rebekah Wyatt. My wife, Rebekah, will always be quick to tell you she is not a writer, but she contributes greatly to the finished product of our books. Rebekah (whose official title in the Wyatt Republic is Minister of Household and Finance) is a voracious reader of Christian Fiction. In the Wyatt writing world, she serves as (among other things) editor, researcher, manager, financial planner, contributor to the story board, plot, and characterization, and of course the final word on all things romantic. So, when you see our characters behaving like ladies and gentlemen instead of blowing snot, passing gas, and belching—thank Rebekah. (Disclaimer: the second half of this sentence was not Rebekah approved.)

Kent and Rebekah's novels have been semi-finalists in the American Christian Fiction Writers Genesis contest and a Finalist for the Romance Writers of America Daphne du Maurier Award for Excellence in Mystery/Suspense. Kent serves as Vice President of the American Christian Fiction Writers NW Arkansas Chapter.

So how did such a partnership ever get started? I mean really, a man and a woman, together, they're so different. Whoever came up with such an idea? Oh. Sorry, God. Great idea by the way. (Disclaimer: the preceding portion of this paragraph was not Rebekah approved). Of course, such an unlikely alliance could only begin in somewhere remote and mysterious—like the flatlands Northwest Kansas.

I was born there. Rebekah was dropped there, like a tornado drops a rare orchid in the middle of a wheat field. Both our early days were, like most young lives, bizzare in their own ways. Mine full of the mundane misadventures of the son of a firmly planted fourth generation farmer, and Rebekah's comprised of the exotic escapades of a traveling evangelist's daughter. When we were in our early teens, we met and fell madly in opposite directions and both skinned our knees. For the few months that her family stayed at our farm, we rode horses and performed magic shows together, but then Rebekah's family was off to the next ministry opportunity. Over the years, we both strayed from God's plan in our own ways and then were thrown together again in our late twenties. In a few months, we were married. God has rescued us from our own imprudence, grown us in our understanding of His plan, and bound us together for His purpose. We love Him greatly because He has saved us exceedingly. Our prayer is that through our stories we might introduce others to THE ONE who longs to do the same for them.

To understand how this whole writing thing began, there is one thing you need to know about Rebekah: She is a faithful helpmate to her husband and selflessly supports his dream far better than he deserves.

There are two things that you need to know about me: I was born a writer, but I became a cop.

As a child on the lonely plains of Kansas, I always enjoyed reading and telling stories to the other kids. When I was thirteen years old I read *R is for Rocket* by Ray Bradbury, and I decided I wanted to write stories like that, ones that haunted you and made you think. John Boy Walton became my hero, and I was going to change the world with my pen. Over the years, I learned that I wasn't Ray Bradbury, but God had given me a writing voice of my own and He could use that if I would let Him. The only problem was I didn't have enough life experience so...

When I was seventeen years old, a car almost ran my mother and me off the road. With my terrified mama holding onto the dash beside me, I pursued the other vehicle in my 1973 Mercury Montego and forced it to pull over. It was the town drunk doing what he did best. He came at me, and I knocked him down and picked him up by his belt and threw him in the back seat of his car to sleep it off. My mother decided that I should be a police officer. She knew that writing nonsense was never going to get me anywhere.

In 1983 she saw an ad in the paper saying a small town nearby was looking for a police officer. She convinced me to apply. But all the time I was being a cop, the bite I received from the writing bug became infected and grew septic. I fed the fever over the years with short stories, award winning poetry and a humorous newsletter that I put out for a growing email list. Another life changing event was when I read *This Present Darkness* by Frank Peretti. It helped get me back on track with my faith and introduced me to Christian Fiction. I had found the direction God wanted me to go with my writing. Foolish fans encouraged me by saying that they loved my newsletters and re-read them when they wanted a good laugh. Many even said I should write a book. With my law enforcement career and my family to raise, I could never commit to writing fulltime. So, I satisfied myself with learning the craft and producing short works. After 32 years, I ended my law enforcement career. I still have many friends walking the thin blue line, and I have a deep love for the profession. But God seems to be telling me it is time to fulfill my other destiny. Now, with God's help, maybe my writing can change the world after all. Where are my old reruns of The Waltons? Look out, Ray Bradbury, something Wyatt this way comes.

Rebekah loves to make jam. If you want to make her Cherry Almond Jam follow this tip. To cherry jam, add 1 – 2 teaspoons of pure almond extract just before putting your hot jam into the jars prior to processing.

You can find Kent on the web at the following locations:

Website: https://www.kentwyatt.org (free stories both real and imagined)
Amazon: https://www.amazon.com/Kent-Wyatt/e/B07GSHF65Q
Facebook: https://www.facebook.com/kentwyatt.org
Twitter: https://twitter.com/authorkentwyatt
Pinterest: https://www.pinterest.com/AuthorKentWyatt/
Goodreads: https://www.goodreads.com/user/show/36911883-author-kent-wyatt
Google+: https://plus.google.com/115005163444293298582
Linkedin: https://www.linkedin.com/in/kent-wyatt-b162b014a/
Instagram: https://www.instagram.com/authorkentwyatt/
Youtube: https://www.youtube.com/channel/UCW_AzksI3It_PSJQFt4oo4w
Hashtags: #AuthorKentWyatt, #SpecialHeroes